Praise for Jane Kirkpatrick

"I highly recommend *Every Fixed Star*. Jane Kirkpatrick's storytelling is deft and true; she breathes life into the long-ago Oregon country with warmth, emotion, and a deep understanding of the region's people and past. With depth, creativity, and inspiration, *Every Fixed Star* provides a fresh view of this period in the Pacific Northwest's history, showing the complicated dynamics between settlers, fur traders, missionaries, natives, and visionaries. Jane has vividly captured the history of the fur trade for intelligent women readers."

—LAURIE WINN CARLSON, author of *Seduced by
the West* and *On Sidesaddles to Heaven: The Women
of the Rocky Mountain Mission*

"Jane Kirkpatrick has a rare gift, for her novels touch both the emotions and the intellect. She fills her stories with living history, each rich detail carefully researched and woven into a very particular time and place— the Columbia country of the 1820s. And yet, *Every Fixed Star* is far from a dry history; rather, it is the moving, heartfelt story of one woman's journey toward accepting her own failings as a wife and as a mother—a struggle common to every woman in every century. Through Marie's 'heart knowing,' we are forced to examine our own hearts and lives and emerge the better for it. Jane's novels are more than 'a good read'; they are a life-altering experience."

—LIZ CURTIS HIGGS, author of *Thorn in My Heart*

"Jane Kirkpatrick has done it again. Her artful manipulation of historical detail and possibility gives us not only a portal to the past, but to the universal truths that apply to every woman. *Every Fixed Star* engages us on an emotional journey alongside Marie Dorion and inside ourselves. This book is—in the most intimate sense of the word—a gift."

—JOYCE BADGLEY HUNSAKER, award-winning author
of *Sacagawea Speaks, They Call Me Sacagawea,*
and *Seeing the Elephant*

Every Fixed Star

OTHER BOOKS BY JANE KIRKPATRICK

NOVELS

Tender Ties Historical Series
A Name of Her Own

Kinship and Courage Historical Series
All Together in One Place
No Eye Can See
What Once We Loved

Dreamcatcher Collection
A Sweetness to the Soul
Love to Water My Soul
A Gathering of Finches
Mystic Sweet Communion

NONFICTION

Homestead
A Simple Gift of Comfort (formerly *A Burden Shared*)

THE TENDER TIES HISTORICAL SERIES

Every Fixed Star

JANE KIRKPATRICK

Award-winning Author *of* All Together in One Place

WATERBROOK
PRESS

EVERY FIXED STAR
PUBLISHED BY WATERBROOK PRESS
2375 Telstar Drive, Suite 160
Colorado Springs, Colorado 80920
A division of Random House, Inc.

Scripture quotations are taken from the *King James Version* of the Bible.

This book is a work of historical fiction based closely on real people and real events.
Details that cannot be historically verified are purely products of the author's imagination.

The floral design on the cover is reminiscent of the Iowa Nation beadwork and is
used by permission of The Museum at Warm Springs, an entity of the Confeder-
ated Tribes of Warm Springs, Warm Springs, Oregon. The design is from a beaded
bag in the permanent exhibit gallery.

ISBN 1-57856-500-6

Copyright © 2003 by Jane Kirkpatrick

Library of Congress Cataloging-in-Publication Data
Kirkpatrick, Jane, 1946–
    Every fixed star / Jane Kirkpatrick.— 1st ed.
      p. cm. — (Tender ties historical series ; 2)
    ISBN 1-57856-500-6
  1. Dorion, Marie, 1786–1850—Fiction. 2. Overland journeys to the Pacific—Fiction.
3. Northwest, Pacific—Fiction. 4. Women pioneers—Fiction. I. Title.
    PS3561.I712E94 2003
    813'.54—dc21

                                     2003002731

Printed in the United States of America
2003

10 9 8 7 6 5 4 3 2

This book is dedicated to

the People of the Iowa Indian Nation
and
Jerry Kirkpatrick.

Cast of Characters

Madame Marie Dorion	an Ioway Indian woman
Jean Baptiste	Pierre and Marie's son, b. 1806, known as Baptiste
Older Sister	Baptiste's first wife (name uncertain)*
Little Marie	Baptiste and Older Sister's first child, b. 1823 (name uncertain)*
Josette Cayuse	Baptiste's second wife
Denise	Baptiste and Josette's daughter
Paul	Pierre and Marie's son, b. 1809
Narcisse Raymond	French Canadian and uncle to Older Sister
Louis Joseph Venier	former trapper and Marie's second husband
Marguerite Venier	Louis and Marie's daughter, b. 1819
Jean Toupin	former camp boy with Hunt; Marie's third husband
François	Jean and Marie's son, b. 1823
Marianne	Jean and Marie's daughter, b. 1826

THE MISSIONARIES

Ignace and Sarah Shonowane	Iroquois and Chipewayan; former hunters at Astoria and friends of Marie
Henry and Eliza Spalding	missionaries to Nez Perce
Marcus and Narcissa Whitman	missionaries at Waiilatpu
Sarah and Edwin Hall	missionaries from Hawaii to Nez Perce

HUDSON'S BAY COMPANY (FORMERLY NORTH WEST COMPANY)

Alexander Ross	factor at Okanogan and later at Fort Walla Walla
Sally	Alexander's Okanogan wife
Jemima, James, and Henrietta	children of Alexander and Sally
Donald Mackenzie	factor at Fort Walla Walla and former Astorian
Peter Skene Ogden	a Snake River brigade leader for Hudson's Bay Company
Julia	Peter's wife
John Work	a Snake River brigade leader for Hudson's Bay

* Denotes fictional character

Josette	John's wife
Pierre Pambrun	factor at Fort Walla Walla
Catherine	Pierre's native wife
John McLoughlin	chief factor for Columbia country, Hudson's Bay, and stationed at Fort Vancouver
Marguerite	John's wife
Tom McKay	son of former Astorian and stepson of John McLoughlin; also interpreter, guide, horse breeder, and rancher on French prairie
Michel LaFramboise	French Canadian and former Astorian, Hudson's Bay
Louis LaBonte	French Canadian and former Astorian; employee of Hudson's Bay
Kilakotah	Louis's Clatsop wife and friend of Marie
Victoria	daughter of Kilakotah and Chief Factor James McMillan
Louis LaBonte II	"Louis Two," son of Louis and Kilakotah

THE FRENCH PRAIRIE PEOPLE

Robert Ewing	Californian and businessman
Etienne Lucier	French Canadian

SITES

Fort Okanogan	present day Washington State
Spokane House	present day Washington State
Fort Nez Perce/Fort Walla on the Walla Walla River	present day Wallula, Washington
Astoria/Fort George	present day Astoria, Oregon
Fort Bellevue/Fort Vancouver	present day Vancouver, Washington
Waiilatpu	present day Whitman National Historic Site
Lapwai	present day Lapwai, Idaho
Crossing, Rivière des Chutes	present day Sherar's Falls, Oregon
French Prairie	present day south of Champoeg, Oregon
French camp	present day San Joaquin Valley, California

He healeth the broken in heart,
and bindeth up their wounds.
He telleth the number of the stars;
he calleth them all by their names.

—PSALM 147:3-4

These earthly godfathers of heaven's lights
That give a name to every fixed star,
Have no more profit of their shining nights
Than those that walk and wot not what they are.

—WILLIAM SHAKESPEARE, *Love's Labour's Lost*

Métier: a French word meaning calling
or finding work to which one is best suited.

"You call a tree a tree," said Tolkien to Eliot, "and you think nothing
more of the word. But it was not a 'tree' until someone gave it that name.
You call a star a star, and say it is just a ball of matter moving on a mathe-
matical course. But that is merely how you see it. By so naming things
and describing them you are only inventing your own terms about them.
And just as speech is invention about objects and ideas, so myth is invention about truth. We have come from God; inevitably the myths woven
by us, though they contain error, will also reflect a splintered fragment of
the true light, the eternal truth that is with God."

—a conversation between J. R. R. TOLKIEN and T. S. ELIOT on the nature
of language, quoted in *Tolkien: A Biography* by Humphrey Carpenter

Part 1

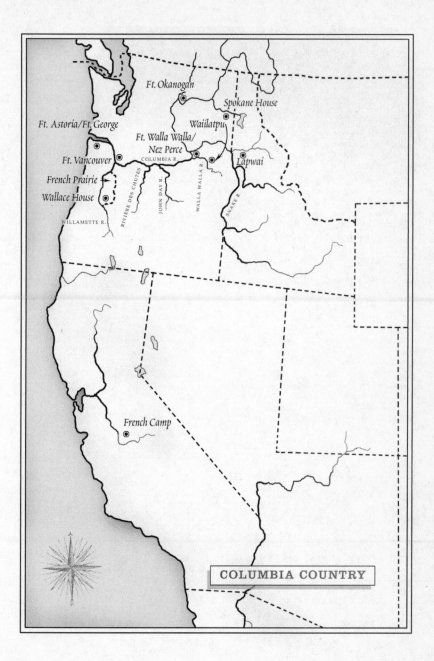

Ft. Okanogan

Spokane House

Ft. Astoria/Ft. George

Waiilatpu

Ft. Walla Walla/
Nez Perce

COLUMBIA R.

Ft. Vancouver

Lapwai

French Prairie

Wallace House

RIVIÈRE DES CHUTES

JOHN DAY R.

WALLA WALLA R.

SNAKE R.

WILLAMETTE R.

French Camp

COLUMBIA COUNTRY

1

The Robe of Regret

June, 1814, Okanogan River, Northwest Territory

Marie Dorion learned to love a place by being present in it. She noticed the taste of dewy sweat on her upper lip, the brush of an Okanogan breeze against her back, the vista of hills rounded like old women bent to their work. The smell and feel of earth as she dug for camas roots in the finger of grasses and the laughter of her son serenaded by the high sighs of the red-tailed hawks dancing in the distance, all named this northwest river place as home.

"A gif, *Mère,* a gif." Paul, her youngest son, shoved his fist under Marie's nose. He opened his palm. "See? Butterfly."

Marie turned to look, lifting his hand. She raised her head at the sound of a distant wail. *A child? An animal trapped?*

"I give gif for—"

"Not now!" Marie Dorion hissed the English words, repeated them in French so he'd be silent. Paul shoved his palm closer.

"I—"

She put her hand to his mouth and whispered, "This is no time for gift-giving." His eyelids blinked in fright, and she dropped her hand, then put her finger to her lips. "Listen," she said. "Do you hear it?"

The child shook his head, no.

"Maybe it's moved on."

She lifted her nose to the wind, walked toward the Okanogan River, her son following. She didn't hear the childlike scream again, but as she pushed back the supple leaves of the willows that lined the stream, she nearly stumbled onto the cause. She bent to the animal at her feet, felt the warmth of its body. The cat must have pulled the animal into the shadow of the willows after it brought the lean doe down. The cougar's claw marks at the deer's shoulder named the beast that had killed it. That, and the cat's eerie cry. Like a rattler's buzz, a mountain cat's wail once heard could never be mistaken for anything else.

"A dead doe," she said, "discarded by a startled cat." She rubbed her stomach. "I'll look at your butterfly later," she said. "This gift feeds our bellies."

Paul's lower lip rolled out. "Gif gone," he said, letting the now dead black-and-orange butterfly drop to the ground. He stomped on it with his moccasins, grinding it into the dirt.

Marie frowned at him. "We have work to do, *n'est-ce pas?*"

She stood up and dragged the doe closer to the water. She scanned the riverbank. The mountain cat could still be there, watching. She and Paul must have startled the animal before it had time to celebrate its kill.

Warmth from the hot morning pressed against Marie. Sweat beaded down her sides, chafed beneath her deerskin dress. She hung her digging stick at her belt.

"We'll fill our water basket *maintenant*," Marie said. "Come. Now you can make noise."

Marie dipped the basket into the river. "Are you hungry?" Marie's sons hadn't had meat of late. The doe's belly ballooned from the heat, but the meat would still be good, if she acted quickly.

Marie felt more than saw the rustle of the willows and was instantly alert. Paul sniffed the air.

"*Oui,*" she agreed. She too could smell the danger. Marie stood to her full height, taller than some of the French-Canadian and Astorian men with whom she'd once traveled. "Make noise, now." She raised her voice, stomped on the dry grass, and forced a laugh while she patted the root basket tied to her belt. She slipped her knife out of its leather case. If the cat stalked them, it would think twice before taking on a tall, noisy woman and a boy who had seen five summers.

She motioned Paul closer to her, to make him less vulnerable, to make the two together seem larger. He shouted, started to hop around, spilling water from the basket she'd handed him. She told him in French, "Make yourself part of my shadow." He obeyed. When she no longer felt the eyes of the cat on them, she patted Paul's thin shoulder. "Good. The cat's moved on. She didn't mean to leave it for us, but tonight we'll have meat. My stomach growls. Yours too?"

Her son didn't answer, but she pushed him before her, back toward the doe. She released the root basket from her belt and bent to her work.

The hide would be useful in trade. And the meat, the meat would feed them. What gift was greater than food for a mother's sons?

Marie felt the animal's warmth through the doe's bristled outer hairs. Dried blood thickened below the chewed remains of the animal's throat. Marie needed to work quickly in this heat. They weren't far from the Okanogan post run by the North West Fur Company, and so she would remove the hide there in the shade of her hut. For now, she needed to take out its innards and cut away the torn meat already forming a dark, red crust at the edges.

She pointed with a raise of her strong chin, directing Paul. "Hold the leg," she said.

The boy walked with his wide gait, still a waddle almost. "Hold tight, *maintenant.*" Marie spoke mostly in English now instead of French. She hoped her sons would learn both ways of speaking. Such abilities permitted status in this Okanogan world peopled more by natives than the Scots or Frenchmen, though those latter Company men, with ruddy, wind-whipped faces, ruled. She wanted her sons to enter this world so they might rule well too. The words they chose would either help that entry or keep their mixed blood from moving freely in the waxed walls of the bourgeois.

When Paul lifted the doe's back leg, she saw the animal's full bag. The doe had a fawn. Marie winced with the image of a bleating fawn somewhere, screaming for its mother. Marie lifted her eyes, scanning. It would be in the area, possibly not far if the cat had killed the doe there, though mothers often distracted danger, leading attackers far from their offspring in an attempt to keep them safe.

The fawn would die now too.

Marie returned to her work. Some things could not be helped.

A powder pouch made of the fawn's hide, one marked by small spots like sun dappled on calm backwater, would bring much in trade.

The doe would be twice the gift then, if they could find the fawn before the cat did.

While Paul held the back leg, Marie used the knife to split the doe's belly. Once again the gift of Sacagawea served her. She'd met the famous interpreter of Captain Clark two, no, nearly three summers previous. Sacagawea had been going home to the Mandan while Marie and her family had been headed west. There beside the Missouri the two women formed a friendship. Both pregnant. Both married to men with French-Canadian blood. Both affiliated with white, fur-trapping expeditions. Both mothers. Both Indian women in a white man's world, guides across relationships if not landscapes.

They were tenderly tied, these two women, despite their language difference, a tie that sustained Marie in dark times. Sacagawea had given her this knife that had been carried on the journey of Meriwether Lewis and Captain Clark. It had served Marie well, even in one of her darkest times when she and her sons had endured the winter in the Blue Mountains after her husband had died. But no time now to think of such things. She couldn't go back, couldn't change what had happened. She'd learn to live with old memories, make them nourish anew, the way a carcass soon feeds new grasses around it, the dead and decaying giving life to the soil. In this new Okanogan place, she'd not be held hostage by allowing those hard times to call her back to a place she'd survived.

She located the center of the doe's belly. It was a rare gift to have meat without the use of a gun or bow. She touched the point of the knife into the soft white crevice below the still swollen milk bag and slowly sliced open the animal's belly from the base of the bag to the arc of the rib cage. She followed a line where the hairs came together in the center. "It is as though the deer were made of two halves and sewn together," Marie said to Paul. "See. We cut at this line." She pointed with the bloody knife.

"*Retrouve le faon,*" Paul said.

"In English," she told him though she'd understood.

"I find the fawn," he told her now, letting the doe's leg drop.

The leg bone cracked against the back of Marie's hand and she dropped the knife into the entrails of the deer. "*Non!*" she scolded. "Stay here. We finish the deer; take it back to the hut. Then we look for the fawn. It will not move. It listens to its mother. You should too."

Paul dropped his eyes. "I listen, *Mère*." He lifted the leg again.

"Only when it suits you," she said.

Her hands reached into the wet warmth of the mother doe, felt for the knife, all slippery now with blood. She found it, laid it aside, and reached in again. Then as though she held the head of an infant, she rolled her hands under the rib cage and over the deer's stomach, bladder, and intestines, seeking the tender strips of sinew that bound them to the spine. If she cut carefully, the entire ball of vitals could be pulled out as one mass. She'd try to save the bladder and the stomach. They could be made into bags that could be bartered for seed beads, molasses, or even a copper pot. A hawk called, and Marie raised her eyes, her hands still gripping the blood-slick knife.

Paul bumped her with his elbow. He poked at the doe's stomach, the bone-digging stick tearing a hole that allowed gas to escape, along with bile and half-chewed grass. It dribbled over the entrails, down into the cavity, staining the meat.

"*Non,*" Marie said, exasperation escaping like a sigh.

"Deer isn't hungry," Paul said in English. "She tosses her food up." He laughed.

How have I raised such a disrespectful child?

Marie stood and reached for the stick, her hands wet with blood. Paul jerked back and the stick slipped from her grasp while her son laughed.

"This deer is a gift to feed your stomach. Not to play with," she scolded.

He waved the stick around at her then, jabbing at her as though he would poke her, too, his wide mouth and sharp little features pulled up into a grimace as he continued to hold the deer's leg while sparring with his mother. "I do what you say," he told her. "I listen to you. See, I still hold the leg."

Marie swallowed, made a choice. She bent back down to her work. Sometimes if she ignored him, his resistance stopped. She could never be sure. Both her boys proved as unpredictable as skunks.

Baptiste, her son with eight summers, challenged her more easily too, since the ordeal on the mountain. He often scowled when she sent him on errands. Yet arguing with the boys only seemed to excite them, then made them stubborn as ticks. They had a rhythm, her sons. They performed a devilish dance with her that spun her around until she felt herself ready to strike, her fingernails cutting into her palms to keep herself from bringing harm. Then her sons would stop, quick as the drummers at a feast dance.

She'd taken to ignoring her sons, hoping that reacting differently would throw them off step. It sometimes worked.

Her sons needed a father's strong hand, but they had none. She'd have to find some other way to teach them to become men or they would never rise in the fur trapping ranks, let alone survive this next winter living here among the Okanogan people and the Scot fur trader, Alexander Ross. That had been her life, always at the mercy of some fur company's whim.

Marie pulled a piece of gurrah cloth from the bodice of her dress. She used it now to wipe away the green specks of undigested grasses that stuck like pitch to the meat. She rubbed the knife handle down on her leather skirt and then scraped at the organs. She finished cutting free the intestines and pulled them some distance from the carcass, then cut the bladder loose. Paul's poking ruined the stomach, but she could maybe save some of the urine from the bladder and use it for tanning the hides. Maybe the bladder could be sewn with sinew and used to hold water. She'd have to see.

"Carry these," she said to Paul, handing him the bag of roots they'd dug earlier that morning. Maybe if she gave him more responsibility he would learn respect. "And lift the bladder. Be careful. It will make a good water bag on hot days." She watched him until he did as he was told. Then she squatted and lifted the deer over her shoulders, holding the front legs and both back legs across her chest.

It was a light load. The doe must have been last year's fawn and had her own first fawn this spring. That infant had lost its mother and it would die. Marie felt a connection to it and to the doe she carried across her back.

"Come, Paul," she said, keeping her voice light. "We see if Baptiste has fish to go with our roots and now this fresh meat."

"The Up-In-Being gives a gif?" Paul asked.

"For no reason except that we are in need of it. Your other mother, Sarah, would say we do not deserve it and yet we are well provided for." Saying such things could make them so. Her friend Sarah would say that as well. Words could make the thoughts come true.

Paul grabbed at the bladder then and forced it into the root bag. "*Attention*," Marie said.

"In English," Paul said just before he gouged the bladder with his stick and took off running.

Urine poured over the roots. Wasted. How could she raise a kind child, an obedient child? *How can one so young have so much venom?* Did the time in the mountains, staying alive, poison this son's attitude?

She'd have to come back for the root bag and bladder. Maybe Paul would carry the water basket. She walked toward the post, hoping Paul would follow in her footsteps. She pretended to be certain of herself. She must find a way to teach and raise these boys who had survived bloody places of their own, who had endured the wrath of men both Indian and non. It was not enough to keep them alive. It was also a mother's job to take out poison, in whatever way she could.

❖

Baptiste Dorion watched his mother from a distance. He'd seen his mother and brother—the last remnants of his family—leaving the shelter of the willows and heading across the grass back toward the fort. Paul trailed behind, dancing close, then dropping back, poking the dirt with a stick. His mother always took Paul with her. Paul didn't help her much, not the way Baptiste could. Even now while she carried a deer on her shoulders, Baptiste could see she didn't have her root basket at her belt. She'd left it behind somewhere. Paul was probably supposed to bring it. He hadn't. He'd be scolded.

Baptiste brightened. He could go get the basket for her. She'd like that. He stood taller, the wind blowing his straight black hair against the side of his face. She'd be pleased if he helped her.

Maybe.

He stared. The fringe of her buckskins barely shifted at her ankles, so gentle were her movements, as though she were the breeze itself, soft and never stirring in an unwanted place.

He started out, stopped. She might scold. She'd told him to help the men fish at the river. He'd do what he was told, not be like that weasel brother, Paul, who skipped ahead of her now.

Baptiste could hear his little brother laugh in his chatter, but he couldn't make out the words or what his mother answered. *Was she laughing?* Paul pretended to talk like a baby, but Baptiste knew he could speak without sounding like his tongue had been stung by a bee. Paul did it to make people laugh, to make the French-Canadians and Scots forget he carried an Indian's blood.

His mother did laugh now. She always laughed with Paul.

Baptiste belonged there at his mother's side, helping. He started toward them.

"You, boy, give a hand here." One of the Okanogan men shouted at him. His mother turned and looked back over her shoulder just in time to hear the man shout again. Even Baptiste could hear the scold in the fisherman's voice. He was sure his mother could too.

He scampered down the bank to the fisherman. Baptiste's family was out of sight now. He wondered what they were doing.

"Good," the Okanogan man told him when he helped pull a big salmon up the riverbank.

He didn't know the fisherman's name, but he'd learn it and maybe get him to tell Baptiste's mother that her son was a good helper and as spirited as a beaver at work.

❖

Alexander Ross had built the rectangular log fort during a fall and winter he spent "alone" as he told it, though Marie knew he'd been surrounded by the helpful Okanogan people. Being alone to a white man meant being the only white man, the only Scotsman, the only clerk to spend the winter while his fur trapping former Astorian comrades explored rivers farther north. Ross, an Astorian-turned, North West fur trader himself, served as chief factor at this post now. He'd even married an Okanogan woman he'd renamed Sally, so he couldn't have been alone much. Marie smiled remembering the ways the North West Company men used words with different meanings, words that sometimes exposed their true hearts like bare skin to wind. She wondered if Ross knew what it meant to be alone.

Marie dropped the doe at the entrance to her hut, aware that even the famous trapper would envy her find.

Paul raced off shouting as he joined other children at play. "We bring in meat," he said.

Marie watched, the exertion of her load drawing her breath. She nodded to Baptiste, her elder son, as he approached carrying a fish nearly as long as himself. The child's dark eyebrows ran together over his nose in their usual scowl. He laid the fish at her feet, winded from the effort.

Marie motioned with a lift of her chin. "Take it to the fires," she said. "Then go look after Paul."

Baptiste obeyed. He was a good boy.

The children in this village played funeral or marriage, both events filled with tribal drama and union, and they played one of them now, Marie uncertain which. From her place, she noticed Okanogan women who stood at fires roasting camas roots or fish. She wondered if they judged the game her sons had chosen, wondered if they'd ask how she'd found meat for her sons. The women talked softly to each other, pointed in her direction. Smoke stung Marie's eyes.

The women here cooked the catch whole, tossed fish into the fires with the heads. Then with long sticks they pulled the fish from the hot coals, some to be eaten then, others to be stored for winter's use. Marie's hands were gouged with deep cuts from handling the fish's sharp fins. One cut looked red and sore, was probably infected. Their ways were new for her. She'd have to make up a paste with horse's urine since she had no salt pork, pine pitch, or cow manure with which to draw out the poison. She bent to check the doe's bladder, remembered she'd have to walk back and pick up the roots, wash off those not spoiled. She sighed.

The children moved their play closer. She watched now as Paul rolled a child of maybe five summers into a buffalo robe. They were of the same age. "Tie tight," Paul said, his little bowed legs making him waddle as he tried in vain to lace the hide and yank the child around who let himself be tossed like a puppy.

Marie supposed this burial ritual healed her sons; a reliving children did of tribal doings, part of life and death. Marie wished the children had played a marriage binding game of celebration instead of the one involving the separation of death. It seemed too close to "the wrapped-up winter" as she thought of it, when she'd secured them inside a robe to keep them safe in the snow-laden Blue Mountains while she'd gone in search of help.

Marie shook her head of the memory. Would time ever cover each fragment of pain that arrived the way ash did, drifting from a winter fire to coat the white snow with gray?

"You try. Get out," Paul insisted. Inside the robe his friend laughed. Paul's voice rose in irritation, "No. You figh! You figh!"

The boy shook his head, no. *"Mort."*

"No," Paul said. "Don't die. You don't die. You wait. Your papa comes. Saves you."

"Il est mort!" one of the Okanogan girls said. "It's how we play it."

Other children pretended to weep now, wiping at their eyes as bigger boys pushed Paul aside and lifted the child in the robe into a sitting position. Little girls giggled at each other, then wailed in mourning, their fingertips covering their mouths.

"What will go with him?" a boy with long hair falling on either side of his cheeks asked. "Do we kill his horse? His dog? He must not go alone to the beyond."

"Maybe his brother is killed. He goes too, so the boy is not alone," Paul said.

Marie gasped. "Paul!"

Paul turned, smiled, then resumed his play. "Guns. Make guns,"

Paul said. He looked around as though to find sticks that might work. "Baptiste?" he motioned then, to his older brother who now stood beside Marie. "Find guns, *oui?*"

"Child's play," his older brother said, moving so Marie felt the warmth of him at her side. He looked at her waist belt. "I go find the root basket," he said but stood still.

Baptiste did things his own way too, Marie knew. Not unlike his father. Always serious, always somber. Marie wondered if he would have been that way if she had stayed back in little St. Louis on the Des Moines River where his father clerked. Her son might have learned to read and write there, to interpret and trade as his father had, find more things to laugh over. Or maybe Baptiste would have found pleasure in plants and insects the way those scientific men did who shared their westward journey from St. Louis to the Columbia and the Pacific Ocean. Perhaps her daughter, Vivacité, would be alive today, her husband, Pierre, too, if they had remained back on the Mississippi River.

"Regret is the robe grief hands you," her Chipewyan friend Sarah once told her. "It promises warmth but gives only weight. It is woman's work to turn regret into something of worth." She must remember that. She must work to put off the robe of regret, turn it into something of value. Marie took a deep breath.

"We should go away," Baptiste said. He still stood beside her on silent feet, watching as several other little boys now wrapped Paul in the robe. Marie felt her throat tighten. *Will Paul resist being tied as he once had, as the day when she'd chosen that way to keep her sons safe?*

"Where would we go?" Marie asked, resting her arm on his shoulders to feel his closeness.

Baptiste shrugged her off and took a step away. "Back to where Papa lies. Mark his grave, *n'est-ce pas?*"

"It isn't safe. It may never be," Marie said. "The Indians there hold hatred. They might wait for us—"

"Take a hatchet to our arms and legs like—"

"Hush," she said, squeezed his narrow shoulders.

"We just go, then." He stood, hands on his hips, elbows out. "Be by ourselves. Bury Papa."

Marie ran her fingers through Baptiste's hair which was as fine as beaver felt and just as thick. "You have some of your mother's ways," she said. "But this time, we stay. Make our place here. We make our own name here."

Marie glanced back to the children. Paul lay still, wrapped in the buffalo robe. He changed his play now to the ritual the children here observed as he acted dead. They carried him in the robe toward the open courtyard of the fort. An older woman who must have just noticed them shouted to the group, shooing with her hands as though they were chickens pecking at seed wheat. "Ayee!" she said. "Go farther away when we are preparing food. Go now." She looked with irritation at Marie as she turned back to her fire where a fish cooked at the outside of the flames.

"You will find another papa for us?" Baptiste asked. Hope whispered through the question. "A more better papa?"

"You look hungry," Marie said. "See if your brother wants some corn bread. Have some yourself."

"I want butter," Baptiste said.

"You remember butter?"

He nodded his head.

"There is a wish we all have," Marie said, grateful for his shift in interest. "We last tasted butter…" She tried to remember.

"St. Louis. With Papa when we left in the big canoes," Baptiste finished.

Yes, three years previous. It had been that long since she'd seen a "neat cow" as the docile milking kind was called. Three years since she'd tasted fresh milk or butter. The supply ship arriving at Astoria—now Fort George—brought rounds of cheese, but that had been the only taste of dairy they'd had. Marie's mouth watered. "We will pretend a cow will wander this way," Marie told him. "Until then, we spread hog's fat on our bread and tell ourselves the story that such fat is butter."

"I miss it," Baptiste said. He grunted then in that way his father always had, and Marie felt a pang of loneliness for Pierre. "I go find the root basket."

"*Bon,*" she said. "I almost forgot, but you remembered."

Baptiste stepped away from her then, pushed aside the hovering children, and pulled at the loose twines holding his brother in the robe. Several smaller boys yelled at him for breaking the rules of their ritual. Paul scowled as his brother freed him, causing Marie to wonder again what might have happened between the two boys those days when they'd been left alone with each other and the wind.

Paul said something close to Baptiste's face, then he ran off in the other direction followed by several of the playing children. Baptiste stared and the look of rage mixed with sadness on his face caused Marie's eyes to pool. How she wished her sons could be friends. Brothers needed to be friends, the older guiding the younger. Baptiste turned, retracing the footsteps his mother had made carrying the heavy doe from the river's edge.

Marie wiped at her eyes now, the tears stinging the cuts in her hand. She hadn't wept much since Pierre's death, though the Ioway, her people, were known by their soft hearts. They cried best in greeting someone not seen for many seasons, in celebrating a longing met, a victory.

Today, though, she felt like weeping: for her sons' journeys from risk to ritual, to fill the distance between her and her children.

As she watched her sons separating, she wondered if perhaps Baptiste was right. Maybe they should go to someplace where no one knew their story, where just the three of them knew what they'd endured. Watching the funeral play almost confirmed it; Paul reliving the days of abandonment when he'd lain bound up with his brother, unable to move, while his mother crawled on for help.

"Non," she said out loud. She straightened to her full height. She had to get clear about what mattered in her life and then somehow find the courage to act on that. Running to a new place was not the answer. Disappearing was not the salve that would soothe the wound. She would make her way here. That was how one lived in a wilderness place, making new choices, naming herself with new, strong names.

Eventually, these Okanogan might accept what she had to offer even though it came from hands whose color was lighter than theirs.

A woman's voice shouted then, and Marie turned back, expecting to be told how to strip the hide from the deer, as if her Ioway way weren't as good as the Okanogan way. Instead, the Okanogan woman pointed and Marie followed her hand toward the Columbia River that ran east of the fork where the fort was located. She squinted to see better.

A brigade that looked like dark sticks floating in a pool of blue wound its way up the wide river. Wind spanked the water, gusting into whitecaps and carrying a man's shout toward the fur fort. The brigade must have been from Fort George at the Columbia, bringing supplies and taking the pelts and hides back for shipping to Canton. The thought caused a lurch in Marie's stomach. It had been her husband's and her plan to go back East, to take pelts and information back to Astor, the man who had set them on their way west.

All that had changed now. In one moment, life as she knew it had ended. She alone was responsible for her sons. She was separated from past hopes, as though wrapped inside a hide tied tight herself.

"Go build a fire," Ross, the factor, directed her. He, too, had heard the shout and had come out of the fort. He fussed at the stiff collar at his neck, brushed lint from his linen jacket. "The brigade will need it."

It bothered Marie, Ross's ordering her when she willingly wished to serve. She wasn't a slave here. She was not his wife. But she set her knife down, walked to bring driftwood from the Okanogan River for the fire circle, her eyes scanning for Paul and Baptiste as she did.

Paul's cluster of friends surrounded him, and he poked at something in the grass with a stick. Marie approached and, as she did, her son lifted a snake, its pale belly twisting against its flight. Paul lunged with it toward the now scattering children.

"Paul!" Marie shouted, her voice sharp and threatening as an eagle's claw. "Put it down! *Maintenant!*" Her face felt hot with both the cook fires and her irritation.

Paul laughed and then tossed the snake, the brown-and-white buttons on its tail weighting it into twisting contortions even as another gust of wind lifted it and carried it well beyond the children. It dropped with a plop to the tall grasses and coiled. Paul ran toward it, stick at the ready.

"Paul! Leave the snake—" Marie began.

"Marie!" A woman's voice carried on a gust of wind from the river. Marie heard it but kept moving toward her son. The snake uncoiled and slithered into the grasses. Marie grabbed at Paul who slipped away from

her grasp, trying to find the snake again. "Marie! Madame Dorion!"
A woman waved her arm now, high above her head and repeated her
name.

"Leave the snake, Paul," Marie told him, turning toward the voice
now as recognition came to her on wings of joy. "It is time to celebrate
and cry. Your other mother, Sarah, has come to visit."

❖

Sarah Shonowane was a Chipewyan woman married to an Iroquois
hunter. Her husband Ignace, their two sons, and more fur-trapping partners, French-Canadian *engagés,* and a sickly woman married to a mixed-
blood man—part Chinook, part Astorian—came in the brigade too.

Marie's tears flowed without stopping as she cried the Welcoming
Song. "My eyes are clear of the dust now," Marie laughed. "And to see
you standing in the sun, this is a gift unexpected."

Sarah wore skin clothes like Marie's and a heavy metal cross she'd
been given by a Jesuit priest long before they'd crossed the Athabascan
region north and headed south onto the Columbia River to Astoria.
"You're staying here at this fort now," Marie said. Sarah shook her head.
"You go home?" Marie asked.

Sarah shook her head, no, again. "The clerk hopes the ill woman
will be cured of her swollen feet and arms," Sarah said. She nodded
toward the invalid being lifted out of one of the canoes. Her hair had
fallen out, and she looked nearly as bare as a weasel, her skin pale instead
of its usual healthy brown. "They hope this dry climate will bring about
a change in the woman's disposition," Sarah said.

Marie and Sarah and others watched as men carried the woman
toward the fort. "Her husband intends to come here in a month or so,
and if she's well, they'll travel back East."

"So you will stay here until then, to help with the healing? This is
good! I've missed—"

"No. We have a place to go to," Sarah said.

The men from the brigade moved into the fort. Sarah's husband
joined Okanogan men near the river, squatting down to talk as they

worked. Sarah's sons stood beside him. They were nearly men themselves now, with strong backs and hair shaved but for a strip in the center
and a spray that rose from the top like flowers held in the hand of a
child. Sarah motioned with her chin to the deer.

"As soon as I finish skinning the hide, we'll go look for the fawn,"
Marie said. Sarah nodded and then bent to help her, a second pair of
women's hands in work another welcome gift.

"We travel east," Sarah told Marie later while she, Marie, and their sons
walked the Okanogan hillsides looking for the fawn. The wind had
stilled, and the angle of the sun made all colors deeper, as though copper
and gold were melted like butter over the land.

"Four cows arrive," Sarah continued, filling Marie in on the gossip
of what had once been Astoria and was now British and named Fort
George. "On a new supply ship. The Fort George people will have milk
and butter now." Marie's mouth watered.

"Cows," Marie said. "They could be more valuable than beaver in
this country."

"My husband says there are wild Spanish ones, with long horns.
They wander up from Mexico. Maybe you rope one of those to milk."

"I lack the bravery for that."

Sarah scoffed. "After how you saved your sons in the mountains?
Oh yes, everyone knows."

"It wasn't me. The Walla Walla people saved them. They did it. And
rescued me, too, a mother blinded by the snow."

"You made the choices," Sarah said. "And you asked God for help
and it arrived."

"Undeserved," Marie whispered. She adjusted the knife at her belt,
brushed at the tall grasses, seeking signs of where the fawn had lain. "My
boys, they witness too much. Paul saw his father's blood…and Baptiste,
he followed me into Reed's hut where the men's bodies looked like that
deer, torn apart by a cat. It's my fault they saw such—"

"Mama!" Baptiste shouted then. "We find it, *le faon!*"

"*Bon.*" Marie looked to where Baptiste stood. It was farther than she'd thought the doe would have gone to lead the cat away from her fawn. "Good!" she shouted.

Both women took long strides to the boys then, and Marie could see the tiny quivering animal rolled into a ball not much larger than Ross's pup. Baptiste bent to touch the animal that lay there, waiting for the return of its mother who would never come now.

"No," Marie said, gently slipping her hand beneath Baptiste's before he touched the skin of the animal and increased its fear that she could almost smell. "I will tend to it." She placed Baptiste's hand in Sarah's palm. "Take him back," she said. "Paul, too." She looked around. "Paul?"

From behind her, like a lynx pouncing, Paul brushed by her. Marie reached for him, missed. She tried to put herself between the child and the fawn. Too late. Her youngest son held a knife in his hand, fist upraised, the knife point gleaming in the setting sun.

2

Children of Faith

The sound of pain bleating across the hillsides pierced Marie as sure as if her son had struck her heart. In one swift motion, then two, Paul had brought the knife down into the fawn's eyes. Marie lunged at the boy, then struck him with the back of her hand, knocking the knife free. Her knife. He'd taken it from her belt.

Marie picked it up and slit the throat of the fawn, stilling its pain. Marie's hand shook and her heart pounded. The fawn would die of starvation even if she had not taken its life. But the look on her son's face, a grimace as foul as spilled bile, sent shivers to her soul.

"Go back to the hut," she ordered. "Sarah and I will bring the fawn. Go!" Paul hesitated, then turned to leave. Baptiste's eyes sought his mother's. "You go too," she said. "Watch your brother."

Marie waited until the boys, single file, moved back toward the fort. She squatted then, her hand still shaking as she began the process of gutting the fawn.

"You should come with us," Sarah said. She squatted beside her friend and touched the back of her hand.

Marie stopped her work, didn't look up. "Raising sons—"

"Sons. They challenge a mother," Sarah said. "It's why we women help each other." She paused. "We can't stay here with you. We go to keep a calling." Sarah spoke her words so softly that Marie looked at her then, the knife still in hand. "Among the people we met when we first came to this Columbia country. Spokane people and the Flathead. They too are trying to find how to live, to raise sons and daughters in this changing place. Trappers stay. More ships come up the river. Everything shifts like poorly packed furs on a windy river. Danger—"

"I'll find a way to raise good sons, to pay off my husband's debt. This is my calling, my *métier.*"

"A butterfly can't go back into its cocoon," Sarah said. "The robe of regret cannot be shaken off in the old ways." She fingered the heavy metal cross she wore at her neck. "Ignace and me and our sons, we go to show the Spokane and their neighbors new ways. You come too. Let us help heal your heart. It will heal your boys too, fill the divided places between you and your sons."

"*Non,*" Marie said. She returned to her work. "A mother binds her sons' wounds. It's what a mother does."

"A mother can accept gifts offered."

"Only if she earns them," Marie said. She shook off Sarah's hand. "I already received the lives of my sons. I deserve no greater gift than that."

Sarah stayed silent, held the fawn's leg, knowing what to do without being asked.

"We know of your courage to save your sons," Sarah said. She leaned beside Marie, her wide hands covering Marie's small ones as she released the fawn. Marie looked at her. Sarah's teeth rested on her lower lip, the way she did in concentration, a reminder of when she used her teeth to hold the hides for tanning. A scar of sorts lined her lips from where she'd bitten repeatedly.

"How did you do it?" Sarah asked after a moment.

"I looked to see where the grass trail ran, where the cat had dragged it—"

"Your sons," Sarah said. "Not finding the deer. How did you keep them alive?"

Marie hesitated. She'd told no one of what she'd done. "I…chose." She swallowed. "I bound them." She adjusted the belt at her waist, slipped the knife that had been her only tool into its sheath. She whispered then, shivered. "Even though I wasn't sure I had enough strength to make it out, to bring back help for them, I tied them up. If I had failed…"

"You were enough," Sarah said, patting Marie's hand. "You always worried."

Marie nodded, folded her hand over her sheathed knife. "Who told you we lived?"

"Those Walla Walla people who found you. Our brigade stopped there at that river to rest. The people had no hides to trade. They're not interested in scratching the waters for beaver. Not when they have fine horses to offer for the company's rifles or copper pots. The partners think them… I search for the word," Sarah said, biting her lower lip.

"They think they act like partners, those Walla Wallas," Marie suggested.

Sarah nodded. "They challenge the North Wester's ways of doing things. But not the way your sons challenge you."

Marie stayed silent. She brushed at the fringe of her dress.

"They have been through a hard winter, your sons," Sarah said. "Now you must help them remember all they knew before. To be grateful for the food given. To kill a living thing only with respect." Sarah hesitated, then said, "It's Paul's anger worn on his face that frightens most, n'est-ce pas?"

Marie nodded, tears springing. "He looked as though he would place the knife into my eyes, into my heart, not just into the fawn's," Marie said. "How could I raise such a child? Maybe Pierre was right. Maybe I treated him too softly. Even when he grew old enough to walk on his own, I still carried him with gentle hands."

"You did what you knew to do." Sarah gazed toward where the boys had walked. "What did Paul witness?" She asked. Sarah rarely asked questions, made statements instead.

Marie jerked her head to her friend. "He saw his father's death."

"Pierre dishonored you, too, his son's mother. Such pain witnessed breeds eyes like Paul's, too," Sarah said. "Your husband hurt you, n'est-ce pas?"

"He stopped," Marie said. "It was better. He didn't strike me again. We were happy. Then he died."

Sarah patted Marie's hand, then fingered the heavy cross she wore at her neck. "I should not stir such painful memories, especially in my friend." Marie fidgeted, looked away, as though checking on her sons.

She tucked loose hair into the knot at the back of her neck, pushed it into the fold.

"Heart questions make you uncomfortable," Sarah said. She used a low voice, then changed the subject. "The partners talk of needs there, that the Flathead and Spokane need more guns, lead, and powder. Their women need cloth and needles. Where we think of going they, too, have other needs, ones the partners miss and cannot trade for. We listen to another voice. One inside us. Inside each of us, Marie. A voice that guides."

Marie stood. "We should see what trouble my sons get into," she said.

"I see them at the canoes," Sarah said. "Maybe they will become voyageurs and the hard muscle work will help them think more wisely. Or tire them out of mischief."

Marie adjusted her position beside the fawn. "You could stay the winter," Marie said. "I have much to learn about beadwork yet. You are a good teacher."

"The mountain was a troubled time for you," Sarah said. "I knew this. I kept you in my heart, spoke prayers for you." She patted her wide chest.

Marie kept her head bent to her work.

"Such prayer talk still bothers like a bee sting, *n'est-ce pas?*" Sarah asked.

Marie nodded. A strength she thought she didn't have had found her in the snowy mountains, had held her close until she saved her sons, herself. But here, in the windless Okanogan evening or during long hot summer days, she relied only on herself, found talk of God could clog her throat like the cold dark mornings when she awoke with a start.

"You come with us," Sarah said. "You come to the Spokane with us. A new start for your sons. Maybe a man with a strong hand to help you lives there. We often refuse most strongly what is best for us. There, no one knows your story unless you tell them." Marie smiled at Sarah. "You were always going. To the Willamette, to that place where Wallace built his post, to that *boise* place, to the Great Salt Sea, the ocean. You—"

"No more. I stay in one place now."

"I feel this," Sarah continued, touching Marie's hand to her heart.

"Something strong pulls at you, the way it pulls at me." She took the basket from Marie's hands, lifted her friend's chin. "Maybe what draws you is a force as strong as those rapids on the lower Columbia and you think you can portage around."

"My mother-in-law once named me Her to Be Baptized," Marie said. "She thought me incomplete. She was right. Only the worthy are allowed the gift of longings met."

"We are created into the intricate weaving of fine baskets," Sarah told her. "The baptismal water simply fills us up."

"I stay," Marie said. "Until—"

"Perhaps while he waits for you to believe that you are worthy, he sends a father to you to help you raise your sons." Then Sarah thumbed tears from Marie's cheeks and kissed her fingers. "We share the salt of sadness," Sarah told her. "The mark of a true friend."

Marie heard Baptiste shout. She walked quickly over the rise in the landscape and saw her son lift the root basket. He'd found it! She waved to him to come and then returned to her work. They worked together then, she, Sarah, and Baptiste. If only Paul could calm himself, they would be a good family, even here, alone.

Marie pulled on the hide again, the fawn so warm. He died in fright. She wondered if Pierre had feared at his death as well. She fought back tears. Sarah wouldn't mind her crying; a friend understood such things. But if she let the tears come, they might wash away her heart, such grief lay dammed behind it. "I teach my sons well," Marie said. "But here, alone."

❖

Marie Dorion awoke with a start into the cool Okanogan dark. Her heart pounded, and her chest felt tight as though rawhide strapped across it. The weight of helplessness gripped her in the mornings, exposed her like a melon split open to be ravished by prairie wolves. She took a deep breath, cool against her throat.

It had happened less in recent weeks since Sarah left. Marie had slept through some nights, found rest drifting over her like the white fluff of the poplar trees that settled onto summer waters. Yes, the darkness befriended if she let it.

Alert now, her eyes scanned, seeking answers. What had taken her from a dreamless sleep? Thoughts of her sons? Sadness over Sarah's moving on to Spokane House, operated by the North West Company? That was probably it. She'd been dreaming of her friend, except that in her dreams, Sarah scolded her. "You knew God during your hard time in the mountains, but you won't let him walk beside you at the riverbeds." It was something Sarah would have said had she been standing beside Marie. It would have begun a conversation about things that mattered. Marie brushed the thoughts away now. She had been given more than she'd deserved already. To hope for more seemed selfish.

Feathery light filtered through the openings of their unchinked hut. Marie and her sons had formed the shelter out of driftwood logs smoothed by the Okanogan River's rushing them from cluttered piles far upstream. Few trees dotted this landscape painted with grasses and low brush. It was a rounded countryside compared to her Des Moines of long ago. Less lush than the land at Young's Bay where she and her husband had spent a year with Sarah and Ignace and the Astorians at the mouth of the Columbia River.

But this Okanogan was a place with few bad memories. Her husband had never walked these hills, had never touched her face here in the moonlight, had never struck her as he once had in those years when whiskey ruled his ways.

It was almost dawn. Marie's heart beat slower as she patted the buffalo robe her sons lay on to her left. Her fingers fluttered over the narrow ear of her younger son, Paul; then sought the face of her elder son, Baptiste, almost nine winters old. Both still slept. They looked so peaceful in sleep. She had to remember they were merely boys, young children. Pierre had said she spoiled them, made them weak like girls. He'd wanted them tough as the leather that soldiers wore around their necks and just as stiff, able to withstand the piercing of a people who took what they wanted without pause.

Her sons were not weak boys. They had shown that in all that they'd endured.

Perhaps one had called out in his sleep and that had awakened her? They were prone to do that since their father's death.

Maybe she'd shouted herself awake? That often happened when she became too warm at night. The buffalo robe proved a good mat but felt heavy during this time of ripening berries. Pierre would have awakened her when she cried out in the night, held her close, helped her know she was safe. She missed that knowing. She missed him.

A blast of wind pounded against the side of the hut, the gust like thunder though she smelled no rain in the air. Another blast struck, skidding loose sand across the dirt floor. A keening sound raised from the distance then, a wail that prickled Marie's neck as though spiders nestled there, beneath the knot of her dark hair. That lynx? Prairie wolves? No, a woman's cry of distress. She recognized that kind of cry.

Hurrying, Marie rolled off the robe, then knelt to pull her buckskin dress over the light gurrah cloth she slept in. She touched her sons' shoulders. They were in a safe place among good people. She and her two sons lived. She had played no small part in that, though when she remembered what she'd done to make it happen despite the harsh Blue Mountains, the drifting snows, Marie's legs weakened.

"Snow is a part of who we Ioway people are," she whispered to her sleeping sons. "We are gray snow." They were Bah-Khi-Je of the Ioways, people named for the soot that drifted over their snow-covered huts along the Des Moines River.

But this was August. She was separated from all the gray snow people on the other side of the shining mountains. Their faces drifted far away as though mere memories lost in smoke.

Marie shook her head, attached her belted knife, and slipped Sarah's iron cross around her neck. Sarah had given it to Marie, just before they headed north.

"But it's yours. You'll need it for your own strength," Marie protested.

"The strength is not in the metal," Sarah told her. "*Non.* It's like the scratching of goose quill pens. The meaning we bring to the words is of more merit than the ink that forms the words."

"Like Ross's ledgers mean more than the scratching," Marie had said. "The scratchings say I owe the North West Company for Pierre's old debt."

"You take it." Sarah pressed the cool metal into Marie's hands. "Practice receiving." Sarah smiled.

Marie wore it now though the added power she felt from it came from the memory of a gift-giving friend, nothing more.

The wail again. It sounded like Sally. Marie's heart quickened as she pushed back the hide door and stepped out into a dawn pink as a baby's tongue. She expected another jolt of wind; found calm instead. The woman's cry pierced it. Marie fast-walked toward the fur post. This was something she could tend to, bringing someone's birthing pain into shouts of joy.

Why hadn't Sally told me her baby was soon in coming? Marie and Sally, the wife of the clerk in charge of the post, had formed a tender tie in these months since Marie had joined the canoe brigade moving from the Pacific—the Great Salt Lake, the Indians called it—to the Columbia's interior post. Marie quickened her pace as another cry sounded.

Perhaps the child came early, as Marie's daughter had. Marie swallowed. She knew about birthing, having brought three children to life within her twenty-four summers. Helping with life was a gift she could give back to people who offered safety for her sons. Skinny-tailed dogs that slept near the huts of the Okanogan answered Ross's dog Weasel's frantic barks as Marie made her way across the garden's cobbled earth. She heard pigs grunt, fenced in a pen near the plot. She stumbled on rocks, her ankles twisted at the hardened furrows. "Oh, whoa," she said, disgusted by her slow pace.

Tips of dim light from candles flickering at nearby huts suggested others were hearing the cries now too.

Marie pushed open the door without knocking, as was the custom. She felt the fire's warmth and smelled the scent of sweat and woman's blood. Weasel, his pointed ears always up, turned to her as he stood beside the floor mat. He stopped barking, his string-beanlike tail wagging as he trotted to her.

"*Que faire?*" Marie asked, then, "*Pardon,*" as she bumped into Alexander Ross.

"*Que faire?* What's to be done?" Ross said. His eyes sank into a face hollowed out with worry. He pointed toward the door. "Get a *sage femme,* woman. That's what we need. Can't you see that?"

Marie saw Sally lying on a mat behind him, the woman clutching her abdomen, writhing in pain.

"I can tend you, *mon ami,*" Marie said. She pushed past the fur trader and knelt beside the square-faced woman, Sally's dark eyes pleading with her to remain. Sally looked so small, too small. Her face, blotched red, was drained of its usual cocoa color. "It will be well," Marie said, her voice low, to soothe. Sally was much too small. This could not be a baby grown complete and ready to enter the world.

Sally tried to sit up, couldn't. Marie reached to help her, her arm draped around her friend's back.

"No, no," Sally said. She shrugged off Marie's help, panted. "Death lingers on her fingers," Sally said in French to her husband, not looking at Marie.

"You see?" Ross said. He yanked Marie up, allowed Sally to catch herself before she lay back. He pushed at Marie's shoulders. "Get another," he said. "One of her people."

"But I've brought babies into—"

"Go!"

Marie looked down on him, but he shoved her now.

"Didn't you hear? *Vous êtes isolée!* Your fame precedes you, woman, carrying stories of death."

Marie looked over his shoulder at Sally's face contorted in pain, her eyes pinched. Then Marie turned and left, lifted her leather dress to better run across the grass to a distant hut, her heart pounding. She could help, but they deprived her! She entered the nearest hut and motioned to an Okanogan woman already gathering up supplies. "Fur post," Marie said, making a sign to show where the need lay. "Sally Ross."

Marie stepped aside as the Okanogan woman left. Marie leaned against the wood hut, catching her breath as she watched the midwife go. She should have known better than to bring her still grieving heart into a place of new birth. Wind chapped the tears on her cheeks. Would it ever change? Would her life ever be wrapped with acceptance again?

❖

Jean Toupin jerked his head, his long dark curls greased, and chased off the flies buzzing around his head without benefit of moving his hands from the paddle of the *bateau*. He worked for the Company now, though not that long ago he'd been a mere camp boy in the employ of the Americans. This trick for dealing with insects while paddling the big boats was essential. Flies were thick and troublesome this time of year.

A *bateau* painted white moved up beside his, and Michel LaFramboise shouted across the choppy water. "We earn our ten pounds of tobacco today, *oui?*" The *milieu*, Michel, stood short and stocky in the center of his boat. *Milieu* weren't supposed to direct the boat's path, but in Michel's crafts, he could either push with the paddles to make his way or tease the *devant* or *gouvernail* into doing what he wanted. Which was what he'd done now, bringing the boat bearing axes and bolts of cloth and seed beads and trinkets up beside the one Jean Toupin helped paddle. Jean's boat carried fewer trade supplies and more bales of pelts as the brigade exchanged goods for furs that would eventually end up at Astoria on the Columbia for shipment to Canton. Well, Fort George they called it now, though Jean had only known it as a post raised and run by partners of John Jacob Astor. He'd been a part of that adventure, launched his adult life traveling across the lower continent with Wilson Price Hunt and that man's sixty or so partners and *voyageurs,* Jean's friend George Gay, two young boys, and their remarkable mother.

The sails had just been lowered on their craft as the stiff wind blew upriver now, pushing them back from where they'd come. The wind so strong. Late afternoon it had happened, just like before, Jean noticed.

"These Columbia River is like a teasing woman, *oui?* She makes us work even if we agree to go in her direction," Michel shouted. He always said *this* as *these* when he used English. Yet even in the midst of winds and high waters, Michel found a way to carry on a conversation.

Jean didn't know much about teasing women even though he was a family man. Or he would have been if he'd had a wife and children to come home to. He had his seven brothers and sisters and his cherished mother, still alive and moved now to Montreal, but a fellow had higher hopes than merely rocking infants as the godfather at the baptisms of his nieces and nephews. He was twenty-two years old. At twenty years of age, he'd believed he would be teary at his own babe's birth, not at the christening of someone else's.

Life was full of surprises. He had learned that. When he'd returned from the Columbia country the year before, his mother surprised him with his own birth year. Somehow in passing she had remarked that it was good a man of twenty had had his adventure and could now settle down.

"Twenty? But I'm eighteen," Jean protested. "The same age as my friend, George Gay."

His mother had turned from kneading her bread, brushed flour from her forehead. "Whatever gave you that thought? You were born in '92, not '94. It was the year of the big plague in Egypt," she said. "Thousands died." She returned to her labors, leaving Jean wondering what happened to two years of his life and why his mother might associate his birth year with the misery of a plague.

But two more years added to his age had gotten him what he wished for: employment with the Company. He'd been first with the Pacific Fur Company of Astor, then with the great North West Company. The Company was family, offering a safe harbor for exploration, a place to come home to with food for his belly and enough adventure to feed his dreams. Yet the Company could be more annoying than younger sisters, and more unsettling in its actions toward its employees than parents to unruly children. They should be off the river by now. But no. The Company said paddle until dusk.

It was strange to paddle downriver, heads and shoulders bent to brace against gusts that flapped the white sails and scraped at their eyes like harsh linen. The blasts pushed words back down their throats. "Every day. At 4 P.M.," Michel shouted. "We should have our rum by four in these country." His square, fleshy face broke open in a wide smile. "We see if we can push ashore soon. Let the middle drive the front." He shouted that in Chinookan, a language Jean suspected the clerks riding as passengers in the boat didn't really understand.

Michel laughed, lifted his red paddle to them. The *devants* in both boats grinned and shifted their crafts closer to the shore. Hours of daylight remained in this August month, but Jean was pleased by Michel's effort to bring them to beach. He hadn't worked as hard all day as this past hour, paddling downriver against the wind.

The clerk riding in Jean's boat shouted now. Jean turned to look at him, and the clerk leaned over the awning rolled at his feet, a finger pointed in accusation. He scowled and gestured back out toward the center of the river. The *gouvernail*, aft, had turned to look too and now pushed the boat back out into the stream. Michel lifted his shoulders as if to say "I tried," then bent to the wind again.

Michel had come out with the ocean-end of the Astor party, back in 1811, and remained in the Columbia country, always employed by the Company, always finding joy in his work. He was older than Jean and boasted of a wife in every tribe who "teach me languages of body and soul." Michel did know a variety of Columbia tongues. Jean watched carefully whenever Michel was brought forward by a clerk to translate. Michel was as wise as any clerk, as skilled, as experienced, and yet he manned the middle of the boats without a second thought, never complaining about "being overlooked." He dreamed, instead. It was good to stand in the shadow of dreamers, Jean thought. A man could be close to excitement without giving up family, ritual, and routine. Jean worked on that aspect of his life, trying to find his place of peace yet never losing sight of some unnamed longing that drew him to these northwest lands.

Arriving back in Montreal after his own time in Astoria as part of Hunt's expedition had been a momentous occasion full of celebrating and storytelling. He'd created vivid pictures of the vast sea, with his tales, the camaraderie of the men building a fort together. He supposed he exaggerated the good times a bit and rushed over the bad. Ladies found the details of starvation and death intriguing if not a bit gruesome. Children listened with wide eyes to those parts of his stories, but eventually he couldn't bring himself to relay them anymore. The pain of that time when men drowned or disappeared without explanation or when he learned of the death of that baby born to the Dorion woman just grew heavier with the telling.

Once or twice, Jean had even found his heart pounding and a bad taste entering his mouth as he talked about the day when the men watched a woman being beaten by her husband, yet the men did nothing about it. In Montreal, the luster of his Western pursuits soon dulled like an unused copper pot.

Then he began relaying stories of the bravery of Pierre Dorion's wife, the one mother who'd joined the expedition. He still remembered as good their time at Astoria when together they'd supplemented the men's meager fare with fish they caught or traded for. In his own dark times, Jean drew on the memory of that good woman whom he thought of with the same fondness as his mother, both strong mothers carried safely in the *par flèche* of his heart.

Now, he worked as a *milieu*, the *voyageur* in the center of the *bateau*. He was taller than most in that position, but not as bulky as a *devant* or *gouvernail* who stood fore and aft. For special occasions, he wore the bright red sash of his mother's spun wool, his ascension sash given at first communion, and used his grandfather's paddle, painted with reds and blues. The middle position he worked at just wasn't compensated as well, no matter the man's experience. The other two positions in the boats earned annually fourteen pounds of tobacco and a knife and axe as well as two blankets, two shirts, and two pairs of trousers a year. He earned barely half. It wasn't fair, but it was the Company policy.

The *milieu* position was rarely appreciated. He'd seen that often enough on Hunt's journey west where those in charge looked right over them, even though they were often the ones with the skill to interpret the signs of the land, or the know-how to befriend the natives if they hoped to pass through with their hair still attached. Hunt had ignored men like Donald Mackenzie. Jean had complained to Michel about this just before they left Jaspar House to head south to the Okanogan.

"You are too much thinking of status, of where men are placed in a boat and who notices," Michel had told him. "A man brings meaning to the work, *oui*? The work does not carry it to the man. It does not matter what the work is. It is the man who matters."

Michel acted as though work was a gift one offered up in return for the opportunity to do it. Michel dug deep in the water for good things to say about work, saying it was something to be appreciated no matter where one was, something to be received gratefully rather than the subject of complaint.

"So we just do as the Company tells us?" Jean said. "Let good men be overlooked?"

"These work is worship, a gift we give, one we give back, *oui*? It is willingness, to do what is asked of us. It is…waiting. We do not always see the results of our work. Maybe not in our lifetime, *oui*? Who knows what will come of a man helping a woman lift a fish from the water, how many will be fed? It is wonder, this work we do. Like the eyes of a child finding a first frog or the way the sun spreads gold across a lake at sunset, a sight we would not see unless we are at work there, paddling our boats. Work is all these, my friend." He'd tapped Jean on his rib cage with his wide paws, spreading that grin like a sunrise over the mountains. "You worry too much about the titles and positions, my friend. Work is a treasure from God, *oui*? Who weighs such a gift?"

Jean supposed he did, weigh his value to men, how his abilities were used. What Jean had learned in his years working for the Company was that no one noticed the most difficult work being done as men paddled one dignitary after another. The honor went to the one who sat with no paddle in hand who was waited on by others.

"Maybe I should have stayed at Jaspar House," Jean shouted to Michel. "Stay in the kitchen out of this wind."

Michel nodded, the gusts forcing him to use all effort to manage the boats, whitecaps building, sending spray across the men's faces.

They rounded a bend and Jean heard a strange sound, like a low growl then rising to a higher pitch. *Was that the sound?* The clerk signaled for them to beach the crafts. "Falls ahead," Michel told him. "See, Spokane await us." Michel pointed with his chin to a handsome band of people standing near the water's edge. In the distance, a few horses ripped at grass, the fall sun shining against copper-colored hides, their long tail hairs separated by the wind.

"What's that I hear?" Jean asked. "The falls?" He'd heard water cascading before, but nothing like this.

Michel furrowed his brows in concentration while the clerk motioned again for them to beach. They pulled the boats up onto the rocky shore.

"These is very strange," Michel said. "It is not the sound of water but voices raised without drums."

Jean listened, surprised at the rhythm of the music. He couldn't understand the words, but the tune seemed familiar, something he'd heard back home, inside a church. They walked up over a rise, even the clerk curious enough to not order the unloading yet.

Before them sat a group of men and women, separated into two groups, singing.

"It's an old chorale," the clerk said. "Hymnsongs, I believe they call it. Sung at chapels across the land. Algonquin. 'Let Christian Hearts Rejoice.' Yes, that's it. The Americans sing at their November feast they call Thanksgiving."

"How'd natives learn such things, way out here?" Jean asked.

"You were seeking new adventures," Michel said. He grinned. "Perhaps you will find these out."

❖

Sally's baby—the one that slipped out onto the mat, so small it was no larger than a thumb—did not survive. Sally told Marie in the morning, her square jaw set firm. Marie could see her friend's wounded spirit in her tear-stained eyes. "She wasn't ready," Sally said after a time. Marie nodded. Sally dropped her eyes while she and Marie wove mats from willows they'd stripped and split. "My baby wasn't ready."

"Some infants' deaths are not the result of a mother's poor choices," Marie consoled.

Sally lifted her eyes, frowned.

"I should have known better," Marie said, thinking of her own lost child.

Ross, Sally's husband, said, "It wasn't your fault, Madame Dorion.

I'm a Christian man. I surely don't believe you brought something bad into that birthing time."

But his words that night had accused, and his eyes accused now just the same while he petted Weasel, the rust-colored dog draped over his forearm. "Sally will be well," he said, his words clipped even in his fluent French. "But there were no miracles. The child is lost."

"Faith is the mother; miracles are her children," Marie told him, remembering something Sarah had once said. She'd thought the words hopeful. Marie added, "There will be others."

Ross turned away. Sally's eyes pooled with tears. They stained the pale green willows spread across her thighs as she kneeled.

Those aren't soothing words. Marie wished she'd kept silent. She wasn't like Sarah who could dispense comfort like swallows of cider given to weary *voyageurs.* Who was she to suggest there would be other children or that in saying it, the pain of the loss of this one could be salved? There had been no more babies for Marie after she had lost her child. Who was she, anyway, to say how life and death worked? Perhaps Ross believed he followed the riverbed like a fallen leaf rushed through spring, with no control over what was meant to happen. Who was Marie to intrude with mere words?

Marie had always set her own canoe into the water, made it go where she wished, even if, like now, it took her to an eddy where she made mistakes that brought pain to friends and separated her further from a place of belonging.

What words could she use to soothe her friend's pain? Marie tied sinew around the fibers, pulled to press the mat flat and smooth. She would weave Sally something, give her a gift as a way of telling her she shared her sorrow and to ask her forgiveness for saying words that cut like a knife.

❖

"Me! Take me," Baptiste said.

"You're too young, boy," Ross said. "This is a man's work, though I admire your willingness. You best look after your little brother, keep him from pulling at your mother's hair. A pronghorn hunt isn't child's play."

"My papa would take me," Baptiste shouted. People listened then.

"You don't have a papa now, so you do as you're told," Ross said. He reined his horse and the group of men set out, followed by several Okanogan men on foot.

"You help Sally in the kitchen garden," Marie said. "Her potatoes will keep us through the winter. Her people don't break the soil, but Ross does and Sally takes his ways. We do too, when it comes to food. You go help."

"I hunt. Men hunt," Baptiste said.

His mother looked over his head toward the departing men. "Do as I say," she said.

Baptiste kicked at a bone, sending it sailing across the grass as he walked. A dog went snarling after it. Baptiste looked back. His mother had gone into the hut. Good.

Baptiste circled around, waited until the Okanogan men were out of sight over the treeless ridge heading north toward what he'd heard his mother call Spokane country. Then he bent low like a creeping thing and moved at the side of the men on foot while keeping out of their sight. He had a small bow and a *par flèche* of arrows laced across his back. He knew how to hunt the small striped deer. He knew how to plant his feet, set his bow. He would bring a pronghorn home for his mother, make her proud of his ability to provide, put something besides potatoes into their stomachs come winter snows.

Birds threatened to distract him. The warmth of the midday September sun brought beads of water to his face. But he crept without being seen, raising his head to make sure he walked alongside the men, close enough to hear them but so silent they did not know that he was there. He would do this for his mother, make her proud.

He smelled smoke.

He stood up. Far beyond, he saw the men on horseback now, and in between them, a small herd of pronghorns. They should be moving closer, but instead the Okanogan men started fires of the dry grasses, the flames licking quickly at the thirsty strands. Like dancing wind, the fire swirled toward the herd. The animals ran away from the smoke. How would he get close to them? A hunter got close to his prey, that's what his papa taught him.

Baptiste ran, high-stepping through the grass now, outrunning the fire, he thought, getting ahead of the flames, moving closer to the herd, his heart pounding, strands of hair streaked across his eyes.

Through the smoke, he could see the herd milling around, with the men on horseback scaring them back toward the fire. He had to shoot, he was so close to the herd. He pulled his arrow from his *par flèche*.

Smoke billowed over him, pushed by the winds. He began coughing, his eyes and throat burning. He couldn't steady his bow, stepped back even farther from the pronghorns. Men shouted and flames appeared on both sides of him now. He'd gotten ahead of the fire starters who circled the herd, still forcing flames. He was inside with the herd, felt the ground shake with their pushing and shoving.

Rifle shots. He spun himself around. The men on horseback fired into the animals. He had to get out. He couldn't take a pronghorn now. His mother would be mad that he had failed to bring one back.

Flames circled them; he sought a break in the fire circle. But he stared instead, lost in the fire's rise and fall like birds lifting with the wind. The flames seemed to call his name, to sing a song as they moved toward him from all sides. He could simply watch it come, waving at him, burning yellow followed by charred black. His eyes stung and he felt sleepy.

An animal fell beside him, its legs brushing against his knees as it fell. He felt the pain of the hooves against his flesh. He stared at the animal. His face felt hot. He dropped his bow and ran.

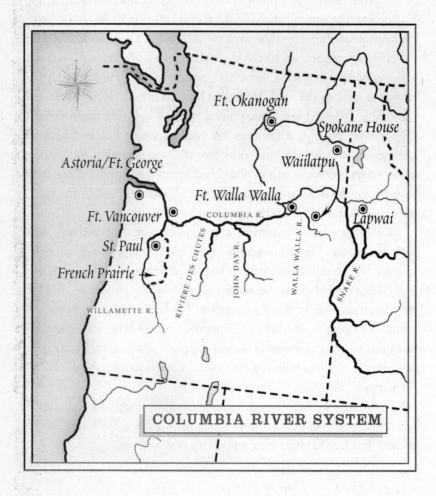

Ft. Okanogan

Spokane House

Astoria/Ft. George

Waiilatpu

Ft. Walla Walla

Ft. Vancouver

COLUMBIA R.

Lapwai

St. Paul

French Prairie

RIVIÈRE DES CHUTES

JOHN DAY R.

WALLA WALLA R.

SNAKE R.

WILLAMETTE R.

COLUMBIA RIVER SYSTEM

3

Priming

The hot season let itself be led like a reluctant colt into cooler nights and balmy days. Berries dotted the brushes in the higher country. Marie filled her baskets, then placed the fruit on the drying rocks alongside the other women. Huckleberries, some as small as the gnats that buzzed around the fort's horses, piled up in the covered baskets lining the perimeter of her hut. Every spare moment she had, she wove baskets or she learned something from the people or the landscape that would help her survive the winter. She watched as the women repaired fishing nets or wove willow weirs. Some of the grandmothers showed her how to place nets in unlikely places where the men might not notice. Otherwise, without a man to fish for her, the boys could go hungry.

Each time she felt tired from gathering driftwood and dragging it beside their hut or her back ached with the tending of fires for drying pemmican and fish or her fingers stiffened from scraping hides, she reminded herself that winter threatened.

She had to take care of her boys.

She had to be ready for winter.

She had to repay her husband's old debt.

Baptiste had confessed his effort to bring home a pronghorn. He'd come back smoky-eyed and smelling of charred grass.

"Where have you been?" Marie had demanded. She grabbed at his leather shirt, yanked him harder than intended. Baptiste winced away from her, bit at the inside of his cheek. *He's afraid of me,* she realized. She released him, her voice softened, "What's happened?"

Baptiste told her of the flames then, that fire helped the Okanogan people hunt.

"The flames danced, Mother. Up and down like old men's knees as they hobble about." His eyes were excited as he talked. It bothered her, how he told the story to Paul. She thought she should scold him, putting himself in danger, maybe upsetting the hunt. Her husband would have wanted her to scold him for his disobeying. But Baptiste had only wanted to do well.

Only later had she learned of the rifle fire and how close it had come to taking her eldest son's life.

"I should scold him for his *désobéissance*," Marie told Sally as the women walked along the stream at dusk, checking Marie's weir. "Someday his not listening to me will hurt him deeply."

"He learned from it," Sally said.

"Can a mother ever be sure what her sons have gained?"

❖

Marie's days were filled with work, with what a mother does. She looked for ways to gain against her husband's debt. Marie recalled seeing an unusual treatment used at Astoria. There, a Kanaka man from the Sandwich Islands had cured a man of the pox. They'd killed a horse and swiftly split the animal's stomach and placed the man in the carcass and sewed him inside, all but his head. When the animal's organs no longer offered heat, they repeated the routine with three or four other horses. Then the Kanaka removed the man and wrapped him in warm blankets for several hours. After the strange routine, the man's ills were gone.

"You're suggesting what?" Ross asked Marie when she suggested doing this for Celiaste, the woman with the swollen limbs and falling-out hair. "Put her limbs into intestines? We don't have that many horses to spare."

"Not horses," Marie said. "Dogs."

"Nonsense," one of the visiting North Westers said. "What good could that possibly do? I never thought that Kanakan cure had anything to do with the horse."

"It's a plan," Alexander Ross told him.

They'd implemented Marie's suggestion only after one of the old men nodded that he'd heard of such a thing too.

"At least we only lose some snarling curs," Ross said. "And I suppose if we succeed, her husband will wield his influence to make us their trade supplier forever. Imagine, keeping the Americans out with dead dogs and warm intestines."

It had taken thirty dogs over as many days, but the woman had improved, and by the time her husband arrived, Celiaste's hair had begun growing back and she could stand with help, and she even took some halting steps leaning on Marie's strong arm. Marie had been proud of the accomplishment. Ross had even taken some money off of Pierre's debt in gratitude for advice and help in the matter.

But her greatest pride, more than gathering up for winter, more than helping cure the woman, was that Marie hadn't struck either Paul or Baptiste since the day Paul had gouged the fawn's eyes. Even when her sons barked at her and sometimes punched her, she told them *non* with firmness, even scowling. But she refused to lay a hand against them.

Pierre had used the flat of his hand to control their sons—and her own flesh, too—and she believed it had not made her sons wiser in their choices, only made them move more quickly to avoid his force.

She would teach respect by showing it, by keeping her face calm. They'd learn that they couldn't distress her, even when they sneered or snarled. They were merely young children who, like dog pups in a litter, sometimes chewed even those with whom they'd shared the same womb. They'd survived much, her sons. They needed time to remake past misery into a present strength.

Marie worked on engaging her sons in helping sew a fox fur into an overshirt with a kind of hood to hold out wind. She patched leggings and tied sinew for snowshoes since Sally said they'd be needed come winter. She prepared her sons for a snow season different from the previous one that had been laced with longing and loss, violence and revenge.

When Marie dried salmon on the drying racks or when she rubbed deer brains onto hides to soften them, she invited Baptiste to watch; gave Paul sticks to rub together to make fire from them. She worked beside her sons. They were tied with tender knots, these three. A braid of three was much stronger than just two.

Baptiste waited now to be told what to do before he used his skinny arms to rub and soften a deer hide. He pushed and pulled against the leather, smiling with the effort of his arms.

"This is good," she told him. "The hide'll bring a fine trade to help us when the snows come." She talked soothingly as he worked. "We'll have a copper pot then, maybe."

"A fire-starter kit," Baptiste offered. "We need that."

"Not if we keep the fire going. You can weave mats while I do bead-work. We'll be inside safe and warm. Show your brother now, let him push on the hide."

"Weaving is women's work."

"Your father knew how to sew up leather."

"For when we hunt and trap," Baptiste said. "We need fire starter then."

"You'll have to stay behind when I set out to hunt," Marie told him.

"I provide," Baptiste said. "Like papa did." He sat back on his haunches, looked up at her.

"We'll have enough food stored," she assured him. "Pelts will give us money against our debt. It's not worth the risk of losing a small boy in the snows here. Sally says the drifts are very deep and the wind still blows and it gets so cold the men sleep with their moccasins close to their bellies or they'll be too stiff in the mornings to wear."

"We need guns," Baptiste said.

"Food," Paul said. "We eat a horse, *n'est-ce pas, Mère?*"

"We don't have a horse to kill now, *stupide,*" Baptiste said.

"*Non,* Baptiste," Marie scolded.

Baptiste pushed harder against the hide now, back and forth, rougher than needed. "I'm cold," he said and shivered then. "Snow makes me cold."

"The cold isn't bad if we're ready for it. Slow down, now," Marie said. "You waste the brains. It is not snow now."

He breathed hard, pushed even harder. *Didn't he hear me?* Paul looked at her, scowled, aware of a shift in the rhythm of work.

"Baptiste. Stop," Marie said.

"Too much snow." Baptiste gasped now, swallowed hard. "Too cold."

When she touched his shoulder, Baptiste startled as though burned. He jerked away from her.

"What is it?"

He blinked several times, worked to catch his breath. "I'm not scared. *Non,* no Dorion is scared."

Marie's mind raced backward. What scared him? What had she said or done to make the boy act this way? She touched his hands gripped over the rubbing stick. She peeled his fingers from it, looking at him. "Baptiste," she said. "It is not cold here now. See? Look around? Leaves are yellow on the willows, almost gone. The grass is dry, but the wind blows it. Hear the wind? Cool, but no snow."

Paul stared at his brother, fire sticks in hand, his eyes the size of stones. "I make fire, *Mère?* For Baptiste? See?"

"Non," Marie said. "He isn't cold, are you, Baptiste? And the hide smells ready for more rubbing." She pulled at the hide's edge so Baptiste could inhale it.

"Why do you do that?" The boy pinched his nose at her as he glared. Then he smiled, cautious and confused, like a man returning from a fit of coughing so loudly he missed words already spoken. He pushed Paul back away from him, and the younger boy slipped and fell, began to cry. "You play with your little sticks over there," Baptiste said. "Mama and I work here."

Marie reached for Paul to help him stand up. He was wailing far beyond his injury, and she pulled him to her, patted his little back. "You're settled," she said. "You're settled now. No need to—"

"He push me! He push me!"

"He didn't mean to," Marie lied. How they could go from a moment of gentleness so quickly to disruption always surprised her. "We'll check on the berries," Marie said. "We'll need them when the snow comes, but you could have a handful now. Would you like that?" Paul nodded, wiped at his eyes. "Good. Take your sticks."

"You'll come back, Mother?" Baptiste asked. His eyes pleaded.

"Un moment." She started to tell him to keep working to ready them for winter, but something stopped her. "I will bring a handful for you, too. Would you like berries?"

Her elder son nodded, then solemn, returned to his work.

As she walked with Paul toward the hut, she wondered if she should have scolded Baptiste for his meanness to his brother. Was that how one learned to treat a brother with kindness? Maybe she still pampered Paul too much. But when she disciplined, she felt as though she cut the ties that held them, even though she always followed with some act to tie the knot again, a special treat to eat, to bring them closer. But perhaps those knots just strained and stretched and didn't hold a thing.

If she didn't strike at them to discipline, and her gifting them with gentleness did not bring change, what could she do? How could she raise them into strong yet gentle men? She sighed. Perhaps a mother couldn't.

Perhaps only a father could.

✧

Louis Joseph Venier threaded the sinew through the bone needle's eye. He was a "tough old bird," as a grizzled trapper once called him. This ritual proved it. Not that he relished it. He didn't. But he told himself that the completion of it alone meant he could always take care of himself. What more did a man really need?

He planted his elbows on his knees as he sat, positioned so the sunlight could pour through the uplifted hide opening on his tipi. He could hear children chattering and a songbird or two twittering in the cottonwoods shading the Little Missouri River. He held his tongue between his teeth in concentration. Even though this was a task he performed by necessity and was always grateful he had, he resisted beginning. He took a deep breath.

"Well, Lune. Since you've found no cure for me, looks like I got to do it again, all on my own." The wolf pup thumped its tail on the dirt floor, its yellow eyes staring at the man who inhaled then stabbed the edge of his wide finger with the needle, breaking through the flap of water-cracked skin. *"Sacre Madre."*

He pulled the sinew, then jabbed at an open V that threatened to ooze with infection if he didn't stitch it closed. He drew the thread at the deep cut, lacing it back and forth the way women wound cradleboards to keep their infants in. He sewed the whole length of his pointing finger, back and forth, three or four times before he tugged the long V closed.

He exhaled, licked his lips, then tied the sinew. He set the needle down and took a swig of rum. "Sustenance," he told his pet. He wiped his black beard with the back of his hand, picked up the needle, and began sewing the middle finger.

For years, his hands had known water, first as a young French-Canadian *engagé* taking dignitaries from Montreal to outposts of the fur trading companies. Then on his own, he'd entered the landscapes of rivers and trees, setting traps, pulling steel teeth apart to remove silver foxes, martins, or tufted lynxes as he made his way in the world as a trapper. A free trapper, it was true. That was something to be cherished. He didn't belong to the bourgeois's brigade, didn't have to take orders from none but himself—and maybe those beaver.

Beaver took the greatest toll on his hands. Each time he set the trap it was deep beneath cold waters where the animals hid themselves, warned each other of dangers, almost humanlike with their looking after their own. Winter winds whipped against his face beside those snow-covered banks, brushed against tanned leathers, hide side out, that warmed his nearly six-foot-tall frame. But pulling the animals out of water required bare hands time after time, hour after hour, setting and releasing. There was no better way. And no amount of pine pitch and turpentine had ever been able to soothe the chapped gouges that lined his fingers like ravines. Even through long summer months when he didn't have to sink his hands in water, the deep cuts remained, promising infection until he discovered that he could sew them up.

"What I need, Lune," he said, pointing at the dog with the needle, a light summer breeze lifting the thread, "is a good woman to manage the hides and a good woman to sew up my hands. Don't you think so? *Non?*"

The wolf dog lifted his eyes but kept his head resting on his paws that touched the man's moccasined toes.

But after all the years of trapping the waters around Hudson's Bay then dropping south to the rivers that the Americans claimed fed the Missouri, he'd found neither a good woman he wished to take to his bed nor a cure for the cuts that pained his hands. And so he sewed alone.

Outside his hut, Omaha women checked the last of the buffalo-hide strips drying on the latticework high above the sniffing dogs. February had been the last hunt, a good one, and Louis had been the recipient of fresh meat as a wintering guest among them. He liked the Omaha, and they seemed to return the favor. Not long now and the traders would be making their way up the Missouri, bringing kettles and trinkets and taking back the Omaha's winter efforts. It was a cycle as certain as seasons. And Louis was a part of it.

He finished his work, the stitching on his left hand always looking a little tidier than that of his right. By spring, the wounds would be healed and, for the first time in years, he'd not have to plunge his hands into cold water. He was making a change.

He crawled out of the skin tent. His eye fell on the lovely Mitain.

He had once thought of courting the lovely, lithe daughter of the Omaha chief. He'd always imagined himself with a passel of children running about, teaching his boys to fish and trap; tickling his daughter's chin with his bristly beard till she laughed. He had imagined himself a good father. Stern, as a man had to be, but able to laugh, especially with his daughters.

But a Spanish trader, Manuel Lisa, had butted into Louis's territory before he even knew what had happened. During a winter past, the man had managed to win the girl's father, the old chief, over. Lisa claimed the comely Mitain as his wife. She'd resisted, Louis had heard. But eventually, the young girl warmed the man's bed as part of *à la façon du pays,* a marriage of the country. With no Jesuit to suggest otherwise, the girl had consented to the marriage of the country.

That next spring, Manuel Lisa left Mitain, her young frame already showing that she carried his child.

"Going on to the Great Salt Lake," Lisa was heard to tell her. "I'll be back, my pretty."

Lisa hadn't gone any farther west than Henry's Fort where he picked up some treasured cache of furs and then returned to St. Louis to his first wife, a European woman. But he'd stopped by the Omaha village to meet his son, and soon all witnessed the left-evidence of another child who would arrive the following year.

That eldest child pulled against his mother's hand now, his two-year-old hand leading her toward the river or some grand adventure. Mitain's infant girl must be in sleeping with the grandmother, at least for the moment. Manuel Lisa'd given a poor impression of the Spanish faith, using the girl as nothing better than to warm his bed, to carry his kin, when, as a good Catholic, he should have cherished the mother of his children.

Mitain's dark eyes caught Louis's as her son pulled her past him. She dropped her gaze to the grasses so she never saw his sign of greeting.

"Her eyes lack a spark, Lune," Louis told his pet. "That Manuel Lisa takes it." The dog thumped its tail on the hard earth floor.

During the long months of the trader's absence, Louis thought to take the girl as his wife despite Lisa's claim; but Louis had heard Mitain's wail when Manuel Lisa left the last time. He knew then that the man couldn't be replaced in that girl's heart.

Besides, she had two children now. "Bringing up another man's child would be like growing up a wolf pup," he told Lune as he scratched at the animal's ears. "Takes many *Sacre Madres* to intervene." One never knew where that offspring's loyalties might lie or when they'd revert to missing what they knew first and hold their new caretaker accountable for their loss.

Manuel Lisa hadn't done much for his children. Like weeds, their father'd just allowed them to grow up.

Sometimes Louis was embarrassed to be a part of that race of men called trappers and traders who wanted to ravish not only the land but the people who'd lived within it, making their way without conscience as far as he could tell. Some wanted them to trap for people as well as for pelts.

Louis checked his own bales of pelts, the ones he'd be trading soon. His efforts at trapping kept him constantly finding ways to take the bounty with the least amount of disruption. He moved out of an area, off a stream, before it was depleted. He made himself a good neighbor. He never took more pelts than what he thought he'd need to trade for his wintering supplies and to put a small amount aside for when he'd get too old to work the trap lines.

He was only thirty. Maybe thirty-one, he couldn't remember exact. But he didn't want to live in a settlement in his old age. No, he was hoping he could see some of what lay beyond the mountains, go where the North Wester David Thompson had set up a post with the Spokane. He wanted to see the waterfalls said to be unlike any along the Missouri system, even grander than the Yellowstone's.

Other unanswered questions pulled him west, too. He'd heard of the Nez Perce and an Indian woman who had translated for Lewis and Clark. *How had that happened?* he wondered. Strange, unexpected things like that always interested him. He supposed it was why he liked books. They gave explanations or at least speculations.

He wasn't sure what he'd do in that western territory, but he'd find something that didn't require him to sew up his own fingers. Maybe after he accomplished his journey overland to the Nez Perce country, he'd go all the way to the Pacific, ride in a ship, and head for Canton, China. Maybe even return to his beloved Terrebonne in Quebec.

For sure, he'd buy a book or two.

The West held his dream, his wish. Wasn't a man, even an older man, entitled to a dream?

"I'm not a complicated soul," he told the wolf pup that whined now beside his hide boots. He still watched the sway of Mitain, her rounded hips covered by a smooth hide the color of a sandy bar. She disappeared from sight, though he could still hear the child's chatter and Mitain's musical response.

Louis opened and closed his fingers, stretching the taut seams at the creases of his fingers. He'd be glad when next year's spring brigade arrived with supplies to take away his winter's work and he could head west. He felt restless here, though he wasn't sure why.

"No, I don't need much," he told his pet. Lune's fur felt thicker than usual, forewarning a hard winter on the Missouri. "So long as I can sew my own wounds up tight, what more could a man want?"

✦

"I play dead," Paul said. "You too." With his fist, Paul poked at Baptiste, who worked a bow into an arc. Paul spoke more clearly now, the winter offering more time together, more time to listen to his mother speak, watch how she formed words with her lips.

"Baby play," Baptiste said. "Go make baby boards. Use a broken oar," he said. "I have work to do, *n'est-ce pas,* Mother?"

Marie nodded. "But his eyes are filled with you," she told Baptiste. "Be gentle."

"He plays death," Baptiste said. "I don't like that game."

"My brother's scared," Paul said. "My brother's scared." He held his fist close to Baptiste's face.

"Paul," Marie chided. "Play what you wish. Let your brother be."

"He needs *Mère* to nurse him," Paul said. "I play on my own." He stomped through the flap of the hut.

"Be careful, Paul…" Marie watched him.

She recalled watching Paul play in the snowdrifts, urging the other children to roll into a robe so he could pretend to tie them. Sometimes he asked them to bind him and his brother. *What darkness stirs his mind?* Marie's sides ached with grief, now woven with ritual into remembrance.

❖

Snow's gone. Good.

"Dig there," Paul's mother told him. "Go deeper."

"I work hard for you, *n'est-ce pas?*" Paul said. He spoke carefully, watching her mouth. She smiled when he talked slow, made the sounds come out the way she taught him. *Does she like what I do?* "I work hard?"

"*Pardon?* Yes, you are a good worker, Paul," his mother said. Her eyes sailed over him through the open door. He turned to see what she looked at. Just hills. She paid more attention to hills than to him.

"Dig now," she commanded.

Paul pushed the deer shoulder blade deeper. His mother should have wrapped the handle tighter to the deer blade; it would make a better shovel. Paul wiggled the handle, and the rough wood snagged his fingers. "My hands are stung," Paul said. He pushed the shovel over the side of the pit. He pulled himself out of the hole. *Will she notice? She never notices.*

"*Pardon?*" His mother said.

"See." He put his hand right under her chin.

She lifted his hand, turned it over gently. He liked the feel of her hand on his. "We'll put bear grease on them later," she said. "Or skunk oil. When the hole is deep enough. I better dig now. You hurt too much, *n'est-ce pas?* Should your brother help again? I'll go call him." But she didn't move. She just stared at the hole. She didn't look again at his hands. She often looked one place but talked at another.

"*Maintenant?*" he said. "You call Baptiste now?" He tossed the shovel into the hole. He didn't like being down there. It was dark, even with a lamp his mother left there when she dug.

"You wanted to dig, Paul."

"They sting like bees." He pushed his open fingers at her, closer to her face. Sometimes she acted like an old dog without eyes, pretending she couldn't see the slivers. "You fix them. They hurt." He raised his voice. "Baptiste can dig."

"Your brother worked all morning," Paul's mother told him. She sounded scolding all the time. "I'll do it now."

"Why dig an old hole?"

His mother breathed out through her mouth. "How many times must I tell you this? Because I don't want the skunks to eat up our dried fish or the smoked meat. I don't want raccoon scat full of berries all over our hut. I don't want my sons to go hungry. So, I dig now."

She said this before? He couldn't remember.

"We were hungry in the snow," he said.

She wiped at her eyes. He could make her cry, he could, he was so strong. But he couldn't make her see his sore hands. Not when he wanted.

His mind wandered. She dug to get rid of the skunks? Skunks were pretty.

But they smelled.

He remembered now. Once he'd cornered one inside the fort's palisade and his brother had yelled, "Grab the tail. You can get 'em that way." Paul snatched at the black-and-white silky fluff. It was tattered with stickers and seeds. How'd they get there? Paul had laughed, then wanted to cry when the smell of old meat hit his face, stinging his eyes, making his mouth taste like ash. His eyes had burned, and he'd dropped the skunk and tried to find his mother, but he couldn't see. He hated not seeing.

Ha! His mother had scolded his brother then. He could hear her, but not see her, and his eyes stung as though slices of ice cut them. His mother lifted him and ran. The next thing he remembered was the water splashing on him and the sound of his mother stepping high in the river. "I'll hold you," she said. He felt the cold, soothing water cover him, his face, his eyes, and then felt the cool air as she pulled him up, cooing like a dove to him. He was safe, so safe. "Poor Paul, my *bébé*, Paul."

Two or three more times she'd bathed him in that way, all his clothes on while she held him. Then she'd stripped his clothes and shouted for his brother to come bury them, and she'd carried him to the hut and wrapped him in a buffalo robe.

He hated that robe.

But this time, she stayed with him and held him. Even after his eyes felt better, he pretended they didn't. It kept her with him. Not as long as he wanted. It was never as long as he wanted.

Sally Ross came and asked to hold him, and his mother had let her. Sally was soft and smelled of roots, but Paul cried and reached for his mother. She took him back. He had made her take him back. And then his mother laid him on the robe. "You stay. I'll be back."

His heart thumped like a woodpecker pounding a tree, and air stuck in his throat. She'd said she would come back. He'd willed her to come back and she had. He'd made her come back so he could breathe again. She put something cool onto his eyes.

His mother had gotten Sally Ross's man to use some of his ammunition to shoot the skunk that sprayed him. His mother said she'd give him some of the skunk oil in trade for the ammunition used. She always traded. He wished she'd trade for sweet molasses. He wanted molasses on his tongue.

Now the skunks were again hiding in the pretty flowers that popped up where the snow melted. His mother said they'd find a better place to hide the food from those skunks.

"Remember, Paul?" she asked. She looked at him now. "Paul? Where did your mind go?"

He loved it when she looked at him with waterfall eyes, all bubbling and wet. "Sally and Alexander Ross had a hole with a door on it inside their old hut. And a ladder so they could go down for food but keep the skunks out. Remember?"

"He's scared of snakes," Baptiste said.

Baptiste always barked words out like Ross's little dog, short bursts that threatened bites but were all boast, no action.

"No!" Paul turned, the shovel still in his hand. "I'm not scared of snakes. They're my friends."

"Wasn't talking about you. Ross is scared of 'em," Baptiste said. "He says he built that pit of his to fool the skunks, but it was snakes that troubled him. He talks about 'em all the time. Even fat branches make him jump when he sees one in the dirt. Thinks it'll jump up at him. Rattle a few stones and watch him howl."

"It's not kind to poke people where their hurts are," his mother said.

"See my hand?" Paul said, shoving his fingers beneath his brother's face.

Baptiste grunted. Then before Paul could pull his hand free, Baptiste pressed his thumb into his brother's open palm. "Don't hurt me none," Baptiste said.

Paul wailed. Not that it hurt so much, but he wanted his mother to see how Baptiste troubled him. His crying sent his mother's accusing eyes to Baptiste.

"You dig now," she told Baptiste as she handed him the shovel. "Give your brother a rest."

Paul sniffed. His mother patted his shoulder. Paul sucked breath in short gasps like a stone skipping on water. He grabbed his mother's legs and leaned into her leather dress. Paul could smell fresh chalk where she must have wiped out a stain from her dress.

He wondered how long he could hold her like this, all his, while his brother had to work. That was all he wanted, just to hold her to him. He squeezed tighter. Whimpered. His mother patted his head. He caught at his breath.

He made sure Baptiste saw his smile.

4

Skunked

Marie watched the man move, a mixture of confidence and caution as he untangled his long legs from the *bateau*. Many more brigades from the North West company had come in this spring, moving inland from Fort George—her old Astoria—meeting others coming south. Men in blue knit hats, wearing sashes. French *voyageurs* with curly greased hair hanging over their necks. Irish clerks and Scottish bourgeois, always assessing profits and pelts.

Marie squinted. She wished she could make faces out before people got so close, but her eyes did not cooperate. Things blurred, like stars watched through tears. She worked in the kitchen garden now, Ross agreeing to her digging and hoeing in return for some of the rutabagas and potatoes at harvest.

Perhaps he'd been here before and that was why he looked familiar. He might be a clerk. Could it be that boy Jean Toupin, who had acted shy with her and had given her a pair of earrings he'd had a silversmith make? She'd accepted the gift and, after her husband died, had traded the copper tubes away for seeds and a new beginning for her sons.

She fingered her ears. No copper tubes hung down to scatter off the mosquitoes when she shook her head. Something else she missed.

As the man approached, Marie knew it wasn't Jean Toupin. It was a young *voyageur* she knew, someone she'd hardly noticed while at Astoria. He'd seemed a mere boy then, though he must have been sixteen or seventeen, only a few years younger than she. He looked older now. Maybe twenty summers. She did remember him liking horses. And the chief factor, McDougall, had sent him on errands that he scampered to accomplish.

Tall, with black eyes that sank like caves into a well-tanned face, he moved like the slow pouring of rum. He gave a confident tip to his blue yarn hat when he saw Alexander Ross approach through the fort's gate, the slightest lift of a smile to Sally as she walked out behind her husband.

Marie tried to remember his name. Mc-something. All the Scots seemed to have that beginning to their names. McKay. Yes, Tom McKay. He was the son of an Astorian Scot and an Indian mother. His father had been killed on the *Tonquin* when coastal Indians had attacked then burned that Astor ship.

"Heading to Jaspar House, then?" Ross asked. The party met not far from Marie. Ross reached up to slap the shoulder of Tom McKay. "Will you go all the way back? See your mother? I hear she's being well taken care of by a young doctor."

"McLoughlin," McKay told him. He made no effort to return Ross's jovial mood.

"Sure and that's the one. With Hudson's Bay, I hear. Our rival. Quite a bit younger than she. 'Tis good she's not alone with the little ones."

Tom McKay stared beyond the Scotsman, his profile to Ross. He scanned the plains between the two rivers. Hadn't Sarah told Marie that the boy, Tom McKay, was one of the men who met with Hunt to tell them that Astoria had been sold to the British? McKay must have been part of the inner circle, part of the decision-making, to be included in such an important meeting.

Maybe he was responsible for bringing the four cows north, a treasure entrusted only to the most loyal of men.

Should I ask him? Will he understand my English?

Other partners joined the men, and the moment was lost. McKay gazed, scanned the landscape, then spoke his words firm, sure, as though he fit first into this wolf litter of fur trapping men. They moved away then from the company of women. Marie felt a tinge of loss.

"Ross has ordered an event," Sally said later.

"What is this event?" Marie asked.

"A celebration," Sally said. "A feast followed by dancing."

"I can help serve," Marie offered.

Sally said, "And you can dance, too. With me if no man invites you. It's been a year."

Marie was startled by Sally's statement. Yes, it had been a year since her husband's death, longer since the death of her only daughter. Sally expected another child soon; Marie was surprised the woman would speak of death with such an easy air. Perhaps it was a sign that she was forgiven for what happened before. Perhaps Marie would be asked to be a *sage femme* for Sally this time.

That evening of the brigade's arrival, women danced shoulder to shoulder in a circle pattern beneath the June moon, their faces lit by firelight. Coyotes howled in the distance. Then a fiddle was drawn from one of the clerk's packs, and soon *voyageurs* and maidens stomped the grass flat. Even children danced in their own little circle while dozens of dogs snarled over discarded bones from the feast.

Marie sat with a blanket wrapped around her shoulders. Other women gossiped not far from her. She knew their names but was not included in their chatter. A chasm ran between them formed of languages unshared. The women at the fort avoided Marie. She assumed they found her unworthy because she had risked her sons in winter, lost her husband to attack. If not for Sally's speaking French and broken English with her, Marie would rarely carry on a conversation with a woman's words.

Marie turned her attention to her sons; she was here to watch them play. She didn't need to be nurtured by Okanogan ways. It didn't matter if no one noticed her. It was too soon for a widow to step into grass anyway. She watched Sally's fringed skirt shift as she danced. Sally wore a beaded necklace that Marie had given her as her apology gift nearly a year before now. And she could see the swell beneath her friend's breast that said the baby she carried was big already and hopefully wouldn't come early.

"You are the woman who lived with her sons in the mountains after the Indians killed Reed's men." Tom McKay stood beside Marie, arriving quiet as snow. He squatted then, pulling on a blade of grass he twirled in his fingers. He stayed close. Marie could smell waxed leather from his tanned shirt. He wore no cap now, and she could see that where the sun touched his upper forehead, his face was a nut-brown color.

Marie felt a hummingbird beating in her heart. Her face heated, and she dropped the blanket from her shoulders, then picked up her beadwork. She ran her fingers over the design held in her lap. He waited in her silence, watched the *voyageurs* and Okanogan women pair up for another dance.

"*Oui,*" she said. "My husband died."

"We are both left behind by acts of our savage kin. I could tell some stories."

"They weren't my people," she said. "Nor your—"

"Scots," he said. "My people are Scots, and my mother's people are part Ojibway."

"So life goes on."

Tom McKay nodded his head once, still looking out at the dancers, never turning to look at her when she spoke. Pierre had often acted that way, as though seeing her face when she told him things would offer no new information than what his ears would hear.

"A *métis,*" he said and nodded toward the children, "like your sons, has lots of stories."

Marie noticed Paul staring at them, no longer playing with his friends. His arms were crossed. She wasn't sure where Baptiste was. She scanned, found him with older boys, eating and laughing. She wished Baptiste would find comfort in his brother's company instead of seeking others. Brothers needed to stay together.

Tom McKay clenched his jaw, and Marie thought she saw sadness swirled with fire in the dark eyes of this mixed-blood man.

"You would dance," he said then, not a question. This time he looked at her.

Marie took a startled breath. Perhaps it would not dishonor her husband for her to take this man's hand and toe-heel, toe-heel to the drums and let him swirl her to the fiddle. The hummingbird of her heart beat faster still.

"I would dance," she said and took his hand.

He lifted the beadwork from her fingers, laid it in the grass, took her hand in his, his grasp firm. The movement reminded her of Pierre in those later years when he was steady like a river's current, yet always watching to see where the river took him, where he might find a rapid he should portage around.

Marie caught Sally's eye as they danced a circle dance, and Sally grinned at her, holding her stomach. Yes, this time, the child would live.

Tom McKay pulled Marie closer to him, and she smelled tobacco, sweat, and sureness.

And then she allowed herself to ache, to feel the longing of a hand touching her, not in pain or counsel over grief, not with the fingertips of a child reaching out to her to feed or nurse, but as a woman, desired. A fog lifted. She heard each fiddler's note, smelled the night fires as though just lit. A smile formed on her lips, and she suppressed the giggle pushing upward like a sneeze. His hipbone touched hers as they faced forward around the circle, his arm behind her. Marie stepped higher, the fringe of her leggings like loose hair in the wind. Tom McKay picked up his knees too, and she laughed out loud with him. Then she leaned into this man she guessed had lived fewer years than she. She drank the water of his tender ways.

"I would come to your hut," he said to her when the dance ended and she returned to retrieve her beadwork. She lifted the coiled basket. She was as tall as he, and he whispered easily in her ear.

She stiffened at his closeness.

"When your boys sleep," he said.

"They stir at simple sounds."

"I'll bring molasses then," he said. "It quiets them." He laughed. "It is as good as mother's milk."

❖

Paul yanked his brother's arm. "See," he told him. "She holds on to that man. We go get her to stay with us."

Baptiste boxed his brother's ears. The wop of air startled, and his brother's fist stung. "She dances," Baptiste said. "Women do that. And now she works her beads. Leave her be."

Paul rubbed his ears. "I'll kill him if he comes close."

"You're a baby," Baptiste said. "You talk big."

"No baby." Paul struck at his brother's arm, but Baptiste jumped back, held Paul's forehead with his hand while Paul flailed toward his brother's chest but met the wind instead. "No baby! I kill him."

An older boy called to Baptiste. He let Paul loose and left his brother to join his friend. Paul stumbled forward with the abrupt release of his brother's hand from his head.

"I watch with cat's eyes," Paul shouted after him. "No baby. You see."

❖

Marie's heart pounded, and she swallowed hard. What was she worrying over? Her sons were asleep on the other side of the hut. Her husband had been dead more than a year now, and for the first time since the massacre, she'd actually welcomed a man's touch to her shoulder, her face. She intended only to be held closely, to perhaps feel the brush of his lips against hers. This man treated her well, honored her worries. He hadn't moved beyond the eddy of her will.

Instead, he'd waited until the camp was quiet, the boys asleep on the robe, before his fingers scratched at the hut's flap and he entered. They'd sat on a mat and talked, his French intermixed with English words. McKay had important connections with the Company, connections that might help Marie's sons to be able to walk in both worlds, like him. It was good for a mother to discuss such things that might benefit her sons. Yes, this was an evening of discussion necessary to keep her boys safe, valued if she wished to someday live without a debt. This time with Tom McKay was nothing more than giving to her sons as a mother should. This was her work, her *métier,* seeking ways to advance her sons. Marie swallowed. *Did she tell herself the truth?* Her heart beat faster.

They spoke of what happened at Fort George, what the North West Company planned, how they worried over the Americans and the other

Brits who owned that Hudson's Bay Company that his stepfather worked for.

Tom McKay didn't boast of his influence or his exploits. He had not even pressed his lips to hers, though she suspected soon he would and that was why her palms moistened, her breath came quickly. Then like a hovering hawk, Tom McKay circled from the wide world of the fur trade to whisper words about himself, his travels, his mother, his father's death. His voice held bitterness with the last, of being left behind by Company orders and learning how his father had died, on duty, by the hands of Indians and the poor choices of an "American ship's captain." He almost spit the words out.

"He set my mother off before he left her," Tom said. Red embers of driftwood burned in the firepit, flashing shadows on his face.

Marie touched his hand. "The stone you carry that you'd throw against the wall of others comes back to hurt you. Such a big stone weighs you down."

Tom stiffened, no longer lounged against one elbow but seated now, still as a heron in backwater.

"To throw a stone against yourself wounds deep," she continued. Still silence.

"I know such stones," she said. "My husband's death. My daughter's. Even my sons are grinding stones for my own poor choices."

He still said nothing more though she could hear his breathing, see the tightening of his jaw release within the shadow. He'd shared something from inside himself, allowed time for her to receive it, and she had offended. It was who she was, always falling short. This was all too new, too uncertain, this using words with strange men. Marie picked at her nails with fingers; dug her nails into her palms now formed into fists. Who was she to be talking as though she had Sarah's wisdom? She'd grown up with her first husband, been around him as a sister first, almost a mere child he'd rescued. He had rarely treated her as his equal, a wife beside him. He had ordered, saw her always as that child.

This man was a stranger, and he'd spoken words closer to his heart than ones her husband had ever shared with her. And she'd offended.

An occasional night sound startled. She thought she heard the thump of a raccoon at the side of the hut, a dog barking in the distance, the laughter of revelers shooting valued ammunition to "put out the stars."

Marie twisted at the knot of hair on the back of her neck. She couldn't bring herself to loosen it, this intimate act done only with her husband. Her hands sweat with the uncertainty of what should come next after such a silence. She'd exposed herself in telling him of her sons as grinding stones.

"The night frightens you," Tom said at last, his hand over hers now, warm, firm.

She shook her head. "Cold."

It wasn't a lie. She did feel a draft and had been cold for a while now. Had the flap on the hut opened? Perhaps Tom McKay hadn't retied it when he came in. Little moonlight showed through. "The closing hide…" she said, keeping her voice low. "It lets air in. I'll light a candle to see if it's tied."

"I'll look," he said, patting her hand as he released her fingers. In one graceful move he unwound his long legs where he'd been sitting beside Marie and crawled toward the door in the darkness. He opened the flap.

"The moon," he said. "*Belle lune.* Come share it."

She stepped around the pit-covering laid over the new hole, hoping she wouldn't wake the boys. They stood outside the hut and looked at the night sky. After a while Tom said, "There is such beauty in your eyes, Marie Dorion. Reflected by the moon."

Wind blew prickles of dust against her face, their clothing. He reached for her fingers then and held them. "We go back inside, *oui?* I tell you a story while I hold you."

She swallowed. Her breath stuck in her throat. *"Oui,"* she said.

He opened the flap. He bent to step in first, took two steps, then disappeared into the darkness, moaning in pain like a buffalo stumbling. *"Blesid Maria!"*

"Qu' est-ce qu'il ya?" Was it the boys, were they all right? Had something slipped in behind them, hurt her sons and Tom too?

Surely the sounds would wake them. *Where's Tom?* But when Marie bent to Paul and Baptiste and she struck the light, they both lay curled on the robe, making sleeping noises even through Tom's outcry.

She heard Tom moan again. She lowered the candle to the sound, and her heart sank with the knowing. Someone had slid off the trap door to the store pit. Tom lay tumbled inside.

Marie's fingers shook. Tom breathed hard, spit out the words, "My. Leg."

Marie turned around. "Can you stand?" she said.

"No."

She eased herself down the ladder into the pit, settled beside him. She placed the candle on the small shelf. She could feel spiders scattering, smelled moist dirt. "If you can step with your good leg, onto the crate," she said. "Pull yourself up. I'll push you. I'm strong." She could see the gouge ripped into the top of his legging, at his hip. She saw white skin, blood, and the sharp shard of bone protruding.

Each jerk must have sent searing pain into him, but he didn't shout out again. Marie pushed with her shoulder from beneath him, and he cleared the top of the pit where Baptiste sat, mouth open. Marie lifted herself up beside Tom where he lay, panting.

"Get Ross," she told Baptiste.

"No," Tom said. "Help me to the fort, tell them…I've fallen. No reason for them to know it happened here."

She motioned for Baptiste to go. The boy stared at her, his face all shadow and dark angle in the candlelight. "Mother?"

"Go," she said. "Wake Ross."

"Let the boy recover from his…night surprise," Tom said.

"I am so sorry. I must have knocked the door ajar when I stepped out," Marie said. "Lifted it free."

"Believe what you will, woman," Tom said.

It couldn't be on purpose. Baptiste wouldn't do something like that on purpose. He appeared too frightened as he backed out of the hut to make room for Tom, who sat breathing hard on the floor, blood oozing as he sat beside the open pit. Marie put a soft cloth to his wound. "Go!" she told Baptiste.

Instead, Baptiste handed Tom the shovel. "Lean on it," he said. Tom stood up with Marie's help and leaned against the handle.

"You don't listen to me," Marie scolded.

Tom's breath came in short bursts of pain. He leaned against Marie as she pulled his arm around her neck. "I'll tell Ross I fell by the dock."

"What happened, *Mère?*" Paul wiped at his eyes as he sat up.

"Did you sleep through this?" She turned, causing Tom to gasp out again in pain.

Baptiste snorted.

"I sleep and dream," Paul said and looked at his mother, his head cocked as though he waited for deserved molasses sweets. He looked so young, so innocent. He was too young to shift the boards that covered the pit. Especially so quietly that neither she nor Tom would have noticed in the night. And he'd slept through it all.

Still, they'd been outside for a time, watching the moon.

Once outside, she helped Tom hobble around the kitchen garden to the fort entrance, thinking of Paul's look as they left.

It wouldn't have taken much to pull the lid back, leave it partway open, while she and Tom turned their backs on her boys. Perhaps that had been the draft she had felt. And when Tom stepped back inside… but it might have been *her* stepping back inside first.

No. Her heart fluttered from newness to knowledge.

She wanted to believe it was her feet that had disturbed the lip of the lid. Tom's injury was *her* fault. How quickly she'd lost sight of her purpose—taking care of her sons, having enough food to survive, paying off her husband's debt. She'd forgotten, sought something for herself, and see what it had gotten.

When she returned from helping Tom, the boys were still awake. They stood when she entered. "Paul, Baptiste," she said, "Do you know how the boards came off the storage pit?" Paul lowered his head. "So. You did this thing," Marie said to him.

Paul moved to stand beside her then. "Skunks," he said. He leaned into her, his head at her thigh, his childish voice like a kitten's purr. "I remember to keep you safe from skunks."

❖

The brigade remained three more days. When one moved south back to Fort George, Tom went with it. They'd exchanged no words since that night, and Marie had heard from Sally that "McKay broke his leg when he stumbled in the night on his way to getting his gear from the *bateau*. He couldn't wait till morning," Sally laughed. "Oh no, he wanted his skunk oil for his chest. He rubs it in to help his breathing. Good thing he had breath enough to shout for help, *n'est-ce pas?* And that your ears were available to hear, *oui?*" She lifted her chin in that way she had that said she knew more than her words said.

Marie stood watching the boats ease into the fast-moving stream. She tasted her own tears. Her sons needed strength, a strong hand. Tom was a good man: wise and perhaps willing to help raise another man's sons. Had her sons—it would have taken them both—set a trap for him, one that might have taken his life and not just broken his leg? A trap that could have just as easily injured her?

Perhaps she had erred by not listening to Sarah, by not going with them to the Spokane place. She'd have to discipline her sons, but for what? She wasn't sure they'd done this, at least she wasn't sure of Baptiste's part in it. And Paul was so young, only five summers. A mother had to be certain if her sons had been disrespectful, had set a trap that injured. A mother had to be sure before taking action, had to be certain to be worthy and just.

She would have to separate herself more from others, give more attention to her sons. It was the gift of her presence they longed for, and in all this living and surviving winter, they'd felt set aside. She'd been selfish wishing time with a man like Tom McKay. Her sons had only been protecting, their efforts gone too far.

This was her fault. She had neglected teaching her sons what mattered, that gentleness with living things came first. She had paid attention to her own longings as she sat outside the Okanogan circle, felt separated and alone. Tom McKay had offered to fill her basket up. She hadn't known it was already full with the loving of her sons.

5

Sojourn

It had been a good placement for Jean Toupin these past two years. He liked cooking and had a good sense of smell, so good that he could identify various spices even when they had no written labels attached to the boxes. Two talents given him that he could put to good use at the fur post called Spokane. Even his height suggested he was better suited for the kitchen than the *milieu* position he'd given up. He could reach the pots and plates lining the tall, crude shelves ending just below the ceilings at the fort. Sometimes they whisked him north in the Company *bateau* to create dishes at other posts, but he liked this post best.

At this Spokane House, the factor named Cox had particular tastes, wanted eggs hardly boiled and his coffee with cinnamon in it. Jean had learned the Scot and British likes and dislikes for appetite and routine. He sorted men's wishes, remembered their preferences so he could serve them better. To serve was worthy work. Mind work rather than hand work, Michel might have said, but honest work and warm in winter. It was also true that few wanted to upset the cook, another benefit of agreeing to be in the Company kitchen. Yes, he'd found a place of satisfaction. He didn't miss the adventures Michel told him about when his old friend happened by. He hadn't made it to downriver forts like the Okanogan or Fort George since he'd found favor in this kitchen.

"There are cows now at Fort George. You could become the herdsman," Michel said while eating his cheek bread, a favorite of the French-Canadians. He separated the two rounded loaves baked side by side. "These cows would give you a new position."

"I'd become a keeper of horses," Jean told him. "But never cows. They're headstrong and devious, slapping their tails in your face. They know what they're doing trying to make a man's life miserable while looking all dreamy-eyed. Clever, that's what they are."

"These Americans, I hear them call them *neat* cows," Michel said.

Jean considered. "There must be more than one English meaning of that word. Cows are anything but tidy. Besides, even tamed Spanish cows are dangerous with their horns. No, I'll remain in my kitchens, even in the hot summers, and far away from cattle."

Michel shrugged his shoulders. "I keep looking for ways to make you a free man," he said. He leaned toward his friend. "I do only work as a free laborer. It is the only way to be in this world. The rest of the time, my native wives keep me busy, and I trap and trade as I wish." Michel looked around as though the walls might have ears. "Even with the Americans."

"Could be trouble," Jean said.

Michel chewed his bread, held a chunk in his large paw, used it to emphasize his point.

"There will always be troubles," he said. "So a man must prepare to die well by living well. He must look after his family and his faith, but he must listen to the fire in his heart and keep it burning."

"My *métier* is to not burn things in the kitchen," Jean said. He grinned at his friend.

"But you take no wife. A man must listen to his heart or he'll shrivel up like an old apple, not even good for cider. You should seek adventures as you once did. Here, in this woman's place, you become heavy before your time."

Jean tugged at the leather apron at his stomach. He was still slender, hadn't gained any pounds. "I like the kitchen work, and my payment from the Company sustains me with a little to set aside for my mother and for another time, for myself. When I'm old. I ask for nothing more."

"You will live your life alone, *oui*? It will be so sad." Michel shook his head, chewed. "These Spokane, they have not found you a woman to warm your bed?"

Jean turned his back to Michel, checked the porridge of peas cooking behind him, the old song of "peas porridge hot, peas porridge cold, peas porridge in the pot, nine days old" running through his head.

"I help you to meet your life mate, eh?"

Jean didn't need a life mate. He enjoyed the company of many women, tending to them. The Company men's wives took pleasure in his care for them. Jean prided himself on remembering little things— about how the women liked their bacon cooked, which child disliked peas, or whether a young daughter wanted her napkin unfolded and placed in her lap or liked two, one for dabbing when the heat of the summer beaded at her forehead. Jean enjoyed the company of women, their sweet perfumes and twitters reminding him of his mother and sisters, he supposed. He liked their chatter about homey things of children and hearth and was often asked to look after little ones while the women stitched. Tending babies was good work, much easier than working as a *milieu,* though now that he thought of it, both tasks were held in the same low regard by the Company partners.

He often forgot they weren't fine ladies of European husbands but were the native wives of Company men. Jean wondered if the women adapted European ways as insurance that their husbands would not set them off someday. Maybe they hoped that when their husbands returned to their place of origin to retire that they'd take their Indian wives with them. But for the color of their skin or their high cheekbones and sculpted noses, they could be French or Spanish or even Russian as far as Jean could tell. Maybe the women secretly hoped the Company would change their rules, in time, and allow the men to take them back without fear of fines, without fear of rejection in polite society.

They all tried to become "small-waisted women," putting aside the leathers of the Indian women who worked pelts. Madame Dorion had first used that term, he remembered. She'd talked of small-waisted women, and Jean always knew just who she meant even when their waists were thickened from childbirth or their love of croissants.

He did still wonder over that Ioway woman, how she fared with that husband of hers.

"Do you remember the Dorion woman?" Jean asked Michel then.

Michel shook his head. "*Oui.* The *voyageurs* call her Madame Dorion. The crew who remember their time with her and Hunt. She lives as a widow now, with her sons. In the Okanogan country, though these I do not know for certain. I never see these woman when we are stopping there."

"Perhaps like me she is stronger alone," Jean said.

"Strong? With no more adventures," Michel said. He shook his head. "You have become as soft as these bread dough."

"*Non,*" Jean protested.

"A man is formed by the challenges he overcomes, *oui?* What challenges you this day, *mon ami?* How will you know at the end of these day that you have lived with your talents well?"

"You eat my bread. That's worthy work."

"*Oui,* but what makes your heart pound, your blood rush into your head? The sight of rivers so swift they take your breath away, ravines so deep you are above eagles soaring. The scent of a woman wearing alder-tanned hides." Michel inhaled deeply through his nose, his eyes half-closed. "Never knowing what the day will bring you yet being grateful for each morning. These is living. No, you are soft, my friend. You do nothing—"

Could Michel be right? Jean couldn't remember when he'd last felt the rush of adventure. Maybe he was soft as bread. But he was…safe in the kitchen. He could perform his work in his sleep. *Maybe I am asleep,* he thought.

"I…I… I'll do something you've never considered, something with danger to it, and risk. To make my heart pound."

Michel lifted his eyebrow, ran his hands back through his shiny black hair. "What would that be, let me guess. You will trap on the side, without the Company knowing, *non?* You will father a child, take a wife first, of course?" Jean shook his head. "It is not baking cheek bread then? No? Something with danger attached?" Michel stared, his dark beard holding dribbles of crumbs. Then his face broke into a grin. "You will go to the Okanogan and meet your old friend, the Dorion woman, *oui?*"

"*Non.*" Jean said. Why had he set himself up for some challenge? Just to quiet his friend, so he wouldn't think him weak? "There's a horse race next week," Jean said. "More than forty mounts will race on the gravel flat beside the river. I'll…I'll ride with the Indians."

Michel looked at him. "These is a dangerous thing. But you have ridden before, eh? What is the risk in that?"

"This week," Jean said, "I put up all the money I have set aside. If I lose, I must start over. What man can start over without courage?"

"Will you bet on someone else, my friend, and throw the race?"

"*Non.* I bet only on myself."

❖

Marie felt rooted to the Okanogan place in the years since Tom McKay's accident. His limp, when she saw him, served as a reminder of what must matter to her now. Marie's days were filled with keeping vows made to herself and her sons, to keep her sons safe, to repay her husband's debt. For three years, she had served only them, given what they needed from her, kept them alive while slowly lowering the debt piled on her husband's account at the company. She trapped beaver, with poor success, adding debt of her own with the purchase of the steel traps but taking the risk that she would eventually repay it and more.

She planted a garden, trading some of the hides she'd taken to the Company trader when the spring and fall brigades made their way north or south for seeds. She kept her boys with her as much as she could, showing them how she had lived back in the Sioux country with her husband's family, sharing stories of her own Ioway people and how they salted buffalo hides or planted corn in the oxbows of the Des Moines. Some things she did not share with her sons. *Not all stories of family should be told,* Marie thought. Nor all choices could be explained, even to herself.

They owned no horse yet, no pig, no chickens. A few pups had made their way to their driftwood hut set away from the fort, but she resisted getting attached to them. She warned the boys as well. "We may need them to feed our bellies in the winter."

Maybe knowing such a possibility existed caused her sons to work harder so that by the second winter, they took in three dogs. The mongrels were loved, and so they were named. Dog, Pup, and Its-owl-eigh,

an Okanogan word for "end of the world." Its-owl-eigh was named by
Sally, who said, "I thought you said it would be the end of the world
before you'd let dogs come into your bed."

"Things change," Marie told her to Sally's laugh.

Marie traded vegetables and hides and the beadwork and baskets
she formed of her own hands. Baptiste stripped bark and bent yew
wood into bows, but the traders paid little for them, saying all tribes had
their own ways with weapons. So Baptiste spent more time tending the
fort's horses, earning marks on the ledger that he sometimes traded for
trinkets. A new bone needle for Marie appeared once "for no *raison,*"
he'd told her. She'd smiled, accepted the gift.

"And I have nothing for you," she said, the words ringing in her ears
as something she'd said to his father shortly before his death.

Baptiste had shrugged his shoulders. He wore nearly twelve summers, and his voice often startled her, going up and down like a prairie
hawk in the wind.

His father had answered her lament by telling Marie that the gift
she gave him that Christmas was remaining with him. She hoped Baptiste could see her presence with her sons as a gift she'd given, wanting
the best for them and nothing more.

Paul still pierced her heart with his difficult ways. He was a stone
that sometimes skipped across the river, sometimes weighed on her
heavy as bone. He didn't jab or push at her as much but had taken on
new, mysterious ways. Once he wound wet rawhide tight around his
wrists and brought them, palms up, to show her, the pads of his fingers
and thumb beginning to swell from the drying sinew. Marie lifted her
knife from her belt and yanked at them, telling Paul not to do such
things, that he was hurting himself, but he'd only laugh. "See how strong
I am?" he said, then scampered away.

Lately, he'd been seen running hard into the fort's posts, falling hard
while other children giggled, or he'd stumble in ways Marie thought
were intentional, especially when the children laughed. Perhaps they
reacted from discomfort of witnessing such strange things, but it seemed
to please Paul, propel him further into risk. Marie vowed to keep him
closer to her side.

She'd seen Tom McKay more than once, from a distance. He often arrived on horseback, riding beside the canoe brigades, though he didn't so easily dismount a horse. He walked with a limp, though Sally said no fever or infection had ever formed in his wound. "Those plantain leaves you broke and pressed against his wound helped him," Sally said. "Too bad you didn't bring in a little more."

Marie avoided Tom when she recognized his gait from a distance; made her way to the garden, out of sight. Separating herself from that shame.

But once when checking her weir at the river, she heard a horse being brought to water. She turned. There Tom stood.

"Your boys have grown, Madame Dorion," Tom said, pointing with his head. He wore a hat with a brim, like some Americans did. He removed it and wiped his forehead with his forearm. He held the hat close to his chest, gave a nod of greeting.

Her sons were downriver, Paul gathering spring willows—unless he'd found another beaver dam. The boy was fascinated by those constructions, pulling at them with sticks, digging down into them to see what was inside. Baptiste watered three of the fort's horses. She heard them sucking water while her son gripped hemp ropes. She hoped her sons wouldn't see her talking with Tom.

"They're good boys, now," she said. "I give them more of my time."

Tom grunted.

Marie wished she'd given Tom a gift those years before, a way of saying she was sorry for what happened. She could apologize, give the gift of words though it was not her way, not her people's way. Still, she had shared words tied closer to her heart with him than any aside from Sarah or Sally or her friend of greatest distance, Sacagawea.

"You do well," Tom said. He pointed with his hat toward the weir.

A salmon making its way upriver to spawn had been channeled into the basket. She lifted the spear lying at her side and with steady hand and squinting eyes, she followed the blur of blushed silver swimming left then right, twisting inside the willow weir. She jabbed once, pulled the salmon still squirming toward the shoreline. She laid it on a rock and struck its head with the handle of her knife, killing it instantly.

"That one got sidetracked," Tom said. "See what *désir* got him."

She looked at Tom. He smiled at her then, a grin as soft as a fawn's ears and just as gentle. He would be a friend, she could see that now, a man who held no grudge to her, a confidante to share words with even though she saw him rarely.

"Bad timing for him, *n'est-ce pas?*" Marie said.

Tom laughed then, his mouth pink inside the dark beard. He adjusted his hat, continued to smile. "Couldn't help himself. You're right. Doing what he was called to do."

She nodded. "Yearning is a part of the journey."

❖

A pewter sky dappled with wispy white hung heavy over the late spring afternoon. When Louis Venier stepped out of the *bateau* at Okanogan, he saw a handsome woman attempting to rope a cow. It was not a neat cow, with short little horns and a bell around its neck, the kind of bovine that expected human hands on it morning and night and switched its tail at flies while she waited. This cow was not the kind of animal he'd seen in Montreal years ago nor the ones who were herded by children in Missouri Territory. No, this was a lean, bony, wild-looking beast with horns like arms outspread that invited nothing but dread.

The woman looked worn from her efforts. Louis stood a moment on the bank, getting his land legs. Such hills as he had never seen flowed with grass like wind across water. The other *voyageurs* with the North West Company laughed and slapped each other's bare backs. It had been a long journey, but they'd made it in record time. They said that only a few more days' travel and the Pacific Ocean would lap at his feet.

Louis wasn't sure it could marvel him more than these mountains had with their snowcaps and gorges deeper than grief.

They hadn't swallowed his grief, though. He'd watched Manuel Lisa come to the Omaha camp and take Mitain's firstborn back to Missouri with him, that coward never witnessing the cries and pleas of his wife. The lout had sent word ahead to have his country wife "removed" so he wouldn't have to see her, but to keep his son in the Omaha camp where he could find him.

Louis had walked beside Mitain for a time after she lost her son, offered her comfort, he thought. But he might as well have been a mongrel dog trotting at her heels. She never noticed him nor gave him any idea she ever would.

Later, Lisa sent word again to "remove" his Mitain but to leave the girl-child behind for him to take. Louis had urged the Omaha trader to ignore Manuel Lisa's order, even if it meant higher prices in trade for the axes and ammunition being brought from St. Louis.

This time the Omaha trader had listened. He warned Mitain, and Louis took her and the child with him, into the high country. Mitain set the tipi, cooked the meat he brought in, and even smiled when Louis bounced the small girl on his knee. But the veil over Mitain's eyes never lifted, and Louis never asked for a marriage of the country. She wore her grief like a shawl no other man could take off.

The following spring when he learned of a North West Company brigade heading to the Columbia country, he signed on as a hunter. They'd wintered at Henry's Fork where the word was Manuel Lisa had once retrieved a cache of furs worth twenty thousand dollars. He'd taken Lune, his dog, with him.

Farther downriver, they'd stopped at Spokane House, ate a fine meal cooked by a fellow French-Canadian. Louis participated in the Sunday services led by the factor and had been surprised to see native people singing hymns he'd not heard since chapel as a boy.

The French-Canadian chef said an Iroquois man and his wife had once done the teaching but they'd moved on before the chef's arrival. The hymns had stayed. "Made me long for a priest, they did, to feed my soul." The chef sighed. "Just one of the losses of living in the Columbia country. You'll get used to it," he'd advised Louis. "Lots of other things we do without, like beefsteak. No beef to slaughter in this country."

He remembered these words when he saw the woman. The beast in front of her bellowed now, twisted like a tossed snake, and brushed dust up from the Okanogan plains.

A man with a limp approached from the fort, began unloading the canoes, nodding, and talking with some of the North Westers.

"She stands up to it, that woman, *n'est-ce pas?*" Louis said to no one in particular.

The man with the limp—someone had called out his name as McKay—looked at Louis, nodded once.

"She's a good woman," McKay told him. "Lucky the man who earns her allegiance."

"Is that one of the Fort George cows?" Louis asked.

McKay shook his head, no. "Wild, let loose from Mexican herds."

A boy, maybe eleven or twelve, rode a scrawny horse and he kicked it toward the cow, reining away with skill when the animal swirled and lowered its head to gouge the boy's mount.

She was brave, the woman, twirling a rope while she stood. He'd heard stories of trappers on the Santa Fe Trail meeting up with wild Mexican cows that roamed in herds pushing their long horns through tangles of brush. "Always want to be sure you kill the beast clean, first shot," one old trapper had told him. "You wound it, and the thing'll track you down by smell. Smart and vile, they are, with minds that don't forget. They'll catch you at a campfire days later and gouge your scrawny body like you was nothing but a hunk of meat about to dribble fat over flames. I seen it with my own eyes, I have."

Louis wasn't sure he believed the trapper's story back then, but seeing the beast now with hooded eyes, snot pouring from its nose, and so agile for such a large animal twisting and charging at the horse, he suspected the tale was true.

Dogs barked and the cow twirled again, tail twitching, head lowered. Another child ran back and forth, shouting, the boy and the dogs trying to force the cow into some kind of corral formed of the side of a hut out of what looked like driftwood stakes. A few other women kicked up their skirts as they ran toward the animal from a safer distance, crying a high-pitched sound to drive the cow past the woman with the rope.

Louis marveled at the woman's steady gaze, her rhythmic swirling of the hemp-twist rope. She stood firm as an oak. As tall as he, taller than the other women, she wore her hair tied back in a ball at her neck, not in the circles of braids behind each ear that the Okanogan women wore. None had braids that bounced on the breasts of the women like the Omaha. *Mitain.*

More women came now to shoo at the cow as though it might be a chicken.

He ought to help her but wasn't sure how he could—or if he should.

The roping woman never wavered, turned slowly, in tune with the cow, the boys and women having successfully driven it into the corral. Sweat beaded on her forehead. Even with the gate closed, Louis judged she'd still have but one chance to rope it and snub it tight around the center post before the beast would charge her or push through the line of upright posts and thus burn the rope through her hands.

She threw the lasso.

It fell short, but she pulled it up quick as a wink and relooped it, swirling it over her head. She eased closer now, ready to step aside if the beast charged.

The cow stopped suddenly, lifted its nose, then lowered it, scraping dirt back toward its belly. It bellowed and glared at the woman who moved like a hunting cat, steady and intent. She held an open loop of rope at her side. Was she trying to get close enough to simply drop the rope over the horns?

"What'll she do when she gets it?" one of the *voyageurs* said. "I wouldn't want to try milking that she-devil. Rum'll quench my thirst better than milk taken from such as that."

"The woman better do it right this next time, eh?" Louis said.

The man with the limp handed a saddle to Louis. He turned to watch a moment. "She takes a long time to learn a thing," he said, then left to carry gear to the storehouse.

"We should help her," a *voyageur* said.

"Looks like she's beyond help," Louis replied as the woman threw the loop, catching only one horn. She held tight, but she wasn't fast enough to snub the rope around the center post. The cow yanked the hemp from her hands, then burst through the makeshift corral as though it knew where the weakest posts stood. It bellowed its way toward the hills, snout up, legs prancing, a good rope trailing from its horn.

◈

Marie wanted to cry, but her anger seared the tears. How long she'd lured that cow toward the fort! How much precious salt had she set out hoping the animal would smell it and come in without restraint? She must have been crazy to think that a wild cow surviving in the brush of the hill country, one who had swum the Columbia, who was as savvy as a fox, would be tempted by something so meager as salt. The cow was too smart for that. And even if Marie had secured it, milking it would have been a troubled time—assuming the cow had been bred and even had milk.

At least they could have butchered it.

"You should have shot it," Tom told her. Like a brother, he offered advice even when not asked. She always listened, believing she owed him something, his constant limp the reminder. But she didn't always do what he said.

Tom lifted her hands to assess the rope burns. "Better get some skunk oil," he said. "Soothe it."

She nodded, a smile lifting the corners of her mouth. "Beef tallow would be good too. If we had some."

"I said you should have shot the thing."

Tom didn't understand at all how much she longed for the taste of milk, of melting butter. Her mouth watered with the thought. Nothing could be better than that, not even the taste of tough beef. But a wild cow couldn't be tamed to milk. Now her sons would do without even meat.

Sometimes she just couldn't face the truth of the situation.

Then this Louis Venier had stepped forward, tipped his dark-brimmed hat and slid his rifle sling around his back. He stood beside her, watching the cow disappear. "Fine hunting," he said, introducing himself. "Not many get so close to a wild cow and live to tell of it."

"Hunting was good. The taking wasn't," she said in French.

He'd laughed, a sound like the steady thumping of a hand against a waterlogged canoe. It came from a deep place, and she turned to look at him. His eyes crinkled almost shut, and he pulled on the dark beard around his mouth. He'd turned to face her. He was a man not afraid to look a woman in the eye, but she dropped hers like a wolf pup succumbing to its mother.

"I'll remember that," he said. "Hunting's good, but the taking isn't. A way to explain when a man comes back empty-handed, eh?"

He'd sounded for just a moment like her Pierre. It was what she remembered best about her husband, the sound of his voice, the lilt of his words, rising and falling like the cry of a hawk. But the laughter was different, and the eyes weren't gray like Pierre's flecked with brown. This man's eyes were dark as a prime beaver pelt.

He swept off his hat then and introduced himself. "And they call you?" He'd spoken in French.

"Madame Dorion," Tom said for her.

"Of Lewis and Clark's journey?"

"My father-in-law and my husband came with them," she said, warmed by the recognition of her husband's name.

"Pleasure to meet you," Louis Venier told her. He actually had to look down into her face, a rarity for her.

"Mère!"

"My son," she said as Paul made his way toward them.

"That's Baptiste, on Ross's horse." She nodded with her chin. "This is Paul," she said. "My baby."

Paul looked with curiosity at the man. Louis Venier nodded his head to the boy, then reached out to shake his hand. "Looks like you teamed that cow well, son," he said. "But you could sure use some better horses than the likes of what your brother's riding."

"We go this spring to get some from the Yakima," Paul told him.

"Well, son, are you and your brother going to drive them back like you did that cow?" He grinned.

"I'm not your son," Paul said.

"Ross approves," Marie spoke quickly. "It's a long journey, but Baptiste goes to help."

"Not you?" Louis asked.

It had been a long time since a man had asked about her preference, to stay or go, or expressed an interest. "Paul stays and helps me collect hemp for the coast trade. I've many nets to weave, and we'll have higua shells white as snow to decorate dresses with fort trade. My sons will trade their labor for mounts of their own."

Her heart was pounding with excitement, words rushed, and she didn't know why.

Louis Venier nodded, and Marie took it as approval, a gift of confirmation that letting her sons make the journey was a right and worthy thing for a mother to do.

"Might be able to use an extra hand or two," Tom said. "You hired on to the Company or a free man?"

"Free man," Louis said. "I can ride. Came out of the Omaha country. Trapped there."

"Beaver?" Paul asked.

"Beaver, s—" Louis stopped himself. "Yes, beaver, fox, otter. Here, boy." He called to a dog that came bounding. "Lune," he said. "Part wolf."

Tom said. "Might check with Ross. I suspect he could use another hand on the Yakima trip. I'll show you where to bunk."

Louis tipped his hat to Marie again, just as men once did in old St. Louis when they met ladies on the street.

She smiled, headed for her hut. Paul walked close beside her, kept looking back. Probably trying to catch a glimpse of that cow. She found the skunk oil, spread the grease on her palms. Her hands shook. She wasn't sure if it was from the pain or the meeting of the man or how close they'd come to having their own cow. Perhaps she'd put salt out for another and when her boys returned with mounts of their own, they could try again.

She walked outside and stood in the shade of her hut, watching the *bateaux* being unloaded. Her eyes looked up to the hills then. July was a hot, hot month here, but in the crevices of the hillside, dribbles of green promised springs running deep. They looked like emeralds in the cleavages of small-waisted women.

"Beaver," Paul said. "He trapped beaver."

Marie nodded. "He might show us how to have better luck than

we've had. No cow I'm afraid. Maybe he'll help us catch more beaver."
She glanced at Paul, trying to gauge his response.

Paul stayed silent, didn't protest.

She drew in a hopeful breath.

✦

Marie found herself anticipating Louis's presence, wondering if she'd
catch a glimpse of him at the corrals or the fur post or along the riverbanks. She watched to see the way he walked, how he used his hands to
talk, the strange scars on his fingers.

Once, he hummed while he watched Marie skin one of the lean deer
he'd taken for the fort. She'd asked to clean the hide in return for chalk
used to remove stains on leather, ran her hands through the new cloth
that the brigade had brought from the ships anchored at Fort George.
Louis talked to her as though he'd always known her, mixing French and
English, pointing, gesturing with his chin. His voice came from the same
deep place as his laughter. He often broke out in song as he worked.

"The music is *bon*," she said. "My friend Sarah sings that one.
Chante faux, though." Marie smiled.

"Out of tune, eh?" Louis held his ears. "The chief trader at Spokane
House, Cox, says some Iroquois taught that song to his Indians there."

His Indians. Marie halted, her knife held in midair. "Sarah was
Chipewyan. She went there. Did you meet her?"

"They were gone by then, according to the cook."

Marie paused, wondering where Sarah had been called to next. She
frowned. Didn't a calling, a *métier*, require that one go and then remain
until the work was finished? She shook her head. Marie served here,
served her sons. She returned to her work, to the rhythm of scraping the
hair from the hide. Where would Sarah and Ignace have gone if they
weren't in the Spokane country or with the Flatheads, teaching the
people the words of God that Sarah said mattered so? Home? Had they
gone home?

Marie scraped harder. Why was she disappointed? Maybe because
she'd thought they'd be close enough to someday meet again. All her

closest confidantes moved on or she moved away from them. Except for Sally. Marie had let Sally come close to her center fire.

"Sarah wanted us to go too, me and my sons," Marie confided.

"It's good country, that Spokane land," Louis said. "Most anywhere in this Columbia country is. Drew me to it, like a bear to honey. But this place, too, could be like home to me, right conditions met."

"I take care of my sons in this place," she said. He needed to know what called to her.

He'd nodded, and she took it as understanding.

He stood silent beside her, the stomp of a distant horse kicking at flies breaking the silence. The wind swirled in gusts, and every now and then Marie could hear the ripple of the river, reminding her she'd need to check her weirs. The hide had eased its way toward the ground as she scraped. She pressed against her knees to stand, needing to pull the hide back up to the securing post.

"Landscape's different in this place," he said then. "People have a different way of doing things. I miss the trees," he said. "More work building a place without trees. How do you do it, without help? Or does everyone help everyone here?"

She didn't know how to answer. She was different, didn't belong. Yet in a strange way, she felt she had been helped, whenever she'd needed it most.

Louis reached to share the load as she lifted the hide back into place. "It's easier to do with extra hands, eh?" She accepted, let his fingers linger on hers, aware of the ridges of scars and the scent of leather on his hands.

That night, Marie tossed and turned in her robe. This was not the time to make a change in her plans, not a time to add the burden of man-loving to her life.

Her sons were finally behaving, allowing her to step one pace behind. They could go with others without her worrying over what poor choices they might make.

She still had much to do to ensure they had adequate supplies for winter, more salmon to dry, more berries to pick, more hides to tan. The willows needed stripping if they were to be made into weirs and baskets, coverings and mats. And she'd made only a little dent in her debt.

No, this was not the time to make a change. Sarah and Ignace might go to a different place, but not her. This was home now, where she'd found the work to which she was most suited, caring for her sons. Her *métier*.

Tears formed in her eyes, pressed against her temples and into her ears. She wiped at them with her fingertips. Where were they coming from, those tears? She recalled Louis's voice, the deepness of it. Sometimes she missed hearing a man's voice spoken just for her ears, warm breath sweetly tender at her neck.

Louis had been a trapper, knew beaver dams and ways. Paul would like that. Louis was a hunter. Baptiste could learn from that. Maybe she should ask Louis tomorrow for assistance teaching her sons what only a man could teach. He'd tell her no if he didn't feel able.

No. This was not the time to ask a man for anything. She pushed the robe off. It was much too warm in this hut. Much, much too warm. She opened the flap, looked at the stars, sought solace there.

Something needed to change. *What would Sarah say?*

She felt an ache as she remembered the face of Louis Venier. Even in memory, she shivered, recalling his touch to her hand, the kindness of his eyes.

❖

Jean Toupin leaned over the neck of the horse, patting it. He spoke softly into the gelding's ear. "Be calm, now. Be calm." He was a sorrel mount with splashes of white at his side like clouds that dotted the sky. "Don't let those noises make you nervous," Jean said. He knew he spoke more to himself than the horse. He'd rented the animal from one of the partners who lifted his eyebrows when Jean told him he'd be racing this week. With his life's savings bet on his win, all or nothing.

The Scot owner had been talking the whole time he saddled "Cloud," jabbering almost, wondering how Jean had let Michel talk him into such a thing. Racing. For money. He supposed even if he lost it was no real tragedy. He'd merely start over, keep working for the Company.

But his goals were loftier than just not losing. He wanted to prove a point to Michel. Maybe to himself.

Jean lifted his eyes over the horse's head, sat up straight. He could count thirty other horses already lined up in the gravel along the river, some prancing with anticipation. If he were merely an observer, choosing whom to bet on now, he'd avoid those. Even with a good rider, the creatures would be tired out and spent and fall short of that needed spurt of energy to cross the finish line first.

The long, flat track stretched out before him.

Jean had two goals, he decided, more important than winning. He needed to get up front fast to avoid the toss of gravel from horses in front as they gouged the track with their feet. More injuries happened from flying rock catapulting into a rider's face than from falling off. Second, he needed to stay mounted. The jostling and pushing could easily toss him under the hooves of the horses.

A Spokane boy named Garry trotted up to him on a big stallion. Garry grinned at Jean now, teased him using hand signs about his "pitiful mount."

"Good horse," Jean signed back, hoping his hands didn't shake too much. He patted his horse's neck again.

Garry laughed. He rode as though born on a horse, and while he couldn't have much more than ten years, he'd be competition for the men. He was light and could form himself over the neck of the horse as though riding as one in the wind. Garry made the sign for *eating* and *stones,* and Jean knew he planned to make Jean do just that.

Jean thought to make a joke about eating Garry's horse instead of stones but decided against it. The Spokane had a good sense of humor but didn't take kindly to talk of having their horses for dinner.

He scanned the other riders. Stiff competition. Maybe just showing up for the race was a win in itself, regardless of the outcome.

Ross Cox, the senior partner at Spokane House, stood with a blanket. Two dark stripes lined the white wool. "Are you ready then?" he shouted. Cox would drop the blanket to mark the beginning of the race. No gunshot to set the animals off. All would be fair. Jean gripped the reins, began applying slight pressure with his knees against the horse. The blanket dropped. The race was on.

6

Prelude

As much as she tried to deny it, Marie was ready to be cherished, and she knew her sons needed a man's wise guidance. Louis Venier, late of Montreal, was a man who seemed able to do both.

Anticipating his presence never failed to stir her. His touch and voice always lifted her spirit. His smile sent an ache to the center of her core.

Most of all, she never wondered when she was with him if she should be somewhere else.

Alex Ross had planned the horse trip to the Yakima and had invited Louis Venier and three other Canadians to go along with him and McKay.

"I'll take the Frenchies and their wives, those who have wives." Alex Ross winked at Louis Venier, and that evening, after the men had been served in the dining house, Louis approached Marie.

"I've little to offer," Louis said. They stood at the riverbank, at a place where water whispered over smooth rocks. "A good dog, *d'habilité* at a thing or two I do well—trapping, hunting."

"Many skills," Marie said.

"And a large heart." He lifted her hand to the flat of his chest. His touch brought a flush to her face.

"Heart knowing," she said, "is the sign for memory. I have memories. My boys have them too. They must be put to rest to make room for you there."

"If you'll have me," Louis said, "I'll stay with you for as long as God allows. Walk beside you while you make room inside that heart for me. Aid your boys to do the same." He reached to pull her closer, blanketed his arms around her. "I give my heart to you, Madame Dorion." His throat sounded thick. "Everything I have I give. Will you accept?"

Marie sank into his strength. She could feel the strap of his powder horn across his back, the brush of beard at her cheek. It had been so long, so very long since she'd been held like this.

"*Oui,*" she said. "With *vivacité.* I accept."

She didn't ask her sons. She believed Sarah would have said she had the right to fill her own basket for a time. Maybe even that she should. The water in a basket must be replenished or it would soon be empty.

"We travel together with my sons to the Yakima. They get to know you there."

Louis nodded.

"It's time I choose something for myself," she told her boys later. "Today, I choose this man to share my life."

❖

Alex Ross presided at the June ceremony. "I'm like a captain of a ship," he told the gathering. "Without a minister of the cloth to bless the union, the chief trader comes closest, and that'd be me." His reddish hair looked pale in the sunlight, and he wore a suit that smelled of herbs meant to scare away moths. He spoke prayers and then, in both English and French, he read from a small book of common prayers, words about submission and obedience and two becoming one.

"Two rivers there," he said. He pointed toward the Okanogan and the Columbia. "Both strong, mighty with a history and coming through a landscape all their own. Then they flow together, become stronger and look different for it."

"Rivers've got lots of rapids in 'em," one of the *voyageurs* called out. "Sure you want to tell them that? Might scare them away?" People chuckled low.

" 'Tis true, 'tis true. But in the rapids we find out who we are, how strong, how quick we think, who needs taking care of, and who takes care of whom. Finding someone to run the river with, 'tis a blessing beyond measure." Here Alex Ross smiled at his Sally and their daughter now, the women of his family painted with red and black bars just beneath their eyes. Sally's belly bulged with the prelude to another baby's birth.

"Sure and begorra, 'tis a gift to find someone who'll stay with us to the end despite the portages and sand bars and high water we encounter, no matter how hard we plan ahead to avoid them. But the Lord is good," Alex Ross continued. "And everything we need to survive the journey has been provided."

He asked both Louis and Marie to repeat a promise that they'd take no other to their bed. "I know this isn't the way of the people here," he said. "But the scourge of this fort is polygamy. Fights and senseless deaths would be nonexistent if men kept to only one wife, no matter how many camps they must travel to. You people believe in a heaven and hell. You believe in the world coming to an end, you—" Sally nudged him. "What?" He turned to her. She whispered something in his ear. When he looked back, his blue eyes were calm pools. "Sure and the Lord would want you to profess your commitment to him and to each other and seal it with a gift. You've arranged for the exchange of gifts?"

Marie reached into her flat wallet purse, newly woven by Sally. Her veil of beads tumbled over her face as she shifted her head. She removed Sacagawea's knife and handed it to Louis. *"Pardon,"* she said. "This is my most treasured possession. It belonged to Captain Meriwether Lewis. He gave it to his interpreter, Sacagawea. It was a trade knife, brought to bring peace to those they met. She gave it to me. It kept my sons and me alive. Now, I give it to my husband that it may keep him alive and bring him peace."

"And you, Venier?" Alex Ross asked.

From a pouch at his waist, Louis offered ivory-handled scissors and a porcelain thimble painted with a scene of tiny horses, running in the wind. "I've got thread, too," he said. He showed her his fingers stitched. "But I suspect you'll do a tidier job on these than I ever have." He held her hand now, and she felt the ridges where the skin had puckered around the stitches. He looked her full in the face. "We're sewn together now with words and promises and blessings. Only death can part us and I'm not planning on that any time soon. We're tied together," he said. "You, me, and your sons, too."

"Well then, let the music begin," Alex Ross said.

Out of habit, Marie touched her waist to feel her knife. It was gone, a part of who she'd been was set aside, given away. It was what she did, give. She might have given away the ring Pierre had given her, but she couldn't, she found. It was a last thing of his. She felt it now inside the flat wallet. And she might have given Sarah's cross to Louis. But Sarah had said it was not the thing itself that mattered, but what it represented that counted, the way a scene painted on skin stood for an event that held meaning.

Louis listened to Sarah's songs, the hymns heard among the Spokane. He might have liked the cross, understood what Sarah said of it. She barely knew him well enough, she realized, to know just what Louis preferred.

But he'd smiled at her offer, turned the blade and handle over in his wide hands. He'd seemed pleased with the weight of it. And perhaps he'd let her carry it still, sometimes. Just as she'd let him use the scissors.

Marie looked over at her two sons standing with a group of boys. They wore their hair as Okanogans now, pulled into a knot at the back, long bangs at the front and even longer strands in front of their ears. Their cheeks were painted with red and black bars. She couldn't see the expression in their eyes, but they stood with arms crossed and legs spread as though bracing for a push or shove.

❖

The horse party—three French-Canadians and their wives, including Louis and Marie, plus Alex Ross and Tom McKay—prepared to leave early the next morning for the Yakima gathering.

"No need for your boy to go now, Madame Dorion," Ross said. "We got men to do the work so we can make better time."

"Madame Venier," Louis corrected. "She carries my name now."

"Sure and it's so. I'll try to remember. But to important things. How soon can you be ready?"

It was said there'd be six or seven thousand people there, and ten thousand horses in the Yakima Valley. Marie felt herself anticipate the journey, the change in routine. Perhaps she'd stayed in one place long enough and could go now, without bringing along her bad memories of the past. She handed the reins to Louis. "Wait for me," she said. "I need to say good-bye to my sons."

"You can't go," Marie told Baptiste as the sun rose up over the river, "because Ross changed his mind. He wants only men who can drive the herds back and women to feed the men and make camps. Not even Sally goes along. Old LaBonte goes. Remember him from Hunt's party?" Baptiste shook his head, no. "We saw him little, but he rides well. His wife will have another child soon. Her nursing child is the only young one who goes." Marie smiled.

"I'm not a child." Baptiste flicked his head back to move the hair from his eyes.

"I'll cut it. Before I go." She reached to run her fingers through the fine, black strands. "With my new scissors," Marie said. Baptiste jerked away. He was almost up to her shoulder; he'd grown so tall during his eleven summers. He wasn't a child anymore, not really.

"We'll be back soon," Marie told Baptiste. "You are old enough to stay behind, to sleep in the hut. Sally will look in on you."

"We don't need watching. We're not dogs," Baptiste said.

"You need to be cared for, just as the dogs do," Marie chided. "I trust you. To look after them and yourselves. It's a big responsibility to watch over your brother."

"I'll leave Lune for you to stand guard if you want," Louis offered.

"Don't need a half-breed wolf," Baptiste said.

"Now wait—" Louis began.

Marie touched Louis's arm. *"Pardon,"* she said. "We go now. The boys know what to do. Look after Paul," she said to Baptiste. "We'll be back in two, three weeks."

"Paul looks after himself," Baptiste said. Marie looked around for her youngest son, couldn't see him. "He plays near the river," Baptiste said. "I'll find him." His last words were softer.

"Merci," she whispered to him. "I'm grateful you're here to watch out for him. He's still young. He needs his brother, especially when his mother's away." She realized she hadn't been apart from her sons since

the time she'd left them in the mountains. A phrase came to her that she'd said back then. "The beloved of the Lord shall dwell in safety by him," Marie said, using her mother-in-law's words. They came as a blessing on her children. Marie touched Baptiste's forehead with her lips to complete the promise that rose from a distant past. Baptiste let her, and she held his face in her small hands.

"Me and Paul could have gone until that Venier chose to go," Baptiste said then. He nodded with his chin toward Louis, who had walked away. Louis sat on a horse, his wrists crossed over the pommel. The horse raised a back leg, kicked at flies at its belly. "We should go and you stay," Baptiste said. "He should go away."

Marie sighed. "Paul was never going. And it's not going to happen your way. Tell your brother I missed saying good-bye, giving him a blessing from his grandmother's heart. Tell him to listen to Sally. I'll bring back horses. This is what matters. The Company needs pack animals and food, and we need mounts to ride and trade. We'll have our own this way, if all goes well. We'll have less debt and will answer only to ourselves, not to the Company. Maybe we'll have more animals because…my husband hunts and herds for Ross."

She brushed at the knot of hair at the back of her neck. She had not called Louis "husband" before this moment. Not even in the night when they'd held each other, skin to skin beneath the one-point blanket.

"Husband," Baptiste said, spitting. He stomped away but said so she could hear, "He'll never be my papa."

Maybe she shouldn't use that name with her sons yet, just call him Louis. The boys needed time. Yes, it was all too new yet, even for her, to use such a name as that.

❖

Paul pinched his nose, then ducked his head under the water. He counted. One. Two. Three. Four. Five. Almost to twenty before he exploded to the surface, gasping for breath. He'd never be able to stay down as long as he needed. He'd have to find a reed to breathe through so he could get close enough. It would be dry once he got inside, but he didn't know how long the tunnel might be, and he had to stay down at least until a count of sixty, maybe seventy, to be sure.

He'd seen his father set a trap in one. No, maybe it was his mother who set the trap. A long time ago. He wasn't much bigger than a beaver then himself. They'd poked long sticks down to find the place where the beaver's tunnel merged from wet to dry so they could place the trap. When they pulled the trapped beaver out the next day, they'd destroyed the hut. But Paul had seen inside. Just a glimpse.

The little rooms inside were formed of sticks and grasses and the yellowed chips of cottonwood. Such a private place those beavers made, and no one could see inside it. Paul wanted to lie down in the dry places where the beaver nested, where they chewed on the barks of trees they'd felled. They had their babies in there, soft little things that grew to have thick tails that slapped the water in warning. But his father had been careful to set the traps so the beaver plunged deep into water when it felt itself trapped. It was what was wished for. It drowned then, didn't ruin the pelt by resisting the jaws of the steel.

Paul plunged back into the water. He wanted to stay there. Even in the dead of winter beside the Boise River, Paul had wanted to remain cocooned by the warmth of a waiting beaver hut.

Maybe if he'd stayed, his father would have remained too and still lived. Then those Indians would not have killed him and the others.

Then that man, Venier, would not have come to share his mother's mat, keep him from going to the horse gathering with the Yakima. It had happened so fast, he hadn't seen it coming. They'd chased off McKay, and his mother believed she'd done it herself. She might have. She might have kicked away the lid to the store pit where they kept the food from skunks.

But she hadn't.

Any other men who had shown interest, he and Baptiste had discouraged too. They'd poked at each other, snarled like wolves, not followed their mother's directions, spit disagreement at her until she turned red and would leave the men's sides to take him and Baptiste back to their hut. She often scolded, but she never struck them, not the way their father had.

Sometimes, if she stayed near the side grass while the dances continued, he and Baptiste would throw rocks close to where people sat or they would grab a bow and arrow and chase around his mother and whoever she sat with until the man would stand and push the air with his hands saying, "Your sons bite the hands that would feed them."

His mother fed them. They could feed themselves now, too, using slingshots and arrows and snares. They didn't need anyone else to tend to them. Neither did she.

Then this one slipped in as an eel. And now, she was off with him while they were asked to play with Ross and Sally's girls. They'd have to wait to drive this one away. It might take longer since his mother had gone through Ross's ceremony, made a promise. She honored her promises.

Venier carried scissors. He'd even given one to his mother. A man shouldn't carry woman things. Perhaps Venier was weaker than he appeared, soft like a girl, even if he did as he said, sew his own fingers up each spring with a needle and thread.

Paul would never take a girl where he was going. No girl was strong enough to swim the tunnel to find a beaver's home. The risk was great if the tunnel proved too long.

But if he made it, it was a perfect place to think and plan. He emerged, took another deep breath. Slipped into the river and counted this time to forty-five. He would do this, find the beaver's home, the perfect place to hide.

❖

They rode through land marked by needle-heavy trees, in the high country where patches of snow clung to the north sides at the base of the trunks. Water in little streams gushed with the snowmelt well into summer. White flowers pushed up through the mat of needles. Marie had forgotten how much she found nurture on the back of a horse. She could feel her legs, her back, even her face more intently. She felt…alive on the horse's back.

To control, no, to work with this animal, was something she'd forgotten. She'd ridden across the shining mountains; later to the woodsy place, that *boise*. She'd walked leading a horse when she and her sons melted into the Blue Mountains, on the edge of survival. She didn't want to think of that animal's fate.

But here, riding with other women, a leg on each side, she felt full. She leaned and patted the animal's neck. It was one of Ross's geldings, the color of a cattail, rusty dark. *"Compagnon,"* she said, "We're friends." She brushed sweat from her face, liked the tart scent of the animal now carried on her hands.

The kinds of trees she saw changed, dribbled out by the arid landscape. Warm sun baked their faces. They crested a ridge marked by greasewood and tall grasses, and the valley floor opened below them. Marie sucked in her breath. She had never seen this many horses all together in one place.

"Oh, whoa," she said under her breath.

"Sacre Madre," her husband said.

"Now, here will be a story worthy of the telling," McKay said. Even Ross marveled at the scene cut by a ribbon of river below them, saying he'd never seen such a mass of mounts in one place.

Horses the color of earth and sun, of red clay and black clustered in groups of two or three thousand, with mounted braves circling them slowly. To the east, skin tipis dotted the valley like wild daisies with only a little more order. Cayuse, Walla Walla, Yakima, and dozens of other tribes met this time of year to trade, choose mates, and celebrate family additions. Smoke rose from cooking fires while children scampered between the hodgepodge rows of tipis followed by skinny-tailed dogs. Drums beat steadily as some danced. A bear tied to a center post bellowed and swiped at people passing.

"Taking bets," Ross said. "Scourges. Polygamy and gambling."

"You only disapprove because you lose," McKay told him.

Ross grunted, reined his horse away from the rim. "We'll ride on down, camp on the outskirts. We can expect a greeting party any time now," he said. "They've been riding off to the side of us for the past two days."

They descended single file down the switchback and settled on the valley floor.

"So now we'll see how well we negotiate for some of those beauties," Ross said. "Unload the packs." The women went to work.

"We'll see how long their memories are," McKay said. "Clarke and Mackenzie won no favors among these tribes by their actions."

"That was years ago," Ross told him. "Clarke was hasty, 'tis true, hanging a man for stealing a goblet he gave back. Mackenzie was desperate for food; he had to kill that Nez Perce horse or starve. Isn't that so, Madame Dorion?"

Marie looked up at the sound of her name, her former name. She opened her mouth to speak, didn't.

"Isn't that so, woman?" Ross persisted. "Reed was desperate for food. And Mackenzie paid a fair price for the dead horse, isn't that so?"

"His rage shot the horse," she said. "Not his stomach."

The French-Canadian LaBonte laughed a deep belly sound. "She always strikes the flint where it gets the most spark," he said. "Even when we come across with Hunt, your woman, Venier—"

The sound of hooves galloping close and pulling up fast broke LaBonte's words. Seven braves in full paint circled around them with several dozen horses. McKay stepped forward and sign-talked. "He wants to know if we're of the horse shooting men," McKay said, turning to Ross.

"Tell him no," Ross said. "It's not a lie. Clarke's long gone. Get those packs open. We'll show them we've brought quality goods for trade. We're peaceable. We have women with us. Tell them that."

Marie directed the two younger women who had dismounted to do as Ross said. One named Cayenne pulled open the packs of pots and knives and cloth and balls and powder while Ross and McKay began the trade talk. Cayenne's child, three years perhaps, carried water jugs to LaBonte, wobbling with the weight. It was almost as it had been before for Marie except this time her husband was not the chief interpreter. McKay was. And she was married to another.

Louis made a rope corral in which to put the horses they'd trade for.

But as soon as goods were exchanged and horses moved toward the corrals, Yakima braves whisked the horses away, whooping and laughing.

"They harass us," McKay said, "if we look weak…"

"'Tis an affront, this kind of shenanigan," Ross said. "But patience wins out. We'll keep going. Eventually they'll see we come only for fair trade. We'll get those horses back."

Marie gathered wood for a fire, but one of the braves rode over to her and signed, "Stop."

"We cook," she told him in French.

"No fire," he said in English, reaching down to knock over the kettle she'd put chunks of dried horsemeat into, meat that they'd brought with them.

"Get out dried fish, maybe," Louis said. "They don't want us cooking horse meat while we negotiate for more."

But even the dried fish was dumped by more braves, laughing. They ripped the packs of food and drove their horses to stomp on them.

"Wait till they settle," Ross said. "Then we'll eat."

For two days, they ate nothing. The braves circled and shouted, replaced by other noisemaking sentries, though they removed themselves as the night darkened, to places unseen, but it still felt as though a cougar watched and waited. Marie slept little. Cayenne's daughter whined. "Get up," Louis whispered to Marie the second night. The fire had dwindled, but a low glow still showed his face. "Wake the women. Put your hand over the child's mouth. Make no sounds. We've overheard. They've a plan to take you three into the bowels of that gathering. Hold you there and trade you. Get them some slave money. You ease on out of here and go as far as you can, as quickly, you hear me?" Marie nodded. "Stay low. Here. Take the knife," he said.

"Non," she told him. "You may need it. We'll make our way to the top of the ridge and move east. Overtake us when you can."

Marie woke the younger women, just girls, really. Cayenne was barely older than Baptiste, and Lisette just a year or so more. Marie wondered how long these mere girls had been with their Canadian husbands, men with faces as weathered as pine bark. Marie signaled quiet and the three eased out on buckskin-covered feet.

Once more, Marie was leaving a husband behind.

❖

The women spent two nights moving back toward home. Marie's stomach growled in hunger, and Lisette hand-signed her sympathy by rubbing her own stomach. Her eyes were narrow as a birch bark canoe. Marie vowed to find a way to know her better. She hoped when this was over they would share good stories of survival and not the ways of widows.

Marie reminded herself that she'd gone longer than this without eating. Food was of little merit so long as they had water, and they'd found streams that cut to the valley and that river that had lined the encampment where their men were. She was glad now, so glad, her sons had not come. Cayenne's child whimpered, and when they neared trees Marie recognized, she used her scissors to gouge out the soft gel beneath the bark, handed the gel to the toddler. A few springs bubbled up in the shade of pines, and they filled their jars, the cold water wetting the basket coils and their fingers while they drank.

Marie kept listening for the sounds of the men coming, hoping she'd see the rise of dust from their horses' hooves.

Nothing.

What would she say to Sally if her Ross didn't return? What would Cayenne do if her man didn't make it? Lisette away from her family of Clatsop people. What did any woman do if her husband didn't come home? Grieve and go on.

The women bedded down the third night in a dimple of land where the terrain changed from a few trees separated by tall grasses and brush to the needle-tree timber closer to home. "I told stories to my sons when we were hungry and had no food," Marie told the younger women. "Sometimes it filled us enough to sleep." Night birds cooed, and in the distance, coyotes sang of their exploits.

The women said nothing, and Marie wasn't sure if their worry and hunger kept their tongues in check or if the words she'd spoken weren't understood. Marie filled the silence anyway with stories of her homeland where corn grew tall and mists lifted from the river as slow as blue herons in flight.

They made no fire for fear of being found by the wrong parties, and eventually, the darkness kept even hand signals from being seen. Marie crawled into her bedroll, settled down. She felt something shiver across her arm. She opened her eyes with a start.

"Ayee," Lisette said as she pushed herself away from Marie's side. "I woke you."

"You lay so close," Marie said. She said it in kindness, but she could tell by Lisette's intake of breath that she must have sounded scolding. "I wasn't asleep," Marie added. "Come. Lay your head here." Marie raised her arm so the girl could curl into the crook of it, her fine hair like a spray of water against Marie's face as she nestled. A daughter would have warmed this place in her heart. Now Lisette would.

Marie stroked the girl's temple, repeating her name. Lisette shifted, sat up, and awkwardly signed, close enough so Marie could see it. "Question, you called?"

"Marie. I'm called Marie."

"Question, you called?" Marie asked. "Lisette, *oui?*"

"Non," the girl said. "Kilakotah."

"Your husband…everyone calls you by this other name?"

"Kilakotah." She pointed to her chest.

"Kilakotah," Marie repeated, and the girl sighed. For weeks she'd called this girl-child by another name. Wasn't that just the way with women, to take on what others said of them until they felt known enough to speak for themselves? "Kilakotah," Marie whispered. The girl shifted in her sleep.

Marie's name had changed, too, now. Could she ask Ross and others to call her Madame Venier? No. Louis wasn't a clerk, he wasn't a chief trader. But neither had Pierre been.

Being called Madame Dorion somehow kept her husband alive in this world, not forgotten. Lisette—Kilakotah—moaned, almost woke. Marie appreciated being called Madame Dorion, too. It reminded her of a time when she had been in the company of good men who said that she inspired them, gave them reason to put one sore foot before the other every day. What would she lose in the changing of her name? She still had Marie. She could even still be known as Marie Laguivoise, the French way of saying Marie of the Ioways.

Louis had bristled over Madame Dorion. She would have to talk to him about it. She would please him. Do what he wished. So long as he did not name her as widow.

❖

The women were awakened by the thunder of hooves on the fourth morning after they'd left the Yakima gathering. A large herd of horses rumbled past them in dusty billows. The Canadians circled around the herd until they were enclosed in a remuda of rope. Louis swept by Marie as she scrambled to stand. He lifted her, and she swung her legs up behind him on his horse, holding him tight. She hooked her fingers beneath his suspenders that held his corduroy pants and buried her face into his back, the rough linen drying the tears on her cheeks.

"You crying?" he shouted over his shoulder to her.

"I sing a welcoming song for my husband," she said.

"Sure glad you got the chance, eh?"

She squeezed him tighter.

Kilakotah's husband stood shyly beside her, watching the reunion. He took off his hat and wiped sweat from his balding head. Gray already lined his temples. The girl slipped her hand into his like a child with its father, and she grinned back at the older man.

"Your husband, Madame Dorion," Ross said later, pointing a chunk of cooked rabbit at Louis, "handed me what I needed at the exact right moment." They sat around a campfire, eating the first hot meal they'd had in five days. Horses stomped in the distance, ripped at grass. McKay lifted his eyes to the west, as if checking to see if they'd been followed. He seemed to be always watching the rear.

Now the stories would come, the tales to regale the women and children. Marie waited, eager to hear what part her husband had played, pleased by Ross's words of praise.

"This chief, Yaktana, rolls in on thunder, turnin' his horse on a watch face. Tight little circle with lots of dust he makes." Ross lifted his eyes to the heavens. "Yaktana grabs LaBonte's knife, right out of his sheath."

Kilakotah's eyes got large with the name of her husband. Marie looked at LaBonte, who raised the knife.

"I tells him to give the knife back or he sails the sky, *n'est-ce pas?*" the Canadian LaBonte said. "He listens not at all to me. Just waves it around my head." He made hand motions to show them.

"Yes, yes. 'Twas a moment fit for a storyteller," Ross said. "All those braves with war paint. Us, staggering and weak from hunger, worried over our necks—and yours—while Yaktana wields LaBonte's knife, a madman slicing the air. I look to McKay. He looks at me. What to do?" Ross wiped his face with his hands, rubbed the rabbit fat into his pants. "Then Venier here hands me a knife." Ross nodded toward Marie's husband. "Your wedding present. Well, 'twas a gift from God, that knife. I grab it and show our knife-wielding villain. 'This is a finer weapon,' I tell him. 'Once carried by a great white chief.' I tell him 'tis a better knife by far than the one he holds, better suited to the hands of a chief than that cheap one of LaBonte's."

LaBonte grabbed at his heart as though insulted, but his grin was wide enough to show all his broken teeth.

"Yaktana takes it from me," Ross went on. "He holds it, reverent like a baby. He turns it over and over. All around is quiet, as still as dawn. Then, the saints be praised, he raises the new knife high and says, 'It's a chief's knife fit for a chief.' He tosses LaBonte's poker back to him, and all around cheer and we go from yellow snakes cowering hungry in the grass to celebrated souls.

"Then he tells me that for such generosity, he'll simply give us the horses. Giving them! And we get most of our trade goods back, too. We separated as friends, with invitations to return next spring."

"The wind blew and a tale was told," McKay said.

Ross took another bite. "Royalty is relative," he said. "We had a king's knife to save our skin."

❖

"You're quiet," Louis said. "Is your welcoming song over?" They lay nestled in a bedroll.

"The knife shouldn't mean so much to me," Marie said. Crickets chirped, and the low fire crackled. She could see McKay riding the first watch in the moonlight. "It secured your lives. That's what matters."

"I'll get another for you," Louis said. She put her fingers over his lips. "I will. I'm a man of my word. You don't know that of me, yet. Though the new knife won't be exactly like that one."

"No," Marie said. "No knife will be like that one. But Sacagawea would be pleased to know what her gift did."

"Your gift, too," her husband said.

She turned onto her side, and he reached his arms around her, held her close, her back to his chest. She stiffened at his touch, hadn't meant to. She wanted to welcome him, always.

He lay silent for a time, then said words Marie had rarely heard. "I'm sorry, eh?"

"Non," she said. "It was no longer mine but yours to give away or keep. Loss brings memories but makes room for something new."

"Not before the empty space is grieved, eh?"

"Not before."

❖

Thirty horses remained in Okanogan. The other fifty-five McKay took to Spokane. Marie and Louis kept three, precious three. Two for the work of making the journey, and one for the exchange of Louis's knife. These horses would not be eaten if Louis had his way. He planned to kill enough lean deer to feed his family so the horses could be the beginning of their own herd that they would someday sell to trappers or to Company men seeking pack animals. Maybe even immigrants. Marie seemed to think others would come eventually. Families, she thought. Louis wasn't so sure of that, but her family had traveled that far. Perhaps others would.

This was his family, these two boys and this good woman he'd snagged. And it did feel as though he'd snagged her, as though he were a tree root covered by water and sand that reached up for her, an unsuspecting boat. He couldn't be sure when she'd break free of him, what flood of water might lift her from him and push her away. But until then, he hoped to keep her with him, eddying in the backwater until she felt fully secure to move out into the main stream with him.

He'd use caution. He had to. He was in awe of the woman. McKay and others told him her story, of her survival on the overland journey and later in the snowy Blues. She never talked about the details, not her husband's death, nor how she and her sons survived. If he even mentioned something of it, to better know the sequence, all that transpired in her life those years before, her look became a closed-door flap covering her eyes. She disappeared behind it. She kept that in her own world. But worlds could be changed by persistence and tender touches.

She could easily live without him. Even he could see that. It never seemed to distress her when Ross hired him to join a brigade going north or south meaning he'd be away from her for a month or more at a time. She stepped up to his horse, kissed him good-bye, and seemed content to do without him, digging at her potatoes, working with beads, riding that spotted pony she'd named Janey across the plains. It had seemed to him an odd name for a horse. He'd suggested a French name. But she said Janey reminded her of Sacagawea and gifts given.

He had no complaints about her as a wife. Why, that first winter they'd been together she was as devoted as any man could hope for in his bed. And yet there was a distance between them, as though she lived in a world of her own, one she'd not yet invited him into. He was a snag hanging tight to a birch bottom boat.

She did talk about her plans, that was sure. She let him in on those, of how she'd be debt-free someday, owe nothing to the Company. He would have talked about ideas more, about what made a man burn with fire, gave him a fullness in his heart. He was more than skin and bones and breathing. She was, too, but the only time he'd seen a spark that said she might talk of such with him was when he'd told her of the Spokane singing he'd heard. She'd said something of her friend being called to teach it. But nothing more. Louis was a man who had ideas about call-ings. Each man had one. It just now occurred to him that each woman might too.

He'd find a book about what drew people toward a *métier* one day. Old trappers and botanists and painters who came up the river with the traders sometimes talked about their reading. He'd never read a book in English.

"Would you ever like to learn to read, Marie?" Louis asked once. He thought her eyes watered, and for a minute he wondered if he'd found a gift he could give her, teaching her letters and such.

But she'd said no. "My head feels too full for my eyes to take in any-thing more," she told him and didn't speak further of it.

He had few books of his own. Hides he might have taken to trade for additional leather-bound volumes now went for things his family needed more.

"A peach," she told him. "See if you can get a peach tree when you go to Fort George next." And she wanted a cow so badly she could taste it. "Count how many cows and calves they have there now," she told him. "They need six hundred before they'll sell or butcher. See how many have grown from those first four so I know how long we have to wait."

"Maybe they'll sell one."

She shook her head, no. "The Company will someday lease, Tom says, but never sell. They want all the milk and butter and cheese for themselves. Someday, they'll ship cheese to Russia, Tom says. No, they'll never let us own one of those. But I will own one, somehow. That Com-pany will never decide anything for me."

"Given up chasing the wild ones?" Louis teased.

She nodded once in that way she had, telling him the subject was closed.

She'd hung on to those horses they'd brought back from the Yakima gathering, too. She'd set Baptiste to work learning boat repairing, a job that was always needing extra hands, and kept a thirteen-year-old from trouble. He used his earnings to supplement their foodstuffs. Paul did his share, chasing dogs from the kitchen garden. Everything they did went to lowering her first husband's nine-hundred-dollar debt and finding a way to keep the horses.

They owned outright two well-formed mares and one gelding that Baptiste had taken over. Both mares were bred back and would foal in the spring. For the one named Janey, Marie had located a big stallion. She hoped she could negotiate the stud fee with Ross.

Louis was pretty sure Marie would go hungry if need be, soften up old leather and eat it during a hard snow rather than kill a horse to eat. Unless those boys were famished. She'd kill one for them if the occasion demanded. There wasn't anything, as far as he could tell, that she wouldn't do for them.

Louis thought he'd made headway with the older boy. Baptiste had a good eye and a steady hand. Together they'd brought in a deer or two that first winter. Baptiste had even grinned when Louis clapped him on the back at the good shot he'd made.

"That animal died respected," Louis told him. "Your pa would have been proud."

Mention of his father almost lost the closeness, but the boy nodded and then went back to tending the kill in silence.

Baptiste had also joined him on a hunt when George Simpson, the chief factor of all the North West Company, came upriver with Tom McKay in 1818.

Marie pushed for that, in fact. To make up for the boys not going to Yakima, Louis suspected. "You tell the bourgeois you have a good hunter to join him," she said. "Someone who would make a good clerk someday."

"Baptiste's a good shot," Louis told her. He bit into a pemmican chunk, scraped the soft chokecherry stuck on his tooth. "But pushing Baptiste as a clerk might not be wise. He doesn't show much interest outside of…"

She'd hissed like a cornered cat. He'd never seen her switch from calm to storm so quickly. "He speaks more than one language. He learns to read at Sally Ross's knees. He knows numbers—"

"I know such things too, and I'm not of the cloth from which clerks get cut. Neither is Baptiste," Louis said. "A good clerk needs to be a wind that lifts another's sail and then makes them willing to go where he wants. Baptiste doesn't have that gift, Marie."

"He has his father's *je ne sais quoi*."

"From what I hear, that isn't all he got from his hot-tempered father."

By the look she gave him, those sharp eyes narrowed and her jaw set firm as a center post, he knew he should have kept his mouth closed.

"What I can't figure is why you're so firm that I stay a free man, that I don't just sign on with the North West Company or any British firm."

"They can't be trusted," she said.

"Yet you push them to take your son on, to educate—"

"On my terms," she said. "My son will be more than a mere *engagé*, someone to be used by them. He will be his own man, use the company. They teach him skills. Then he can work for the Americans."

"The Americans won't ever come here in force, Marie," Louis told her. "You know yourself. No neat cows allowed. No little farms. This will always be Brit controlled. And when the British and Americans agree on who occupies what of the Columbia country, the Brits will have the upper hand. They're the mother country, Marie, and the Americans are wayward children." He grinned. "You know the strength of mothers and how little power wayward children really have."

She'd turned her back on him, went about the work of brushing her mare.

Paul was another story. His pointy ears located much lower than his ferret eyes, the sharp chin and wide-gait walk, that sullen slouch, all set the boy apart. He didn't know how to smile in any kind of friendly manner, at least not to Louis. And the stare he gave his mother—admiration tied up with tight strings of possession—formed a pit in Louis's stomach when he watched the boy. As soon as Paul saw that Louis was watching him, the boy's face changed to scowl of darkness. He was as unpredictable as a spring squall.

Worst of all was that Louis's wise and loving wife, Marie, didn't seem to see it.

◆

Paul struck his mother across her mouth. Louis was stunned at the act. They'd been quietly eating, sharing a meal. Paul's attack shot like an arrow into an otherwise still air.

"Mine," Paul said. "You gave Baptiste my salmon." He'd grabbed what had been his mother's food and attacked the hut's flap as though it resisted before leaving. Louis's wife wore the finger marks on the side of her cheek.

"The boy needs control," Louis told her. She'd done nothing in response to his violence, given Paul no consequence for such disrespect. "Authority. He needs to know how to treat people with respect."

"I shouldn't have been so hard on him earlier," she said. She tenderly touched the side of her mouth. Her lip was split. "You didn't see it all. You only saw his lost temper."

"Over a piece of fish," Louis said.

"*Non*. It was not about the fish. It happened this morning. I need to find a better way to correct him when he's rough with the horses. I didn't give him a chance to explain how the sores got there. I should have—"

"*Assez,*" Louis said, putting his hand up to stop her. "You wear his choices like an ill-fit robe. It does him no good. Nor you." She'd lowered her eyes, returned to peeling the roots in her lap. The tip of her tongue probed at the split place on her lip. Louis dug in his pack for a tin of pine pitch. He scraped a piece on the end of a knife. He pasted a dot of the black stuff onto her lip.

"No more," she said, waving him away. "The pitch takes too long to wear off."

Louis hadn't thought her vain, a woman who worried over her looks, but he could see now that she did. Or perhaps she didn't want people's eyes drawn to something that might suggest mistreatment.

"He has been through—"

"What?" Louis said. "What has he been through that a dozen other children have not? Tell me this, woman." He pointed through the open flap at young boys and girls working, sitting talking to their elders, gathering fire wood, spearing fish. "Others lose their fathers and they survive. Paul has you. Some of them are all alone, Marie, their fathers and mothers both dead. Or they are stripped from their mothers by slave traders or worse. They don't demand the way Paul does. He acts as though we all owe him."

"We do," she said, then whispered, "For what I put him through."

"Blesid Maria," Louis said, throwing up his hands. "He hit you, Marie. No one deserves that. Have you no limit to what you will endure?"

"A mother knows no boundaries," she said, her eyes pooling as she looked up at him. "Especially for her youngest."

He stared at her for a time until it came to him what he must do. What he had in mind couldn't happen any too soon.

7

Finger Plays

"Maybe if you took the boys back to where their father died, maybe then they'd say good-bye in a good way," Sally suggested. She'd begun curling her hair with twisted rags at night. The ringlets hung down and bounced now at her ears. Marie wondered where she'd seen such a fashion. "All the fighting inside them would crawl out and stay there in that place of bad memories."

The two women cooked black moss that they'd gathered from the pine trees at the headwaters of the Okanogan. Sally's children sat in the dirt, digging with sticks. "It's ready to put on the rocks," Sally said. "Oh, you remember," she added when she saw that Marie had already begun the pounding process. "You have a good memory. I show you once and you know a thing. Now that I can write, I scribble it down. So I won't forget when I learn a new thing. What do you do when you forget?"

"I don't," Marie told her.

Sally laughed but stopped when Marie didn't join her. "I'm sorry your eyes keep you from studying the letters," Sally said. "Maybe your eyes water from the smoke."

"We Ioways are just good criers. My eyes watered even when I looked at the maps Hunt showed me. The scribbling blurs. I blink often to keep the water from washing my view. It does little good. Even before the snow blindness in the mountains. But this," she lifted the clump of black moss, flattened it with a rock on a wider rock, then formed it into a cake. She threw a few dried huckleberries into it now. It would taste good when it cooled. "This I can remember how to do. From the smell of it and feel of it. That's how I remember to make this *squill-ape*."

"The hard cakes store well for winter. You could take some with you if you went to that *boise* place, for your sons to leave bad memories behind." With a new copper spatula, Sally pulled more stringy moss from the outdoor ovens, laid the mass on the rock for Marie to pound and shape. The stack of sun-dried cakes grew larger. Marie began filling her baskets with them.

"It was interrupted, their death songs, yes?"

Marie nodded agreement. "My sons and I had no time to bury their father's bones."

"Aha. Then you go next spring maybe. Mr. Ross tells me new trapping brigades are ordered by the Company. To take beaver and martin and otter, with many horses, men, and women. Even children will go. They'll need women to handle hides, salt them, and move the camps. You wouldn't be the only woman this time. Maybe your Louis will go too. As a hunter. He's trapped, yes?"

"Who leads this expedition?" Marie asked.

"Donald Mackenzie," Sally told her.

"The one who shoots Nez Perce horses? He's back?"

"He goes to the Boise River, where your husband's unburied bones lie. He'll build a fort among the Nez Perce, on the Walla Walla River, too. When he goes to the Walla Walla, we'll go along. You come too. I'd miss you if you weren't there, Marie."

Marie smiled.

"I'll ask my husband," Marie said, pushing against her thighs to stand. It was good to work beside a woman. And if she went back to the Boise with a brigade, she wouldn't be the only woman this time. She'd have no babies to worry over, no worry over a daughter being born too soon. Like before.

❖

"No," Louis said. He sat with the boys on cut-off stumps they used as chairs in the hut. Louis had rechinked the walls to make the hut warmer for the winter. He'd pounded old, bent nails straight and lined one wall with them. His felt hat hung on one. Baptiste's bow on another. "We stay here. I have a bad feeling about that Mackenzie and Walla Walla."

The deer already had thick fur and, when skinned, rolls of fat lined their backs warning that this winter of 1818 would be a harsh one. Marie knelt on a mat placing white beads onto a leather garment. "Not unless ordered to by the factors. We won't leave here. It's home." Louis held his hands up for Marie to see her own handiwork in sewing up his winter cuts. "My hands are healed at last," Louis said. "Your skunk oil soothes well. I thought it was the cold water that split my hands, but cold, dry air cuts the skin too."

Marie nodded, placed her small hand inside his for just a moment before returning to her work. "We know the ways of this Okanogan country," she said.

Louis said, "Such a large brigade as Mackenzie takes, two, three hundred horses, eighty men, their wives and children, invites trouble. They take out too many hides, leave nothing for the people there."

"So many Company men are meant to frighten the Bannocks and Shoshone," Baptiste said. "The numbers are for safety. We go as free trappers. We only take what we need." His voice still cracked when he talked, but he spoke with new confidence.

Louis shook his head. "The size threatens. So many invaders make the Shoshone defend more. That Mackenzie is said to strip the rivers like grasshoppers on leaves, leaving nothing for those who live there. No," Louis said.

"I'll go," Baptiste said. "They can use my help."

"We stay here this winter. Together," Louis said.

"He's scared," Paul said, pointing his chin at Louis.

"Paul…" Marie raised her eyebrow. She touched her tongue to the hard piece of pine pitch still on her lip.

"Fear stirs a stew," Louis said. "Keeps it from boiling over. Fear is a sign of caution, which you need."

"*I'm* not afraid to go," Baptiste insisted. "I'd learn, Mother. Maybe find Papa's bones and put them to rest. For you. I do this for you."

Marie let her hands rest on her thighs. Should she let her son bring an end to his father's dying? Did going home for him mean going to where his father's bones lay? Did he have to go home before he could find comfort somewhere else?

"You go for a learning time, eh?" Louis said. His tone held curiosity, not conclusion.

Baptiste nodded, "If you went too—"

"That man does women's work only. He uses scissors not guns," Paul said. He pointed to Louis. He never used Louis's name, Marie realized. "I'm not afraid to go where my father dies. I'm no woman hiding—"

"Paul!"

"Mama takes a woman to bed. Mama takes a woman to bed," Paul crowed the words. "That man grows soft in Mama's—"

Louis struck the boy with the back of his hand, the sharpness of the skin-to-skin contact shattering through Paul's taunts.

"*Silence absolu*," Louis said, "in case you don't understand English." His nostrils widened and his jaw jutted out like a hard rock in water. "You will keep your mouth closed of such words. Your mother deserves more, even if I don't."

"More what? More of you, woman?"

Louis struck him again.

Marie's stomach was a knot at the end of a swirling rope. She'd been here before. This same mistake, here, again. She'd chosen a man who struck boys. *Am I next? Did my eyes fail to see this? Did my mind close like a trap just so I could find warmth in a bed robe?*

Paul touched his face with his fingers. A half-smile slithered up toward his right cheek, now streaked with white from Louis's blow. Louis hadn't drawn blood, but the boy's eyes watered, and the imprint of Louis's fingers branded his face.

Her youngest son, the one with ten summers, let out a wail then and ran to her, grabbing her around her waist, his force against her bringing her into this moment. His arms shook. His head pressed into her. He was just a child, a boy. "Shhh, now," she said. "Shhh," her fingers gently patting his cheek. Yet he didn't look hurt. He looked almost…satisfied, as though filled with power when Louis struck him. He was a cat who had finally annoyed a dog enough it had snapped. Was this a lesson she'd taught her sons?

"*Non,*" she said, patting Paul's head as he cried. She pulled his face back. The tears were real. He did have a bruise on his cheek. "*Non,* no. This is not good, husband. Not good."

"You're right, woman," Louis said. "It's not." Then her husband of mere months walked out of their hut.

❖

Louis would have given anything for his wife to weep in his arms. Instead, that night, Marie lay with her back to Louis.

He hated the boy for making him do things he'd never done before. He'd struck a child. Twice, in front of the boy's mother. He had sworn he'd never do such a thing, and now he had. He hadn't signed on for this, not the constant challenge of these children. Louis had never thought of himself as cruel, never imagined he could get into a biting match with a ten-year-old. How could he have hurt a smaller soul? Why, it grieved him to take an animal in a trap.

Louis's face burned hot. This boy, this child, made him see a side of himself he hadn't thought was there. *Mon Dieu,* he prayed. *What kind of man am I?*

Was it jealousy? No. He'd wanted to protect Marie from the taunt that she'd chosen a weak man. He'd wanted to defend himself. But what kind of man used force against a child, even if tempted?

She lay there now, not asleep. He knew that from the sounds of her breathing. He dared not pull at the blanket, didn't want to disturb her. He tried to imagine what it must be like for her. Was she trying to forgive herself for those months long ago when something happened, he didn't know what? Maybe she carried the blame of their father's death though he couldn't see how. A man made his own choices. Everyone said her husband's death was a massacre, retaliation perhaps, for something the man named Mackenzie had done.

But she and the boys were the only survivors. Theirs were the only words of witness.

He wondered if his life with these boys would have been different if they'd been of Louis's flesh and blood. If they'd have grown up with him, had some good to mix with the bad. If he'd known them as infants, as his own, maybe he'd have more patience with them. If only he would get a nod back from them, some little indication he was more to them than a wall they had to break down to get to their mother. Maybe then he could have had more…tenderness toward them.

Baptiste at least was civil to him. They'd even shared a pipe and sat as he had with his own father when he was Baptiste's age. Two men looking out over the landscape, just thinking.

With Paul, Louis had no such heart knowing, nothing to draw on in his memory to help him when that child pushed at his limits.

Louis rolled over now, lay on his back. He'd always been able to fix a thing.

Maybe this boy wasn't fixable. Maybe Paul could sever the tie Louis had made with Marie. As with Mitain, Louis couldn't make her stop loving that Manuel Lisa despite the rat he was, stealing her son, trying to take her daughter. Maybe he couldn't help Marie see the trouble stirring in her sons, either. Louis couldn't give her eyes to see with both love and clarity. She saw the surface. He wanted her to look deeper into what lay at the bottom of a spring-fed pool. Maybe it wasn't even his place to try. Maybe he just swirled muddy waters better left stilled.

He touched her hip. "Marie…" She flinched. *Is my wife frightened of me?* "I seek your…forgiveness," Louis said into the darkness.

"He is my son," she said after a time. "You've no right to ask me to set him off."

"Non," he told her. "Truth is, I don't know what to do, eh? Don't know what'll become of him if he keeps on this path. Or of you."

"Or of us?"

She spoke the last so softly he wasn't sure what she'd said at first.

"What do you want to become of us?" Louis said.

She lay silent. He ached with her silence.

"A man and wife with a family. Maybe start our own?" he asked. He couldn't tell if she was crying. "Maybe I should just go with Mackenzie to Boise." Louis sat up. He felt her flinch again. "Get me away from here, give us some time, eh?"

"He is my son," she said and pulled at the blanket, covering her shoulder. She moved farther away.

"And it's not fair. To ask a woman to choose between a husband and a son."

"*Oui,*" she said.

"I don't ask such a thing of you, Marie," he whispered.

"Not in your words, but in what you do."

He considered. "Maybe," he said. He was in a wilderness here, trying to mark a trail for her, for himself.

He never heard her breathing change, didn't know if she slept. The distant sounds of wolves mourned into the night. He stood finally, walked to the door flap he pushed aside. He gazed at the scatter of stars in the sky that promised dawn. He couldn't change Paul. He couldn't give Marie what she needed in order to stand up for herself against her sons. He could only change himself. A man was responsible for which rivers he decided to run and who went with him.

And for when he decided to beach the craft and walk away.

❖

Jean Toupin's shoulder burned whenever he tried to lift it. In the months since the accident, he'd managed to use that right arm to stir a few soups, but it still sent searing pains into his back whenever he tried to reach too quickly to pat the jaw of a horse, reminding him that he couldn't. He couldn't even scratch the animal's ear.

He shook his head. *Stupide.* He'd won the race but lost much more. Even though he had anticipated the blankets being tossed at the finish line, the other mounts so close behind him had pushed against his, disrupting its rhythm and gait. He'd won all right, but he'd been tossed forward, jamming his shoulder as his palms hit the hard-graveled ground. He'd felt as though his arm had been shoved into his back, and he actually heard a tearing sound coming from his own body.

Michel had pulled him from the pebbles shouting, "You win! These is magnificent!" But even months later, Jean still couldn't perform his kitchen work as he had before, and now the factor had assigned him to tend the horses, something he could do with his left hand. Or so they hoped.

But what use was a horseman who couldn't use his right shoulder to toss a rope or even reach behind to scratch his own back? So much for taking a risk. *Stupide.* He'd never again let pride talk him into doing something so risky. He had a fat bank account, but for what?

The horse nudged him. "You are a good one, my friend." At least he enjoyed the animals. But they'd retire him, send him back to Montreal if he couldn't perform his duties. The horse blew air threw its nose. "Maybe I set a new goal here, to lift my arm to scratch your ear. An inch at a time." What else could he do but start over?

❖

Marie wasn't sure when she knew. Perhaps the knowing arrived with the aching in her legs. Certain smells grew more intense, and she sometimes wanted to bathe twice a day instead of every morning, clues of the changes her body forewarned. Still, that intensity of scent often happened after the winter when they'd spent so many hours inside, keeping the flap closed. Smoke from the cooking fires permeated everything, so the close quarters might have been the cause of her discomfort.

With sand, she cleaned the fish baskets that had grown unbearably smelly, beat on the mats, and laid out new, fresh ones woven from the pile of hemp she'd harvested the spring before. Ross said it was the year 1819 on his calendar. Not long ago, they'd walked through shoulder-high snowdrifts when they went to the fort to celebrate New Year's Day, just as the French-Canadians liked to, with singing and dancing. Ross dispensed shots of good rum.

Spring would soon crawl around the corner like a cautious cat and with it Marie and Louis would mark two years of marriage.

But it was longing for the taste of an apple that truly told her. Even an old crumpled fruit that might have been discarded back along the Des Moines River would have been welcomed like a son long away on a journey and finally returned home.

She wondered how to tell Louis or if she should.

They hadn't spoken of the incident with Paul after that night when Louis had left the hut. She'd held firm her choice not to let the boys go to Boise, and Marie vowed she would not let her husband leave the hut wounded. She would follow him, ask him to return, even if the words she said didn't soothe. There was no marriage if a man walked away and didn't come back.

Louis had come back the next morning, surprising Marie with new needles for her sewing kit. "We mend together," he'd said.

It seemed to her, Louis had made some slight adjustments around Paul, allowing the boy to have time with his mother without the competition of her husband. Louis and Baptiste shoveled paths through the snow, led the horses to wind-swept hills for food, talked easily with each other around the evening fire. The two of them got along. Not Paul. Paul was a weighted stone on a deep-set fishing net.

During the worst winter months when the Okanogan winds howled drifts into piles resembling remembered cream, the hut held tension thick as hog fat and twice as common. Few words were spoken then. Louis sewed leggings, repaired moccasins, helped Marie cut out the boys' clothes from hides. Paul mumbled something once to her about women's work, and it bothered her that one so young could separate men and women in that way, as though a woman's ways were somehow less important than what a man was asked to do. Louis helped in the hut. A man could and should learn to serve others. Louis was more a man for it, not less.

Her family sometimes walked the deep drift paths to Kilakotah and LaBonte's hut or to the fort to visit with Sally and Ross and their brood. Those that wintered together became a kind of community bathing in familiar waters. Those arriving on the spring or fall brigades, rushing in then out, would never understand this tender tie of people held together by experience. The separation of Indian and non, Okanogan or Clatsop, took on less weight in the winter where each supported the other to stay alive until the thaw.

Once when the wind had howled and the snows swirled into distant dust devils, the boys had stayed with LaBonte and Kilakotah's family for four days. Kilakotah had a new baby, and Marie had come to help deliver the infant they named Louis LaBonte II, as though the name bore more weight with a number attached.

With the sudden change in weather, Marie and Louis had returned to their hut to keep the fire going, check on the dogs. They laced snow-shoes on and led the horses to the frozen stream to break ice for them while hanging on to a rope attached to the hut. Lune walked upon the crusty snow beside them, the wolf-dog almost disappearing from sight in the chalk landscape.

A wool blanket close to her eyes kept the stinging snow from Marie's cheeks, but she could see little in front of her. She remembered the snow blindness in the Blues, gripped the rope tighter.

Back in the hut, stomping snow, the dogs dancing around them, she and Louis warmed their hands at the fire. "Here I have a rope I made with my own hands to help me find my way through the snow," she said. "Sarah said she prayed for my safety each day, but it's my rope I hang on to now."

"I do that too," Louis told her.

"You have a rope?" Marie said. She pushed at Its-owl-eigh with her foot, gently setting the dog away from her ankles where he'd plopped.

"*Non.* I keep you in my prayers, Marie."

His words had warmed her, and then without the presence of her sons to keep her always alert, the two had laughed together, sat on the robe, eating dried meat. She'd warmed to Louis's touch.

"*Demande grâce,*" he'd whispered, as they later lay coiled beside flickering flames, dogs snoring from the far side of the hut.

"*Oui,*" she said. "But forgiveness is not mine to give."

"It is," he told her. "I don't deserve it. I have never struck a child, not once, Marie, until Paul."

"I hit him too," she whispered, glad he couldn't see her face in the darkness. "So we both seek forgiveness." He kissed her, a whiskered soft-ness. "I worried you might hit me too," she risked then. She felt him wince.

"Never," he said. He pulled her to him. "You are as precious to me as my own bones. That you would even wonder—"

"I'm pleased you didn't go with Mackenzie to that Boise River."

"You noticed. Baptiste was disappointed."

"I didn't want you to stay here if you had a mind to leave."

"I'll never leave you," he said.

She could live without him, she was sure she could, though she'd miss him, oh, how she'd miss him. He probably didn't even know that. Perhaps he thought she welcomed him to her mat because she was lonely, not because she'd chosen him to be there. She'd meant the vows Ross had had them say. She would stay with Louis till death, if he let her. But she'd have to find a way to keep the stone of her son and the smite of her husband's hand from igniting a fire.

Still, inside their hut, she kept a distance between her and Louis when Paul was around. Paul acted tamed as a wolf pup willing to curl at her feet, then. Through the winter, the tension seemed to have seeped with the heat out into the cold.

Baptiste, too, scowled less, she thought. He was really a good boy, did what she asked. In fact, she sometimes didn't even notice he was there. Or maybe it was because he wasn't there as much. He had offered often to help with the horses at the post.

Marie hoped Louis understood why she moved away from him in Paul's presence. Louis had his own river to run, and perhaps she wasn't meant to be on it with him all the time, at least not while she had sons still in her hut.

But she wasn't sure how to tell Louis about this new knowing.

Then Louis saw the swell beneath her breast.

Both boys were in the hut, Baptiste working on a bow and Paul sharpening a leg bone into a blade. A drizzly rain spit snow outside, and a spring brigade had moved upriver and beached just the day before. Louis put his hand on the rise of her belly as she bent over the fire. "We'll soon have a child," he said. He smiled. "My plan works."

"You planned for this?"

Paul stopped what he was doing, knife held in midair.

"You'll be a good mother," Louis continued. "What do you boys think of that? A little brother or sister comes into our hut."

Baptiste shrugged. Paul said nothing.

Marie looked at Louis, wanting to be certain he didn't jest, that this infant would be truly what he wished for. She found no judgment on his face, only a soft smile creating an opening in the black beard.

"Mackenzie sends for more horses," Baptiste said. "We'll help take them south?"

"Where'd you learn about that?" Louis asked.

"McKay. He came with the brigade. Says they met a courier from Mackenzie."

"Mackenzie's still alive at least," Marie said. "That's good. The winter's been a harsh one, and they're still at the *boise* place, alive."

"They need remounts," Baptiste said.

"Hopefully not for supper," Louis said, his deep voice laughing.

"My knife, Mama?" Paul was suddenly beside her. He handed the leg-bone blade to her. "It's sharp, *n'est-ce pas?*"

Marie shook Louis's hand free as she bent to face her son. Paul handed her the bone, and she turned it over in her small palms. He'd twined leather strips around the base as a handle. The workmanship was good for one so young.

"You've done well, yes, Paul." She handed it back to him.

"So, what do you think about a brother coming?" Louis asked him. "Will you be a big brother to him, then, Paul?"

Marie shook her head at Louis, her eyes warning.

"Yours now," Paul said, pushing his knife back to her. He glared at Louis. "You need it. To keep the baby safe."

Marie turned back to her task, uncertain how to respond to her son or her husband. After all, Louis hadn't said she *was* already a good mother, only that she would be.

❖

Baptiste and Louis saddled up along with three *engagés*. "Maybe Paul should go with you," Marie told Louis.

"His feathers might lay better in a flock, eh?" Louis asked. Marie smiled. "You think I can smooth his edges by just having him around me."

"If he sees others treating you with respect, he'll do that too. Time together heals."

Louis grunted. "Keep him with you. He can have you all to himself for a time. Before the baby comes."

"You're generous," she told Louis.

"Or *le fou*," he said.

"On Hunt's journey, for a time, there was a plant man named Nuttall. The men called him *Le Fou* for his foolish ways, but he cured sickness and stopped a senseless fight between Manuel Lisa and my husband."

Louis's eyebrows rose at that, and Marie sensed that he wanted to ask her more about the disagreement, but Ross signaled their leaving.

Just then, the men from the Spokane country who were herding the additional horses they were taking south rode up. When the dust cleared, Marie noticed that one man rode with awkwardness, his right hand resting on his thigh, his left holding the reins. "Madame Dorion?"

Marie squinted into the speaker's face, which was shadowed by his hat.

"*Oui.*"

"Jean Toupin," he said. "The camp boy."

"You know this one?" Louis asked.

Marie felt herself smiling, her face growing warm with remembrance. "*Oui.* He walked Hunt's trail with us. And welcomed us to Astoria."

"I once gave her a pair of earrings," Jean said.

She reached for her ears, dropped her hand quickly. The holes where earrings once fit were covered over now with a film of skin.

"I'm sorry. I had to trade them," she said.

Jean laughed. It was a man's laugh, not a boy's. "Then they served well," Jean said. "Who could ask for more?"

8

Right with the World

Marie and Paul did work well together that first day after Louis and Baptiste and her old friend Jean Toupin headed south. Paul helped her plant the seeds in the garden, and he scampered without hesitation to bring food up from the pit. When other boys called to him to set snares for rabbits, Paul shook his head no and smiled at his mother. This was really all he needed, Marie decided, time with her to be reassured of a mother's love.

"Louis was right," she told him. She brushed at his hair, pushed it back from his narrow eyes.

Paul could be as still as a mouse in the sagebrush while a rattlesnake slithered by. He did that now, his eyes unblinking, not a muscle twitching.

"Louis said it was best if you stayed here with me while they were gone. I thought you might want to go with your brother and him."

"I stay here. To take care of you."

"Oh, you chose, did you?" Marie smiled. She pulled at the lengths of hair that hung on either side of his narrow face. His pointy ears pushed through thin strands. "You forget that I am still your mother who is in charge, *n'est-ce pas?* I decide what is best for you."

"*Oui,*" Paul said. "You are still my mother."

❖

Sally often took over her husband's responsibilities of greeting the brigades when Ross was off following the Company's orders to explore, secure, negotiate, and trade with natives. Ross was gone now, to the Willamette place where Marie and Pierre and her sons had enjoyed their first winter in Oregon country.

With Ross gone, Marie spent more time in Sally's presence. They often rode together across the hills, loaded roots into bags. "Janey would bring a pretty price in St. Louis," Marie said patting the neck of her horse. The animal had spots across her rear that looked like a snowball splattered against red earth. The women sat, hands over the pommels, reins loose in their fingers. Marie warmed with her "Sally time," as she called it. And now that she shared the news of a coming baby, they had more to exchange than gossip.

"You'd never sell her," Sally said. "I know you. Do the St. Louis women ride as we do?"

Marie shook her head. "They sit behind their husband, their legs to one side, hanging on to him and a handle more narrow than a bucket's. They squeeze their fingers and look sideways as he reins the horse forward. They stop when he does; they go where he goes."

"Like our marriages, yes?" Sally said. Both women laughed.

"We ride in the same direction, but we see very different things," Marie said. "They see what's ahead, and we see what is happening now."

"We should bring Kilakotah to ride with us next time," Sally said. "Her boy has a hard cry that pierces the night. I think she doesn't rest much."

"She doesn't make enough milk," Marie said. "We need a cow."

"We're fortunate to have goats," Sally said. "Or she would have nothing to offer."

"I hope to have enough with this one," Marie said, patting her stomach. "But we should get a cow from Fort George," Marie ventured. "Your husband could make such a request."

"They hold the cows like cards, close to their chests," Sally said. "It will be a while before we are allowed one here."

At the fort, Marie helped cook and clean, often eating in the separate dining room with Sally and any of the other wives and children of clerks and traders making their way north or south. If they spoke French, Marie followed easily, though her English had improved greatly with Sally's help. She might never be a bourgeois's wife as Sally was, but she learned the ways of such women. She noticed the intricacies of the fort procedures, how food was stored or ordered, what arrived by ship and when.

Sometimes, she even helped with the work of stacking barrels as she stood taller than a number of the *engagés* and could reach top shelves.

Any extra work Marie did went to pay Sally for the instructions she gave Paul—and Baptiste when he was there—in English and reading and writing.

"I will ask Ross to teach your sons the catechism too," Sally told her one morning after a lesson with her own children and Paul. Even Kilakotah had started making scratches in a sand-filled box, her son bounced in his board across her knees. "Such instruction would be good for them. Kilakotah says she'll come."

"No," Marie said.

"No? A son who might be a clerk someday should know all the ways of those he works for," Sally said, "if not for his own good."

"Any extra I earn must go against Pierre's debt," Marie said.

Sally stared at the ledger sheet. "How did your first husband come to owe so much?" She marked a paper, reducing Marie's debt. Sally would show it to Ross when he returned so he could adjust the official ledger.

"The Company forced him into the debt. I'll get us out."

"Will Louis help?" Sally asked.

Marie shook her head. "It's my debt, made before Louis. No one can pay it but me."

"If your boys trapped, you could repay the loan faster. They're of your first family, they belong to the debt."

"Paul's too young, and Baptiste is interested in horses and bows and arrows."

"I see Paul near beaver huts when we are fishing," Sally said. "He seems to know the ways of beavers. I see him swim once. He stays under a long time. He must find a reed to do that, so he can breathe. Kanaka people can do this, from their time in warm waters of the Sandwich Islands, diving for oysters. And Paul isn't too young, Marie. Work is a way a child learns to be generous, giving to others and to himself. Work is not only for the wonder of it. Maybe this is what he misses. He doesn't know how to be generous, so he finds trouble where he shouldn't."

Marie considered. "Maybe when Louis comes back, I'll ask him to take Paul out to show him how to set traps."

"Ask Louis about the religious instruction," Sally said. "Your sons will need such learning to survive in the Company."

"I decide such things for my sons," Marie said. Sally lowered her eyes, then changed the subject. "Perhaps they won't need to work for the Company; they can find another way to care for themselves. They won't need religious instruction then."

She wasn't sure why Sally's suggestion annoyed her so. Perhaps it reminded her too much of the years when she was young and Pierre's mother had insisted she become baptized, had called her, taunting almost, "Her to Be Baptized." It was as though only the friar's water could wash her into completeness, lead her to her *métier*. Marie resisted still the giving up and giving in to the baptismal water. She did not need it. When the boys were older, they could decide such things—if they ever faced a challenge that required the benefit of baptism.

"There are no priests in this Columbia country," Marie told Sally, "so my sons have no need to learn of what priests do."

Sally nodded, but her dark face deepened in color. "I meant no harm, Marie," she said. Sally dropped her glance.

Irritation must have ridden in on Marie's words. Marie looked for better words, but her giving basket stood empty.

❖

The men returned in record time. "The clerk they sent had nothing to think with," Baptiste told her. "He left his head at home."

"Jean Toupin?"

Louis shook his head no. "He was all right. But they failed to post a guard, and we were raided," Louis told her. "Two men died. We lost the horses, but Baptiste and me and your Toupin friend, we got twenty back."

"I can imagine Mackenzie's fume when you arrived with so few," Marie said.

"Some of the Indian raiders died too," Baptiste said. "I took one out myself. His back bled red."

"You should not be so proud of killing another," Marie said.

"It was in defense," Louis said.

"His back attacked?" she said.

"You killed someone," Paul said. His small eyes sparkled. "Tell me. Tell me."

"We arrive safe and in time," Louis said, dismounting. "Our going was for nothing anyway, as Mackenzie met us."

"Mackenzie was attacked, Mother," Baptiste said. "By the same people who killed Papa."

"You don't know this," Marie told him. "You shouldn't tell tales."

"Likely he's right," Louis said.

"Tell how you killed one," Paul demanded.

"Later," Louis said. "This talk upsets your mother."

"He has other plans, Mackenzie does," Baptiste told her. "He will build a fort at Walla Walla, on the south side of the big river."

"In the American section?" Marie asked.

"Jointly held," Louis reminded her, that one eyebrow lifting in correction. "But yes, moving brigades from there, into American and Mexican territory. The word is the Company is to make the area a 'fur desert.' Take all the pelts they can to discourage Americans from settlement and frustrate any American fur companies thinking of trapping."

"Did you shoot him?" Paul asked. "Tell how you killed—"

"A fur desert. Mackenzie knows no limits," Marie said.

"I wonder sometimes if anyone does," Louis finished.

"What was it like to watch him die?" Paul said.

❖

Mackenzie began building on the Walla Walla River, an event that changed Marie's days.

The Okanogan fort bustled with the new arrivals of French-Canadians and laboring Kanakas once from the Sandwich Islands and now spread across the northwest by the Company. Partners sent men from various outposts to join in this adventure that McKay said was to be the finest fort in all the Columbia country. Few of the men stayed at Fort Okanogan for more than a night before heading south to help Mackenzie. Marie watched to see if maybe Sarah and Ignace might return from wherever they'd gone. But no one mentioned having seen the Iroquois family.

Even Kilakotah scanned the new arrivals as though searching for someone. She studied Indian faces, a look of longing haunting her eyes. Sometimes she looked much older as she stretched her neck to see better. Wrinkles in her neck showed that Marie had never noticed. Marie ran her hands over her own throat.

Something more stirred inside Marie when she watched her young friend's seeking. It reminded her of another time when she'd been missing something, someone. She must not think of that time before even Baptiste was born. She shook her head as though to empty it of sad thoughts.

Marie worked in the kitchen with some of the *engagés* who served as cooks. She could handle the heavy copper pots and seldom showed signs of tiring, even though the seams of her dress had been let out wide to accommodate the anticipation of her child.

Louis was dispatched to bring horses again and carry messages back. There were challenges at Walla Walla, more than when the Astorians built at the mouth of the Columbia. At least, that was what McKay and Ross and other partners implied within earshot of the women. Men's voices often drifted down the narrow hall between the men's dining area and where the women worked to prepare the food.

"They're felling trees a hundred miles upriver and floating them down for building," McKay said. He chewed on a piece of goat meat, a string catching on his chin. "And the Indians there are wanting to charge them. For the trees, the land." McKay shook his head. "Mackenzie has a way of riling them, that's for sure."

Wintering heat supplies would take extra effort to secure, too. Repairing boats there would be troublesome so far from good timber. Hammers and furnishings would come from back East, around the horn to Fort George and then upriver.

"I'll tell you the story," McKay told Ross. "Mackenzie wants it to be grand, to show the Americans. He's even making peace with the Nez Perce, buying them all nature of trinkets to quiet them down."

" 'Twill serve him well if he's faithful, then," Ross said. "Winning them will keep the Americans out and discourage settlers."

"No way wagons can come across those mountains," one of the other clerks noted. He stabbed a piece of melon with his fork just as Marie moved in to remove his empty plate. "Think there won't be too many settlers in this rough country, I should say."

"Unless the French-Canadians decide to remain after they retire from the Company," McKay said.

"Sure and that'll be thwarted by the policy," Ross said. He sighed. "All must return to where they signed on—Canada. Not likely they'll come back here at their own expense across the mountains to farm."

"Unless they leave their wives and children here," McKay said. "They'd come back for them. I would. If I had a family."

"Well, we should," Ross said. "Yet, the Company's quite canny, really. They encourage alliances to calm relations with the interior tribes, but they discourage taking the women and children back with them, which causes even greater outrage."

"Of course, they won't take their native wives with them," a clerk said. "How would she fit in there? The men will find another bedmate soon enough. Plenty of women awaiting the romance of a man who's lived in the Columbia country. Isn't that right, Ross?"

Ross cleared his throat. "Not much farming here unless we can get water to the plantings in a more timely fashion. But in that Willamette country, where the ground's black as coal…"

Marie could hear no more as she slipped out into the kitchen. The scrape of chairs and the loud calling of a crow outside the window broke Ross's voice. She wished she could have heard Ross's reply. An ache inside her stomach made her wonder what kind of world she was bringing a new child into. So many changes, dangers. She wondered if Sally knew what would happen in this changing land.

"Mackenzie wants 250 horses there eventually," Louis told her. He chewed on the *squill-ape* recently soaked in water. They still had a good supply of the moss cakes.

"All this moving back and forth. Does it mean this fort will close?"

Louis shook his head. As a free man, Louis rarely ate at the fort's table, relying on Marie's ears to gather up gossip like crumbs at the clerks' feet. She found the crumbs, but it was his job to interpret what they meant.

"There'll always be need for this fort," Louis said. "The Okanogan has a wide drainage. Makes a good fur collection place. And not far from Spokane, for fresh mounts to be exchanged when people ride overland." He chewed again. "But the Fort among the Walla Walla will be the main place soon, for exchanging hides and supplies."

"Perhaps you could take Baptiste with you again," she said. "He brings back wages he applies against the debt. He's a good boy."

"I'd help with the debt, Marie." He'd offered before, but she'd only bristled.

"It's mine to pay off."

Louis nodded. It was as he expected. "Paul wants to go," Louis said then.

"He's talked with you?"

Louis nodded. "Quite pleasant he was. A surprise. Maybe he's learning to adjust, finding a place for me—however small—in his life. I'll take him, leave Baptiste. He can be more help to you here. If the baby comes early, send him or ask him to send that new Frenchman Narcisse Raymond to get me. He's a good man, that one."

"This one takes its time," Marie said, patting her stomach.

"Paul'll have a new *enfant* to challenge his place soon enough. A time away might help him ease into it."

Marie considered. "All right," she said after a time. "He may as well begin learning that he won't be the baby for much longer."

❖

"It won't be so bad, Paul," Marie said. "See. You'll get to ride Janey all that way, help the other men keep the herd moving. You'll watch her colt, make sure she follows. Mama wouldn't trust her to anyone but you. It will be an adventure. Maybe you'll see things you saw when you were much younger, when we were found by the Walla Walla people."

"I don't want to remember them."

"They were good to us. You played with the children and—"

"I don't remember."

"You'll do fine," Marie said. She patted his knee. "I made new leggings for you, you're getting so tall. And we'll braid strips of cloth into the horse's mane." Marie pulled out the fold of gurrah cloth she'd dyed and redyed with chokecherries until the pale cloth bled red. "See. To go with the black and red bars we'll paint under your eyes."

"Let Baptiste wear Okanogan paint. I'm Sioux, like my papa."

"Sioux and French-Canadian and Ioway," Marie said. "You come from good stock."

"Cloth, but no paint. Louis doesn't wear paint."

"He's right," Louis said.

Marie smiled. Perhaps this would be a good trip for them, ready Paul for the new baby. He seemed to realize at last that Louis was here to stay, a part of making their lives better.

"Tie the cloth on my wrists, too," Paul said. "Louis too. We make it a ceremony."

She did as he directed, her husband holding his hands up so she could knot the soft cloth on each wrist, leaving streamers to flow in the wind. "Save enough for the horse's mane," Paul told her when she doubled the strips that fluttered like flags.

"Good thing the horses are accustomed to such things. There," Marie said, finishing up the last knot. "I'll save the rest for the manes."

They walked out then, Louis with his arm around Marie, Paul run-walking ahead. Even Baptiste strode with them, holding Paul's horse for him while his brother grabbed the mane and pulled himself up.

"Like he was born there," Louis said. "A natural." He, too, mounted, and Marie tied the red cloth into both their horses' manes.

"We tie the ribbons every time now, Mama," Paul directed.

Marie nodded agreement. She shaded her eyes from the sun as she looked up at her husband. He leaned to kiss her, and she stood taller to take his face in her hands and hold him for a moment.

"Me too, *Mère*. Good-bye to me, too," Paul demanded.

Louis released her as Marie stepped over to Paul, kissed him on the cheek he bent for her. "You be a good boy," she said and stepped back.

From behind her, Louis ran his finger down the center part of Marie's hair. She turned to him, holding her abdomen where she felt the baby move. She laughed. It felt good to laugh loud and full, to be done with grieving. She anticipated this new life, her new life with Louis, with Paul coming around to acceptance and a baby joining this mix.

"*Mère*, again," Paul said. "Kiss me again."

She laughed and did.

"Paul worries he'll lose his place," Marie said softly when she turned back to her husband.

"He thinks the last will be loved best," Louis said as he put his face close to hers. "But he doesn't know yet, that only goes for kisses."

❖

Marie pushed the infant out of herself, firm and wet against an Okanogan hillside warmed by a summer sun. Her groan of delivery sounded like a hawk's sigh, even to her own ears. It echoed against the bare hills, rolling above the dimple of already yellowed grasses where she squatted. Panting, she massaged the new life and watched the infant take in air, making a sound like the gurgle of spring water falling over rock.

A blast of wind struck at her, and she nearly lost her balance. The Okanogan hills were scrubbed by steady winds this time of year. A hawk hovered above her. In the distance, she could see people, little sticklike forms near the river where songbirds would serenade, dancing from willow branch to branch. Baptiste would be there. Paul's horse nudged Marie with her nose.

Marie cleaned the baby's tiny nostrils with her fingertip while the infant's fingers splayed like the branching of a spring stream rushing. So tiny. So perfect. The fingers moved in a delicate dance. The infant sneezed, then took in breath as Marie stroked the soft down of the baby's arms. Marie looked around for Baptiste to see if he was well occupied with the rest of the fishing party. With soft grasses she'd pulled earlier, she wiped the baby dry and wrapped her in a gurrah cloth.

Sally Ross had told her she should remain behind, that she looked to soon give birth. "I know the signs," she told Marie.

But Marie didn't want her child arriving inside the confines of the hut beside the fur post. She wanted the baby to breathe the air fed by grasses and warmed by a June sun that brushed the open sky. The land-scape would midwife this infant as it had her last child. But this one would live.

"Oh, shhh," Marie said, kissing the smooth forehead. "Daughter of my heart." She sang her welcome song. It was a girl! How she'd longed for a girl! Not to replace the one she'd lost those years before. No one child could replace another. Marie's heart beat faster, a memory searching.

For seven years she'd longed for a girl-child and now, here she was with hair like Sarah's sons, dark and standing up already.

In the distance, Marie could see a dog scamper beside Baptiste, its shadow small. Noon. It must be noon. She had squatted here a long time; rising and falling with the arc of pain, wind whipping the fringe on her leather dress.

But the baby had arrived, full of life, and in a little while, she would have milk to feed her. Marie inhaled the scent of her daughter, her liv-ing daughter. "She is a plump, round-faced girl with hair the color of prime beaver hide, soft as sable," she said out loud as though the infant's father could hear, as though her first husband needed an introduction and the knowledge that at last, a healthy girl had been delivered. She felt a pang of guilt that she had thought of Pierre first.

But now, her only regret was Louis not being here to meet his child.

Marie allowed her first daughter to settle in her mind. "Move over, Vivacité," Marie whispered to the memory. "I will make a new room for you inside my heart now, as this one finds her place of belonging."

Marie wanted to breathe a prayer of thanksgiving, to the One Sarah said made all things happen for good. But she held back, not wanting to bring attention to One so powerful, not when more than once Marie had sent a blaming arrow his way. Besides, when she noticed the good things, they didn't last. It was better to simply let them pass, unnamed.

This time, no husband looked at Marie with pleading eyes, suggesting she could not keep the child alive. This time, no expedition waited for her to hurry along on the only horse. This time, she birthed the child alone. Memory ached into her side.

"Regret is the robe grief hands out," she told the child. "No warmth."

This was a time to celebrate, to fill a basket up, not consider its weight. "Your other mother, Sarah, she tells me to send heavy thoughts to the wind, to make room for lighter ones. So for her, I thank the Lord for this gift given." She kissed the baby's cheeks. "I'm afraid to take in the joy too long," she told the baby, whispering through her lips against the infant's temple. "Good things never last. Powerful One is jealous and takes human pleasures back."

Marie knew Sarah would disagree, but this was her experience. She hadn't received the joys that Sarah had, nor had she learned how to hold them in her heart.

Marie's hands massaged the infant. She held the baby to her breast. "Soon," she said. "You will eat soon."

Marie bit the cord off then and tied a knot close to the child's navel and stood to expel the afterbirth. She buried the circle of herself in the rock-dribbled dirt.

Next to her chest, the infant felt firm. Would it be safe to name her, to admit she already loved the lips as thin as pumpkin seeds, the eyes the color of strong tea? She could call her Louise, perhaps, after her father.

"Maybe I name you for your sister," Marie said. "Vivacité."

She heard a hawk screech and watched as the wind held it in one place in the blue sky. "Perhaps I should call you Her to Be Baptized, as my mother-in-law once named me," Marie said. And for the first time Marie heard the name as one "who was called to something," as Sarah had been, and not just a name of one unworthy.

Baptiste approached then, riding a horse that neighed to Marie's mount. "You have a new sister," she told Baptiste. She held the baby up to him with both hands.

Baptiste sat silent. *What should a fourteen-year-old boy say?*

"Paul will tell you to send it back," Baptiste said.

"The youngest always feels left out at first," she said.

"He'll think it's squirmy," he said. "It'll eat too much."

"No, no," Marie said. "She'll bring joy to us. Your father will be happy."

"My father is dead."

Marie nodded. She pulled the baby into her chest. The infant tried to stretch inside the cloth, and Marie opened the thin linen so the boy could see his sister's face.

"Can I touch her?" Baptiste asked.

Marie hesitated, then said, "Gently. You're a strong brother."

And the boy was gentle. As he stroked the baby's cheek with the pad of his finger, Marie realized she'd been holding her breath. "I like babies," he said. He looked up at her. "Did I have a big brother? When I was little?"

That longing again, a knot in her stomach. She kept her heart stilled. "Paul—"

"We'll help him like this one," she said. "He'll see that the basket is big enough for three children, for all three. Maybe more. I can take enough out of the basket to make room for more."

"For your Louis, too?"

"Louis, too."

The hawk cried out. Marie looked up then to see the bird as it faced into the wind, still in one place, going nowhere. Then just as quickly, it dipped into the breeze, made the slightest adjustment in its wings as though to let the challenge pass. It allowed itself to be carried upward. A slight adjustment, and the breeze lifted him to where he wished to go.

"Paul will adjust," she said, hoping it was so. "We will all need to resettle with this new baby girl."

❖

His child. The tiny, breathing being was his child. Marie presented the infant to Louis when he and Paul arrived back from Mackenzie's Walla

Walla fort. He watched Marie's face as she held the child close to her breast. For just a moment, Louis understood Paul's jealousy, his desire to possess Marie's heart, to make no room for any other. Could a woman love a child that much and still have room in her heart for the infant's father? For another?

Louis shook his head, took a deep breath. No, this was his daughter. It would be different with his flesh and blood.

He watched Paul now, the boy as sullen as an ox. He seemed so old at times, his face so serious, always scheming, never joyful. He walked slump-shouldered. With his wide gait, his feet dragging heavy. It was as though he carried a weight too large for even Louis to lift off. Not that the boy would allow anyone to take it, whatever it was. Paul'd been civil on this journey south. He'd given one-word answers to questions, followed most directions without comment. But he'd been distant, unwilling to see the adventure in the journey. The only excitement he'd shown had been when they'd sighted a beaver lodge on one of the tributaries. Nothing else seemed to intrigue him.

"See there," Paul had said when they'd come near the dam. He kicked Janey. The horse startled forward at the abrupt move of the boy. The red gurrah strips of cloth fluttered from the horse's mane, Paul's wrist. "There must be a large one inside there. Think of the branches they pull in through their tunnels." He looked around, pointed to the trees felled by the rodents. Then they had heard the large plop like a rock being dropped, and Paul said, "Hear it! That's him! I go look for him."

"No, Paul. We've got horses to attend to. People waiting on us, eh? No time for playing. You're a big man now."

"Want to find that beaver," Paul said.

"Not now. When we come back," Louis said and other *engagés* signaled them to return to the herd.

Paul hesitated, and Louis wondered what he'd do if the boy simply defied him, rode away to pursue the beaver, and ignored what he had to say. He felt his palms get sweaty.

He had no talent with children. Perhaps that was why Mitain had kept him at a distance. Maybe she knew he couldn't bring another man's child up well in this world. Maybe he'd been wrong to think having his own child would make a difference.

But Paul hadn't challenged. He'd reined Janey away from the stream, jabbed her side again with his heels, and yanked on the bit. Louis thought to correct him as Marie's horse had a soft mouth and didn't need such pulling to comply, but decided he had pushed his luck enough in getting Paul to turn aside from the beaver chase. It was always a question, whether to step over something with Paul or stand his ground.

After that, they'd had no other conversations except the one-word responses when Louis asked a question or gave an order. It was like traveling with a snake; he was never sure when it would stop moving steadily along, when it would coil to strike.

Now Louis watched with caution as Paul pushed his way to stand beside Marie. He should see and hold the baby before Paul, Louis thought. Then he corrected himself. What kind of man was he to be so possessive that he thought the first gaze should have been his and not this boy's? Surely he was man enough to wait a boy's turn.

Paul barely glanced at the infant, then said, *"Fille."*

"Yes, a girl," Marie said. "Your sister, Paul."

"I had one. She died."

Louis watched a shadow cross Marie's face. Paul treated his mother like old leather. Again, Louis wondered if he should intervene, decided against it.

"She is nearly *impeccable*," Louis said, leaning in to view his daughter, a movement that interrupted the pain in Marie's eyes. When Marie opened the thin cloth for him, he felt his throat thicken. "Nearly *impeccable*," he whispered, his finger pressing at the cloth to reveal his daughter's tiny chin.

"Not perfect? What's wrong?" Marie said.

She looked over Louis's shoulder as he took the child in his large hands, the scars of his fingers snagging on the fabric, the red ribbons hanging loose like reins at his wrists.

"She has my nose instead of yours, eh?" Louis said. "Otherwise, she is perfect."

Marie smiled. "It means she'll be a fine cook, able to season the meat well and tend to her husband and her family."

"As her mother does," Louis said. "As her mother does."

Marie smiled at him, and he felt as light as a bird. He could do this, raise a daughter. Perhaps even easier than if he'd had a son.

He placed his daughter back into Marie's arms, then put his own around the two of them. "You have given me the greatest gift a man ever receives, other than your love," he told Marie. Her eyes watered with his words. He felt her tears on his forearm. She leaned back against him, the sweet smell of her hair rinsed with some kind of herb filling his senses.

Paul thrust Janey's reins at Marie, nearly throwing them at his mother. "Your horse needs work," Paul said. "She reins her own way. I want a gelding to ride. No more weak-willed mares." With that he'd stomped away.

❖

They named the baby Marguerite, after Louis's mother. "It's a mother's name, eh?" Louis said.

Marie never loved him more than at that moment. Louis understood her work, how much she longed to have her life recorded by the gifts she gave to home and family. To name their daughter with a mother name, from her very first beginnings, spoke of the value Louis saw reflected in that mothering work. She did that work now, poking at the outside fire while Louis held the child.

"Your mother raised a good son," Marie said.

"My brother thanks you for the compliment," Louis said.

"You have a brother?" she asked, turning to him. It had never occurred to her before, whether he had a brother or a sister.

"*Non.* I make a joke for you," he said. "I was the only child. Our Marguerite will have it different, eh? She will be the first of many." The infant's long fingers curled over his one. He bounced it lightly, staring at this child. "And when the time comes for her baptism, she won't have to change her name, then. She will always be known by a mother's name as a woman should."

"The priests will be a long time coming to this place," LaBonte said as he approached with Kilakotah and Louis Two. "Maybe we have them baptized together. Same day, them being born the same year and all."

"Louis Two was born before the New Year's rum," Marie corrected.

"What do you say to that, Venier? They were almost in the same year."

"Their baptisms could be," Louis said. "The first of many. A man finds reward in God allowing him to help create, *n'est-ce pas?*"

"This is true," LaBonte said.

Sally insisted on a dedication service with Ross presiding. "Not official now, you know," Ross said. "Just a dedication. I'm no reverend."

"We can sing songs," Sally said.

"You know," Ross said. "'Tis the strangest thing, those songs. Some of the Flathead sing them. And the Spokane. Even pausing on the Sabbath to sing. Now how'd they know to do that, way up there in Spokane country?"

"This is acceptable," Louis said. "We sing and say a blessing. For now, eh, Marie? Someday the priests come and our Marguerite will have a real baptism."

She'd nodded, saved from the choice of whether to have Marguerite baptized or not. If she did agree, perhaps Louis would ask the same of her, that their marriage be properly acknowledged. That would require instruction, judgments by the priests, and baptismal water. A baptismal ceremony would be insufficient to cleanse Marie of all her failures as a mother, failures any could judge by simply watching her sons.

No. Her sons still suffered from the trials she'd exposed them to by her poor choices. Paul cut at her heartstrings with the sharp knife of disrespect, and Baptiste lived with a wall around him, separated, as though still tied inside a buffalo robe.

Still, she had received a healthy daughter. She'd been given a new chance.

9

Heart Knowing

Life with a daughter was different. Or perhaps it was having an attentive father that made the change, Marie couldn't be sure. But she felt more laughter bubble up with this child, more joy in seeing her roll over, more delight in her coos as she spoke to her mother, her eyes always watching. Marie couldn't remember Baptiste or Paul behaving in these ways, cooing and calming with their own fists to their mouth. But back then Marie had been busy tending hides, and her mother-in-law had cared for her sons when they were small. Other, wiser women, spent time with her children.

Marie wished she'd watched them more closely, to learn their lessons.

"Who would think they learn so much?" Kilakotah said. The two women's infants slept in baby boards propped up against the side of the hut while Marie and her friend dug potatoes from the kitchen garden plot. The mixed-blood families were allowed to plant and harvest for their own use. And they repaid the costs of seeds and tools by returning half the produce to the fort's stores. They worked twice as hard for half the harvest. It was the way of things at the Company's forts.

"Louis Two sits up alone?" Marie asked. She slipped the shovel beneath the potato plant, reached, shook off the dirt, then laid the tuber in a basket.

Kilakotah nodded. "He eats so well he's like a fat tick who falls over. But he puts his hand out now, and pushes back up and looks all proud. Like he shot an arrow and hit a mark."

"Marguerite makes sounds that mean she's hungry, wet, wants us to move her, wants to see something different," Marie said. "She makes demands, but they're easily met. She stretches up, to see far away."

"She likes to ride?"

Marie stood, pressed her hands against the small of her back to ease the strain of digging. "She always falls asleep. That's what I'll do when her teeth break through and she fusses," Marie said. "Take her out across the hills."

"A good excuse to ride a horse," Kilakotah said. Others might still call her Lisette, but she would always be Kilakotah to Marie.

Marie's boys had been calmed by traveling here and there with their father in canoes when they were babies. Sometimes Pierre drank; sometimes he was gentle as a kitten. Home had been Marie's mother-in-law's hut. Marguerite would be raised on horses, in Marie's home, with Louis's guidance. Marguerite would learn to ride astride the way Indian women did instead of sitting on a soft pillion and hanging on precariously behind a husband.

Marguerite would have older brothers offering protection too, once they adjusted to her presence.

Marie scanned the landscape for her sons. Baptiste bent beneath a horse, filing at the animal's hoof while Louis hovered over him, pointing. Baptiste learned, paid attention. He even laughed at Marguerite's blinking eyes. "She teases," he said.

"It's what women do," Louis had told him to Baptiste's agreeable nod. The boy responded to Louis's words; while his mother received only grunts.

Marie glanced around and realized she hadn't seen Paul for several hours. Maybe he played with Jemima Ross, Sally's child. Marie scanned. No, he couldn't be with her; Jemima worked beside her mother hanging cloth dresses on the line beside the fort.

Marie's stomach tightened. She'd have to ask Paul where he'd been when he got back. His constant disappearance without alerting her gnawed. What was he doing, gone so long?

Marie wondered if he noticed how Marguerite's eyes followed him in the hut, how her arms reached up when he bent over her. He never tried to pick her up, but Marie was sure she adored him. He just didn't seem to take in her loving him.

"Rivers woo him," Louis said once when Marie spoke of Paul's disinterest in Marguerite. "It is the only thing I find that consumes him."

"Perhaps he'll follow in your footsteps," Marie said. "Seeking beaver huts to look at and study."

"As a trapper? Maybe," Louis answered.

But she could tell by his response that he was wary of making any predictions about Paul. "Maybe the water Paul knew first back on the Missouri will lend him work that molds him. His mother certainly hasn't been able to shape him well," she said.

She remembered that conversation as she dug potatoes with Kilakotah. Louis Two rocked forward, squealing for his mother's attention. She picked him up.

"Pierre said I spoiled my sons when I picked them up," Marie said. "That I teach them to be soft when I listen to them quickly. Life is hard, he always said, and they must learn it."

"That's not my people's way, not while a child is yet in its board, Kilakotah said. "We want a baby to know they are as precious as blue beads. How would you treat your most prized possession if it called your name? No. Love is what we teach in the board," she said. "That everyone is loved. Even when some are not with us."

Marie glanced at her, but Kilakotah dropped her eyes.

Marie had lifted her sons up, carried them well past the board time. And Paul was now as distant from her as if she'd let him wail. Both of her sons. She had not done well with those children. Still, Marie's time with Marguerite gathered her to a place of comfort even while her heart expanded, like dress threads being let out to make a better fit. She had friends to share small news with about her daughter's progress and a husband who adored them both. This was new, a joy.

"I shouldn't name it," she whispered to Marguerite later that morning when she placed the board at Janey's wither, grabbed at the mane and swung herself up onto the horse's back, her buckskin dress creeping up over her brown thighs.

The hills stood sharp against the clear sky, as though cut with the marriage scissors Louis had given her. She loved crisp mornings that invited riding. But if she named that joy too loudly, she was sure it would disappear too. The horse would stumble. A snake would coil across their path. The ties that kept Marguerite safe would loosen and release the child before Marie could save her.

Her only hope was to imagine the worst nightmare, believing then it would not happen. They'd ride to find Paul now. She imagined her son with his foot caught in a trap or lying in a daze from a fall from his horse. If she imagined the worst…

Paul sat beside the river, his leggings rolled up beside him, his bowlegs still wet with leaves stuck to the calves. His breech cloth was stained dark from water. *A beaver dam.* She might have known he'd be there, swimming around as though he were a beaver himself. "At least he's safe," she told Marguerite asleep in her basket at the horse's flank. See. She'd imagined the worst and it hadn't happened.

❖

Sally often reported on the evening tea routine of her and Mr. Ross, a ritual that followed the factor's meal.

"I am a fine listener," Sally told Marie. "And Mr. Ross does love to talk."

Several of the women worked on beadwork or wove flat wallets out of willow root bark. Marie and Louis and the families of the French-Canadians and their Indian wives lived away from the fort, but in the late afternoons, the women would gather. Sometimes, Sally read while they worked, her words taking on a teaching tone. "This is the year eighteen hundred and twenty. The Americans and British have agreed to joint occupation. Both nations will live side by side inside the Columbia country."

"Louis says the Brits discourage American trappers and any settlers who might want to farm south of the Columbia," Marie said.

"The land is good north of the river," Sally said. "Anyone with any sense will settle there anyway. Now let's do our English lessons. The word for *willow* in the local language is spoken as 'sally,'" she said. "We make sally bags. In Chinookan, they're *aqw'alt.*"

"The Clatsop call them *wapaas*," Kilakotah said.

"We should write them down," Sally said. She laid her needlework aside and bustled to a small desk where she took parchment from a little box. She tapped a quill pen, reached for ink and powder. "You try writing?" She pushed the quill toward Marie.

Marie shook her head. She repeated the words in her head, to make the sounds stay with her even if she couldn't picture how they appeared on a paper.

"We'll find out what the Nez Perce call the bags. Or the Cayuse. We'll be going south to Mackenzie's Fort Nez Perce soon," Sally said then. She'd set the writing utensils down, and Marie wondered if her love of language might be more for show than anything. "More words to sift and sort." Sally smiled at Jemima, who was deep in concentration, the child's tongue poked out between her lips.

Marie's beadwork formed a floral pattern she sewed onto soft hide.

"The Company pushes to finish that fort," Sally said. "Mackenzie has trouble with the Indian workers. They want payment for the timber the men have cut. They've even refused to sell the men food until it's settled. Mackenzie needs more hunters, Mr. Ross tells me." Sally clucked appreciatively over her Jemima's pen scratchings. "Your Louis might be asked to go," Sally said.

Marguerite fussed in her baby board, and Marie laid her beadwork down and picked up her child. She held Marguerite at her breast. The infant suckled well and, since her birth the previous summer, already weighed as much as a wild turkey stuffed with corn.

"You'd come too," Sally said. "We'll all go. It will be a bigger place, that fort."

"This Okanogan is large enough for me," Marie said. She patted her daughter's back, heard her burp. "Who stays here to run this fort? Maybe my sons will be better able to find a place here if so many others go south."

"It's always a worry, isn't it?" Sally said, suddenly serious. "If they go with the Company, our sons will not rise well, what without schooling back East. And if they don't join the Company, what's their future? Mr.

Ross says all the Iroquois and free trappers are as useless as perfume at a skunk hole."

Marie put her finger into Marguerite's mouth and the infant sucked. Tiny eyes the color of acorns gazed back at her. Marie blinked. She'd known someone else in her life with acorn eyes. Ah, the camp boy Jean Toupin, the giver of earrings. His eyes were the color of acorns.

"More choices live in a larger fort," Sally said. "Even for your sons, Marie. Marie?"

"I'm listening," Marie said. She continued to gaze at her daughter.

"The Indians at the Nez Perce fort will not be allowed inside the palisades to trade, as they are here. They'll have to leave their made beaver pelts at an opening in the wall, Mr. Ross says. The blankets and cloth and kettles will be kept behind an iron door. Mr. Ross says we'll claim that land one day, for the British, and the fort's successful operation will make that happen. You come, Marie," Sally insisted. "It would not be the same without you there with us."

"I once left when I should have stayed," Marie said. She thought of Sarah's offer, much like Sally's, and wondered if she should have gone with them. How did one know the right choice to make?

"You could sell your beadwork more easily there," Sally told her. "More customers. Walla Walla, Umatilla, and Nez Perce, Shoshone, Cayuse, Snake, all kinds of bands. Here, there are only us few Okanogan and sometimes the Spokane who come down." Sally paused. "You can earn more to put against the debt, Marie."

Marie hesitated. Did Sally think she was driven only by her debt?

"I think we stay here. Not go to Fort Nez Perce," Marie told Louis later as she stirred the stew. He'd been out late, bringing in a lean deer and two plump grouse, well past the time when the men gathered to eat together. He hung his powder horn on a nail in the wall, leaned his rifle near the center post.

"Mackenzie will lead a brigade out, and Ross is to be the chief factor at that fort. A man named Cox comes here to run this one. Your friend Toupin has experience with Cox. I think we go south. I'd rather hunt for Ross, as a free man, than work with Cox."

"But they won't let us inside the fort," Marie told him. "At Astoria we couldn't sleep inside the palisades, but we could be cooled under the roofs during the day and see the men putting up the flag. Mackenzie—"

"I've heard this, eh? Indians kept out and our men kept in. Hard to know who is more contained."

"Where will we live, if you go there for the Company?" she said. "Me and my sons? Inside or out of this new fort? Sally will be inside and—"

"You're my wife. Your sons are my sons; Marguerite mine as well. Ross will treat you right as the wife of a French-Canadian."

"This Okanogan is what Marguerite knew first," Marie said. She stirred the stew too hard. It spilled, and she jumped to avoid the stain. "She needs more time here to belong," Marie said, wiping at the spill.

"Winters are milder on that Columbia," Louis said. Marie still rubbed at her dress. Into the silence, he plucked at the feathers of the grouse, the tiny rip as the skin resisted making a sound like a baby popping her lips. "And the Nez Perce have good stallions. The best. Your herd would grow there, Marie. They plan which stallion to match with which mare. The animals don't run together without a plan. Marguerite can come back here when she's older. To make her place of belonging known." Louis put his hand over hers, halted her scrubbing.

Marie didn't look at him. She wondered whether going or staying was the best to do. The smell of cooked venison filled the hut now.

"Getting a cow from Fort George will take less time…when that time comes," Louis said then. "They speak of a disease, anthrax, that breaks out in the East. Cows die back there. Getting more cattle out here will take longer. Maybe they'll have to bring stock from Mexico or the Sandwich Islands."

"But they'll be even more valuable," Marie said. She looked at him now.

"Even more valuable."

Marie served up the stew in a wooden bowl, then stood in the doorway of the hut, the leather flap loose in the late evening heat. Everyone seemed to think she made her choices based on trade. Would her beadwork get more in the Walla Walla country? Would she be able to find a cow so she could sell milk and butter? Were these the choices that now guided whether she moved or stayed? Was that all she'd become? A woman who traded just to get some possession, just to get out of debt?

No, she made her choices to advance her family, that was why she did what she did. It was what a mother was expected to do.

Sarah had said all women made such choices, men too. "All who are made up of more than just skin have an empty place inside them that only God can fill up," Sarah'd said. Her friend told her to listen to that inner voice. It was why Sarah had moved on to be with the Flathead and Spokane. Where had she gone since then, Marie still wondered. Perhaps that voice had talked Sarah away. Marie tried to imagine how she'd recognize such a voice or if she'd have the courage to follow it.

"We can always come back here if the fort life is not what you want for your children," Louis said. He stood behind her now, arms around her.

"Change our minds?"

"Sometimes we're allowed," Louis said. He moved beside her. He ran his finger down the center part of her hair.

Marguerite fussed, and Marie bent to lift her from the mat she lay on. Marguerite grasped Marie's fingers, the child's hands so long and delicate. They'd milk a cow with ease someday. They'd carry a bucket and bring prosperity to her husband's family someday. Marie kissed the child's fingertips, the nails as small as fish scales.

Marie turned to Louis. She kissed him. "Who's to say what new voices we might hear in a new place?" she told him. "Besides, every daughter's fingers should know the feel of a churn, and her tongue, the sweet taste of butter."

Louis grinned. "You'll go to stay with me, then."

"We go," she said, "to move closer to the cows."

✛

Everything changed with the move.

Marie felt consumed, taken in by something larger and uncertain. When she gathered roots, when her sons had their lessons in English, when her daughter took her steps, all changed. She'd always noticed new things, made them her own, but here, the shift in routines unsettled. She

felt a kind of watching, as though she were a cougar following the movement of others. She hadn't known that the familiar gave such safety.

Paul's ways changed too. He was gone even longer now, rarely said
where he'd been when he joined the evening meal. With twelve summers, he strutted almost, an awkward gait that brought snickers from
others when Paul wasn't looking. He would strike out quickly if he
heard their giggles. They acted cautious, those children. Marie sometimes heard them call him "Rooster" and imitate his strutting walk,
chest out, legs bowed. She'd frown at them and they'd scatter, but they
left behind the pain held in a mother's heart.

Even Baptiste spent more time in the lodge of the Cayuse camped
outside the fort. Marie had met few of them as yet, spending most of
her time with Sally and Kilakotah. Louis had secured a place for them
inside the palisades. Another change.

Baptiste's work took him farther too, with more horses for him to
tend. Once she'd heard the music of a jaw harp, twanging the little wire
while someone breathed some dancing tunes. She'd squinted, scanned,
and when Baptiste walked by, she asked, "Was that you playing, Baptiste?" Her son had merely grunted, moved farther away.

Marie watched as Mackenzie led out brigades of Hudson's Bay
employees and free trappers into the Snake River country. "I hear some
Huron and more Iroquois go north, too," Louis told her. "The Company became their common enemy, so now they make their way there
with the Spokane. Some say they bring more Sunday songs, ones they
sang when they poled the big canoes out."

"Where do they learn them?" Marie wondered. She gave a chunk of
tallow to Marguerite to gnaw against, hoping it would help her back
teeth come through.

Louis shrugged his shoulders. Maybe Sarah's inner voice left behind
the songs, calling the boatmen to sing.

Sometimes, when Marie rose beneath early morning skies brushed
white by pale moonlight, she thought of all those men back East who
touched lives even in this western place.

"The Indians, those Huron, deserted Mackenzie. They're not reliable," Sally said once. Marie suspected that she repeated the words of

her husband while the women scrubbed carrots from the new kitchen garden. "Company men and free men can take three hundred beaver traps with them and set them into streams. They could drain the timbered mountains. But only with reliable men. Those Huron aren't."

"But their women handle the hides," Marie noted. "The free men don't bale them. Neither do the Company men. It's their women who make them rich, and those women are like us, Sally."

Sally dropped her eyes, her fingers fluttered at the handkerchief she lifted from the lace at her wrist. She directed Jemima to the outdoors to bring in more carrots.

"That Simpson, your Ross's boss, he doesn't notice that," Marie said. "Maybe the Huron and Iroquois chose to leave the Company because they're wiser. They can see what the Company's policy will do to our people. All people."

"We're…different, Marie. We've joined with husbands who will take care of us. Besides, my husband says it's best to use only Company men," Sally told her in a voice that reminded Marie of the day she'd been asked to leave while Sally lost her baby. A judging voice, not to be questioned. "He'll want to hire now, only Company men."

At this new fort, Louis hunted, bringing home deer, *yaamash,* in the local language; and in the evenings, he helped Marie weave mats and baskets, sew leather clothes he carried later for trade at the fort.

"Women's work," Paul said, watching Louis tie the sinew that bound the leather seams.

"Louis has a gift for needle and thread," Marie defended. She smiled at Marguerite, who waddled after a leather ball just outside the door, squealing as she reached it. The dogs yipped and chased.

Louis cut the sinew with his knife, split it down the middle to form a slender thread. Marguerite squealed again, and Marie stood to see if she was troubled. She wasn't, just rolling with the dogs.

Paul pulled a knife from a sheath at his waist, ran his finger as though to check the sharpness of the blade. He scoffed as Louis used his knife to cut sewing sinew.

"And my husband finds good willow root, and looks for the right kind of grass when he's out hunting. It's a gift to make baskets both beautiful and useful, *n'est-ce pas,* Louis? Louis doesn't ride blind like some, only looking for what interests him. He keeps his eyes open so he can—"

Louis patted Marie's hand, shook his head at her.

She dropped her eyes. She must remember: Louis was a strong man without need of a woman's defense against either the Company or her son. He wasn't challenged by change.

At least the delight with her daughter hadn't changed. And slowly the routines of this new place would comfort.

❖

The seasons, though distinct, melted into one another at this Walla Walla River. A wide eddy of water, wide as a lake, marked the changes. Skiffs of snow sometimes accumulated beside the willow-lined stream, but few heavy drifts clustered as there'd been beside the Okanogan. In the spring, roots were easily dug from the banks. In months when the Okanogan country would be still buried in snow, this land had new blue blooms in the shadowed folds of the hills, only weeks after Ross served the New Year's rum.

Marie learned the new names for the roots she dug. *Pyaxi* was the narrow root the color of pale sun that she piled into her round basket hung from her neck as she bent. A Umatilla woman said the word meant "lives forever," because the roots stored so long and so well. One handful in the winter, when mixed with dried salmon, would fill a family's stomachs for the day. Marie gathered large bags of them through the spring and dried them for the winter. Little Marguerite joined her, waddling here and there but always staying within the sound of Marie's voice. A daughter never strayed as far as a son.

A leafy green plant pushed out of the ground, one Louis said tasted like celery. *Latit-latit* named that plant Marguerite ate fresh in the field. By evening, it rushed through her stomach like a spring flood.

One of Marguerite's first words was the word for water, fresh, life-giving water that brought the salmon in the spring. *"Chuush,"* Marguerite said. She sipped from a buffalo horn spoon of water Marie held to her lips.

They'd been at the spring gathering when her daughter spoke the word, and Marie felt warmed that the landscape taught such words, signs of her daughter's good thinking in the season of new beginnings. Marie nearly forgot they were at a place where she'd once grieved the death of her first daughter. Now Marguerite's learning made her name this a good and happy place, not one of mere grieving.

For several weeks each spring, not far from the fort, the region's tribes gathered to dig roots, to pay homage to all that had been provided them as they survived the winter. They said thanksgivings, celebrated, and traded. The air stayed balmy, wind rising only in the late afternoon and usually settling in time for the dancing that went on far into the night.

There, Marie found her Umatilla friend, Calming Water, who had opened death's palm and helped teach Marie how to fill it with gifts after Vivacité's death.

"A new child," Calming Water said with a mix of Chinook jargon and signs after the two women recognized each other across the moccasin-flattened grass. Marie pressed her hands to Calming Water's face. Tears formed in the woman's eyes. "Your girl," Calming Water told her later. "She'll make a good berry picker with those long little fingers."

Marie nodded, pleased she could understand so much of the other's words. "And good for milking cows." She made the motion with her own hands. Calming Water frowned, and Marie wondered if she'd ever seen a cow milked.

Throughout the gatherings, Marie watched carefully each knife worn at the waist of a Yakima man, any man, to see if Sacagawea's gift might reappear and perhaps she could earn it back in trade. In the two years of gatherings she'd attended, she'd seen no sign of the blade. It was an emptiness she expected would never be filled, and she chastised herself not for the giving of it to Louis but for hanging on to the wish that she might still have the use of it, might still be reminded of the woman who gave it whenever she watched Louis pull it from its sheath. Perhaps she hadn't truly given it as a gift but had only meant to loan it.

The gatherings were welcomed interruptions from the days at the fort, filled with tending children, making clothes and food, doing women's work.

Marie sometimes took small pleasure in the seasonal work, let the rituals of gatherings and family fill her up. She even listened with new ears at the stories read by Ross on Sundays. Ross called it "reading day." They all sat and listened, a French-Canadian named Narcisse Raymond offering interpretations in Cayuse and Walla Walla words while Ross spoke. Indians were allowed inside the fort for services but not to trade. Even her sons sat cross-legged and appeared to listen. Did they understand Ross's words, some of the signs? Both boys used more English than she did. Or did the meanings of the words float above them as they did her, precious sounding but distant as stars?

Sometimes at night, she'd listen as Louis held Marguerite in his arms and told her the English names for those stars. He spoke of mirrors used to help sailors find their way by recognizing their flickering lights.

"Do the sailors know the stars' names?" Marie'd asked Louis once.

"Not all of them," he'd told her. "Just the ones they learned to love. The ones that help them find their way."

❖

Baptiste stood with his hands on his hips, elbows out as he watched her make her way to the river, a basket of washing on her hip. She swayed when she moved, almost a whisper of a walk, and the fringe of her dress brushed her calves just as his mother's did. When she was out of sight, he took the jaw harp from his pouch and moved closer. The metal instrument felt wet with perspiration.

He knelt, peered between the willow leaves. He could see the sunlight shining against her greased hair. Tight braids she wore. The center part looked chalked, it was so white. She took pride in her person, walked proud as a Cayuse girl. This was good. Maybe too good. She might have no interest in a *métis*. Maybe she'd resent his living inside the fort as though he were a white man like Louis instead of one with mixed blood.

She set the willow basket down, crossed her arms as though to pull off her skin dress before she scrubbed the garments. Women did that, to save their clothes from getting wet. He hadn't thought of that. He'd only wanted to give her a gift of music then disappear. His heart pounded.

She lowered her arms, kept her dress on, then leaned over and knelt. She began scrubbing against a rock, humming while she worked.

Older Sister they called her. Firstborn. Like him. A fleeting thought raced through his head—had there been another son, older than he was? No. It was only a dream, looping around itself, perhaps to fill the void of his missing father.

He swallowed. Even as Older Sister worked she had a rhythm, as swaying as spring grasses. *How old is she? As old as Paul? Older? Surely.* He'd play a song for her. He put the jaw harp to his lips, suddenly embarrassed by the twanging sound, the less than lofty heights he'd aspired to yet couldn't produce. A mournful fiddle would express his heart; a wooden flute, but not this vibrating wire. What had he been thinking of?

Older Sister turned toward the willows. He felt blood throb at his neck, but he kept playing. Would she laugh at him? Would she leave? Would she be angry that he watched her at work? He'd never seen eyes as dark as sable look so bright, so clear, so young. He let the jaw harp fade from his mouth. Could she tell he imagined her kneeling beside him, his arm around her waist, holding her close, the sweet smell of her breath mingled with his?

"Why do you scowl so?" she said when he stopped.

He sucked in between his wide front teeth, swallowed, forced himself to open his face, smooth his brows and smile.

"That's better," she said. "Now come make music beside me while I work. It will make the day go faster."

❖

Louis was still assisting in the transport of horses between the Flathead area, Okanogan, Spokane House, and this largest fort in the Columbia country now, this Walla Walla. The North West Company had merged itself with its rival Hudson Bay, and taken on its name. Louis worked by contract, not as an employee of the Company. Ross needed as many horses as they could handle to give in trade for what beaver pelts the Indians brought in. And the horses provided consistent meat for the fort, a practice that served up a constant irritation to the tribes.

"We were raided," Louis told Marie when he'd returned from one such trip. He cooled his horse with short, intense strokes of the brush. "Two men killed. They're angered by Mackenzie's stripping of the rivers, and they'll do whatever they can to disrupt the trade. Ross thinks the Americans put them up to it, to discourage the Company."

"Were they men we knew?"

Louis shook his head, no. Marie was relieved. Deaths cut deeper with a known name attached. "There isn't enough game for everyone to provide for their families," Marie said. "That's why the tribes attack."

"The Company isn't just trapping for food, Marie. They want to make the sector a fur desert," Louis said. "A desert means nothing left, eh? So the death of a few French-Canadians or Scots, whether free man or working for the Hudson's Bay, is of little consequence to the Company. Stir things up, that's the name of this game these Americans play."

"A fur desert?"

"Only in the American sector. What Hudson Bay thinks will be given to the Americans." Louis had cooled the animal as he worked, the horse no longer wearing the white line of lather across its chest. He'd calmed himself, too. "Maybe these decisions are beyond men like me, eh? I just do what I can, day to day. Get back to you safe. That's my job."

Marie nodded, but this second raid bringing horses south concerned her. She didn't want to lose another husband. She didn't want to lose another child. Perhaps they should move back to the British sector, north and west of the Columbia River, move to safety on the Okanogan. If any place on earth was truly safe.

"He was a good man, that John Day," Marie told her family as they ate their evening meal. She remembered the Virginian with fondness, a man who'd been helpful to Hunt on the journey west. "Tom McKay says he lost his mind somewhere near a river about halfway between Fort George and this one."

"Must have been weak to die of being crazy," Baptiste told her. His voice broke at the end of his sentence. A high-pitched crack sometimes brought redness to his neck when he talked. He cleared his throat. "The bad thing was over with, but he still carried it in his head. *Stupide.*"

"We never know how we'll react until we face great challenges. John Day faced them," Marie said. "You don't know of that time before. The Indians tortured him. You were little then."

"Baptiste thinks like a girl," Paul said. He tore at a piece of horse meat, a stringy strand hanging loose and unnoticed over his lower lip.

"Tom brought other news, too. His stepfather, John McLoughlin, has been ordered to come to old Astoria, Fort George, to clean it up and make more profit from that site."

"A good man, is he?" Louis asked.

"Tom's never met him. Nor his younger sisters. They'll all come from back East. And Fort George will be as it once was, an important fort."

"They'll keep men at that fort, boatmen, mostly. But before long, they'll see the value in moving the fort across the river into what will be Brit land," Louis said. "Anything south of the Columbia River will be argued over. Besides, since the sickness and deaths of the river tribes, there are more people closer to this Fort Walla Walla than the ocean. Getting furs to an inland site would be easier and make getting goods from the north there easier, too."

Marie handed Marguerite meat she'd cut into little pieces. Some of the women chewed the meat first, before giving it to their children. Sally said it was because so much fish softened the children's teeth. Marie's children had tough teeth, so it was a practice Marie resisted. "I wonder what they'll do with the cows at Fort George?" Marie said. She watched Marguerite grind her meat.

"Milk them, I suppose," Louis said. "I don't think they'll sell any or trade any away." With his fingernail, Louis flicked at dirt caught in the carving of his powder horn. He'd finished eating and now polished the horn with a piece of soft calf hide. He called it "vellum," and it was as thin as parchment. "You know the policy about that."

Marie nodded.

"But cows get loose," Marie said. "And maybe people who live outside the palisades find them."

Louis grinned. "You think you can get your boys to milk cows?"

Baptiste shook his head no. "Too much shade under the belly of a cow," he said. "I like sunshine on my work."

He smiled, and Marie thought he might someday be enticed to milk.

Paul uncrossed his legs and scowled at Louis. He motioned with his hand to his brother and moved outside. Baptiste followed.

"I'll milk them myself," Marie said. "And keep the butter, too." She handed Marguerite another piece of meat. "They'll need hunters," Marie said then. "If they move old Astoria inland. They'll need men to move more horses. John Day no longer hunts for them."

"You'd go back to Astoria, after…"

"My bad memories don't live there," she said. "Not many. Mine live at the *boise* place, that's where I'll stay away from. Tom says they could use people to tend the horse herds, the pigs and goats. And Kilakotah comes from that place. Her father is a Clatsop chief and—"

"You resist for weeks this move from Okanogan to Walla Walla. Now we make a good way for our daughter, your sons behave better than before, and you want to move again?"

"For a good reason," Marie said. "I go when the reason is good. And besides, I am beginning to grow too easy here. I notice only the good things, the roots and the gatherings, the fine growth of my daughter and sons. I stop looking sideways, left and right, to make sure I'm not struck unexpected by a rattlesnake asleep in the grass."

"You don't trust the good things that happen to you, eh? A daughter. A husband who does women's work without complaint." Louis smiled at her. "Sons who are sour but who are learning new things."

"When good things outweigh the bad, it's a sign of future trouble. I'll trick trouble by making a change now. You nearly died, husband, with this last raid. Two men did," she said. "We go to Fort George with McKay's stepfather and make it a good place. It will be like going home."

10

Stones

"I'm staying here," Baptiste said.

Marie sat with her family in the hut after they finished their meal in the main dining room. Marie and the women had eaten, then cleaned and readied the table for the following day. Marguerite pulled at Its-owl-eigh's ears, and Marie shushed them with her finger to her mouth.

"I left nothing at Fort George I need to go back for," Baptiste said with a smile.

"He has a woman he visits," Paul said. "They make babies."

Baptiste frowned at his brother.

"Paul," Marie said. "Treat your brother with respect."

"He plays with girls," Paul said.

Baptiste shook his head, looked away.

Marie stared at Paul, turned to Baptiste. Why wasn't the boy defending himself as he usually did? She'd never imagined Baptiste as a man or that his constant absences from her table meant he was eating at another's. Marguerite was just a toddler. She couldn't think of herself as a grandmother. No. Surely Paul taunted.

"Is this true?" Marie asked.

Baptiste shrugged. "The girl is true."

"Who are her people?"

"Her uncle's Narcisse Raymond. She's Cayuse."

"A good horseman," Louis said. "Narcisse is." He lowered his eyes, and Marie knew her hot face must betray her dismay.

Baptiste sucked spittle through an opening between his front teeth. It was a habit, Marie noticed of late, that made a sound like the squeezing of water from soaked hides. He did it while he gained time to speak.

"You wait until you are able to care for her and her family. You wait until you do the proper things," Marie scolded.

"I don't have enough to trade for a bride's price. All I earn goes to pay off a debt, remember, Mother."

Baptiste was fifteen. He was strong and had learned at Louis's side, but he couldn't live on his own. Not with a wife. He was too young. He needed watching… No matter that should he take a wife, live with her people, he would learn of her ways, be tended by that girl and her family. A good husband planned ahead, provided.

Once he moved to another's hut, he'd be gone from a mother's life, her influence. Although right now it seemed she'd had little influence for good.

"She shows a baby," Paul said then. "Baptiste makes a baby."

Baptiste slugged his brother in the shoulder then, a sound that stung and caused even Marguerite to lift her eyes and form her mouth into an O. Her lower lip pushed out. Paul howled, holding his arm. Marguerite began to wail.

"It's true," Paul whined.

Marie raised her eyebrows at Baptiste while she lifted her daughter. "Oh, shhh, now. It's all right. Baptiste?" He looked down.

She'd have to find out if this was so. Kilakotah or Sally told her things, or a dozen other women who mixed their French and English with a language the river people called Chinook. But this, a child coming into the world, one fathered by her own son, this news had not reached her ears in any tongue.

Perhaps the other women protected her from it, didn't want her to feel badly about her son's poor choices.

Had Baptiste so little regard for his own child or the mother of that child that he would act without regard for how to protect them, be responsible to them? She looked at his lean body, his wrists outgrowing the length of his sleeves. His face had the first brush of a beard; his hair held a wavy shine that reminded her of Pierre's. The small bone in his throat stuck out like a sharp stone in a dry riverbed. He was still too young to be a father.

She would find out about this girl, but she would also make plans to take him away for a time, until he grew older and could live for more than comfort. Yes, it was time they moved from the shadow of this Walla Walla fort. She should have pushed for it sooner.

"We'll talk later of this, Baptiste." She kept her voice light, enthusiastic. "For now, we make plans to go to old Astoria, Fort George. Louis will take us there, yes, husband? It will be a good change. We can work in the cow barns."

"Not me," Paul said. "I know these rivers here, the Cayuse and Umatilla. If Baptiste can live away from here without being noticed by his mother, then so can I."

Did Paul think she didn't notice him?

Baptiste twanged the single wire on his jaw harp. *So he does play it, probably for the girl.* Paul lounged on the woven willow mats, rubbing his arm, a half-smile sent to his brother. "You will go," Marie said. She set her jaw, glared at both sons. "My sons will go where I say. Do as they're told. I have need of you there."

"No, woman, you listen." Paul unfolded his legs so quickly Marie blinked. He stood, leaned toward her, his narrow face close, his eyes angry slits. He breathed as hard as a spent deer. Marie felt her heart pound. *Am I afraid of my own son? Are both my sons so foreign to me? What have I raised?*

Marguerite cried harder, and Marie's hand shook as she stroked her daughter's hair at the back of her neck. She didn't break her son's stare, didn't back down.

"Paul," Louis said. He touched the boy's arm.

Paul swirled, a cornered animal, lunging. He swung his palm back. Louis jerked away to avoid the blow that just missed the side of his face. "I don't go, woman," Paul said, "I don't do what a *woman* tells me to do. I have no need of you."

❖

"Make the red ties, for the manes," Paul said. "The way you did before."

Paul and Louis would make a trip again to Fort Okanogan, taking horses from Fort Walla Walla to that farther post.

"As I did before," Marie said, feeling encouraged that Paul wanted a past pleasure.

Paul nodded. He'd been...*charming,* that was the word for it, since his outburst of a few days before. He'd stormed out of the hut that night and not come back until morning. Marie had gotten up often to peer out into the blackness, hoping to hear the sound of his horse. When he returned, he smelled of the river, and she knew he must have slept beside it. He gave no explanation, but brought her willows of the kind she liked and wove into baskets. "For you, *Mère,*" he said and smiled his lopsided smile.

She didn't bring up the move to Fort George again, though she and Louis talked of it when the boys were not around. "We need to go soon," she said. "To take Baptiste from foolish mistakes and give Paul new people who might take to him. Besides, it is a good place. There are plants that heal the stomach there. The rain makes the land green and lush. It reminds me more of my Des Moines than this place."

"Montreal is green."

She nodded agreement though she'd never been to his country, had seen only paintings in some of Louis's books. "There are huge fish there," Marie continued and remembered Sacagawea's story of the giant one that washed up onto shore. "And there are grasses deep enough for herds of cows to get lost in...and I could help find them. We all could help find them. The hut at Young's Bay might still be there."

"It's been what, nine years since your husband built it?"

"We can build another, if need be. You, me, Paul, Baptiste."

"Marie..."

"Paul will be better when he is in a familiar place," she said. "And Baptiste, too. Maybe with the new factor coming, McKay's stepfather, Baptiste will find a way to work with more respect given him for his efforts than he gets here. McKay was once young there at Fort George. He's risen within the Company. Baptiste can too."

"You dream too—"

"You take care of this duty for Ross with the horses. You and Paul. Baptiste works to fill the water tanks for the fort this week. I'll find out about this girl. If Paul has made a story and there is no child coming, when you come back, we all go."

Marguerite raised her hands, and her father lifted her onto his thighs as he sat atop his horse. Marguerite had long dark hair that the wind played with. She had some of Louis's curls, though they were looser, spent. Marguerite ran her finger down the scar on his pointing finger, all the others, too.

"Parle," the girl said.

"Talk," Marie corrected. "Tell him you want to know how his fingers got hurt."

"Um." Marguerite hesitated. "Papa?"

"A long time ago," he said. "When my hands were wet in cold streams in the winter, my hands cracked. Wide open, like a big mouth, eh?" Louis opened his mouth wide to show her. She stuck her fingers into his mouth, pulled on his lower jaw. He laughed, took her palm and blew in it. She giggled. "I come in, build a fire, and then I sew them up. Sometimes the thread holds long time, eh? Other times, only a day. The cracks get wider and then infect, get gooey as tree gum." She wrinkled her nose. "Then I decide to sew one last time. No more, I say. No more trapping. I come to this place west and meet your mother, *n'est-ce pas?*" Louis looked up at Marie. "She sews them just once but it is a good stitch. The knot stays tight. Nothing can break it. Only a scar remains to remind us of what was once, eh?"

"I scar?" Marguerite asked. She rocked back and forth.

Louis laughed. *"Non, non.* A scar marks pain," he said.

"Maybe her birth," Marie said. "There was a little pain at her birthing." She smiled.

"You are remembered in here," Louis said and he touched his heart. "You live there so while I'm gone, I can feel your heart pounding as though one with mine. When you hear your mother's heart and your own, Marguerite, you think of mine beating somewhere, thinking of you, eh? That way we keep stitched together."

"I'll remember that, too," Marie said. "When I hear my heart beat, I'll think of you."

"Let's go," Paul said. He twirled the reins on his big gelding, a horse Marie had worked with, not traded away, so Paul could have him as his own. The animal stomped, the red ribbons flashing in its mane. Paul's wrists and Louis's both wore the red strips of ceremony Paul had started those years before.

"Paul and I'll be back soon as we're able." Louis kissed her. Paul kicked his mount, left Louis behind. "I'll talk with him about our going to Fort George, but maybe he is ready to stay behind here. Maybe your sons are ready to be separated—"

"*Non,*" she said. "All three will be with us. It's the right way. They don't know it yet, but I do."

Louis gently squeezed the point of her chin. "A mother knows, eh?"

"Everything," Marie said.

And for that moment in her life, she believed it.

❖

Marie located the girl, rode to the scattered camps around the outside of the fort while Baptiste worked the water brigade. Louis and Paul had been gone three days. She didn't expect them back for another week, so it was a good time to explore the Cayuse camps.

Many of these families that lived in the circle of dust beside the fort were not the wealthy horse owners who bargained well with Ross and the other traders but rather were people who might have been their slaves. The men ran errands for the traders, sometimes carrying dispatches of mail packets. Mackenzie had instituted the practice, knowing native runners could get letters and such through country that the Company riders and brigades couldn't. The women often washed the corduroy of *engagés* and used the meager wages to trade for items to supplement the staples of roots and fish. They usually owned no horses, had lots of dogs and children, too. Those who had the fewest resources often had the most children, Marie noticed.

As she rode out, stopping at each of these small camps, Marie would say the girl's name. Older Sister. People would shake their heads and sometimes point in the direction of another village. At one camp, she came upon a dark-faced Cayuse woman with black eyes.

She was about ten to fifteen miles east of Fort Walla Walla, a lovely place of lush green that others called Waiilatpu, when they pointed her in the direction of a tipi with poles poking the air. It surprised her that Baptiste could have made his way there. When could he have? How could she not have known?

Perhaps Older Sister's family had camped near the fort and had just recently made its way to this green place. She wondered what Baptiste found inside this family that had made him follow.

Marie watched as a slender girl brought willow roots to her mother for weaving. She appeared to be the eldest of six or seven children who scampered about. Dogs sniffed at Marie's horse as she rode up. "Older Sister?"

The girl looked up and smiled without the usual caution one might show to a stranger. "Mother," she said.

The word startled. Had Baptiste told her she'd be coming? None of the other families she'd visited had implied they knew who she was.

Marie could see what her son found attractive in the girl. She stood tall, her shoulder-length hair loose and draping down from a center part. Her upper lip lifted, two tiny mountain peaks divided by a deep impression as perfect as a raindrop hovering on a leaf. And she had a confidence about her for someone so young...and she did look young.

Older Sister reached up as though to take Marguerite from her basket hanging on the side of Marie's horse. Marie allowed it, pleased that the girl noticed the child and wanted to help the toddler down. Older Sister had compassionate eyes that met Marie's gaze, but they lacked sparkle. *Was the girl tired?* she wondered.

Two children hung on to Older Sister's skirts, and they looked so much alike Marie wondered if they might not be her own children. Could the girl be already married? Did Baptiste know? No, they must be younger brothers and sisters. Perhaps Older Sister took interest in Baptiste for the help she thought he'd be in this lodge of women and children. Marie knew people talked of Louis's skill at women's work. Maybe this girl thought Baptiste would do as much. She didn't know her son well if that was what she hoped for. When Older Sister bent, Marie watched her waistline. She showed no evidence that she carried a child. Marie sighed with relief.

There'd be time for grandchildren, time when her sons were mature men, ready to commit to a family and their wife's people. Time when her sons would be ready to fish and hunt and even sew leather if that was what it took to be grown men rather than lounging near the stick games, hoping to win trinkets they could take in trade.

This was good. No baby. Baptiste had made a good beginning though he was young. She had time, to talk with the mother to be sure the girl was chaperoned. She had time to advise Baptiste about the ways of men and women and the mutual respect each deserved. Maybe he had learned some things by the way Louis treated her. Maybe she could take a deep breath and trust that she had done some things right by her sons, that she was raising up a good daughter.

Paul's face came to her mind, the slyness in his eyes… No. He, too, was doing better. As long as he was unprovoked, he could handle himself well.

She'd tell the mother of her worries and that Baptiste was going away with them to Fort George. She'd tell the mother that in time, when Baptiste was older, their families might weave together, make a good mat. In time.

The mother said something to Older Sister then, and the girl sighed, set Marguerite down, and turned to take two smaller children with her along a well-worn path Marie guessed led to a nearby stream. Her mother was a washerwoman. Marie saw poles now, with lines that clothes lay across catching the afternoon breeze.

Older Sister turned back, motioned Marguerite along. Marie nodded agreement when her child sought permission with her eyes. She was a thoughtful child, this Older Sister. She might well be a good fit for Baptiste.

"They call me Marie," Marie said and signed. "Question, your name?"

The women talked, two mothers sharing time. She found Older Sister, when the girl rejoined them, both shy and loving to Marguerite. She decided not to tell her of the move. Let Baptiste. Instead she offered a gift; invited them to come to her and Louis's hut to share a meal.

Marie and Marguerite started back, warmed by the visit.

A horse ridden hard headed toward them.

"Madame Dorion! Madame Dorion! Come quickly. There is trouble," Ross said. "So much trouble."

Marie felt alarm. She'd taken in joy with the company of Older Sister and her mother. Now, she'd pay the price.

❖

Marie tried to make sense of what Ross told her, and his coming himself rather than sending LaBonte or even Baptiste to bring her the news. "A mistake," she said. "Louis is dead? How?" *Where's Baptiste? How can this be?*

The words roared in her head while the river flowed beside her without sound. Canada geese that had spent the winter broke the glassy water, fluttered then slowed, followed by their quiet V. Their necks arched, and they clustered their goslings together as the horses splashed through the ford toward the fort.

The gates were opened wide by the time Ross and Marie reached the palisade. The guards must have been watching for them. The heavy timbers closed behind them with the swoosh of a weary woman sweeping a giant hearth. Marie reined Janey up. Dust pillowed up where Sally stood, a handkerchief to her face. She dabbed at her eyes.

Both Baptiste and Paul stood beside horses, Paul's gelding lathered from an obviously hard ride. Other free men and Company men who'd left to bring the horses from the northern fort held their mounts now. They stood, heads bowed, talking in small clusters. They wouldn't look at her.

"Papa?" Marguerite said.

"Hush," Marie told her as she handed her daughter to Sally's now upstretched arms. Her friend's eyes were red and puffy.

"Let me hear this from them," she told Ross. She nodded with her chin to the Company men who'd ridden out with Louis. Her eyes scanned the open yard, hoping against hope to see him, to find that Ross had misled her without knowing.

Paul rushed at her as she dismounted. *"Ma mère,"* he said. *"Ma mère.*" His use of the pet name brought her eyes to him. His face was streaked with dirt and tears, and his eyes darted left and right as though he expected a blow from some unknown place to hit him any second. She held him to her, an arm around him while her eyes searched for someone who would look at her. Even Baptiste looked away.

"What's happened?" she asked LaBonte, who approached now, his felt hat twisting in front of him with his big paws.

"Can't make sense of it," LaBonte said. "We didn't know we were being followed. Shoshone have been miffed ever since Mackenzie started trading guns and ammunition with the Flathead. They must have traded some to the Blackfoot, who used 'em against the Shoshone."

"Shoshone? They did this…thing?"

"We don't know, Madame Dorion," Ross said. "We can't be certain, 'tis true. Just a tragedy, a terrible one."

Paul wrapped his arm around her waist. She peeled his hands from her. "Tell me what you saw," she said. She shook his shoulders. "Tell me what happened."

"I got away," he said.

"And I'm glad," she told him, pulling him again into her chest. She patted his back, could feel the blood at his temple against her chest, throbbing rapid as a rattlesnake's buzz. "Calm down, Paul. Tell me now."

Paul wailed and LaBonte answered, "Paul and his pa took a string of a dozen or so of the horses to water. They were the last batch to go down."

"The rest were grazing steady," one of the free men told her now. "We were making a cold camp, hoping for an early start, being only four, maybe five days out from here. Had the herd and were heading back. Everything going well, for a change," he continued. "You can see they're a good looking bunch of mounts."

She hadn't noticed the horses when she rode in with Ross.

The horses made it but not Louis?

"Seems as though they dallied. Took longer than usual to drink. Getting dusky dark, it was. We was about to go check on Venier and your son here, when this one comes riding wild saying his pa been taken along with a couple of horses."

"Taken? What do you mean, 'taken'?" Marie asked Paul. She held him away from her, her fingers pressing into his bony shoulders.

"They rode in fast, all painted up, swinging hatchets, *Mère*, swinging wide with cuts at him like at Reed's camp, a long time ago, remember? He tried to put his hands to protect his face, and the red ribbons blew in the wind, and those men, they chopped at his arms with blood and the horses scream and he yells at me to ride hard back, get help." He took a breath. He didn't blink as he talked, and his words ran together, a whirlwind of fast-moving dust.

"Did you see him…fall?" Marie asked.

"They take him. They kill him and they take him, pulling him up on his horse and running the others out of the water where they were drinking. They whoop and howl and scream and my horse turns and turns around, all scared, too, and I fall off into the water and get all wet, but I'm not scared." He swallowed. "I get back on and just not sure what to do and they ride off with Papa slumped and bleeding, all slumped and bleeding."

"Did he fall off? Didn't he fall off? You got to him, you brought help to him?"

"By the time we got there, it was dark," LaBonte said. "Don't know how long it was before Paul reached us. Morning, we tracked the blood, but it led right into the river, along with the horse signs. We rode a ways, watching either side for where they'd taken them out to go overland. Then maybe four, five miles upriver, we found the horses, grazing. All of them. Easy as you please beside a big beaver lodge. Even the one Louis had been riding was just standing there, head low. Strangest thing. His horse was covered in blood, no question about what your son saw. All we can think is that they lifted him from the horse and took him. So sorry, Madame Dorion, so sorry."

"But why? What would be the reason?"

LaBonte shook his head. "Maybe something scared them off. Or they had second thoughts about taking the Company's horses. Maybe when they saw young Paul here head our way, they figured there were more to come after them than what they'd bargained for. So they left the

herd and just took the evidence they had that they'd done harm to anyone. 'Cept for that horse, of course. Who could blame them, then?"

"No evidence of any kind. No Louis?"

He lowered his eyes. "Sorry, Madame. Didn't mean to be cruel."

"But…there's nothing to prove that Louis is…dead? Or who did it?
Or why?"

"Sorry, Madame."

She turned back to Paul. "Do you remember anything about them,
which direction they came from, the color of their face paint? What
kind of horses did they ride? Can you describe the hatchet? How many
there were?"

Ma mère, ma mère, ma mère." Paul was sobbing now, shaking, and
she knew the thought of the massacre he'd seen must have brought back
all the old heart knowing, memories more than he could bear. He'd told
the men "his papa" had been taken. He'd never called Louis "Papa."
Could he have mixed up what happened those years before with the
tragedy he'd witnessed now? Maybe Louis was still alive somewhere.
Maybe he'd fallen off and the Company men had overlooked him in the
brush beside the river. She had to go look. She had to find out for herself. Ross might not let her go look, but Louis was a free man and she a
free woman. She would do this for him, for herself.

❖

"It will hurt too much," Kilakotah told her. "And what can you hope to
find so late now?" Marie tightened the cinch that held the saddle in
place on Janey's back. Four days had passed since the news arrived, more
than a week since the attack. That was how Marie thought of it, an attack.
Kilakotah bounced Sally's newest baby at her hip, held Marguerite's
hand. "You shouldn't go alone."

"I'm not going alone. Paul's going to show me where it all happened. And Baptiste will ride guard for us. My sons and me, we'll find
out what happened. More people will only attract attention."

"Mr. LaBonte says this is not good," Kilakotah said, her voice soft as a song. She'd once told Marie her name meant "Little Song Bird" in her native Clatsop language, and her voice reflected that now, a soothing Marie welcomed. "He agrees to take you. If you insist on going."

"He doesn't know what Paul knows."

"But you said Paul should not be reminded of the death, that it brings back his father's death. And you, alone there…this isn't wisdom." The horse snorted and stomped at flies clustering on its belly. "We need no extra horses covering what happened by their hooves."

"I need to know if what Paul saw was what really happened or if he's remembering something else. Mixing it up. Maybe Louis escaped and he's trying to make his way back and we can go there and help him."

Kilakotah's eyes held pity.

"Don't," Marie said. She looked away. "Don't. This is mine to do."

"Wear the widow's name," Kilakotah said, patting Marie's hand. "Pretending you're not won't make it so."

"I don't wear that name well." The name should fit like a watersmoothed stone in the palm of her hand. Instead, the word and the wonder of how this might have happened again weighted heavy as a robe.

Louis, gone. A second husband lost to her own race, her own people. Her chest constricted tight as wet rawhide. *I must attract disaster.* No man should stand so close to her. Perhaps not even her sons were safe with her. Paul might have died too if he hadn't made his way to LaBonte and the others. The thought sent cracks through her otherwise stone frame.

"I've done what I can do here," Marie said. "I've swept the dirt floor. I've cooked *luksh* but didn't taste it. I mixed salmon with the camas roots, but never felt filled. It's time now I moved, did something to put a final face on this."

Marguerite patted Marie's face as she held her and rocked, wiped at the tears that fell not for a welcoming song but a leaving one. Marie kept looking at the palisade gate, willing the heavy timbers to open and reveal her husband riding through. Or walking. She'd take him walking or even being carried if only he'd come back. If only she could live over the last day she'd seen him. What had they talked of? How had she been with him? Kind? Irritated? "Let LaBonte go with you," Kilakotah said.

"He can ride to where they found the horses, to where they turned back with them. You may find no answers."

She wanted Louis back. The ache split her heart in half. How could she live knowing a second husband might be found by wolves or cats? A widow needed a final wrapping to rebind her heart before she could let her husband's spirit go.

Kilakotah's eyes searched, stopped at the sight of her eldest son sitting in dirt. "I'll look after Marguerite. I have enough milk for two." Marie nodded, grateful.

Kilakotah didn't look at Marie when she spoke now. "Sometimes, my people ask that the widow give herself to be buried with her husband. She has nothing more to live for, they say. Or they will choose a child to join the father on his journey." She took a deep breath. "LaBonte says this will never happen to me or our sons. If he dies, he already makes a plan for us. Did Louis have a plan for you?"

Marie's stomach knotted. Old fears tangled. She pushed aside the memories of her first husband almost leaving her behind in St. Louis, of not knowing if she was being set aside the way Indian women sometimes were, like Thomas McKay's mother had been. She'd pushed her way west. She'd found a way to make her first husband take her.

And she'd survived when Pierre hadn't. She'd done what she could for her sons, then and later when she'd joined with Louis. But they'd had no plan. Not for how she'd live without him. What mother with a child still suckling at her breast imagined herself without the baby's father?

"I stay behind," Baptiste said as she finished saddling. She motioned for Paul to mount up. "I'll take Louis's place tending the horses here at the fort."

"You come now, with me," she said. "To see this place Louis died at."

Baptiste shook his head. "I do more good here." Marie stared at him, her head spinning with frustration and grief.

"You go to your Older Sister," she said. "That's why you stay here instead of helping your mother."

He shrugged his shoulders. "I'll see to Marguerite. Me, and Older Sister."

Why did he…? Marie felt shaken like a gourd rattle, hollow with dried seeds where her heart had been.

"If we are not back in ten days, you come seek us," she told him.

Baptiste nodded. Then he cupped his palms so his mother could step into them and up onto her horse. He patted her leg with his hand, then pushed his hat up away from his eyes. Were those tears? No, just dust he wiped. She pressed her heels into Janey. Paul's horse galloped close behind.

❖

Marie imagined finding Louis as they journeyed north. He'd be resting in the shade of a juniper or pine. Or they'd find evidence of where he'd dragged himself to the shadows of a rock and there found a pool of water to keep him, knowing Marie would come seeking. She rehearsed the words she'd say, the tender holding of him, his head pressed against her breast. At times, the ache of it became so real she caught herself speaking out loud, saying his name.

"Qu'ya-t-il?" Paul turned. "What's wrong?" he repeated in English.

She shook her head. How could she tell a boy of such longings?

The journey north gave Marie time to watch and consider. Her son Paul and Louis had ridden together, fast then slow, but at least they'd ridden out, had formed a kind of tie, however fragile the strand. Paul had cried and grieved what had happened, hadn't he? Yes, when she'd first learned of the attack. He must miss Louis too.

And yet as she watched Paul ride in front of her now, his hair knotted in a roll at the back of his neck and his sharp ears sticking out through the black strands that framed his narrow face, he didn't appear cowed or beaten by the witness of the killing. He rode confident, shoulders straight, one hand resting on his left thigh. He pointed to birds in flight, a rabbit that huddled in the brush. Once she thought she even heard him laugh when a hawk dove then lifted, carrying a grass snake in its talon.

Paul didn't appear troubled by their approaching a disaster place. He rode pushing forward like a herd mule, demanding to be first. She wished he showed more…remorse. It would mark him as more…innocent.

A strange word.

She scolded herself under her breath. This was just his way of grieving. She grieved differently. That was all. Kilakotah's people grieved by adding more loss to the pain. Each made this journey in his own way.

Still, Paul had never expressed a single regret about Marguerite not having a father now. He'd not said a single word about Louis's passing, only about the attack and his own survival of it. Nothing about Louis's death.

There. She'd said it to herself. Louis was dead. Her husband no longer lived. He'd left her behind. She was a widow then. She'd been set off, by death.

❖

Each night, Marie and her younger son slept beneath the stars. Marie counted them until she fell asleep. Sometimes, she lay still staring when the silver sunrise worked its way over the hill, her mind filled with thoughts of Louis and her loss. Staying awake was better than that emptiness of waking and remembering. She'd survived one husband's death. She knew how to do this. She just didn't want to.

Paul slept untroubled. No nightmares. He'd had them after Pierre died. For months, as she remembered. He was only four then. Perhaps living through that made this an easier transition. Each took that journey at their own pace, on their own stream.

After the fifth night out, they approached the place where Paul said they'd been when the attack happened. She was surprised to see they were at the Okanogan River, far upstream where the pines grew tall and underbrush of berries filled in the empty spaces. "It's a wonder you didn't lose more horses," Marie said. "The foliage is so thick here."

In her mind, Marie had imagined the horses being moved south, closer to the Columbia where the terrain met with wind rushing through wide open spaces but also where spring grasses were swept clear of snows. Had they invaded the territory of a tribe? Had the Company men acted foolishly, the result being her husband's death? Perhaps she should have asked LaBonte to come with her. Maybe Paul didn't remember accurately.

"Why were you so far into the timber?"

Paul shrugged his shoulders. "This is where Louis takes us."

They rode beneath hanging branches, cut through thickets of willows and along muddied banks. The water level of the river fluctuated as the thaw pushed water from the melting snow in the mountains. Marie could see where the shoreline had been wet the day before and was now dried. Maybe they'd see something the men or Paul hadn't seen before.

"We watered the horses here." Paul reined up, pointed as they came into an area with less brush close to the water. The bank was gradual, and Marie could see why it would be a good place to watch the herd.

"How many horses?" Marie said.

"Twenty or thirty."

"That many? But you only brought back fifty or so. You were watering half the herd, just the two of you? Why?"

Paul hesitated. "That many returned with us," he said. "We only had maybe ten or so that we watered."

"Oh," she said. They rode slowly along the bank, Marie's eyes squinting for clarity, to see something the men might have missed. "I'm surprised LaBonte and the others didn't come looking for you sooner then, with so few horses to tend to themselves and your being gone so long."

"The Shoshones came from out of those trees there," Paul said. He pointed. "Louis was here, where we are. The Indians came up and chopped at him, at his face. He put his hands in front." He showed her. "His eyes were big."

"And where were you?"

"Here. I was behind him, here."

She couldn't picture how Paul could see Louis's eyes if he was behind him or how he could see where the Indians came from at this position. *He must be confused. The startle of it, the fear for his own life must have warped his memory, even after so short a time.*

"But how—?"

"They rode out that way," Paul said. He licked his lips. His breath came short. He kicked his horse, splashed into the stream, left, then right, the water rushing against his horse's legs. He turned his mount toward her and nodded. "They pushed the horses before them. So many pushed them. And they grabbed Louis while they rode. Off that way. Around that bend."

"Did you try to follow them? If you headed back to get help from LaBonte, how did you see what they did with Louis?" she said. "Or where they went exactly? Are you imagining what they did, Paul? Please just tell me what you know you saw, not what you think must have happened."

"I tell you what I saw, woman."

The words came with such force she felt struck. She could think of nothing to say. He reined the horse and started at a gallop, splashing up the stream. "Paul, wait." He didn't turn back.

Marie followed, more careful, watching both banks, her eyes scanning, heart pounding. She rode closer to the right bank, planning to ride close to the left bank on the way back. Paul rode down the middle, never looking to the side.

Nothing. No signs of anything. Kilakotah was right. It had been too long. She tried to memorize the sights and smells then, the feel of the breeze lifting her hair, the trickle of moisture growing beneath the heavy knot at her neck. *Oh, Louis, I hope you have a resting place on this water, that they gave you that at least.*

They'd ridden several miles when she spied a beaver's lodge. A good-sized one. And beyond, a meadow opened, suggesting that the river had changed course here. "That's where they found the horses," Paul said. "His too. No sign of the Indians. Nothing but our horses."

She put her hands to her eyes to shade the sun glare on the water. Where would they have disappeared to, all those Indians on horseback? And why not take the mounts they'd come to steal? Why only take a man, a good man who had done them no harm? It didn't make sense. It just didn't make sense.

She dismounted and walked around the meadow, hoping to find some remnant of her husband, something he might have dropped to indicate he was still alive, to show them a way to follow him. A crow cawed, another answered. She half expected to hear the plop of a beaver tail sending out a warning. But there was only the sound of the water rushing over sticks. Just the silence, interrupted now by Paul's horse twisting his head and the bit rings clanking.

She rode up the other bank, circled out, and worked her way back, hoping to see something, perhaps a new grave, his powder horn, something that marked his having been here and died. There was nothing. She reined her horse toward the stream.

"So, this is where you will be remembered in my heart," Marie said.

"Eh?" Paul said.

"I was talking to Louis," she told her son. "Telling him I would remember this place as a quiet resting place. He trapped beaver for a time and left that way of living to come and be with us in this country. I know nothing of his people. We were his people."

"Good. He has a beaver mark his days then," Paul said. He nodded with his chin toward the beaver lodge nearby.

"If this is his resting place. There's no sign of it," Marie said.

"He took up women's work," Paul said.

"Yes. The work of loving a family, of providing for them, of living with kindness. Such is women's work. And men's too." She stepped off Janey and let the horse rip at grass. "This is a good place to put him in my mind and let him rest," she said. "Green. Fresh smells of spring. Water rushing."

She made the sign of the cross for Louis then. When had she done that last? For Vivacité. She would have to be the one to speak last rites to speed his journey, as he'd want. She didn't even have a way of telling his mother. She didn't even know if his mother still lived. If she did, she would wonder always, never knowing what had happened to her son. A mother always wanted to know such things; even if her sons grew gray and wrinkled, they were still sons.

And then her eye caught something lifted by the wind. Just the hint of color. A red piece of gurrah cloth fluttered near the water.

11

For Company and Kin

"Louis was here!" Marie pointed. "There!"

Paul rode closer along the upper bank where the beaver lodge formed a deep pool. Marie heard but didn't see the plop sound of a beaver signaling distress. She turned back to the ribbon of hope that fluttered. She inhaled the wet mud, memorized the flotsam of twigs and sticks that had captured this single strand of wish.

Paul jumped off and stepped onto the mud hut, pulled the strip of cloth from the thatch. He had nearly fallen then, using his fist to balance. He made his way to her and laid the shredded ribbon in her palm.

Something about the touch of the cloth brought a comfort she hadn't known she needed. Louis had worn this thin thing at his wrist; she had tied it there for him. Or perhaps she'd woven this strand into the braid of his horse's mane on that last day. She looked at Paul.

"Bloodstained," Paul said.

Dark splatters like dried mud stuck to the cloth, now dried by the wind. "So much blood," LaBonte had told her when he'd given her Louis's horse. "He's gone from you, now then. You must accept, *non?*"

Perhaps now she could, holding this cloth, in the spot where Louis must have spent the last moments of his life. She could begin that journey to what would be.

The Shoshone must have wanted to make a point, that Louis and the Company's men had invaded their land for the last time, that the Hudson's Bay Company had somehow violated a boundary and they'd paid a price for it. Louis had, at least. Even as a free man he wasn't safe from the Company's consequences.

Marie looked around her. She didn't fear for herself or for Paul. There'd be no challenge in killing a woman and a boy. They might have kidnapped them, but no message would be sent by their deaths. Women and children meant nothing to the Company.

Marie mounted up, still trying to make sense of why they would not have left Louis's body behind. Perhaps they'd burned it, though she'd seen no evidence of a funeral pyre either. Nothing. Even animals scattering a body's bones would leave evidence. Louis had vanished. Only this piece of cloth stuck in the top of a tangle of sticks remained, windblown, with dark spots of blood. If it had been in the water, they would never have found it, or the blood would have all washed away.

For three more days, she and Paul camped beside the river, returning to this place where a beaver hut grew beside the water. Paul chattered like a squirrel about beavers and their habits, how last winter he'd clubbed one they had netted and they'd pulled a live one onto the ice. His eyes would sparkle as he spoke. Marie's eyes ached with the clash of his excited frenzy in the midst of her wounded debris.

They found no other evidence of Louis.

Marie might have stayed forever near this river where her son prepared the fires for her so she could soak the dried salmon cakes in water. Paul even soaked his own without complaint. She sat distracted, staring, trying to understand what she'd done wrong, what part of her needed purging that caused her to draw disaster to herself, like a leech set to skin.

"I fix for you," Paul said, pushing the cake at her. Marie worked at smiling. Her son did "women's work." All men did if they wished to survive, but somehow if a woman was present, it became her task to do it, suddenly a challenge to her sons or husband if they were asked to lift a hand to help. Women's work might weaken them.

Louis had not weakened. He hadn't chosen this spot to die in either. The Company men must have worked their way too far north with the horses, and so the Shoshone or maybe Spokane or Flathead or a hundred other peoples who wished to protect their families from invasion had found them. Had found her husband, Louis, and made his dying a message for the Company.

For a moment, the thought of going where Louis was now welcomed. As Kilakotah's people sometimes did at death, it seemed a peaceful way to end the emptiness, to put a salve over the wound stabbing at her heart. Baptiste had his life, a way to break the waters ahead of him with Older Sister and her family. Paul was resourceful. Even now he rode out of her sight, seemed ever interested in the formation of the beaver ponds and where the animals might enter. He'd learn to trap, become a free man, perhaps a hunter. His father had hunted. She could see that now. They'd do well enough without her, her sons. They had their father's ways. What had she given them?

She could just slip into the wide end of a boat and quietly paddle herself into the river, slide the oars and poles over the side, and let the water take her where it might. She'd close her eyes and feel the drift of the stream against the canoe, hear a Canada goose rise up, a merganser flush. A breeze would brush against her face, and at night, she'd look up and stare at the dozens of stars. She would will herself to stop breathing.

It would be easier than swimming up through the pain that would flood these next days and weeks and months. She knew those days. They were as familiar as skin.

Her sons would be better off without her. She brought harsh things into their lives, this mother did. Bruises and deaths. And all the prayers of her friend Sarah, of her former mother-in-law, even those her own mother might have spoken as she ran fevered to find the Jesuits, had not kept her from causing harm.

Two husbands dead now. One daughter.

Sarah would tell her she had done this once before, this coming back from distant painful places. She would tell her that her memories, faith, and friends, however distant, would carry her through those places until she could walk again. "We are not alone," Sarah might say. "Whether we invite others in or not."

But Marie was alone, so alone. Again.

Kilakotah would remind her that Marguerite longed for her, that a daughter needed a mother to help see her through, that for her daughter's sake she must not close her eyes and lie back in a boat headed for the sea. She mustn't drift out into the river, never setting an oar to seek a distant shore.

Kilakotah was young and didn't know the choices this mother made that caused another daughter's loss. Marguerite would be better raised by Kilakotah and LaBonte.

Marguerite.

Her daughter's image came to her, the tall child with an oval face, wide eyes, and tiny hands that patted at Marie's cheeks when she suckled. Marie's breasts ached. She still nursed her sometimes, for the pleasure of those soft gathering times together. Selfish.

Marie wrapped her arms around her waist as she felt herself tremble. Her fingers, cold, were white as bone. She was such a selfish woman, so selfish.

This was her task then: to face the fact that she was selfish, too selfish to be a good mother. She would raise Louis's daughter, to keep her from harm as best she could. She'd begin now to move away so her daughter would not catch sparks set off by her mother's dangerous flames. She would see Paul and Baptiste formed into men who would tend their families and hold tight to those ties. She should not expect joy. She should not expect a hopeful life where a man served his family for the length of his wife's years.

How Sally and Ross lived with such care of each other, how Sarah and Ignace traveled to shared callings was not the way of things between most husbands and wives. Those couplings were rare, like brightly dyed grasses woven together into valued baskets. Hope for any one woman was not a promised gift. A life free of trial was not a part of a mother's name, any mother's name.

Wind fluttered the gurrah strip now tied around Marie's wrist. She fingered the bloodstained cloth. This was all she was worthy of, then: something to touch and smell and see, a gift to remind her she was once loved by Louis Venier.

❖

That Older Sister plays at coupling, Paul thought. *Because she is firstborn, she thinks she's better.* He watched the second sister, Josette, do as much work as that older one, but no one noticed her. No one called her name with lightness, only when they needed something. It was that way with firstborns. They expected the sun to bow down to them. The eldest always shone and forced the others to remove their coats if it got too hot around him.

Where were the men of that household? Had Baptiste gotten rid of them all? Not his weak brother, his older brother. Paul watched the Cayuse encampment from a distance. Perhaps he should court the younger sister. Perhaps the women would take good care of him when he brought home venison. He could be a better provider than his brother.

His mother said she'd met one man in this family. The uncle looked after things. Bride's prices were negotiated with the uncle, a French-Canadian. With so many to feed, they would be lost without the uncle. Paul smiled. Perhaps Baptiste would have his "firstborn" reward now, having to take care of so many. He would be too busy to lounge around his mother's lodge. It would serve him right.

Paul reined his horse away from the willows. The area used for waste smelled strong, and it surprised him to find the Cayuse camp here. They'd been at that grassy place, east, but they'd moved closer to the fort. That would make his brother's travels easier.

Paul squeezed his knees together and his horse jumped, ready to run, when Paul noticed dust rising. He relaxed. His mother riding Janey. He reined up, stayed in the shadows.

His mother wore widow's clothes, a dark cloth wrapped around her head. So did this Older Sister's mother. No dresses covered with beads and shells that look like puppy's teeth.

He watched. His mother dismounted carrying a basket of *pyaxi*. She had roots to spare? She gave away his favorite roots? She lifted Marguerite out of the traveling basket. Everyone fussed over the girl. First or last. The middle was never noticed unless they performed amazing things.

❖

Fort George no longer lured. For Marie, the thought of starting over there, of convincing Paul he should come with her and Marguerite to the place where they'd once lived at Young's Bay was as draining as the long walk with water baskets carried on her shoulders from the river to the fort. Instead, she would work here, find the way to feed her family, prepare for winter, and do this without burdening another.

Even if Paul agreed to go with them, Baptiste, it was clear to her, would not. Her eldest son acted as though he had no mother now. He spent all his time at Older Sister's camp.

Marie watched carefully when the girl and her son walked together, when he cupped his hands for her to mount his spirited horse, to see if the seams of her leather dress were strained. They didn't seem strained. Still, he spent so much time there, often not returning to his mother's hut until long after the moon had risen. Lune whined when he entered, missing his master.

If Older Sister's mother did not provide supervision for her daughter, got distracted with so many younger children, fell asleep before sending Baptiste home, bad choices could be made. Marie had failed to instill discipline in her son or he'd be home, not winning a young girl before he had the bride's price.

Two mothers failed their children. Two mothers would be judged. One baby might arrive.

At least it didn't appear that Older Sister carried a child. Paul had been wrong about that. Marie would need to say something to her Baptiste, but Louis's death gave her little emotional reserve. Any talk about her son's choices promised to reflect her own poor choices when she looked in the mirror of her son's eyes.

At least Paul had been less troubling to her since Louis's death. He'd hovered around. He ran errands, chased chickens into the pens, gathered eggs for the fort, even shoveled dirt clods in the kitchen garden so her watering ditches between the rows reached roots of corn and the tangled vines of peas. Paul never once mentioned it as women's work. He even looked after Marguerite at times, and while the child sometimes cried in his presence without provocation—at least none Marie could see—her daughter followed Paul around like Ross's Monterey dog trotted after Sally's youngest girl.

The only drain Paul had placed on her these past few months had been the repetition of the story of Louis's passing. The boy never seemed to tire of talking about it, of how the Indians' horses sounded when they came rushing from the hills, of how Louis shouted for him to get help, and of how he had waited to see if he could rescue Louis rather than run and hide. "As a coward would. No brave one would run for help when he had his own axe and hatchet," Paul told her. "My hatchet was bigger than—"

"I can't hear it again." Marie put her hands to her ears.

Paul dropped his eyes. "I thought you'd be glad he wasn't alone, Mère. Aren't you pleased Louis didn't die alone?"

Marie frowned. Of course she was glad Louis hadn't been alone, but perhaps if her son had gone for help sooner…no, she mustn't hold her son accountable. She must not blame her son for the unanswered questions, the unspoken judgments.

She must learn to think of other things when Paul repeated, couldn't seem to stop his story. She heard the rhythm of his words but not their meanings, so that when he truly needed her, he would stand in front of her and glare. "Mère. You do not listen."

She'd agree, nod her head, and give attention to him. But sooner or later, his need always brought the conversation back to Louis's last days, the red cloth at the beaver house, and Paul's surviving when his step-father hadn't.

"We should go back to Okanogan," Paul said once. The thought soothed.

"No, but we'll build a hut as we did there, out of drifted logs outside the Walla Walla fort," Marie said.

Out of that had come the choice to build a new hut outside the palisades. "We'll live farther from the fort. We won't have to watch the comings and goings of others through the wide gate." She determined to do it before Mackenzie asked her to leave. She knew he would. A woman alone caused trouble for the Company at so large a fort, especially a woman once married to a white man. Even she knew that when Pierre had died, Fort Okanogan had been small enough and distant enough that few men came by to offer themselves to her as a husband.

Even Louis's arrival and drift into her life had been like snow slowly gathering at the corner of a palisade. It was expected over time and comforting to others for its gentle ease.

But here, in this large fort where trades went on through holes in heavy walls and those people with darker skins remained outside unless invited in, here, without a man at her side, she caused suspicion. Some trappers would tell themselves they were merely tending to a poor widow woman when they lounged near her lodge. But Marie knew most sought someone to scrub their linen on the river rocks or gather roots enough for a belly-filled winter. Women's work was the work of surviving, and those who had a woman willing to share their lodge had more fat on their thighs and fuller cheeks than those who bragged that they "survived the country alone" or with their horse and dog.

Already, a coon-capped man or two had lingered near her hut, arguing over this or that in her presence the way her sons did to gather her attention. She'd gone about her work, grateful she had tasks to do, holding Marguerite's hand in hers while she ducked her head past their gesturing arms and headed for the garden, preferring the company of weeds to willful men.

She would move, before such men began arguing, before the rum they allotted themselves brought them scratching late at night, before Mackenzie or any other European man told her she had to go. She would decide such important matters on her own.

She had enough skins and lodge poles for her family's tipi and plenty of mats and a few furs to line the perimeter and hold the tipi's skins to the earth so no wind lifted up and under when snow came. Her four horses gave her wealth and assurance of survival if the winter lasted past their supplies. She could trade for what they'd need. The hearthstones and andiron to hold the copper pots were easily moved, and Sally and Kilakotah said they'd help when the day came.

Marie picked a site north of the fort, close to the Columbia, on a bench slightly above the water. Grasses promised grazing for the small herd; a garden could be carved out of it the following year. They'd go back and forth to the one she'd planted in the spring inside the fort's walls to harvest. Both Paul and Baptiste could help dig out the site a foot or so into the hard ground. Marie would set the poles around the circle, wrap the skins, and when winter came, they'd be warm inside.

"I have things to do," Baptiste said when she first told him she needed help.

"This is one of them," she said, her gaze unflinching.

He grunted his assent and motioned with his chin to Paul to retrieve the shovels. The boys worked well with her that morning.

Then Older Sister came by carrying fresh berries in a basket at her hip. She offered the plump, dark berries to Marie, then turned quickly toward Baptiste. Had the girl's mother sent her with this offering to soothe the way for news?

From her back Older Sister lifted a second basket that she handed to Baptiste. Marguerite waddled over, and Older Sister squatted down to let the child grab a handful of berries that she smashed black against her mouth.

Baptiste smiled. He nodded his head as he wiped his forehead with his forearm, then spoke so low to Older Sister that Marie couldn't hear the words the two exchanged. Once, the girl giggled then glanced quickly at Marie. Older Sister dropped her head, the summer sun making her dark hair shine. Shy, she was, yet wanting to please.

For just a moment, Marie remembered her own journey into the hut of her mother-in-law. She'd been about Older Sister's age, perhaps a little older. Marie had offered her future mother-in-law nothing, had nothing to give.

For the first time, Marie wondered if her mother-in-law, Holy Rainbow, had sought permission to bring Marie to her lodge. Maybe she'd been ordered to do it by her husband. Or perhaps she'd simply done it on her own, offered the gift of her home, her presence, to soothe a girl found grieving.

And what had Holy Rainbow felt when she realized her son Pierre had taken this young girl to bed? Perhaps she'd thought the girl stupid, not for choosing her son but for allowing herself to become with child. Or maybe Holy Rainbow felt at fault, for not better protecting this girl rescued from a death village and warmed beneath her family's robes.

Marie's hands felt suddenly cold, drained of blood, white as bone. Her heart beat harder and she felt her breath coming in short bursts. *Some memory, some disease lives in a memory there.*

"Mother?" Baptiste asked. "Are you *mal?*"

Marie startled at his voice. Her hands shook.

"Merci." Marie took one of the fat blackberries Older Sister offered her. She held it between her fingers, put it shakily to her mouth.

The girl said something in a language Marie didn't understand. Apparently Baptiste did. "First fruit," Baptiste said.

"Pardon, a special gift. Are the bushes near here?"

Baptiste translated again, and the girl blushed, said something to him. "She will show you when it pleases you. You're better now?"

Marie nodded. *What upset me?* She took a deep breath, tasted the berry seeds on her tongue.

"They're very sweet," Marie said as she ate another. She could add them to cornmeal or sweeten the salmon cakes with them.

Older Sister spoke again. "What did she say?" Marie asked.

"She says they may not be as sweet as those to come later. But it is her pleasure to see a smile on the face of the mother of her baby's father."

❖

"What is the bride's price?" Marie spit the words out as Baptiste watered the horses at the river.

"Three horses. Her people are Cayuse. They admire good horses, and they say what we have are good. Otherwise it would be five. Ten made beaver, for trade. And two laying chickens and venison. They have a large family. Many younger."

"And you bring them another," Baptiste's mother said. "Two, counting yourself and the child."

Baptiste nodded. "It will be more work for her, and for her mother." He shrugged. "Women's work."

"What if Older Sister came to our lodge?" Marie said.

Baptiste jerked his head to look at her. What was she suggesting? Was she so lonely without her Louis that she couldn't bear to let her son leave? Or did she worry over Paul? Maybe she didn't want to be alone with him.

"You would do this? Give up all but one horse? The price would not change if my wife moves to—"

"I know, I know. It's not offered to trade her value down. I don't lower the gift."

"Why then?" Baptiste pulled on the horses' halter ropes to slow them from drinking too fast in the summer heat. He sucked air in through the space in his teeth. "Is your tent so lonely without Louis?"

Marie's eyes lifted to his. Was his mother angry? Hurt? What?

"Maybe I put her to work helping with Marguerite," his mother said. "Maybe she offers extra hands for weaving mats and doing bead-work. Her effort would replace the traded horses."

Baptiste grunted. "Another hand to pay off the debt." His mother reached for Janey's rope, stood by her at the water's edge. The animal drank the water, a sound as soothing to Baptiste as the rustle of wind through the leaves of spring.

"Maybe we have more horses than what we need to get from here to there?" she said. "We can walk. You can hunt and help feed us. There is no merit in accumulating more than what is needed to feed ourselves and those we call our own."

She makes a sacrifice for me. Why?

"Paul will not give up his horse," Baptiste said.

"It's not his. All we have was given as a gift, Sarah would tell us, *n'est-ce pas?* Wealth is not what fills our lodge." She pointed to the berry basket Older Sister had hung at Janey's withers. "Sweet berries are provided." She pulled on Janey's rope then. "Besides, we'll have more horses in time. And I'm not yet done raising my eldest son, a task a mother should finish before he begins raising his own." She brushed at her son's hair, pushed it away from his eyes.

Baptiste stepped away from his mother. "I'll speak with Older Sister," he said. "See if she thinks this could work."

In silence, he led the horses back toward the hut. He wished he could give his mother the gift of appreciation he knew she wanted from him. Yet something held him back.

✛

Two rock towers marked the Columbia River at Fort Walla Walla, reddish spirals of basalt that rose into the sky like sentinels for the wide plains beyond. The river masqueraded as a lake here, wide with waves lapping at the shore. Jean couldn't understand why he didn't remember this section of river. Hadn't they trudged by the rocks with Hunt? But Hunt's party had meandered so far and had even split up in order to survive. Who knew whether the bedraggled band of *voyageurs* had passed here in a dense wintry fog and merely missed the rocks; or whether they'd never come to this river at all. He'd ask Mackenzie when he saw him.

It had been awhile since he'd had time to talk with the big man, to watch him ever moving, his red hair flying. Even when Jean had brought the horses down a year ago, he'd only seen Mackenzie for a minute. Mackenzie always had places to go. Making a fur desert took time.

Jean had watched after the man's scent hounds when they'd crossed the country with Hunt. The dogs were distinguished by musical barks. A new breed, porcelain hounds they were. He'd helped bury the one and watched the big Scot cry. It'd be good to meet up with the man he'd come to admire. Mackenzie always learned something from his mistakes. Wasn't that the mark of a man after all? Not that one never erred, but that his errors spurred new soups, new ideas, new adventures that led to a better life for those he loved. Yes, it would be good to see Mackenzie.

They beached the boats at the dock that slipped out into this part of the river that masqueraded as a lake. The land around them rolled bare as a baby's bottom, no trees to speak of, only jagged ridges shadowed into low rolling hills. Stark, this landscape. Jean tried to lift his barrel with his right shoulder, winced, then grabbed a *par flèche* with his left, instead. He walked past several workmen who approached to help carry goods from the *bateau*—some natives, and others in the familiar Company garb of corduroy and sashes.

Up the bench toward the fort, Jean paused. Before him grazed several hundred horses ripping at grass, their muscled necks arched to the slender stems. As far as he could see, the animals dotted the wide plain that dipped then spread out toward bare ridges. He was in good horse country, that was sure. Mackenzie wanted Walla Walla to be the central site for horses just as Fort George was to be the cattle place. These horses were magnificent. Wide chests, reddish rumps with spatters of white; others dark as dirt with white blazes on their faces and feet. They stood lean and shiny, wind separating their tail hairs.

"The horses cut the hair of the hillsides, *oui?*" Michel said, standing beside him.

Jean nodded. These were working animals, ready to transport men and materials into the places where canoes couldn't go. They weren't all Spokane horses. These were bigger animals. The Indians must have been actively breeding for size. Jean watched two race the wind. They were faster, too. Perhaps Mackenzie had gone south to Monterey to bring back such fine animals. Such a herd did the former Astorian proud. Jean could just imagine the tales he'd tell about the building of this herd, the various tribes he had to calm to acquire them. This was a good place. Jean had made a good choice to come here.

They passed through the six-foot wide gate made up of heavy timber. Again Jean felt his jaw drop. The sheer size of the place was a wonder. "It must be a hundred feet at each section," he told Michel. "Look at the thickness of the logs. Bigger than at Fort George."

"Mackenzie has outdone himself with these one," Michel said. "Is he keeping others out or himself in?"

Alexander Ross came out of the factor's house followed by a woman who must have been his wife, all dressed with lace at her wrists and a brooch at her throat. She held a baby, and two little children peeked out behind her wide skirts. *They must eat well at this fort,* Jean decided. Not a small-waisted woman in sight, though Ross's wife was comely with her cocoa-smooth skin and eyes that welcomed with warmth. Ross pointed to the gentleman's dwelling, urging Michel and Jean and the other *voyageurs* there while he invited the clerk into the house.

"Mackenzie'll be sorry to have missed you," Ross told the clerk. Jean turned, eavesdropping, wondering when Mackenzie would be back.

"Mackenzie tires of these place?" Michel said.

A look of annoyance flashed across Ross's face as he turned to see who had spoken. Michel grinned. "Mackenzie pales in the shadow of such a magnificent fort, *oui?*" Ross hesitated, then smiled back. No one was ever upset with Michel for very long even if he did speak without being spoken to.

The clerk said, "We were under the impression that he would be here, that there were problems—"

"Took his leave to the Red River country, he went. 'Tis a shame. He'll be missed," Ross said. "The Company came upriver from Fort George, sending him back East. He left almost immediately with a return brigade."

"You mean he isn't coming back at all?" Jean said.

Ross frowned. "Let's get these unloaded, shall we? So you…gentlemen can eat and turn in."

"It was why I agreed to come," Jean complained later to Michel. He had his bedroll out under the canopy in front of the gentlemen's dwelling house. They'd eaten pork and biscuits yellowed by a good egg.

"Go back, then," Michel said. "Or on to Fort George. Maybe these James Birnie at the river dalles will take you on at his trading post, if you long to spend time with a Scot." Michel laughed.

Sometimes Michel made light of too many things.

"I'm off to Fort George myself," Michel said. "Maybe I'll become indebted to the Company and set my own traps. A few good years in that Willamette country and a man could be on his own."

"I'll loan you whatever you need," Jean said.

Michel waved him away. "Even Mackenzie didn't go south far enough. Much is untapped. Come with me, Jean. You have too little to cause wonder in your life."

"As a free man?"

"These is a risk, to go as a free man. Too much for you?"

Stars sprinkled the dark sky like cone sugar flecked over cocoa. The air felt heavy, not cooling at night the way it did farther north. "I've spent my life with the Company," Jean said. "They even let me work as I could in the kitchen, hoping my shoulder would come back." He rolled his shoulder as he spoke, holding his elbow with his left hand.

"Not as a free man, then," Michel continued. "I do not think I will be a free man, either. There are advantages to being under the Company's wing, clucked as a good hen. But to get the best from the Company, one must be bold. Be a large cat; a man cannot merely stalk or skulk, he must leap at times. He must convince the Company that it will benefit them for a man to do what he pleases, *oui?*" Michel pulled his wool socks from his feet, waved the scent away. "I tell them there is reason to include me to go south, that I learn languages from the women mostly and that is where information is best discovered, *oui?* A little risk, maybe, but so much more information, so much more opportunity, and yet I perform my duty."

"I'm just a kitchen hand who sometimes rides a well-trained horse," Jean said. "I wouldn't inspire confidence in a negotiation." Jean couldn't imagine a clerk looking to him for advice about this or that, the way they might seek out Michel, even if Jean did speak another people's language with ease. The Company had been his life, but it did restrict the possibilities. He'd been at Spokane for years because that was where he'd been assigned.

"You do not think these through, my friend. If you wish to remain a cook, these is good. But if you wish more, then you must say to yourself what you wish. Only then can you say it to others with a loud voice: 'I will be these for you, sir, and you will be pleased I am willing to be your servant, *oui?*'" Michel struck his chest as though raving in triumph, and Jean smiled into the night.

"You think the Company would make a job for me that way?"

"Leap. These is the spirit. What is it you would ask for, even if Mackenzie were here to hear it?" Michel sat up, leaned on one elbow, just the slightest light from the lamp inside the window casting a shadow against his face, his interest in his younger friend both encouraging and rattling.

"Ah…to stand beside the factor and interpret for him," Jean said. "To make a man understood to another man. To advance the work of the Company as they bring a better life to the people it serves."

"You think the Company is in the business of service?" Michel asked, but then he rushed on. "Say these then to Ross. In the morning.

Say you will do these things for him to make him a successful factor at this Walla Walla Fort. Then do it for him. Otherwise, he sends you back with supplies, over a route you have already been."

Jean felt his hands grow wet, and his heart beat a little faster. Could he convince a man such as Ross that the Company had need of him not as a kitchen chef or *milieu* but as an interpreter? It would be a step up in the Company. Jean sighed. Michel could convince a man like Ross, but not Jean. He lacked authority. Michel wore confidence on his wide shoulders. Still, maybe Mackenzie's not being here as expected could be converted to a benefaction, rescue from a disappointment. Interpreters were in the business of conversions of sorts, weren't they?

❖

"You give us very little time," Sally told Marie. "A new brigade's arrived. Mr. Ross has a dozen things to do. Must you have a ceremony now? Couldn't it wait?"

"No," Marie insisted. "My son has chosen a wife. We have the bride's price, and the family has consented. And the girl already…" Marie made a motion over her stomach.

Marie looked beyond Sally's gaze, wasn't ready to see the judgment in her friend's eyes. Oh, many women started their families young, that was not unusual. But Marie had hoped Baptiste might choose a factor's offspring or a clerk's, or that he would have waited until he had secured the bride's price for himself.

"How will Paul take this new arrival, do you think?" Sally asked the question as though in passing. She waved to her daughter, who played in the courtyard with Marguerite. Blew her a kiss from the palm of her hand.

"The baby doesn't look to be born until the spring," Marie said. "There's time for Paul to be ready for this change. And he does well with Marguerite."

"I meant Older Sister's joining you. Paul prefers…to have room around himself. And you," Sally said. "Baptiste's wife may challenge that for him."

"This will not be a pebble to stumble over," she said. "We have lived through large boulders that threatened to roll over us and break this family apart, and we are still here together. No. We will add Older Sister as easily as we added…"

"Louis?"

Something in Sally's tone sent a warning. "As easily as we added Marguerite," Marie said, not at all certain why Sally's words hit like a fist to her stomach.

❖

"Not now, not now. I've too much to organize. McKay from Fort George brings word that they wish fifty horses as soon as they can be delivered and through the Wish-ram country. I'll send LaBonte…" Ross was talking to himself almost.

"Or, perhaps I could assist," Jean said. "I know some languages of these river people."

"LaBonte's wife is his ticket through. He's known there, and we have other issues to attend to here. McKay speaks the languages well enough. His mixed blood serves him."

Jean remembered a McKay, a young man not much older than himself. His father had died when the *Tonquin* sank. Could the McKay that Ross spoke of be this man? Jean would have to ask, but later. He couldn't get distracted by the past: Jean had to focus on the future.

"Sir," Jean said, standing to his full height of nearly six feet. "I would seek appointment as an interpreter to attend Monsieur LaBonte in taking the horses to Fort George. I have experience with horses. I know the native languages in that region. I've already been to Fort George along this very route."

Ross frowned. "You've just come in from—"

"I was here before, delivering horses. Before that, with Hunt and Mackenzie and all the rest coming across," Jean insisted. "This isn't new to me. I seek—"

"You were with Hunt?"

Jean nodded.

"Well, 'tis a tiny sphere we inhabit then, lad. You must know the Dorion woman, then."

"I had the privilege to travel with her for a time, yes. She's Madame Venier now, I imagine."

"It's her wedding affair I'm arranging."

"Sir?"

" 'Tis why I've so little time to be discussing your future what with my wife atwitter over wedding vows needing to be said in the midst of the Company's efforts. Sometimes these natives—"

"Madame Dorion marries again?"

" 'Tis a confused man you are. She's newly widowed. 'Tis her son's marriage. But the woman pushes and won't take no for an answer." Sally interrupted him then, pulling on his shirtsleeve. She whispered something in his ear. He pulled out his timepiece, flipped up the cover. "Very well. 'Tis decided. You'll go with LaBonte to Fort George." He looked up at Jean. "Michel will be assigned as well. Prepare meal bags. Be ready to leave at first light."

❖

Marie knew she ought to know him, something familiar in his gait as he approached. She squinted. He doffed his knit cap while loose black strings of curls as twisted as tobacco framed his long face. His powder horn lay strapped over his chest that was as muscled as a *milieu's* would be, yet narrower than most. He introduced himself as a *milieu* just arrived from Spokane.

"I know you," Marie said.

"And I you, Madame Dorion." He pronounced it as Pierre had, *DeRoin*. Few did, and she stopped her eyes from searching his face for memory and truly looked at him. That was when she recognized the eyes, those acorn eyes.

"I learn of Monsieur Venier's death just today," Jean said. "I am sorry for this loss." He bowed slightly at the waist.

His voice no longer cracked as it had on Hunt's expedition. Now it sounded smooth as well-tanned leather, rich and firm. His beard was trimmed, full and curly but tight at his cheeks. She smiled at him then, and felt suddenly shy. *"Merci,"* she said. "You arrived with the brigade?"

"And leave soon, with Monsieur LaBonte and McKay, to take mounts to Fort George. That McKay, is he the boy whose father died on board the ship?"

Marie nodded. "Many of us stayed in this Columbia country, despite the claims it made on those we love." He stared into her. "You still work with horses then," she said. "You had a way with them. I remember. That and slicing salmon and drying sturgeon."

He grinned. "Had I known you walked through a wilderness place without Venier, I would have delayed departure, to talk of old things."

"Do they need a *milieu?*"

Jean shook his head, no. "I go as…interpreter," he said. "Overland. As with Hunt. As your husband did."

It surprised her that LaBonte would need an interpreter, what with Kilakotah going along. And McKay certainly knew his way along the river. Could Jean be boasting? No, he'd never been that way as a boy; she didn't expect it now of the man.

"You've earned an important position in the Company," she said.

"My first time." He cleared his throat. "Ross says your son marries."

"But not so wisely. The girl's young." She waved the thought away with her hand. She wouldn't complain now. What was done was done. She made her voice light. "My daughter will have a playmate before long." Jean turned to where Marie looked, pointed to Marguerite. "She wears shoes when no one else does."

Children gathered in the courtyard where Older Sister's family sur-rounded their daughter, beads like waterfalls draped over her head, down over her eyes. Marguerite wore leather-bottomed shoes.

"Two husbands I've said good-bye to. Two I've lost and never buried. I am an old coin now," she told him. "Used up and if lost, one not worth finding. *Pardon.* The marriage begins."

"You have a daughter." His voice held surprise.

She nodded, watched her son gather with his future in-laws. "I leave now. I hope your journey goes well."

He dropped his eyes, and his cheeks above his beard reddened.

"Yours as well," he said. Marie heard a boyish wistfulness inside the man's voice, a certain kindness.

❖

"You gave him to me," Paul complained. "You said he was mine." If he raised his voice she sometimes cowered and gave up like a mouse to a hawk. "You give yours. I keep mine."

"Your horse belongs to all of us, Paul. Now I decide he goes to Older Sister's family, as part of the bride's price."

"You keep your Janey." Paul spat the name out. "You're selfish, old woman. You care only for yourself."

"A brood mare will bring us more later. If we give her up—"

"My brother should pay his own bride's price." Where was his brother anyway? Off pretending to be a man while he, Paul, was asked to sacrifice for his brother's pleasures. He knew this would happen. He knew it! After all he'd done.

"We are a family," his mother said. "We make our family stronger with Older Sister coming here. Her mother will miss her hands helping them. This is just."

"Baptiste doesn't leave and go there? Why doesn't he go there?" Paul could feel his heart pounding and his voice growing higher. He had to sound calm. When he shouted, his mother sometimes raised her voice too. It frightened him. He didn't like to feel fear.

"I have asked Older Sister to come here and for Baptiste to stay, to help his mother and his family. We are without a husband or father now. They have an uncle to help, but the horses will make it easier for Older Sister's family to live without her. We're grateful we have them to give."

Paul could feel his head hurt, a pressure building against his temples. He was always the last to know, always had to work hard to be heard. If she included him earlier in decisions that affected him, he'd have more time to help her find better solutions to these problems she created. But no, he always learned last as though he were a child no wiser than Marguerite. Not telling him was what riled him, forced him to defend his rights.

He jerked his head back so the hair stuck behind his ears. Even his hair hurt at times like this when he could not get her to listen to him. Sometimes words, the right words, could change her mind, but he didn't always know what those words were. His mind jumbled. He had to act, had to do things to make his mind slow down.

"We surrender our horses so Baptiste can have a woman to warm his bed? This is what you want me to give my horse up for?"

"It's the right thing to do," his mother said. Then firmer, "It's what will be done."

He hated it when she used that voice, a tone that allowed no passage through it. He picked up his axe and began slinging it toward the center post where the horses were tied outside their lodge. The *ka-chunk* sound of its hitting soothed Paul, though the horses pulled back at the noise. They whinnied, not liking this activity.

Paul's mother winced, and he walked with fast strides to yank the axe from the post, then stepped back to toss it again. "I could get food enough for us," he said. "See how I use a hatchet. Let Baptiste go to his mother-in-law's tent. It will save us from having to feed them too. I'll make sure we have enough to eat. I'll trap beaver. I'll—"

"The bride's price must be paid no matter where Baptiste lives," his mother said. "Please, Paul, for your mother." Her voice was gentle. She was giving in to him. She was weak and whining. He hated it when she whined.

"I keep my gelding who is big and strong and will take me far out to bring in deer meat. I even trap this winter for you. I need a big horse then. Not your little Janey mare."

"Paul…the trade is made. The mare's bred back. In time you'll—"

"No!"

Something deep inside him burned from his gut up through his throat. His head felt like a pine tree blowing up when hit by lightning, as though exploding from the bottom but split down from the top. His shoulders strained. His body felt strung like a too tight bow while his fingers dug into his palms.

Don't come close. Don't come close.

He grabbed for the hatchet. The horses danced into dust. He tried wrenching the weapon from the post, but it was lodged deep. The horses pulled back, whinnied and snorted, yanked against their tie ropes, dust swirled at their feet.

He strained at the axe, his heart pounding. Something pressed against his head, his eyes. He felt tears push against his nose. He couldn't pull the blade out! He couldn't do what he wanted! Everything battled him.

"Paul," his mother said, her voice soft.

She'd once said they would all go to Fort George with Louis, that even her sons would go, but they hadn't. None of them had gone because he hadn't wanted to leave.

He heard her raspy breath. No, it was his own breath. He must remember. Things had changed before. They could change again. He could make them change.

"Paul, *pardon*," she pleaded. She reached for his hand.

Don't touch me don't touch me don't touch me.

He didn't want to hurt her, he didn't, but when she whined it was as though it wasn't his *mère* at all but another voice… He heard a sound from his own throat. His arms quivered from both hands gripped at the hatchet handle as though around a neck. He couldn't hear what she said through the buzzing in his head. He smelled her closeness, her softness, the scent of her fear.

No, no, no. It's your strength, Mère, your strength keeps mine in check. Back away, away!

He sucked in air. He pulled out the axe. He must silence the voices in his head.

12

Twisted Strands

Marie felt as twisted as rope. She wished her son and Older Sister had waited. She wished she had the bride price to hand over before the joining ceremony. She wished LaBonte and Kilakotah could witness the ceremony. Their presence for her son would have tied the day with a tight sinew of celebration, taken away the tinge of worry and regret that hovered around her like restless gnats at a feast. The presence of friends at such honoring rituals made them stronger in the memory and troubled anyone considering too easily detaching. Such responsibilities required a pause for longer thought.

But Kilakotah had ridden off with her two children and husband, and Marie had no way of knowing when she'd ever see her again.

Marie tried not to think about it.

Her life seemed twisted with the strands of coming and going.

Perhaps she'd pushed things too quickly for Baptiste. This would only be his sixteenth autumn. No, it was the right thing, this public witness to his obligation born of ardor. She just wished Kilakotah had been with her as a witness. She'd married young too; so had Marie.

Marie hadn't realized how much Kilakotah's friendship meant to her until she no longer had the young woman's presence just a path away. Sally, too, she claimed as a friend. But Sally listened with only one ear and was always taking a breath to answer while Marie still formed her thoughts into words. Sally talked with her husband, Ross, about women's ways, which wasn't always wise. More than once a worry shared between the women had ended up at the Company's table, leaving Marie with an uncomfortable stomach. She imagined such a discussion had prompted Ross to try to prevent Marie from riding out to where

Louis had been lost. She'd had to remind him that she didn't work for the Company and her husband had been a free man, not one who had signed his life over to North West or Hudson's Bay.

Kilakotah would take in Marie's worries and never spread them. She was a friend like Sacagawea was, where the language of their beginnings mixed with French and English and limited signs that sometimes faltered like a hesitant bird, made sharing hopes and fears go deeper. Perhaps the words kept the women from taking the other's burden as their own and instead allowed them to come beside the other to share the load.

With her silences and nodding head, her hair pulled tight at the top of her slightly sloped forehead, Kilakotah would have helped Marie quell the bees that buzzed inside her, soothe the worry that made her fingers turn white with cold even in this August heat.

Or maybe she just envied Sally her warm feather bed in winter, or her seat on a high-back chair before fine china at the factor's table.

Marie was not an envious woman; she didn't think she somehow deserved what Sally had. It was the comfort she longed for, the look of contentment that smoothed Sally's round face while Marie's face wore wrinkles of worry.

Paul had not attended the wedding ceremony.

He had slammed the axe into the ground, then mounted his gelding at the center post and ridden off, swirling away from her in a cloud of dust that blinded her to him.

She shouted, watched him ride away.

She wore outrage lined with sadness over an undergarment of relief. The relief concerned her most. What kind of mother would be grateful her son had ridden away, refused to participate in a family gathering? A poor mother, one ready to set a stone down, live with her shame, if only for a moment.

Marie had been sure Paul would return when he cooled down. That was what she told herself. It permitted her to attend the ceremony, wear the face of a woman pleased with the arrival of her son's wife into her lodge.

She told no one that it felt good to not anticipate Paul's surprises at the ceremony. What kind of mother could feel relief at such things?

Paul still hadn't returned by the time the bride's price had to be given to Older Sister's family. Finally, it could no longer be delayed.

"We deliver two horses now," Marie told Older Sister's uncle Narcisse.

Baptiste chewed the side of his mouth, his new wife with eyes downcast. A father would have worked out these arrangements. A father would have tended to such things. She would have to do it with no Pierre to help, no Louis in her life. A brother might have assisted… "We are short the gelding, but we will bring him…before the week is out."

Narcisse's beard grew unevenly; a scar marking his right cheek caused the growth to swirl. Marie found her eyes going there first, to avoid the pity she knew she'd see if she looked at the man's face. "Agreeable," Narcisse said. The story of her son's outrage toward her and his riding off with a part of the bride's price had already spread throughout the fort.

Her face felt hot, her fingers cold. "When my youngest son returns…"

"My wife's sister and I have discussed this," he said. "Our daughter begins well with your son. Two horses of such quality are honoring for my sister's daughter's marriage." He paused. "You bring us the foal from your mare next spring," he said. "It will be enough."

"Without the gelding?" she said.

"It will be enough. Just the colt. No more. We do not need the gelding."

"But—"

"A gift is given when it is received," Narcisse told her. "Accept this. That's how you honor the bride's price."

Sacagawea's words of long ago echoed in Marie's mind. "Kindness is the beaded belt that binds all together. Expect kindness. Whatever you give out will be returned."

Had she given anything out to Narcisse Raymond and his family that he should be so generous now? Marie tried to remember. She'd done nothing to warrant such a gift.

Perhaps it was given in pity, her youngest son's demand on her considered a stone weight others hoped to help bear.

"I'll accept," she said. "But when he comes back, I'll bring the geld—"

"No," Narcisse said, holding up his hand to silence her words. "It is my place to change the bride price. Your place to accept it."

A blend of hopes and lifted shame spread through her. "So unde-served," she whispered. "I accept it. For my son's sake. Thank you." Her voice cracked. Tears pooled in her eyes, and when she looked to see whose warm hand now touched her shoulder, she was surprised to look into the eyes of Older Sister.

❖

Baptiste and Older Sister spent the next few days sleeping in a separate hut, joining in with meals Marie prepared. She tried to keep the tradi-tions as they should be. Marie's own marriage with Pierre and with Louis had lacked this time of gentle resting and discovery. She smiled at her daughter-in-law's chapped cheeks, evidence of many kisses.

Marguerite scampered about, making mud pies she baked in the sun. She shared them with Older Sister, happy to have found a friend. Baptiste's wife often sat beside the child, patting the dirt. Marie won-dered if it might be the first time the girl had been permitted to play, her first days that weren't taken up in the care of younger brothers and sis-ters. Her name had made choices for her: Older Sister.

Marguerite slept close to her mother now, her soft snores soothing. The sounds and smells differed with just Marie's and her daughter's breath to warm the tent. The dogs were banished to the outdoors dur-ing the hot months, though they left their fleas behind.

Marie kept waiting for the sound of Paul's gelding, the scratch of his hands at the flap; even his barked words of gruff greeting would be wel-comed. She'd tell him they could work something out, that Narcisse had given them a different way.

But no scratching woke her; no rider rode in to surprise her.

Worry formed like a worm in her stomach, twisting itself so that she sometimes couldn't breathe when she thought of him, of what he'd been through, of the last conversation they'd had. She should have found a way for him to keep the gelding herself. He had given up so much, seen so much to strip his soul of gentleness, and then his mother ripped something he loved from his hands. No wonder he ran off to recover. No wonder he needed time away. She hadn't given the possibilities enough thought before she insisted the gelding be given. One could not force a gift. She should have known better. A mother should know her own son.

Surely he hadn't left because Older Sister was coming to their tent. No, he'd been angered by Marie's insistence about the horse. He needed time to cool.

When he hadn't returned by the second day, Marie saddled Janey and rode out with Marguerite sitting in front of her. They found no sign of him, no lone rider resting in the shade of a distant tree. No boatmen recalled seeing him. It was as though he'd vanished, her son. Simply disappeared.

"We should be drying fish," she told her daughter. "Gathering berries. So much to do before winter, and now here we are looking for your brother."

"Paul hides," Marguerite said. She sounded scolding, then with the confidence of a child added, "We find him. Make him eat last." No doubt the worst punishment she could think of for his thoughtlessness.

Marie patted her arm, chastised herself for complaining in front of her daughter. She must keep her worries to herself, perhaps ride out or ask her questions without Marguerite around so her daughter needn't know how much her brother's absence wounded.

❖

At the next morning meal, Marie sent Marguerite to the sleeping tent of Baptiste and Older Sister to tell them the food was ready. She watched Marguerite put on her leather-soled shoes just to scuff along the path to her half-brother's lodge. The shoes had been worn by Sally's girl, Jemima, and no longer fit that child. They'd come from back East, Sally said. "Hand cobbled," she'd boasted.

Marie hadn't wanted to accept them since she had nothing so fine to offer in return. But Marguerite saw the shoes, slippers almost, and held the soft leather to her cheek, her dark brows lifted in question, the firelight dancing in her hopeful eyes.

"Very well," Marie had told her, and the child jumped around the tent then, the fringe on her buckskin dress bouncing above her knees.

"*Oui,* Mama, *oui,* Mama, *oui!*" she'd sung in her little voice. Marguerite started to pull them on over her dirty bare feet then stopped. Instead, she carried the precious slippers to the river, set them down and scrubbed her small feet before placing the hard skin of her feet inside the leather.

"What will I do when she outgrows them?" Marie said, mostly to herself.

But Sally answered. "It's a good sign she chooses European ways. When she goes to school in the Red River country, she'll walk with familiarity and not stand out as a child carrying Indian blood."

"You offer two amazing thoughts in one speaking," Marie said after a pause.

"Jemima and James will go to that school," Sally said. "Mr. Ross insists."

"Does he insist no one knows they are raised as who they are, as Indians?"

"Yes," Sally said. "He says it's how they'll marry well, their education and conversion to Scottish ways."

"Mama?" Marguerite touched her arm, drawing her back to the present. "You day sleep," she said.

Marie smiled. "I remember a story from your Aunt Sally, on the day you received your shoes." She nodded with her chin to her child's feet.

"Baptiste and Older Sister come soon," Marguerite told her after she'd made the meal announcement at Baptiste's tent. "They talk, but when I come in, they act asleep," she added. "Lay all quiet, but they're awake."

Marie poked at her cooking pot, waiting. The marriage had done nothing to increase Baptiste's conversations with his mother. He still rarely spoke to her, even during meals.

Marguerite held a stick for Lune. Marie winced with the memory of Louis and his bushy-haired dog sitting outside watching geese rise from the river. A hundred times a day, still, she thought of him. How long after Pierre died did it take before every scent and sound stopped reminding her of him? She couldn't remember.

Lune gripped Marguerite's stick with his teeth. He growled, but his tail wagged so hard, his whole body moved. The three-year-old laughed and pulled the dog, still hanging on, outside. Fire crackled into the silence.

Marie missed her sons, missed Paul. He was like an ember that sometimes got enflamed and leapt out of control. But the watching and waiting of loving hands could keep the flames from devouring everything around it, could cool until the embers burned just enough to stay warm, but never burned to bring pain, and never burned out. That was what she'd hope for while she waited, searched. That Paul would return before he brought more pain or burned out.

❖

Michel sang, his voice booming out across the river that was as smooth here as vellum. Jean wished they'd had this kind of stillness when they'd been in the boats instead of fighting the wind to paddle with the current. Here not even a breeze brushed against them when they pushed the herd forward. There were fifteen of them, not counting Kilakotah, the children, and one or two other wives. Enough people to manage the horses, at least for the moment.

Jean failed to join in the singing, instead aware that it felt good to be sitting astride a horse. Yet he felt soreness in his buttocks and wondered if he had something for a poultice to treat it when they bedded down that evening.

"I will walk for a time," he shouted to Michel, who nodded and relayed the message forward to McKay, the clerk in charge. At least walking and leading his horse, Jean had time to think.

These animals were green broke. They hadn't had men on their backs often. They shied at rabbits that scattered or at the shadow of a hawk. Even the one he rode after several hours still pranced and twisted worse than a nervous girl at a New Year's frolic, so he could rarely let up on his guard. The animal yanked on the reins, jerking his arm, and Jean stepped back to talk softly to him, trying to see what strange thing had startled it this time. *A sun-bleached bone lying in the trail.* He led the horse around it.

The thing was, he often couldn't tell what upset the horse, what made it giddy or shy. Not unlike women, he supposed.

He thought of Madame Dorion now, the sadness that filled her eyes. Twice widowed. And he'd heard rumors about her youngest son being a difficult one. She deserved better than that after all she'd been through. Back when he was Hunt's camp boy, he'd made it his personal mission to keep her and her children safe. He was glad to do it since her husband didn't seem to notice the danger she was often in. Sometimes, the danger *was* her husband, his affection for the drink.

Jean's timing was always off. Just a boy he'd been back then, not able to do much of anything to increase her comfort. She'd cut his hair and mended his socks, and he'd thought of her in a motherly way, cared for her in the way his mother had taught him to treat a woman. He'd enjoyed helping her with those young boys; felt he'd helped her when he took Baptiste with him to look after Mackenzie's dogs.

At Astoria he'd enjoyed sharing the occupation of supplementing food for the Astorians. Marie and he had lessened the discomfort brought by the resupply ship's delay, too. She hadn't waited around wringing her hands as some of the clerks had, wondering if they'd have enough food or not. She was resourceful. He remembered that. And he admired that in her. She'd even made a poultice out of horse urine and mud that had eased the men's sore feet. He chuckled to himself. He'd make some that night. He'd place it somewhere besides on his heels.

Together, Madame Dorion and her woman friend, Sarah, and Jean had dried enough fish to extend the supply to the hungry Astorians, and Madame Dorion had even had some left over to place against a debt.

As he remembered, she often talked about her husband's debt. "Debt is the slavery of the free" some Latin scholar had once written, or so his mother told him. Or maybe it was a Proverb, about not being a borrower or a lender that his mother discussed. "Never be indebted to another." He never had been. He remembered how the debt drove Madame Dorion, though it never seemed to change the behavior of her husband.

Jean tried to remember the man. Volatile. Unpredictable with a tendency to outrage over little things. And yet he'd fought for the woman to keep her horse when some would have eaten it; he had put her needs before his own. It was the only act that had raised Jean's esteem of the man.

Kilakotah's boy ran up beside him. Chubby and good-natured, he asked to be set on the back of Jean's mount. "He's green broke, now," Jean said as he lifted the boy. "Hey, you've ridden a little, now, haven't you?" The child couldn't be more than four years or so, and yet he settled himself like an old man accustomed to sitting on a horse's back.

"I ride with Marguerite," he said. "She stayed home."

Jean thought now of Marie's daughter. Baptiste's half-sister she'd be, the one who played at Fort Walla Walla wearing shoes at the joining cere- mony. Jean wished he could have stayed. Not sure why McKay was in such a hurry to head out.

Marguerite was a pretty child with a heart-shaped face. She didn't act shy around him as so many Indian children did. She was almost bold coming up to him. She touched the fringe on his sash and stuck her tiny fingers into the ridges of the corduroy at his ankles and looked up at him with eyes the color of tea.

"Your mother makes this?" she'd asked in English. He'd expected French and thought it an odd question from a little child. She listened carefully, wrinkled her brow in confusion when he told her no, he didn't know whose hands had stitched it.

"Papa stitches," she'd said.

It wasn't something he'd known about Louis Venier. He hadn't seen the man stitch anything except some good escape routes when they'd transported horses together those two times. He'd heard rumors about the man's last journey. He wondered if those tales had reached Madame Dorion or if she set aside anything that reflected poorly on her son. He'd have to ask LaBonte.

Jean looked ahead. The herd and those moving them had dipped out of sight in one of the many ravines that carved their way to the Columbia on the south side of the river. Jean pulled his horse up, stepped into the stirrup, wincing as he tried to raise that right shoulder. Would he ever remember that he couldn't do what he once did?

"We're riding double," he told the child. "We best catch up, eh? Before your mama comes looking for you."

He shook his head of the mosquitoes, brushed them from the face of the child. Pesky things. Almost made a man consider wearing earrings to chase them away. He'd have to do that if he cut his hair off, which he sometimes considered doing. It would keep the fleas and lice out, that was sure. He frowned. Live ones were crawling in the boy's hair, shiny and clean as it looked.

Jean shook his head again, recalling an earlier time. It was such a boyish thing to do, giving Madame Dorion those ear trinkets years before. His face felt hot even as he thought of it. And yet she'd taken them and seemed pleased. He'd felt the slightest tinge of regret that she hadn't kept them. Ridiculous. If the gift wasn't given to her with gratitude for the little things she'd done for him, a present for her to do with as she chose, then what had he hoped to get from the giving? What kind of gift was it if it wasn't freely given? What kind of a man offered something and then made a judgment about what was done with his offer?

Jean winced at the pain as he sat the saddle, his right arm resting lightly around LaBonte's boy. If Jean had indeed found a new occupation, if he did want to stand beside chief factors and interpret for them, negotiate through difficult places, he'd probably be going with supply brigades, moving men and mounts and materials here and there and spending much of his time in the company of horses. Was that what he wanted to do? Oh, he'd keep his word; he'd help deliver the horses to the fort. But rather than stay to look after them and interpret there beside the ocean, he'd see about coming back this way to learn more about the tribes closer to Fort Walla Walla. After all, Astoria had LaBonte, and McKay certainly spoke Chinookan with ease. And he'd heard they'd be moving the fort or starting a new one on the north side of the river since the area they rode in would probably one day belong to the Americans rather than the British.

Now that he thought of it, Mackenzie's choice of locale for Fort

Walla Walla smacked in the face of the Americans. A fort north and west of the Columbia would have said, "We plan this land for Britain." Instead, Fort Walla Walla said that the Brits would go where they wished, even with a joint occupation. It would take a bold leader to carry out the British mandate south of the Columbia, and the little Scotsman Ross didn't really hold that kind of vision, at least not that Jean could see.

Maybe Jean could be of more service back at the Walla Walla with Mackenzie gone now. He could always supplement his interpreting work by caring for the horses or cooking. They needed better training. A good trail horse couldn't afford to startle and sashay at every little twitter in the grass. They had to trust who rode them to get them to whatever post they headed to, had to believe their rider knew the way and wouldn't let a horse reroute on its own. They were not unlike a parishioner meant to follow a faithful priest, he supposed. Each had to trust, be willing to be led.

Jean could be of more use than just doing one thing well. The past had a way of teaching if a man took note of its lessons. Why, he had remembered what Madame Dorion put into that poultice she'd made. The whole brigade would be happy with him if he offered that as a gift!

❖

"You look for Paul." Baptiste's mother said as she scraped at a hide. "You know the languages. I've heard Sally say her husband thinks you'll soon speak Cayuse as well as Narcisse Raymond does."

Baptiste grunted, but it pleased him to know that Ross noticed his skills. Sometimes, Baptiste thought he knew the Cayuse words better than Narcisse, but that was no matter. Ross wouldn't rate a boy higher than a man.

But he was a man now. Though he'd never made the journey as his father's people had, seeking time away, to move from boyhood to beyond. He'd made the passage, sweated, and purified himself with steaming water and the plunge into the Walla Walla River. He'd done it at Waiilatpu, the grassy place, where Older Sister had lived, farther away from the fort's bustle. He'd seen the world differently after that, as a man saw things. His discovery of Older Sister followed.

These River Indians had different ways to do things, but he was sure if his father had lived, he'd have approved of this path taken.

"Is that your worry?" His mother again.

His mind had wandered, taken off on a path of its own. If he waited, she would fill in what he had missed. "Her time isn't due for maybe two, three months. You could find Paul by then and be back. Bring him back."

Baptiste shrugged. He wouldn't say yes or no to her now. Once spoken, she never eased up, wanted whatever he'd agreed to do to happen before the sun set on the words.

"I promised to be with her when the child comes," Baptiste said. "As you say, she's young, Mother. She needs her husband at her side."

"You're a good husband and a good son. You go now. Try to find Paul, make him understand that the bride's price has been changed. You owe him this. It was your bride's price. Tell him he can keep the horse. If you don't find him, you come back to be here, for your wife. You have time. She stays here and we come to know each other, a mother and daughter, *oui?*"

He said nothing.

At the sleeping hut, he told Older Sister what his mother wanted. Older Sister never pushed him. He stood with his arms crossed, bracing for her protest. "When you cross your arms," Older Sister told him, "I know you have closed your thinking to me. I won't open a flap you want closed."

He hadn't known his body told tales. He lowered his arms then, and she smiled. "When I asked if you wished to live in your own hut, it was a question, not a way of telling you what I wanted. Not a way to make you do something." She sat in the sleeping lodge, stroking one of the pups that were now full-size. He still thought of them as pups. "When you say your mother wants you to find Paul, what you do is your choice, not mine. Not hers. Do what you do because you choose it," she said. She patted the robe beside her, pushed the dog away. Baptiste dropped his arms and lowered himself next to her, folding his legs.

She snuggled against him, the swell of her belly warm against him. "Do what you must. Just know that I never want you to drift away with your thoughts," she said. "Unless you take me with you."

He'd reached and pulled her to him. He kissed her.

His wife was different from his mother. Her loving came on lighter wings.

❖

To Jean Toupin, Fort George looked threadbare as an old woolen sash. Rain-streaked boards of the dwelling houses stood weatherworn while the roofs, once yellow with fine wooden shingles, were now covered with moss and fir needles caught in upturned splinters.

"They do not take such good care of these place," Michel noted. "I think maybe while I'm gone, they make improvements to welcome me back." He grinned.

"It's on the south side of the Columbia. They expect the Americans to have it someday," Jean said. "They won't improve what Americans might get."

"My stepfather's to come out and build a new fort on the north side." Tom McKay said, gesturing across a wide bay to a point of land that showed some evidence of activity. He stood with one knee bent as though to give relief to his bad leg. "A farm's there, where the hogs are, at least most of them. But the weather is still disagreeable many months of the year. Cow barns are on this side. Pretty precious, those. I suspect we'll be moving livestock and men inland before too long."

"Astoria, Fort George, looked very inviting after the overland journey with Hunt," Jean Toupin said.

Tom McKay looked at him, nodded. "I forget you have that story under your sash," he said. Tom's knee buckled. He caught himself before falling and remounted his horse. "Living through disaster binds people."

"We all live through these hard times," Michel said. He swept his hand to indicate the fort.

"I didn't remember it as so bad," Jean said.

They moved the horses into a corral, then met a man named

Beignoit who said he was an interpreter. It seemed to Jean that everyone was an interpreter and that the title failed to carry the weight it once had when the Company was newly forming at his post.

"He talks too much for a man with these title," Michel commented later in the men's sleeping quarters. "Beignoit says he knows who sleeps with which man's wife while the other is away."

"Don't think that's something I'd discuss," Jean said.

Michel pulled a twist of tobacco from his side bag, bit it, and chewed. "Especially when the man he speaks of is the clerk in charge of Fort George who is off working and his wife was once promised to the very large lover she is now with."

"Isn't there a policy, that the Company is not to take Indian wives, at least not officers or clerks?" Jean asked.

McKay adjusted his hat. "Didn't stop Ross," he said. "Nothing's happened to him back at Walla Walla." He paused. "What happens to the children, now that's another story."

As the weeks went by, with the daily drudge of moving the horses to meadows in the coast range of mountains, managing them through thickets of oak and red alder, Jean found himself thinking more and more of what had made this place palatable. This week Jean worked the kitchen; next week he rode horses to the meadows again. He went where the Company assigned him.

The breeze this time of year was balmy, and it rarely got sweaty hot. Flowering plants spattered the dense foliage, paint blobs on a palate. He hadn't even lived through a long winter the way most of the sea crew and overland parties had. He'd have that to look forward to, if he remained.

It wasn't so much the uniqueness of the landscape that he'd remembered when he'd left Astoria behind those years before. Not the crab apples he'd picked and stored or the bark he'd made into a tea that helped his stomach; and it wasn't finding the black gooseberry and cooking it into a fever-easing porridge that he remembered. When he saw the berries and crab apples again, their uses had come back to him, even the proportions of some of the recipes he'd concocted to the hearty grunts of the men.

No, it was whom he'd been with when he discovered those uses that came to him now, that tinted this place differently. The presence of people kept a place in his heart. It was why he'd returned to Montreal, to see his family. It was why he'd enjoyed Spokane House. The scenery engaged; but it was his friends there who sustained him.

Even now as he rode up into the meadow, reined a horse into a fast trot to turn a mare and colt out of the trees and back into the herd, he realized it was LaBonte or Michel or others stationed at the post who worked with him that came to mind at the end of the day, how they'd helped each other accomplish their tasks. People made the places.

So why had he wanted to leave here all those years before? His friend George Gay had wanted to go back to New York, maybe even return to Gloucestershire where he'd been born. Jean was easily influenced by his fellow camp keeper and his persuasive British ways. But he suspected more it was because he was homesick. He missed his mother and sisters, the smells of perfumed soaps and rose hip–stuffed pillows. Their giggles and twitters and admiring of an older brother built a man's ego if not his character.

On the journey overland, Madame Dorion had been the only woman he'd talked to for months. They'd formed a kind of friendship, he'd thought, though she never asked a thing of him. It was always him receiving something from her.

Jean removed his cap, wiped his brow with his forearm. Could he still be cow-eyed, gaping over a woman old enough to be his mother? But was she? He calculated, guessed she might be six or seven years his senior, nothing more than that. And what was age anyway in a place where in short years, boards weathered from yellow lumber into brittle splintery lengths of pewter gray. It wasn't the aging in the years but the wisdom in the aging that mattered, and most folks said he'd always been older than his years.

LaBonte signaled him, and they began the journey back toward the fort where the horses would be corralled for the evening, safe from marauding mountain lions and cunning Clatsop or Tillamook who might be seeking horseflesh they could use in trade. As they approached the fort, Jean noted that the huge cannons had been positioned to point toward the land and not the sea. That focus surprised him since almost every story of danger or disaster at Astoria had originated on water, not inland: the loss of the *Tonquin,* the threat of the Brits in that war of 1812. And yet the fort's factor feared the natives, inland. The very people who'd lent them aid, teaching those who'd listen of their ways, like the Indian woman, Madame Dorion.

"We'll have *wappato* and leeks these night," Michel told him riding up beside him. "You can smell the fires, *oui?*"

Jean sniffed, nodded yes. With the scent came the memory of a woman pulling the slender grasses from shallow water, breaking off the bulb, and later cooking it with leeks. *Wappato.* He hadn't eaten that in years, yet just the smell reminded him of Madame Dorion, the woman who'd introduced him to it. She wasn't afraid to learn from those around her, to take on new ways if that would help her family.

She might have received some gain for surviving the attack against Reed. The Company might have compensated her for the loss of her husband, given her a fresh start somewhere, even if Dorion had been a free man. Yet she still had a debt to pay, LaBonte told him. The Company hadn't done much to ease her burden, despite her loss. But she hadn't complained. Even LaBonte said she never complained.

Jean's stomach growled. "I hope they have good hunters," he said. "A little meat to add to the leeks and *wappato.*"

"If not, maybe you suggest they convert interpreters to hunters, *oui?*" Michel said. "Maybe not so dangerous an occupation. Monsieur Beignoit might wish he had changed his title; he was found murdered," Michel whispered. "They suspect the lover who has little appreciation for the interpreter's loud mouth. Interpreting can be dangerous, *oui?*"

Pierre Dorion had been reassigned from interpreter to hunter, Jean remembered that now. Why did everything remind him in some way of the journey overland and that woman?

❖

Marie laced the *shaptakai* onto the back of Baptiste's saddle. She'd painted the image of a horse on the leather suitcase herself. "Dried salmon enough to last you," she said.

"I put berries in the *squill-ape,* as your mother calls it," Older Sister said. She stood with her small hand upstretched, rested it on her husband's thigh. "Something sweet. For when you stop at night."

"I'll think of you," Baptiste said. "That's my sweetness."

Older Sister blushed. "Come back soon," she said. "With or without your brother."

Baptiste nodded. To Marie he said, "You will be disappointed if I come back alone."

"You'll have done what you could to make a new ending," she said.

"Your effort is a special gift," Older Sister told him. "A part of the bride's price."

Baptiste looked at his wife. Marie couldn't remember when she'd seen such gratitude in her son's eyes. Had she ever? Had she ever given him words that made his heart sing as his wife just had?

She looked with new respect at Older Sister, felt a twinge of grieving for the son she'd lost who now acted as a husband.

That husband reached down, caressed the side of Older Sister's cheek. He leaned over and put his hand to her belly. He whispered something to her that Marie couldn't hear. The girl lowered her eyes and smiled as she stepped back.

Baptiste lifted Janey's reins, pressed them against the horse's neck. He tipped his hat to his wife, his mother, and rode off.

Marie put her arms around the girl and they stood watching. Marie believed she saw tears in her son's eyes; knew they pooled in Older Sister's.

"He is a good man," Marie said. Older Sister nodded, wiped her eyes.

"I don't like being left behind," she said. "I would go with him except for what is best for my baby." She rested her hands on her belly.

Marie pulled the girl closer. "Baptiste will be a good father," Marie said, hoping she'd shown him, too, how to be a loving parent, a giving brother.

Older Sister said, "I only feel alive when I am where he is."

13

Divided Stones

Paul probably went north, back toward Okanogan. Still, Baptiste's brother could be cunning, try to anticipate where someone would find him and do the opposite. So Baptiste chose to go downriver, maybe as far as Fort George, asking along the way. There'd be more brigades to talk with in that direction, too.

He'd had no luck, though he rode all the way to old Astoria. It had changed in the past nine years since they'd left it behind. He couldn't even find a trace of their old hut at Young's Bay. He'd come back upriver, crossed to the south side and asked after Paul at the falls on the Willamette where Indians speared fish. Nothing. He was heading home after three months. He'd make a stop and then go north if his mother insisted he keep searching and Older Sister had not yet delivered.

With his forearm, Baptiste wiped his forehead of sweat. October could be hot during the day and yet cold enough at night to cool out a deer carcass. He'd seen small herds disappear into the puckered valleys of hills. Older Sister had told him to make an adventure of this, not to see the journey only as obligation. Shooting a fat buck would make it an adventure.

He wished he could have taken Louis's horse instead of his mother's mare. Janey was a sound animal, but he might have pushed harder with Louis's horse. He missed the animal. Narcisse had distributed the bride's price quickly though, to family. It was as it should be. Someday, he and Older Sister would receive back some treasure, perhaps when their daughter married, if they had a daughter. Meanwhile, he had this sturdy one to ride and she'd done well, for a mare. Good brood mare.

Baptiste preferred hunting in the open country, not in the treed areas that lined the streams here. The big hillsides where the deer scraped loose rocks caught his ear before he even saw them. He'd seen a small group of does skitter over a knoll, stop, look back. He listened now, turned to the left where a talus slope eased down the hillside, giving the look of poured molasses in the midst of pale brown. The does had looked back that way. They were waiting for the buck.

Baptiste still couldn't see a big deer, but he could hear movement. He dismounted, pulled Louis's rifle out of the scabbard. He pulled the cap of his powder horn with his teeth, measured the charge, then dumped it down the barrel. He fitted a ball and rammed it into place, then laid the rifle across the saddle as a brace.

The buck was moving again, hunkered down behind sagebrush clumps that masqueraded as trees. Browsing, that was what it was doing, slowly making his way behind the herd of does and small fawns.

Beyond rolled the Columbia, the late afternoon sun turning the blue to blood red mixed with shades of gold. Baptiste watched as a brigade beached in the distance. Maybe he'd join them tonight, take shelter in the company of men. They might have seen his widemouthed brother with his narrow ears. Memorable, his brother was, in more ways than one.

Baptiste supposed if he had a son who disappeared he'd want to know what happened to him. He wished he was more worried about Paul, but they had little between them except blood. Older Sister said it was a great loss that he had nothing more, no brother to rely on. "You must be the older brother," she told him. "Take the lead in things. Especially now when your mother has only you."

Sometimes he wondered if even that was true. He had that looping dream again, where a boy brother talks to him, tells him they share a grandmother, a mother and father, too.

But his mother said he was the older brother, just as his wife was Older Sister, and that meant rules and rituals not expected of the youngest.

Baptiste turned back, caught a glimpse of the buck now and closed one eye to aim. He'd have a hot meal tonight and some to share, and a hide to take back to his wife.

He took in a deep breath.

He heard a blast then. Baptiste watched the animal drop. A man whooped. It wasn't him. He hadn't fired a shot.

✦

Marie heard the sound and rose from the mat. The sound came from outside. She thought maybe it was Paul returning, or Baptiste, perhaps. She bent to push back the flap, stand into the night cold, a blanket wrapped around her shoulders. As her eyes adjusted to the moonlight, she heard the groan and saw a form lying not far from the lodge.

"Lune," she whispered. She moved quickly to the dog's side, but it made no move to lift its head or turn to her. No fast breathing before going. The dog had simply lain down and died. "Oh, Lune. Louis loved you so. Marguerite will be so sad." Here was one more loss, one more explaining to lay before her daughter who still awoke in the morning asking when her papa was coming home.

She lifted the animal and carried him away from the hut, where Marguerite wouldn't find him. She'd bury him in the morning, maybe let her daughter help. Perhaps that would make the passage final. She wasn't sure she could endure a question of when Lune would come back.

She'd just started back when she heard the cry, this time from inside the hut. It was Older Sister! The girl never cried out, never complained.

Marie ran, kicking the blanket out around her knees as she sprinted. She'd heard that sound, long years before, with Sally's baby, when it had come too young, too soon. The skin at the back of Marie's neck prickled.

"Mother," Older Sister called out. "My mother." Marie ducked into the sleeping tent where Older Sister and Baptiste had made their home before she sent her son looking for his brother. The scent of blood filled her head. The girl must have been in labor for some time. Perhaps that was what she heard that woke her. Perhaps it hadn't been Lune's breathing his last at all.

"My mother." Older Sister was crying now, her face hot and sweaty, hair sticking to her neck. Marie lit a lamp, gasped at the pool of blood.

"I'll send for her," Marie said. She left the girl, only for a moment, to go awaken Marguerite, whose eyes were big as biscuits. "Marguerite! Wake up. Go find Josette, Older Sister's sister. Quick now. Don't put your shoes on. Get her and her mother. Quick now, like a rabbit."

Marie scooted her out the door, grabbed a pouch of herbs, ran back to Older Sister, knelt beside the girl, the woman, the mother. "It is too soon?"

Older Sister shook her head. "Aiyee!" She arched in pain, panted. "I push at him, but he does not move. I push for hours. But it's too soon. I try to hold back, too. Keep him with me—"

"Why didn't you call for me?" Marie asked. The girl looked weak, too weak.

"I don't…want to…bother," she panted. "I do this, alone. I help my mother when her babies—Aiyee!"

Marie's mind raced. What would stop it? Or was there a way? She was so small, this woman-child, and bleeding. Too much bleeding.

Oh, what will help; what will help? Another child lost. It couldn't be, not now. Tamarack tea. "When your mother gets here, I'll make tea. To stop the labor. Now I hold you, change the way you lie. That may stop—"

"Now!" the girl screamed as she sat. She expelled an infant, the cord tight around its neck. Marie knelt before Older Sister, pulled at the slippery tie, held the infant barely larger than her hand. It was a girl, dark as a raven. Marie cleaned the infant's mouth with her fingertip, blew air into her lungs and she made a screeching sound resembling a cat almost.

"Is he, alive? Let me see his face."

Marie said, "A girl. You have a girl."

"Name her," Older Sister panted.

"You and Baptiste can name her. When he gets back," Marie said.

The infant moved in Marie's hand, sucked in breath. She had no fingernails. She was still growing.

Marie felt something wet at her knees. More blood. Too much blood.

"I go now," Older Sister said. Her voice was breathy, her eyes dreamy. Her hand gripped Marie's wrist. "Name her…Little Marie. Until she chooses…a name of her own."

❖

"*Pardon, pardon.* I believed I was alone here, aiming at this animal," the French-Canadian told Baptiste. The man had made his way down toward the talus slope. "I notice the sunlight against your rifle," he said. Then he squinted. "You are Jean Baptiste Dorion, eh?" He pronounced it differently than most, and Baptiste knew then who he was.

"Jean Toupin?"

"*Oui.*" He clapped Baptiste on the back. He stood taller than Baptiste, lankier, too. "I'm heading back to your Fort Walla Walla. We can ride together. This will be agreeable? We'll share the meat."

"That's generous," Baptiste said.

"It's nothing. God provided the deer, and the Company the means to take him; it is my duty to share him."

"I'll help you dress him out," Baptiste offered, and Jean Toupin accepted.

They worked together, the two men, mostly in silence, but each knew the routine. When they finished and had the deer quartered and tied onto the horse, each carrying half, they led their animals toward the Columbia. Now they had time to talk.

Jean Toupin told him he was heading back toward Walla Walla to meet John Work. "He comes new to this country and I'll work with him. As an interpreter. I know some of the languages here. You do as well. You like this *métier,* being an interpreter?"

Baptiste nodded. He wasn't much to talk about what he did or how well he did it. It was one of the things he treasured about his life with Older Sister. He could talk with her about anything. This man seemed pleasant enough. He'd tell him some of what he worked at.

"I've been looking for my brother," Baptiste said. "More than interpreting for anyone. My pa did that work. Grandfather, too."

"I know the name well," Jean said. "I have not seen your younger brother." A breeze carried the deer scent to Baptiste's nose. He looked back and brushed at bees already taking their share.

"No one has. He seems to have hidden himself well. I'll go to Okanogan next."

Jean nodded. "Your mother. She is well?"

Baptiste noticed a change in Jean Toupin's manner when he spoke of his mother. He wasn't sure what it meant, but it was different. "She's well," he said.

"I much admire your mother, eh?" Jean said.

"A lot of people do."

"I hope to speak with her when I return. About a...transaction. You think she'll meet with me?"

"Depends on what you're selling," Baptiste said. "She isn't much into higgling."

❖

Everyone cried, long, deep cries. In her mother's lodge, Marguerite saw nothing but knees and feet rushing here and there, hands damp from the cloths they placed to their faces. Older Sister's mother sat holding her stomach, rocking, crying. Marguerite hid in the back, bundled up in the buffalo robe where she wouldn't get bumped or stepped on. She'd brought Older Sister's sister who cried but had patted Marguerite's head too.

Sally came. Marguerite's friend Jemima said her mother lost a baby once. They never found it.

But this baby had lost its mother. Marguerite didn't understand that. Older Sister was sleeping in her hut.

The baby, Little Marie, wore dark ash. It had been the color of her hair at first, but it was lighter now. Marguerite's mother fed it with drips. Jemima said it was goat's milk.

It lay beside the fire in a basket. Marguerite got up to sit beside it. Her foot was longer than...it. The baby. It didn't move much. Just opened its mouth like a tiny bird she'd seen once when it fell from a nest. Poor baby. It needed its mother. Marguerite looked at her own mother. "When's Older Sister getting up?"

❖

"What can I say?" Marie said. "What can I say?"

Baptiste's mouth was gripped tight, as though to open it would force words out into the world that might never be taken back. Her son had just ridden in, accompanied by Jean Toupin. Janey had been ridden hard; she was lathered, breathing heavy. The news had been sent downriver in hopes that he would hear, come.

"I don't want to see it," he said. "Just her. I want to see her."

"Her body's been tended to," Narcisse told him, stepping up to him. "She's at Waiilatpu. A good place. You must tend to this child now already five days old."

Baptiste had never looked so ripped apart to her. His shoulders hung on his frame, and his eyes darted here and there as though seeking comfort from somewhere, anywhere.

"This happens," Narcisse told him. "Living and dying."

"She was so young," Marie said.

Baptiste turned on her then. "Her youth is not the cause of this. You sent me away; that's the cause of this. If I had been here, I would have known, could have helped. She would not have suffered, bled to death in her own bed while her mother-in-law slept."

Jean Toupin put a hand on Baptist's shoulder. Her son jerked away. "Baptiste—"

"Your mother did what she could," Josette said. "My sister wanted the baby. Your baby. She asked her to be named Little Marie. Older Sister loved your mother, Baptiste."

Baptiste spat, his fists at his side, his body a storm, raging. He shook his fist at Josette's face. The girl didn't blink. "You think she loved the baby more than her own life?"

"You are filled with sorrow," Josette told him. "Too full now, to see the gift of your daughter."

"That will come later. Baptiste...I..." Marie stumbled. Her own grief so wrapped up in her son's.

"Because of your precious Paul," Baptiste said, his voice shaking. Marie knew he would say something now, words she didn't want to hear, words he'd someday wish he hadn't. "Who probably killed your own husband." She felt tightness at her temples, as though she might explode. "You don't even let yourself think such things. No. Nothing to harm your precious Paul."

"Baptiste—" She reached for him.

"And now the two of you have killed my wife."

He shoved Narcisse out of his way, headed out into the night.

This was worse than losing Pierre, worse than not knowing what had happened to Louis or to Paul. Here was pain she shared with her son, the loss of a lover and friend, and yet she could not walk beside him in his grief.

She had sent him away to find Paul.

❖

Jean Toupin met with the factor, went about his work a day or two, always thinking of the woman. At last he gathered courage to wait outside the lodge for Madame Dorion. He wouldn't bring up his transaction. Not now. This was a woman who needed staking; she needed a strong presence to hold her up. Not a stake so rigidly attached that the plant risked being pulled from its roots nor tied so loosely it couldn't raise its head to sunshine. Just one willing to be there, standing beside.

He passed by the tent of the girl, Josette, who helped her mother with washing now. He sucked on his pipe, let the smoke drift around his face. *Should I even be at Madame Dorion's lodge?*

"Have you seen Lune?" The small hand tugged at his corduroy.

"Who is Lune?" Jean asked. He looked down. Marguerite, that was the girl's name.

"My papa's dog. He hasn't come home," she said. "My papa neither."

Jean nodded. "It's hard to wait for someone you love, isn't it?"

Marguerite nodded. "See my shoes?"

"They're very *bon*," Jean said.

"They're warm too," Marguerite told him. "We have a new baby," she said.

"How do you like that?"

"It's like having a lion."

"A mountain lion?" The child nodded. "You've seen one?"

"I walk and it follows me," she said. "It lays down to sleep and I find my *mère*."

"Tell me how that baby's like a lion," Jean said, intrigued.

"When it sleeps it's soft and I pet it. But then it wakes up and it makes howl sounds and then they put her next to *my* mat and it cries louder, and I don't know if she'll ever stop crying." She caught her breath. "It'd be better if I didn't wake it."

"Sometimes it is better to let lions sleep," Jean said. "Even baby ones." She nodded and placed her hand in his.

"Let's go see if we can help your mama with her lion."

❖

Marie hovered over the infant. She had to keep her alive, give everything she could to make sure this infant did not die.

She put warm rocks inside cloth and centered the baby between them inside a willow basket. She had no hair. No fingernails. As fragile as a butterfly. The baby's skin coloring had become the color of old leather, getting lighter as it took in breath. She had been nearly black and blue at birth. Her tiny navel twisted dark like the twirl of a melon plant. When it turned black, it meant the melon was ripe. Maybe it would mean Little Marie would live, had ripened enough to survive.

Little Marie. Marie could hardly call her by that name. But Jean Toupin did, as soon as he came into the hut. "Little Marie," he said. He didn't lean too close as some might; he didn't put his face to the baby's to breathe her air. He didn't put his hand where fleas might jump and bite. He just said her name with a softness that made the baby pull her fingers to her face. He made her real and not just a tiny offshoot of her mother.

"Little Marie is in good hands," he told her.

"I'm no *sage femme,* even though the infant lives. A wise woman would have found a way to save the mother's life too."

"It isn't ours to give life or take it away," he said. "We have the privilege of creating, but then we are set off, all parents are set off. Even grandparents. We get put aside, and what we love goes another way. We walk with them for a time, but," he shrugged his shoulders, "a good parent knows our children walk on alone."

"You are a father," Marie said.

Jean shook his head. "A brother of many. But, like Baptiste, I'm the eldest. We watch our elders more closely, compare ourselves with them for the time when we have no little brothers or sisters to watch. We learn new things. We always fall short, *n'est-ce pas?*"

She certainly fell short. If giving to her children was her *métier,* then she had yet so much to learn.

"Why does your arm swing funny?" Marguerite asked Jean.

Jean rolled his shoulder. "Got myself tangled up with a horse," he said. "Won a good race though. Just lost the usual use of this arm."

"Does it hurt?" the girl asked.

"Not much. Restricts me some."

Marguerite said, "Mama, where's Lune?"

Marie's eyes pooled. She'd forgotten about the dog. "He's... I... Behind..." She looked at Jean as though her eyes might tell him, might beg him to find an answer for this child. She had nothing more to give.

The baby made a squealing sound, and Marie peered at her more closely. Would this child live? Marie had to do all she could to make it so. Someday, Baptiste would want his daughter. Someday, he might forgive his mother for what she'd done, making him go away when he was needed most. She had to keep this child alive. Wasn't that what a mother was, a bridge over which her children traveled from pain and disappointment onto joy and love?

Jean Toupin had been talking. She hadn't heard him. *"Pardon?"* she said.

He shook his head as if to say, no matter.

He scanned the lodge, stopped as his gaze landed on a single china cup.

"You wish tea," she said. "I've forgotten to offer—"

"No. I'd like to fix you tea," he told her. "I'm good with food. And I'm good…" he raised his chin toward Marguerite "at disposing of… problems." He nodded in the direction Marie'd looked when she tried to talk about the dog. "If you'd let me help."

He found the water basket, dropped the hot rocks from the fire into it and poured the water into the single cup. He dropped the tea leaves in and handed it to Marie. "Sit," he said. "You drink."

And Marie did, sinking into a sigh of wonder as her hands warmed around a cup offered in kindness.

❖

"There's a letter for you, Marie." Sally fluttered the parchment with the wax seal, fanning herself after her rush up the path from the fort to Marie's lodge. "The Indian runner brought it. And he told Mister Ross it was all paid up. At the other end."

Marie furrowed her brows. She held a tiny paintbrush in one hand, a paper of vermilion in the other. Painting the tiny pictures on one side of the flap had been a way of easing the emptiness of these past months. She'd just finished outlining a small circle that would become the sun. She'd begun in the center of an imaginary circle, the way she remembered her mother-in-law, Holy Rainbow, telling her calendars of the Sioux were kept.

The year of her beginning was a block of whitish gray, of snow, to represent the Ioway people known as gray-snow people and how her heart had been icy cold with the dying of her mother and her sister.

"You'll run out of room with all you want to paint," Sally said, pointing with the letter.

"Is it from Paul?" Marie tried not to sound too hopeful, but she couldn't imagine anyone else who might write to her. But how would Paul get money to pay the various Indian runners that Mackenzie had trained to deliver "talking paper" from place to place? She'd always thought it odd that Company men needed ammunition and many men to move through Indian country safely, but little pieces of paper, that often carried more weight with their words, could ride through with only a single rider to protect them.

"It doesn't say where or who it's from," Sally said. "Just has your name on it."

"Oh." If Paul had gone back to the Okanogan or even east to the Missouri River country of his father, no message would come by an Indian runner. It would come by brigade, down from the north.

"Shall I read it?"

Marie hesitated. Who else could she ask to read it? And would Sally keep it to herself, that what was inside was only for her eyes and ears? Marie's mother had gotten a letter once, long years ago. She remembered that one of the Black Robes had come to read it, one of the priests, and her mother had wept.

Her mother cried often after that letter, wiped her eyes as she worked clay, leaving little bits of red on her cheeks. She told her daughters that the tears kept the mud moist and would make the pot strong.

She couldn't remember ever seeing her father after that letter arrived.

"You always take so long to answer, Marie," Sally said. "I purposefully speak in English to give you practice, but perhaps I should have asked in French. *N'est-ce pas?*"

"I've never had a letter sent to me," Marie said. "I don't know the custom for such things. Will what you read stay—"

Sally clucked her tongue. "The one who reads is like a riverbed, Marie. She just holds the words but lets the meaning flow through. I'll not say a word about whatever is in here. It might be good news. From Paul, maybe. You could use good news."

Marie nodded. Baptiste's baby cried, and Marie unwound her legs to attend to the child. She lifted Little Marie from the blanket and bounced her at her breast. "Marguerite, find some dry moss, please?"

Marguerite stepped on tiptoes that pushed out through the slippers, reached for the basket holding the moss. Marie laid the infant down on soft furs and swabbed the baby's bottom. She was aware of

Sally's impatience, but Little Marie must come first. When the baby was cleaned and wrapped in dry moss, Marguerite motioned to be allowed to hold her. "Sit," Marie told her, then handed her the child.

"Baptiste grieves still," Sally said. It wasn't a question, just a statement.

Marie nodded. "I was wrong in thinking he didn't know the meaning of his marriage vows or that he took them too lightly. He took them to his heart." She patted at her chest with her fingers.

"Older Sister was a sweet thing," Sally said. She sighed. "And you were good to her."

"Not long enough," Marie said. "I should have died. She had a new life ahead."

"You have Marguerite to tend to," Sally told her. "And now a grandchild, too."

"Older Sister's mother claims her soon," Marie said. "But she lacks the strength from weeping over her daughter."

Little Marie had gained good weight on the goat's milk in the past several months. She'd have done better with cow's milk, but that was not to be. They'd survived the winter. At this time of spring root digging, Marie knew that soon the grandmother would come for the baby, not as a replacement of the child she lost, but as a way of keeping Older Sister alive in her heart.

Marie would let her go freely, almost with relief that she could safely deliver a child to the hands of those who would love her. Grief followed Marie, sat itself on her hearth, refused to be swept away. Sometimes Marie wondered if even Marguerite was safe in her presence.

But then she'd see Baptiste carrying wood for his mother-in-law's fire or bringing in a deer for their meal, and she'd recognize a young man who harbored hate in his heart for her, but who had done the right thing for his wife's family. So despite the trials his mother had put him through, he'd taken on the role of a son-in-law with tolerance if not warmth. Once the baby was with him, Marie and Marguerite would survive alone.

"Shall I open it?" Sally pushed the letter toward her. Marie looked at Sally and nodded. *"Bon,"* Sally said. "Maybe it will be the start of a correspondence and you'll try again to learn to read. You could, Marie. I just know you could. You're wise enough."

"My eyes," Marie said. She motioned Sally toward the letter and away from trying to convince Marie.

Sally slipped her finger the color of cocoa under the orange wax seal and lifted the letter flap. "We should read who it's from first," Sally said. "That will change the meaning of the words, knowing who says them."

"No. Read from the beginning," Marie said. She returned to her painting of the sun. She would paint a river flowing through it to mark the rivers of her life, the Des Moines, the Mississippi, the Missouri, the Snake, Okanogan, and the Columbia. She'd add the Walla Walla last, for it was along that river she was rescued and her boys were saved. Blue often faded into the leather. She wondered what she might add to the mashed berries to keep the stain vibrant.

Sally shrugged, took a deep breath, read silently.

"Are there no words?" Marie asked.

"I'm practicing. I don't read as swiftly as Mr. Ross." Sally cleared her throat. "It's from Monsieur Jean Toupin." Marie frowned at her. "He says this one comes in the dispatch from Fort George East. *'Later, I will come myself, when the Company permits it. I write to tell you that I have assumed your debt. A separate letter goes to Mister Ross to read the ledger and send me the account so I can transfer into yours what is needed.'* He writes with a fine goose pen. All the letters are even," Sally noted. "Mister Ross says this is a sign of patience and good breeding. I try to get my letters even but—"

Marie raised her hand to stop Sally's flow of chatter.

"'Please consider it a gift for those months you gave care to me as one of Hunt's party. I wished to discuss this with you when last we met, but other matters pressed. There is no requirement except receiving. Nothing more.'" Sally said, "Oh, Marie. Now you can send Marguerite back to school with Jemima. Your beadwork won't go just to repay your husband's old debt."

"The beadwork was not just for that obligation," Marie said. "It is a joy I have to make such things that feed my children. They bring trade for seed. For clothing. For horses. I make gains despite lowering what I owe. I get it done myself. It is what I do, what any mother would do when her husband has died."

"Yes, but you see? His generosity frees you. How wonderful. I didn't even notice him when he was here. Was he the tall one? What would move a man's heart to do such a thing?"

"I don't need his generosity. And there will be more; it is not a complete gift. No rose grows without a thorn."

"But they have lovely fragrances, those roses. Mr. Ross gives gifts without expecting anything back, just to enjoy the aroma of overflowing. Don't you do things for your children without hoping for a repayment?"

Marie said. "I only know that in this world, all good things are followed by bad and to accept the gift of the seed means the winnowing must happen."

"You won't have to work so hard."

"My work is who I am," Marie said.

"'*There is no requirement except receiving,*'" Sally repeated. "See. It's a gift. Without any repayment." Sally pointed to words that just ran together in Marie's eyes.

Marie shook her head. She laid the red paint down, and with the side of her knife, she swirled the thickness to add texture to the center of the sun.

"At least let me finish," Sally said. "He says, '*No requirement except receiving. But it is also my fervent hope that you consider this letter as an invitation to start anew. For I see you not as a woman to whom my mother extends gratitude for your care of her son during a long, hard journey across the continent. I see you not as a mother with a son she has raised and with a boy and a daughter still growing, but as a woman whose company I find rest in. When next we meet, I would discuss these issues further, taking them to conclusion.*'"

Sally reread the last words to herself, her lips moving as a woman in prayer. "Why, it's a marriage proposal," she said, looking at Marie.

Marie said nothing, just painted. It would be best to not think of what he'd written. She should just paint, let Sally be excited until she went away. Then Marie could consider alone what he had done.

"It's cause for celebration. This generous man wants you to become his wife. I'm sure of it. What will you say? This is *bon, n'est-ce pas?*"

"It's as I told you," Marie said. "There are always thorns on roses."

"But that doesn't mean you'll get poked when you receive one, Marie."

Marie grunted.

On a piece of old torn hide, she wiped the paint from the knife blade, then picked up the black color to circle it, to make the sun stand out against the hide. Even while she painted she had to agree that the presence of dark dye outlining a shape always made the inner, lighter color stand out. Were the tragedies of her life simply dark outlines against her brighter spirit? Were the dark times defining lines that helped her know what she was made of, what lay in her center?

Perhaps Jean Toupin had seen something of her center, of the fire that burned within. Now he offered a way to free her up, as Sally said. To be free of the debt meant she could move toward things that mattered instead of seeking freedom from what had held her hostage. But what did move her forward if not the debt? Her sons were separated from her. Little Marie would soon be gone. If she gave too much to Marguerite, that child might end up pained as her older brothers were. *Can I live with the uncertainty of being freed of such a debt?*

"I can hardly wait to tell Mr. Ross. What will you tell Monsieur Toupin, Marie? He'd surely want an answering post."

"There is always a price," Marie said. She knew this. If she accepted his generosity, pain would follow. It was the defining line of her life.

❖

Baptiste raced the horse full speed, liking the feel of the wind on his face, the movement against his legs as the horse grabbed at the steep bank, lunged up the hill into the Blue Mountains. Baptiste could smell the sweat, could almost sense the horse's desire to take him where he wanted to go even though the rocks spilled down around his legs and the hard earth offered little to push the journey forward. When he felt only the hardness of the dry ground as the horse's hooves struck the earth, his mind took him to a different place. When he tasted blood on his lip where he gripped his mouth, in that taste and ache of physical pain he could forget the aching of his heart.

It had been seven months since the death of Older Sister. Seven months since he'd felt the sting of words sent by his mother telling him she was dead.

At least he hadn't had to look at the face of his child much since then. His mother had seen to that by keeping her in her lodge. When Baptiste saw the infant out with his mother, he made himself scarce. Older Sister's family always needed help, wood brought to them, stakes set around a garden plot. Anything to get him away from his mother. His leaving to help Older Sister's mother was natural. His own mother couldn't condemn him for not being there for her.

He knew that would be changing soon. His mother-in-law, a woman he spent little time talking with as was the custom, wanted the infant for her own now, in the lodge where Baptiste had moved to help his wife's family. And Baptiste would let that happen. He'd let the women decide such things.

The baby especially made his stomach ache. People said she was a pretty baby, his daughter. He could only see that she had been too willing to come into life and so had taken her mother's.

"Hold up!" He got the shout from the rear, from Older Sister's uncle, Narcisse.

Baptiste and his horse reached the shady place near the top of the ridge. He pulled up, dust settling in puffs around his horse's legs. The horse blew hard, then shook its head. Baptiste let it move out of the shade toward the tall grass.

While he waited for Narcisse, he pushed his hair back behind his ears. The thin strands never tangled, not even in the wind. He wore them loose, free, not tied the way some mixed bloods did, not cut off the way Tom McKay wore his, like a white man's hair. Baptiste's hair said who he was, and he was the son of a Sioux father and an Ioway mother. The Company men could just accept that about him or stuff it in their vest pouch.

His mother had always worried too much about what would happen to him, where he'd fit in, if he would at all. All those reading days he'd sat listening to Ross read Scripture. All those days his mother had insisted he learn of church ways had meant little to him. They'd comforted Older Sister. But they hadn't saved her from dying too young.

His mother spoke of a changing world he needed to be ready for. Baptiste laughed. There was no getting ready for anything. Hadn't the last seven months told him that?

He and Older Sister planned a life together. His grandmother, Holy Rainbow, would have wanted his wife baptized, the children too, if there had been a priest. Even his mother faltered at the thought. He never could understand that about her, the way she stiffened at religious talk. She'd said she'd prayed for their safety that time in the mountains so long ago. He'd heard her breathe French words to God when they escaped after his father's death, so why was she reluctant about such things? Maybe it was a woman's way. Maybe if Older Sister had lived, she'd have walked him through the tangles of beliefs.

Older Sister had been willing. They'd spoken of such things. His mother might have thought he talked only with his passion for the girl, but he'd wanted to bring joy to Older Sister's eyes in many ways, not just when they shared a robe. He'd promised her he'd be a good provider, a protector, a loving husband. He'd watched his own father change over time. His father found a resting swale in an otherwise rolling landscape of his life. Louis Venier, his mother's second choice of a husband, had been a good man who'd never raised a fist to him, never spoken with cross words. Baptiste missed Louis, something he'd never tell his mother. She'd think him weak if he did. But he'd shared his missing of the man with Older Sister. He'd promised her he'd be a gentle father.

Older Sister and he had held their own ceremony before making the decision to join together, a ceremony he would have had a priest perform before he ever touched Older Sister as a wife. But there'd been no priest.

There'd been no priest when Older Sister died, either. And somehow, Baptiste felt the weight of that upon his own shoulders, a failure as sure as if he'd left his young wife unprotected.

Maybe it was punishment. Perhaps they'd been meant to wait to form the marriage tie. But he'd insisted. Maybe her death so young was brought on by his own impatience to love her, to begin a family of his own. He wiped his face with his hands, shook his head. No, his mother never should have sent him after Paul. He would have been there, might have saved his wife. And now that baby reminded him each day of what he'd done by doing his mother's bidding.

Narcisse rode up, took his felt hat from his head, and wiped his forehead of the dirt and sweat. They'd come to ride the perimeter of where they'd burn the grasses. For years here, Narcisse had told him, the Cayuse and Nez Perce torched the ground of dry grass so the deer would have fresh sprouts in the spring and so their hunting in the fall would be successful. So many fires burned that from a distance the air around the tamarack- and fir-dotted mountains wore a hazy color the Company's Scotsmen called blue. They'd even changed the mountain's name to it. That was just like the Europeans, always naming something the way they saw fit, as though the name given by the people who'd lived there longest had not been offered up in love. "The Cayuse only name what they love," Narcisse told him.

This trip to the Blues had two purposes: to mark the spring burn area and to hunt, to bring back venison or elk. The two men would use their weapons even though the Company refused to trade ammunition and guns with Indians. Even Tom McKay had not been allowed to trade for a weapon but had been allowed the "use" of a rifle from the Company warehouse. Narcisse, as a French-Canadian, had one. And since the guns had been left behind when his father died at the time of their breathless escape, Baptiste had Louis's, though he'd heard rumblings that the Company worried over a mixed-blood having such a weapon.

His mother had once had a gun. He'd seen her shoot a deer or two when they wintered on the Willamette River long years ago. Since then, she'd never had the wampum, the currency, to barter for another, even if she'd known a source. So he'd done without—until Louis's death, instead learning to use his bow with skill to help his wife's family and his mother's. He was surprised Paul hadn't taken the weapon with him.

Narcisse put his hat back on. "We'll ride together. That way." He pointed. "You ride too fast and hard, Baptiste. Think of the horse."

When Baptiste didn't answer, Narcisse turned in his saddle and stretched his arm to the south. "That way," he said.

Baptiste's eye scanned the area, then looked back. He frowned, stared at Narcisse's *par flèche*. "You carry something new," Baptiste said.

Narcisse nodded. "I traded pelts with the Russian American Fur Company. They're willing to trade for weapons," Narcisse said. "And they gave four times what the Hudson's Bay Company offered for made beaver."

"Four times?"

Narcisse pulled the rifle out and handed it to Baptiste. "Good weight," Baptiste said, turning it in his hands.

"We'll bring in plenty this time," Narcisse said. He hesitated then, "You take it." He pushed back the gun Baptiste attempted to return. "Maybe you'll not push your horse so hard if you have a new thing to think of."

"Russian American Company," Baptiste said, lifting the rifle to his shoulder, looking down the sight.

"Aha." Narcisse nodded.

"They trade rifles and ammunition. Even to Indians."

"Aha." Narcisse nodded.

"Forbidden Company trades," Baptiste said, lowering the stock from his shoulder. He looked at Narcisse. "They will also trade liquor then."

Narcisse looked aside. "Not something a good man plans for," he said.

"I've never claimed to be a good man," Baptiste said. "If I can get enough beaver trapped this winter, I'll plan all right. To soak my sorrow instead of hoping my horse will ride me through it."

14

The Silent Speaking of Stones

Jean Toupin anticipated. He had a new adventure awaiting him, and it wasn't just related to the woman. John Work, said to be not much older than Jean's thirty plus years, was sent from York country to the Columbia country in the spring of 1823. He'd actually joined the Company at nearly the same time as Jean, that was what Jean'd been told. But Work had risen through the Company ranks to clerk status while Jean was still merely an interpreter. Horseman. Hunter. *Voyageur*. Cook. Even hog hound and milkmaid could be added to his various roles as he'd been dispatched more than once to the farms in service to the Company. Fort Langley, north, and Fort George had the cattle exclusive.

But John Work was of Scotch-Irish descent, while Jean was French-Canadian, and therein lay the distinguishing difference for advancement, or so Jean told himself.

Jean had pushed for change, for some months. He'd finally secured permission from Fort George's chief factor to return to Fort Walla Walla. Jean didn't think the decision came from any persuasiveness on his part but on the arbitrariness of Company movements of materials and men. A brigade taking supplies to the interior forts would be sent off, later in the year, but the ship had just recently left its cargo. He was to meet John Work at Walla Walla and take direction from him.

The brigade headed east. Jean went with it.

At least being at Fort Walla Walla would give him time to see if Madame Dorion—what was he to call her?—had received one of his letters, to see if she had accepted his transfer of accounts, to see if she was still there and willing to at least talk.

After he'd sent the parchments, he'd wished a dozen times he'd pulled them back.

"You decide these letters should be sent after much prayer and provocation. It was a good decision, then," Michel assured him. "The decision, it stretches like an old sash worn over time, but it still fits when you tie it tight around you, *oui?* It still holds you up."

Jean agreed, though at times he wished he hadn't told Michel of what he'd done or said related to the woman. But Michel had a reputation with the ladies, and Jean needed both his wisdom and experience.

When he'd first told him, Michel had clapped him on his back, had raised his voice in song and made Jean's cheeks hot. But his enthusiasm had given Jean's boldness hope. "So you think it is all right, what I've done?"

"Even if she does not have you, it is a good gift to give someone, to free them of obligations not of their making. If she does not see this, it will be sad. It will mean she is not as wise as I think she must be to have survived with her sons as you say."

"Might be wise enough to turn me down as a suitor," Jean said.

"Ah, love," Michel told him. He clasped his hands over his heart like a lovesick girl. "It takes on the faces of a sad dog, a happy, panting one, a barking, annoying scamp, but it never loses its face. Even when love looks to disappear, it doesn't really go away. It forms new. You had a different love for these woman those years ago. Now…" He lifted his arms to the sky. "All the world is yours, these is true, *oui?* She was a friend first. These is a wonderful thing between a man and a woman, to have a friend to fall into love with."

"She may not see it that way. She's made no effort to send a letter back."

"She is shy, perhaps."

They'd been assigned to slop the hogs, and Jean stepped aside now to avoid the largest pig mistaking his foot for the pile of salmon skins and the mix of old molded cornmeal.

"You must have courage, my friend, courage." Michel laughed as though the status of Jean's heart was a thing to be made light of. But then he quieted. "Very, very smart often stands right next to very, very *stupide,* my friend. They pass into each other the way a stream comes into the river. But a man does not know if he is next to very smart or very *stupide* unless he has the courage to be there to feel the river push against his legs."

Michel had told LaBonte of Jean's letter-sending and later lament, and then even Kilakotah had patted his hand one day and made the sign for love, which was fondness signed with greater force. She crossed both hands across her heart, fists softly closed. "Love," she said, her voice high and breathy.

Jean sat on a log chipping at a block of wood, carving it into something, he didn't know what. Sometimes he waited to see what the block of wood told him as he held it in his hand, waiting for the image he was to form. Other times, the wood chips flew from the object, forming little amber snippets that stuck in the ridges of his corduroy. He pretended not to know what she meant, but she patted his shoulder again and made the sign for *long time* with her two hands passing each other like boats on calm water. "Ma-rie," she said, making it two words rather than one. "Long time."

"You two are friends?" he'd said, looking up at her.

He signed something to her, and she shook her head. "I only know *love* and *long time*." He remembered that she knew Chinookan more than signs, and he practiced using that language with her now. He'd wanted to appear annoyed, and yet her presence did comfort him, she and her gentle son who hovered close to her skirts.

Later when he'd gotten the news from the factor about his returning to Walla Walla, it was Kilakotah he'd told first.

"You bring her back to this place?" she said in Chinookan.

"Too far ahead for me to plan," he said. It was the best answer he could give her.

Finally, in the fall of 1823, nearly a year since he'd left Fort Walla Walla, well over six months from when he'd sent the last letter, he was headed back, taking boatloads of hawk's bells and knifes, bolts of cloth and metal spoons for trade; and sets of china and stuffed pillows for the factor's quarters. He was to stop at Fort Walla Walla and remain there until Work arrived. Once that happened, Work would decide Jean's fate if the woman hadn't already decided it.

As they made their way along the Columbia River, it struck Jean that he had never headed east along this river before. It took on a new perspective, traveling upriver instead of down. He often rode, but sometimes, he acted as the *milieu* again. He poled and pulled, but he also couldn't see the sand or gravel bars that stabbed the river like wounds until it was too late. That obligation rested with the other boat positions, so Jean could scan the landscape without guilt. He looked for the spot McKay spoke of, not far from the mouth of the wide river entering from the south. It was a good site for a fort, let alone a farm, as McKay planned. And the river itself, the Willamette, the Hudson's Bay people now called it, must drain a mighty area to be so wide here, run so thick with fish and water clear as tears.

At the place where water cascaded down a five-mile-long chute between black boulders where Wish-ram and Wasco Indians stood on platforms to spear and then net huge fish, the men portaged. It took fifteen men to carry even one of the heavy cedar-bark canoes, empty. They completed the portage without trouble, losing neither man nor material, and paddled on, giving Jean ample time to wade deeper into worry.

At the mouth of another river, one of the men shouted, "John Day's River." Jean remembered the Virginia hunter who had traveled with Hunt. "He went crazy," the *voyageur* said. "Indians found him here and brought him back to Fort George all weepy, they say, and out of his thinking."

"This is where they found him?" Jean asked. He looked at the meandering river blending a darker stream into the Columbia at its mouth.

"Weak American," the *voyageur* finished.

They made camp then, at the base of high ridges dribbled with reddish rocks and sparse grasses. Old yellowed flowers growing close to the earth dotted the cracks. Jean could actually see the heat coming off the rim rocks, as the days were warm even though the nights cooled as expected for October. The ridges resembled layer cakes dribbled with dark crumbs. He'd come through here in January with Hunt's party, and the rocks had been dusted with snow. Now they were burnt brown by the sun and rare rains. John Day's River. Day was a good man to have his name attached to a big body of water such as they camped beside.

Even if he had lost his mind. Lesser men would've gone insane much sooner.

The *voyageurs* prepared the evening meal of cold pea purée, hard-boiled eggs, and cheek bread made of two rounded loaves crusted together. After the work of portaging and paddling, each *engagé* also received a glob of butter to spread on their bread. A real treat. Later, Jean walked the sandy shoreline that licked the slow and meandering stream. He picked up small pieces of driftwood. No trees marked the hillsides, so he knew they must have been nearing Fort Walla Walla. Or this region shared a similar landscape, so different from Fort George's.

Smooth rocks with rainbows of color swirled through them interested him. He bent to lift one. How did the layers of red slip in between the halves of gray? It looked like a piece of bacon stuck between crusts of biscuits. What brought these two chunks of rock together and melded them so tight they became one, were one? Like a parent to a child, they were joined.

No. Children separated in time. More like a husband to a wife, two separate parts somehow brought together, never to be separated in the eyes of God. Except by death.

That was what he was hoping for with this woman. What could meld this woman, someone he so admired, to him? Was such a joining even possible? He bounced the rock in the palm of his hand.

Probably not.

Without Michel around to remind him of what he hoped for, that wanting something good and being generous were worthy efforts regardless of how they turned out, without his friends to keep his thinking clear, his mind took off on a journey of its own.

"Life and death are part of the same river, Jean," Michel would tell him. "So we must live fully, as God intended, until we die, not wait until we are ready to die before we begin to live. God is the river; we are the riverbeds he flows through. She will have you. She will kneel at the riverbank with you. I have faith if you do not."

"She might see my paying her expenses and asking for marriage as a trade," Jean said.

"You will have to clarify these. When you see her," Michel said.

"Sometimes what we do is interpreted in different ways than we intend, *oui?* These happens between us and God too. So we ask for help to understand. You tell her these thing."

Jean put the rock that was half gray and half charcoal with a layer of red stone between them into his pouch. He pulled the leather thongs to tie it shut and strapped it around his chest. He put his most precious things in that little bag. He'd remember he picked that stone up at John Day's river and that it told him that two could become one if they understood each other, if they were joined by something strong.

Jean thought later, as he stared up at the dizzying array of stars, that he should have contradicted the *voyageur's* judgment of John Day. Jean heard coyotes howl in the distance, and when the breeze rustled dried plants, he reminded himself that was what it was and not some rattlesnake come calling. It was too cold at night for them to be crawling about. There were dangers here, but tonight the snakes weren't one of them. John Day may have been just one of a thousand men who would come west, make only a small mark, and then die. But he hadn't been weak, and Day shouldn't be forgotten. A man never knew what challenge God might hand over in the dead of winter after a starvation journey of two thousand miles. Even a French-Canadian might falter if the conditions were right.

Here he was on a voyage—again—of almost that many miles, coming down from Spokane House, arriving at the ocean, and now back east toward Walla Walla. He hoped he wouldn't falter. He wasn't starving now, that was sure. In fact, he'd grown an inch or so. He was almost too tall for the *milieu* spot. Didn't think a man could keep growing past the time he gained suspenders, but the ready eggs and milk and cheese from Fort George's farm had served him well. He'd appear different to Madame Dorion…the woman…than he had the year before. He had to discover what to call her.

❖

"Mister Ross is quite intrigued," Sally told her. "No, I didn't say a thing about it. Mister Ross raised the subject." Sally stitched on a quilt piece while Marie melted deer tallow she would pour into tin forms for candles. Beef tallow would have made much better candles, but they had none and wouldn't for years. The Company's cows hadn't reached six hundred yet. At least some of the forts now had oxen to help with plowing, but milk cows remained harbored at the coastal fort.

"I suggested that it must have been as a result of Monsieur Toupin's sharing Hunt's journey with you. And your husband," Sally said.

Marie felt her face redden.

"My, I think it's a wonderful gift. Wonderful."

It was not embarrassment but shame Marie felt, for receiving something so undeserved. Sally told Marie the debt had been paid, her account wiped clean. The weight of the gift bore down on her as though she carried a rock in the flat wallet worn at her waist. Not as heavy as the weight of what she carried in her heart about Paul, about Older Sister, about Baptiste's distance, about all the gifts she received and then lost, but still heavy just the same.

"This tallow doesn't melt well," Marie said, her voice irritated even to her own ears.

"You don't have to raise your voice," Sally said. "I'll be silent."

Marie wasn't sure why Sally's chatter sometimes grated on her like pebbles in her moccasins. Or maybe it was Jean's latest letter, saying he'd be back soon and had further matters to discuss. She carried worries as stones and couldn't sort out the wonderful gifts from those that felt like cost.

She'd found a way this past year to push life's sadness into a ball that sat in her stomach. It was there, but she could live with it, push it around just a bit when it became troublesome. Until Jean Toupin's letters arrived for Sally's readings. Then anticipation pushed heavily against her solid ball of sadness.

Marie had accumulated extra food she didn't need. She had enough to keep her and Marguerite well fed. Even when she extended some to Older Sister's family, she had food left over. She couldn't remember when that had happened before, when she'd had enough to give away.

And the beadwork that she took in trade at the Company store allowed new purchases instead of lowering her debt. Cloth. She could make her daughter a cloth dress. She'd purchased tanned leather from back East, cowhide leather. She took Marguerite's little shoes apart and used them as a pattern for a new pair, one much larger. She stuffed the toes with moss, hoping they might last a year or more before the child's toes pushed out to the air.

After Josette came to claim Little Marie for her mother, Marie soothed her grief by making forays, asking after Paul. She even paid for letters to go to clerks at forts in Athabasca, Langley, and farther east, asking, always asking if anyone had heard of Paul. She answered Marguerite's question about Paul and Baptiste and Little Marie as best she could. Separations had no good explanations.

Once, while they traveled out, she even asked if someone might have seen Louis Venier. She knew he was dead, but if he wasn't, if he'd been taken captive, he might have been like John Day, lost in his mind for a time, but wandering still.

Nothing. No word on either of those losses. No confirmation that her husband died; none that her son still lived.

Through it all, Marie kept an accounting of the gift. Jean Toupin might change his mind and want the gift returned. She wanted a fair ledger for him when he came.

At night, when she pulled the old buffalo robe up over her and Marguerite, and she listened to her daughter's soft sleeping sounds, she would sometimes allow herself to feel the awe of being free from the debt, of having more than she needed, of no longer wanting. Then she'd quickly push away the sigh of satisfaction arising from such unearned wealth. It wasn't right to experience joy when her son was missing, when two husbands had died, when an eldest son grieved the passing of his wife, when someone else had paid her way. She'd remember the words of Jean Toupin's letter then, and the weight of the stone would shift in her basket. Familiar, warm, tender, and undeserved.

She'd been told as a young girl that she was strong. Even as an adult once or twice men had marveled at the way she could lift a saddle to a horse's back with one hand or carry a bale of furs on her shoulders at least for a short distance from the *bateau* to the warehouse without breathing deep. The old trappers who prided themselves on their strength would watch, move the lump of tobacco from their lip to their cheeks so they could talk, and say, "Will you take a gawk at that one? Pack more than my hinny, the woman does."

They usually thought she couldn't understand them, maybe that she was deaf since she never made an indication that she heard. An Indian woman learned early to pretend she hadn't heard the insults spat her way. She hadn't appreciated being compared to a pack mule. She'd told Sarah of the trapper's words.

"He was marveling at your strength," Sarah had told her. "You could take it as a slap or as a…salute."

After that, she'd seen that, yes, she was strong physically. But outer strength had nothing to do with what was inside where her strength felt no greater than a feather drifting in breeze.

"What will you do when he comes to claim you?" Sally asked.

"What? I didn't agree to *à la façon du pays*."

"He said they weren't related, that you needn't marry him. Do you want me to reread the last letter?"

Marie shook her head. She remembered it, word for word. She just couldn't believe it. "Too much I've wished for and the wishes get washed away in the middle of the trail."

"We need to keep hoping for things, don't you think?" Sally said.

"Beef tallow for candles, then. Wish for that," Marie said.

❖

Marie watched a harvest moon rise over the bare hills, washing out the starlight. Big geese that flew in formation the way a mallard family breaks the water made calling sounds as they rested on the river. In the daytime, they flew thick as flies in the skies, never faltering despite winds that buffeted the bluffs swirling up whirlwinds of dust.

Though it was late in the night, the winds still howled, hitting the lodge in sharp whacks like slaps of an angry man's hand.

Marie heard Janey stomp in the corral, her colt at her side. Until weaned, she remained with Marie, but soon the stud colt would be led over to Older Sister's family. It was as it should be, another debt paid. Another blast struck, followed by the puffing out of the tent as air seeped under the ridgepoles. Embers perked at the center fire that lit the interior like a soft sunrise. Marie smelled rain in the air but couldn't hear anything pelting the leather tipi except soft sand blown by the wind.

Janey whinnied then, as though to a familiar horse. Could it be Paul, after all this time? Over a year? Marie sat up, knelt at the tent flap. What would she say to him? Could she tell him about all the nights she'd lain awake wondering if he was dead or alive? Did he think her so heartless she wouldn't miss him, his presence, wouldn't wonder what had happened? Her mind churned a hundred possibilities.

Sometimes, she imagined Paul being taken in by a friendly family, Shoshone or Umatilla. At the fort, she'd watch to see if any of the riders looked as she imagined him a year older. And once, she was sure she'd seen his narrow frame racing across the hillside in the distance. When she mounted Janey and headed after him, dogs barking at their heels, the boy turned and she saw the surprise, the fear, in the child's eyes. It hadn't been Paul.

But if Paul were just outside now, she'd welcome him, open her arms, bring him back into the fold. How many times she'd imagined it, hoped for it. She knew what leaving someone behind meant, and what it was like to be left behind.

Paul should know she'd only wanted the best for him, had been worried about him. Angry at first, yes, then saddened, a grief so deep she sometimes couldn't take in breath.

Baptiste would welcome him, too, wouldn't he? Now that she thought of it, her elder son rarely spoke of his brother. But he had his own loss to live with, his own rocks to carry with Little Marie growing up without a mother. Josette, Older Sister's younger sister, carried the baby about as though she were her own, but Josette was young, that child, and more like a sister to the baby than a mother.

Yes, if it was Paul, she would open the flap; she'd cry an Ioway greeting song and widen her arms to him, welcome him in, all forgiven. She closed her eyes and, without thinking, sent an arrow prayer, up high to meet a target. *Let it be my son. Let it be my son.* She drew back the flap and looked out into the night.

"Paul?"

"Mister Ross is going without me," Sally said, stumbling through the tent flap, the wind whipping her skirts. Marie's fingers felt the thick paint of the design she'd painted onto the tent. She pulled the flap shut, tied the string. "He won't let me go," Sally sniffled. " 'Tis for men and women who'll work the hides and handle the furs, he says." Sally wiped at her eyes with an lace-edged handkerchief. She huddled near the fire, her teeth chattering. "He acts as though I don't know how to do such things."

"You have experience."

"He doesn't think so." Her eyes pooled. "Too hard work, he says. My hands will get blistered and all the glycerin will be 'for naught,' he says." She hugged herself, rubbing her arms, the blanket around her acting as a shawl.

"You'll be needed here. You run things," Marie said. "He knows this."

"There'll be a new factor. He'll bring his own wife." She picked at a piece of lint on her cloth skirt, straightened the high waist that fit tightly just beneath her breasts. White women's clothes looked good on Sally's slender frame.

"He doesn't want to remind the men of my…Okanogan family."

"You are Okanogan."

"I don't deny it," Sally said. She sat up straighter.

"The new chief factor, Thomas McKay's stepfather, he has an Indian wife," Marie said.

"Does he?" She sniffed, wiped at her nose. "I didn't know that. I should have. How is it you do?"

Marie shrugged. "McKay was at Astoria. A young boy, when I was there."

"As Toupin was. Have you decided what you'll do yet?" Sally asked.

Marie shook her head. She poked at the fire. "You wish something warm?"

Sally looked around. "I haven't ever been here, not since Older Sister—"

"I have elderberry tea."

Sally nodded, wiped at her nose again. "I don't want to be left here while he's off for six or seven months. The Company sends him as though he were a horse." She bit out the last words. "I can't make Mr. Ross listen to me. What will I do? What will we do?"

Marie thought to tell her of her own days of deciding when Pierre first told her he was going west, the names she took on in such choosing so long ago. She chose silence instead, thinking of her earlier question to herself, of what she'd do if Paul came back. Yet she knew, some questions weren't questions at all, but revelations, meant to be unveiled only by the one doing the asking.

❖

Marie awoke to an ache, a longing to hang on to a sweet dream. Here had been a hand, warm and gentle on her hip as she slept. In her dream she had called the name of Jean Toupin and he had kissed her ear. "Where are the earrings?" he'd said.

"I sold them for the good of my sons," she'd answered.

"Then I will find you another treasure that you must keep forever, for you have done well by them." He had kissed her ear again, her neck. She'd giggled, brushed at where bushy beard touched her skin. It felt more like a lick, and when she brushed at him and rolled over, she woke. Its-owl-eigh panted over her, drool dripping onto her cheek.

"Oh, whoa," Marie said and sat up, brushing dog hair from her neck and face.

She lay back down, patted so the dog would lie beside her. Its-owl-eigh turned three times, then plopped. Marie lay awake now, remembering the dream. More, she remembered the sweet warmth she'd felt with the words of Jean Toupin. She imagined his face, how he stood with one shoulder held lower than the other. His hands on hers when he handed her hot tea on a cold, desperate day. He was a good man. And she was ready to receive him.

❖

"I walked a shoreline," Jean Toupin told Marie. He stood before her tent in the November dusk, his fur-lined jacket held closed by a wide belt

strapped around his middle. He wore fringed leggings and not the corduroy of his countrymen. "I kicked out a few small sticks. Whatever
drifted there must have come from great distances, during high water."

Marie nodded. He'd begun the conversation without preamble, no
hello or nod of recognition. He'd simply stepped down off his horse as
Marie came through the tent flap. Her hand held the knot of hair at the
back of her neck and she looked up at him, surprised that he'd truly
come. Her heart beat fast, this moment finally here.

Jean looked different. A fuller face, square with a high forehead. He
seemed taller somehow though she didn't imagine that could be so. He
had the tiniest of lines like streams flowing into his acorn eyes. He held
something in his hand and he flipped it between his long fingers. Then
the words, French words, maybe to be sure she could understand him.

"I found this one. Not even very large but rubbed smooth by its
travels through rivers and rocks." She gazed at the driftwood carving
shaped like a cow.

"And sand," she said.

He smiled. "And sand. I wondered, to myself now, how such a perfect shape could come of all that rolling and tumbling. It must have
come a long, long way," he said.

"Is it heavy?"

"Heavy? No. Doesn't seem so." He pressed his fingers around it. It
fit inside his palm. "Alder maybe. You think alder? The wood grain has
an oak look to it too, though. If I had carved it I could tell by the way
it gave up its shape. Wood has a story, eh? But I don't want to cut into
it. It's impeccable the way it is."

"Clay has a story, many stories," she said. "And the colors of paint.
And beadwork designs. They have stories."

"Same as wood, then. Kind of unveils itself as you work it, cut it,
and shape it. But this, that it should look like something so common.
What's the likelihood of that? Something so everyday, so recognizable,
coming out of the river, all complete. Just lying there, waiting to be
picked up." He shook his head.

She reached for it, held it. The lightness surprised her. "It's not so
everyday a shape. I haven't seen a neat milk cow in the fields for seven

summers. We tried to rope a wild one, Paul and Baptiste and me, our first year in Okanogan."

"That would have been a sight."

Marie smiled. "It was. And we failed at it. Did you see the stock at Fort George?"

"See them? I milked them, got kicked by them, licked by their calves. Even churned butter a time or two."

"Butter," she said, and her mouth watered. "I have a child who has never tasted butter."

"They'll start shipping it inland soon. Maybe bring calves here."

"They won't let us have them," Marie said.

"No."

"I'll have one, one day. I will," she said softly. "Even if I must go into debt for it." The word caught in her throat, and she started to hand the driftwood piece back to him. He waved his hand, palms down, to decline.

"Keep it," he said. "It's yours."

"You give too much," she said. She smiled.

"Just a little piece of wood. Something picked up that I didn't even carve myself. I take it as a special find. My mother always said to keep my eyes open for the unexpected good, the little treasures."

"It might hold a sliver in the wood," she said. "Sometimes things look perfect but they aren't." She teased a bit. It had been so long since she'd said *coquette* words. Would he notice? Did she do it well?

"It's too smooth to hold a sliver." He reached to rub his thumb over the surface, forcing her to open her palm wider, the carving lying in the flat of her hand. She was aware of his closeness, his care not to touch her. "Not a rough edge in sight." He looked at her then. "And if there was, I'd file it down quick as a lick. What I'm good at, smoothing things out."

His eyes bore into her, reached a place in her soul. She looked away. "I found it near a river they named for John Day. You remember him?" She nodded. He still rubbed his thumb over the driftwood, came close to touching her skin, didn't. "Always thought him a good man," Jean said. "Tender to the little ones, met his obligations. For an American, he was all right."

She started to pull away, but he closed her hand over the driftwood, then held her fingers clasped in his. She let him, savoring the sense of him.

"Keep it," he said. "My gift."

"I have nothing to give back."

"You give back when you take what I offer," he said. "How long will it take you to learn this?"

He kissed her fingers then, and tears formed in her eyes. Then one by one, he lifted her fingers until her palm was open again.

"I'll fill it often if you let me," he said.

"It's a small hand, not a very worthy one."

"None of us merits a thing," he said. "If we received what we deserved, I'm not sure we'd name that as a gift."

She ran her thumb over the driftwood, lifted it to her face and caught the scent of his hands on it, the scent of him.

"Marguerite, Little Marie, Paul? They're here?" He looked past her, toward the open flap.

Marie shook her head. "Marguerite sleeps. Little Marie is with her father in her grandmother's lodge. My Paul is…gone."

He watched her face, then after a time said, "Could snow." He turned his acorn eyes from her, scanning the sky. "No stars out tonight, eh? Turns cold."

"You should come inside, then."

"Soon as I tend the horse," he said. "Earned him. Part of my pay for working at Fort George, but he's new to me yet. Haven't had much time to know his ways. Don't know how'll he behave with your mare there."

"He looks to be of good stock. She hasn't been bred back yet."

"Good spirit, too. More time I spend with him, the stronger but gentler he seems."

She pointed with her chin toward the corral. He nodded. She watched Jean's back as he stepped to the horse, loosened the saddlebag he'd tied behind the cantle, set it down in the dirt. He pulled at the cinch and slid the saddle off, setting it up on end, the striped saddle blanket lay over the top of it barely brushing the dust.

"I'll bring those inside," she said and bent to pick the saddle and blanket up.

"Merci," he said. "I'll bring in the bag." He led the horse to the corral.

Marie stood for a moment, the weight of the saddle on her shoulder. She heard the soft jingle of the horse's bit as Jean loosened the bridle. She turned and went inside, knowing he would follow.

Setting the saddle and blanket off to the side, she lifted the robe up over a sleeping Marguerite, stirred the fire pit for added light. Then she brought the carving to her face, smelled the scent of leather and sweat that lingered. A cow. She smiled. How had he known she longed for a cow? Jean loved to give. She would have to learn to receive. She turned the natural carving of the driftwood cow over in her hands. It was so light, the gift so unexpectedly light.

And at that moment, so was she, inside and out.

Part 2

15

The Company We Keep

Marie handed Little Marie back to Older Sister's mother, who stood outside the hut on her way to Marie's wedding. Marie missed the child more than she imagined. Josette looked after the child well, Marie knew. Still, the loss of her dimples and dark eyes greeting Marie in the morning caused a piercing in Marie's heart. She never got enough of the baby's pats to her cheeks.

"I go to get ready," Marie told Baptiste's mother-in-law. "Thank you for letting me hold this little one. It is a gift in my day." Marie looked around. "Is Baptiste here?"

"No," Josette said. "He helps my uncle. I'll ask him to come see you."

"He's busy, then," Marie said. "He'll come when he can." Marie dropped her glance and hurried away.

❖

It was the last joining ceremony at which Alexander Ross officiated before heading out to the Snake River country leading his brigade. Older Sister's family, several of the *engagés* and *voyageurs,* a few of the free trappers, and some of the Iroquois who'd deserted Mackenzie and now trapped or moved about as they pleased from fort to fort attended the event.

Baptiste did not.

Marie preferred a simple joining, just her and Jean and Ross, but Sally would have nothing of it. She insisted that Marie be bathed in the traditional way. She gave Marie a cloth shirt and skirt and new leggings to wear.

"You must have family as witness," Sally said. "Mister Ross says our spouses are placed in our lives to tell us things we're to know from the Creator. It's what holds a marriage together. That and the faith a good man won't set a wife off."

"Are you worried over Mr. Ross not honoring his vows to you?" Marie asked.

Sally shook her head, no. "I spoke up and told him what I feared. He had no idea. It's good to speak up, Marie."

Marie smiled. She'd told Sally she wanted no big event for her wedding.

"I have done this twice already, with family there, and still, I was widowed. I come to this place empty-handed once again," Marie said.

"You're rich beyond measure," Sally said. "I see the way Jean looks at you. He'll take good care of you, Marie. He'll bind himself to you like a rawhide rope."

"I would marry in the Ioway way," she said.

"We're in a new place, Marie. We do things different. Even I have to make new traditions here, tie a little sinew from the Okanogan, from the Scots. Even from these river people."

"Jean wishes we had a priest."

"Not this far out," Sally said. "Maybe we should send word to your friends. Mr. Ross says they're on the Clearwater now."

"Sarah and Ignace are that close?"

"Not so many days' ride, east, Mister Ross says."

Too many days for sending word before the joining. And yet excitement welled up inside Marie, knowing they were near.

"You smile a young girl smile," Sally said. *"Bon!"*

Sally placed a veil of tusk-shaped shells and beads called dentalium over Marie's head. "You'll need to adjust the blue beads between the white shells," Marie said, "so all the beads are spaced evenly."

"I know," Sally said.

"Marriage in the Ioway way," Marie said, "my father would take me to my mother's sisters for dressing. And my suitor's uncles would send over many horses, maybe twenty. My father would give them to my eldest brother to give to my brothers or brothers-in-law and the rest to chiefs or braves. Through the year, they would give back gifts of equal value so none of us was too wealthy or too poor. The Company should think this way."

"Do you have brothers?" Sally asked. She stepped back to view the veil.

Marie shook her head, and the tiny beads and white shells shimmered before Marie's eyes, blurred by their closeness. "No more. My clan was the Cow Buffalo and our subclan was known as Road Maker. We made a way through things."

"Well, see, change is in your blood."

"On my wedding day, my father would tell me not to talk to my father-in-law, and my husband would be told not to talk much with my mother for the first year. We'd have a feast, and my father would give gifts that would also be returned in that year to show we would always have enough as long as we gave away. And we'd live a time in my mother's home."

"You would have been happy?" Sally asked. "My father made sure the match I wanted with Mr. Ross was one I wanted."

Marie looked at her friend. "Happy? My father would have wanted me safe," she said. "And my mother would have wanted the marriage performed by a priest. I don't know about happy. Only the worthy deserve to be happy."

"I don't think…well, are you?"

Marie considered.

Sally commented into the silence, "Reading those letters from him, I know he wants to take care of you. He admires you, Marie. He believes you've earned happiness."

Marie nodded. "I am. For today. I give it as a gift to my new husband."

"A new thing named on your marriage day. You've chosen Jean, all on your own. To be both safe and happy."

A feast was planned. Sally told Marie she'd never had a groom take such an interest in the meal. "He's a master at seasonings and spices," she said. "He's made a sweet potato–dried peach compote that has never so stimulated my tongue. Cinnamon, he said."

"And butter," Marie whispered. "He saved a small amount from his last expedition."

Sally wrinkled her upturned nose. "I suppose I should tell Mr. Ross. But I'll suggest it as a wedding present."

It was a Presbyterian service, as that was Ross's experience, and Jean Toupin agreed. "At least we don't have to wait three weeks for the marriage banns to be read before we can wed."

"Presbyterians are speedy at some things," Ross said. "Though deciding on something isn't one of them." Several of the clerks laughed.

Sally nodded an exaggerated agreement as she stood behind him. "I was referring to the elders deciding things at Presbytery, Mrs. Ross," he said, as though he had eyes in the back of his head. "The poor Americans who have adopted the same procedure for their Congress will be higgling for years before the border north is settled. 'Tis a pity. And much debate about the trade system with the Russians and Americans, too. Ah, well, that gives us room to do as we please while they while away their time."

"When the priests come, I'll be seeking another service," Jean told Marie. "You know this? And you will need to be baptized if you're not."

She kept her face without emotion. She didn't need baptism. It hadn't saved her mother from distress. Besides, only the worthy could be baptized. Everyone else must wait until named *impeccable,* perfect. She was many choices away from perfection. But she wouldn't tell him those truths today. Today, she'd chosen joy.

For now, they were making a public statement of their commitment, of Jean's intent to keep her in a marriage of the country. She would keep him, too.

"God makes the third part of these vows," Ross told them as they stood in the courtyard, surrounded by old trappers and traders, Cayuse and Umatilla. Even the Scotch-Irish clerk named Work watched the proceedings while English and French-Canadians formed a semicircle around them. " 'Tis God who'll hold the two of you together," Ross intoned, his Scottish accent growing stronger as he took on the formal tones of ritual. " 'Tis not ta be broken now, by any man or woman in this life."

"Nor by the Company either," someone in the back shouted. People laughed.

"Nor the Company either," Ross said, and he winked at Sally.

And so Jean Toupin took Marie L'Ayvoise Dorion Venier as his wife.

He handed her a *shaptakai,* later, while guests ate and a fiddler played. The leather suitcase had been painted with bold designs. "I was told the husband provided gifts to the bride," he said. "Including the wrappings."

"Sometimes the container is as valued as what's inside," Marie said.

She opened it. Inside she found a drilling tool and white mollusk shells called dentalium like those used in her veil and valued for trade. Papers of paint lay folded to keep the colors vibrant. "So you can create things," Jean told her. A thick, three-point trade blanket covered something heavy. Marie lifted it out of the stiff leather case. "A gift the river gave," Jean told her. It was a rock with a red layer that ran between two halves of gray stone, one side just slightly darker than the other. "These two sides are tied together, in stone."

"Our sign," she said.

Jean nodded. "We are stones held together with faith."

"Does this mean we take the buffeting while God stays safe between us?"

Jean scratched his head. "God is what holds us together while the rock is tossed into smoothness."

She held the rock in her hand, bounced it. "I'll try to find God there for you, husband. In the center."

❖

His wife counted the years. Jean watched her use the paints to make new marks on the leather calendar that lined the tipi she set up when they traveled distances digging roots or picking berries. He tried to get her eyes to look forward, not back. It was who she was, she told him, a mother looking back on the year her son left.

"Why this way, eh? Why not count from a gifting time? Paint grander moments on the calendar. When Little Marie was born, eh? Or when we were both ready for each other?"

"A time of tragedy past must be witnessed."

"Witnessed but not worshiped," Jean complained.

"If I notice good things, something bad follows," Marie told him.

"Something good, too," Jean said. "It's there, as certain as the trouble."

Marie was thoughtful. "This is the year Sally says the Company counts as 1824. Little Marie begins her third season, and Marguerite celebrates her fifth June."

"Good," Jean told her.

"And when our baby arrives, we will add another."

❖

Jean acted as midwife for his son's arrival in the fall of 1824. "François is a miracle," Jean said. "First this *enfant*, beige as soft leather, is of my own blood, and then after all this time I am at last a family man." He wished his mother could have met this child, his sisters claim the babe as nephew. He'd write to them so they could know and add it to the family Bible.

It worried him to have no baptismal water for the child. He bore some guilt for pretending to be a priest, sure that this home baptism would not protect the child from harm. He said nothing of his concern to Marie. Marie had not protested, but neither had she encouraged the ceremony. Jean made the sign of the cross in prayer to mark the birth.

When Baptiste brought fresh venison to their hut, Jean showed him the child. "You've been baptized, yes? You can act as godfather. My son will need a man to lead him, to act as uncle and guide him in religious ways."

Baptiste shook his head, no, and left before his mother could even see him.

Jean didn't know if Baptiste had been baptized or if the thought of being a godfather was more than he could manage. Baptiste's reputation for whiskey was well-known, though Jean had been careful not to mention it to Marie. The boy grieved himself into deeper pain.

Baptiste wasn't around much. Jean would invite him, but he would cross his arms or stand with his hands on his hips and grunt. "I visit," he'd say, but he rarely did when Jean was there, and Marie never spoke of his having come while Jean was away.

So his son had no godfather to witness his birth, to promise to look after him and care for him should something happen to his father, to be a part of his spiritual education even while his parents lived. "I'll ask LaBonte or Michel to have this honor when I see them next," Jean told Marie.

He wasn't sure when that might be. Just as it had been a miracle that Jean was present for his son's arrival and to plan a baptismal service, it would be a miracle if he saw his friends again before the baby turned one. John Work and other Company men moved him between Fort George and the new fort being built on the Columbia now called *Belle Vue*, sending Jean here and there, busy as beavers moving logs down ridges and dragging sticks on water.

Jean hadn't wanted to leave Fort Walla Walla without Marie, but she'd said plainly she wouldn't go.

"I know this place," Marie said. "When to plant seeds and how the sky looks to tell me to cover the plants so they don't freeze before harvest. I know the skies here and when the wind will lift and thump against the tent and when it'll calm. And Sally teaches Marguerite English letters. And I have a grandchild growing up here. Sometimes, I even understand some of the Sahaptin language spoken by the people. This can't happen in other places with much moving around."

"Sally Ross is pretty vocal about not liking being left behind while Ross takes out brigades. She'd be happy to go along with her husband." Jean cinched his horse, using his stronger left arm to roll the stirrup back and jerk it tight. This woman's strength was colored by streaks of stubborn.

"If you trapped, my hands would have work to do, but you don't trap now. You build structures and paddle and transport and work on boats. We would only be extra weight for you, my daughter and our son."

"Warmth in the robe at night," Jean teased.

"Your son grows like a beaver here," Marie said. "See how fat he gets. He crawls like one too, waddling from side to side. A mother knows what's best."

Jean grinned at the image, let her change the subject. François was more a turtle than a beaver, but she was right. François was healthy here. And if she joined him, she would just have to follow other men's orders, wouldn't really be a part of the effort the way women were on the trapping brigades. He hadn't thought of her as wanting to be a part of the achievement of an adventure, not the way he did himself. He'd thought having the children circling around her knees or showing Marguerite how to prepare beaver tail or jerky or keeping her husband's arms filled with warmth would be enough for a woman—if she did her mothering work beside her husband.

He hadn't thought of Marie as having a desire for any other kind of occupation, that where she did a thing might matter. He still had much to learn about this woman he'd taken as a wife.

"Your son won't have the familiar in which to be brave and try out new lessons if we follow you here and there to Fort George and this new place, too. A child grows where he feels safe, especially if he's to risk new things."

"We'd be there. He'd know us."

She clamped her jaws in that way she had of telling him no more discussion would change the outcome. Jean sighed, uncoiled his legs, and stretched, then lifted his son and blew against the boy's bare belly, just to hear the child's laugh. He'd savor this moment, take it as fuel for the work he was asked to do now since his wife would not go with him.

❖

Baptiste pursued a way to live with his sense of separation. He resided outside the fort, staying with his wife's family in a place he'd become familiar with. He'd made it his home. He built a fence around his heart so his daughter could not enter and break it.

He didn't want Little Marie to reach for him, to clutch at his clothes. He didn't want to be near her when she crawled toward him, if he rested on a robe. She cooed and made sounds and acted as though he was someone she wanted to spend time with. He'd startle and leave, claiming he needed to check the horses.

He stayed separate from his mother, too.

"You don't come over much," his mother said once when he brought a quarter of meat for her. He'd shrugged his shoulders. "We would be pleased to see you more. Not just when you have meat to bring us or wood for the fire."

His mother didn't sound scolding, but he took it that way. He watched her bend to her work, a piece of red gurrah cloth tied into the back of her hair knot. She always wore that, ever since Louis's death, or had it been since his brother had left?

More than once, he wished Paul were still around so that he wouldn't be the sole target of his mother's interest, so he could lay the blame where it really belonged, on his thoughtless brother.

"You look thin," she'd told him the last time he'd brought her meat. She squinted in that way she had.

"I'm building new structures for the Company. I'm strong, Mother," he told her. Her fussing felt heavy as fog. "No need to worry over your son."

"Maybe not this son," she said. Baptiste felt his face grow hot. He lowered his head, and the long, straight black hair that he could nearly sit on covered his eyes and his cheeks so she wouldn't see. Lying on his back, her new baby cooed and kicked. Babies. Everywhere. "Have you ever heard from him?" she asked.

"Don't you think I'd tell you?"

She hesitated. He pulled his knife at his waist, began sharpening it with a stone he took from his pouch. "Maybe you'd say," she said. "But brothers might keep secrets from their mother."

"Not these brothers," Baptiste told her. Then: "Enjoy the meat." He stuffed his knife into its sheath.

He did occasionally wonder what had become of Paul, but the boy was savvy, had always been so. While Baptiste didn't know why Paul had taken off, he was sure he'd left of his own accord and hadn't been lured away and then sold to some neighboring tribe. If he had, whoever had taken him would've soon brought him back. Besides, Paul looked French-Canadian more than Indian, and he could well have gotten hired on using the name of Dorion for currency. At least for a time.

"Maybe you and François will be closer brothers," his mother said. "Here. Hold him." She handed the boy to him, his legs pulled up under him then pushing down. François could stand on his own with a little support. Baptiste took him, felt the soft flesh beneath his armpits while he held him at arm's length. "Marguerite misses you, too," his mother said.

Marie returned to her work. She cut a chunk of the front shoulder of the deer, then paused at the opening in the meat that marked where the bullet lodged. She pointed with her knife. "No arrow. Where do you get ammunition?"

"Narcisse gets it," he said. "I trade for other things. Things that make me laugh." He smacked his lips.

She looked up at him and frowned at the way he still kept the child out from himself, the baby's face quizzical. François started to squirm. His eyebrows thick as caterpillars flinched in then out, his mouth taking on the shape of O.

"François likes to be held to your chest," she told him. "Hold him closer or he'll cry." Baptiste bent his elbows to bring the boy in. The child smelled sweet, his chest dressed in soft buckskins and his bottom covered with moss held by gurrah cloth.

"Your children should make you laugh, Baptiste. You won't need the other. You laugh so little."

"I'm well taught, Mother," he said. The child squirmed, and his face began to pinch like an old melon sinking into itself. Baptiste felt his mouth go dry. He didn't want to hold the child to him. Any child. "I hear Narcisse call me," he lied. "And I need to speak with John Work."

"You're going with a brigade? With the Company?"

"It's time I saw places without bad memories." With that, he set François down, harder than intended. The baby wailed while Baptiste ducked his head out of the tent.

He hadn't intended to leave until he told his mother he was. It was time to go. He downed a swallow of rye from his stash of whiskey. It burned through his gut. He'd head back East, sign on with the military, be an interpreter as his father had been. He'd seen this country. Maybe the Americans would even pay for his information, for what he knew about the Columbia country. No decision about the borders had been made yet. Maybe he could influence that somehow.

He took another swallow. It took so little for him to feel the numbness that cradled. His mother and his brother, they fueled his drinking. Perhaps, he'd go look for his little brother, find him under some board crawling with lice. He doubted even that would please his mother. No, nothing that her elder son could do pleased her. His mind felt fuzzy and tight. He'd look for his lost brother. And maybe, if he found him, he'd make sure Paul never came back.

✥

Marie's life settled into a rhythm similar to the time before she became Jean's wife. Her husband followed the orders of John Work, dismantled Fort George, helped move it to what was now called Fort Vancouver, leaving behind the lovely French *Belle Vue*. She raised his son without him, brought Marguerite up as she saw fit, without the intrusion of a stepfather.

When Jean came home, she listened to the tales he told, how they'd twice moved the new fort. "The new factor, McKay's stepfather, says the first place'll flood, so we build so far up from the river that we get dizzy from the height. Then he has us move all the buildings closer to the docks. McLoughlin's a commanding force," Jean told her. "But like all Scots, he has his way, and lesser men to carry it out for him."

Marie listened, treated him with respect, but when he asked what his son had learned while he was away or what Marie had taught him, Marie drew a fence around them, put Jean on the other side. "The Irishman Peter Skene Ogden, he comes through with brigades. He has a pretty wife. Indian," Marie said.

"Ogden makes crude remarks about 'half-breeds' and 'savages,'" Jean said. "I never know what's best to say those times." Jean helped her in the garden plot as she pulled corn for grinding.

"Two years now we get a good crop at this plot," she said.

"I always wonder how his wife, Julia, must feel when she hears such things. She understands French and English and can keep her face as frozen as a winter stream whenever men talk near her."

"We learn that early," Marie said. She handed him another cob of corn. "Ogden says the Iroquois desert him for the New Englanders because the Americans undercut him."

Jean snorted. "I suspect it has to do with the man's ways of controlling more than American currency."

"You work for such men," Marie told him. François waddled now. Marie watched to see if Marguerite would give up her writing in the sand with her stick. "Your brother," Marie shouted, which sent Marguerite chasing him to make sure he didn't get too close to the river.

"There's little choice, Marie."

"You might be a free man. My first husband was a free man."

"Your first husband had no safety while he worked. He put you at risk, you and your sons."

"Maybe Baptiste has chosen this," she said. "Maybe he works for himself now. He could take his child with him, then."

"He told me he was heading back East."

"To visit his grandmother, then. He'll be back."

"You tell yourself what you wish, woman," Jean said. He carried the armload of corn to the site where she would dry it and later grind it into meal. When he returned he said, "If I was a free man, would you travel with me, with my son?"

She wasn't sure. There was safety here, near the fort but still outside it. She was free to do as she pleased here, able to keep Jean where she wanted.

"Did you load the seven cows and bull onto boats?" Marie asked. She motioned with her arm for Marguerite to bring François closer. "Were they gentled enough for that?"

"You didn't answer my question," Jean said. "Would you come with me if I was a free man?"

"Did the cows have calves at their side? See how your boy grows." She lifted the boy and handed him to Jean, who was soon distracted from his questioning.

"The calves didn't let their mothers leave their sights," Jean said, his smile broad as he held his son who pulled on his father's ears. "But the bull, well, he had his own ways of doing things, let's say."

"To be expected," Marie said.

"Not really. He was driven the same as…oh," Jean said. "I don't always know when you tease."

"There's much you don't know of me," she said. She lifted her chin, let a smile escape.

"It's the way you want it," he told her. "Or it would be different."

Later, as they lay on the mat side by side, Marie wondered over his questions. They'd become friends, she and Jean Toupin. Perhaps these separations added to that, the coming and going forcing them into different knowing. She saw him new each time he returned. There was a certain guest quality that warranted welcoming songs. She'd drop her eyes in shyness, feel her heart beat like a hummingbird's when she accepted his fingers to her chin as he lifted her face to his to kiss her in greeting.

She scented herself with lavender and gave sweets to the children so they would run to her first when they sighted a brigade on its way, so she could be ready for him, bathed, her hair knotted smooth at the base of her neck, that red cloth strip tied in. She always offered food he preferred. He would hold his son, feel the weight of his own flesh and blood bounce on his knee. Marguerite, never a standoff, tumbled onto his lap too, with ease.

The robe they slept together in always warmed. She never turned her back to him, and yet she kept a distance in a quiet place of her heart, a distance he might penetrate if she spent more time with him, had to negotiate daily the world of her domain.

Jean usually brought Marie some small trinket, some little gift to mark the passage of their time apart. The gifts made her uncomfortable but she accepted them. To please him. It was a price she owed him, for her keeping them apart.

❖

There were few options in this western place, Jean noted. One could be a free trapper and sell to either Americans or British companies or the

Russian American one; desert and join up with an American company, or work for Hudson's Bay. All choices were about the Company, and the Company was about making money, nothing more or less. His wife just didn't understand that. The best thing he could do for his family was work for the Hudson's Bay Company. Hadn't he been able to construct a wood house for his family? Hadn't he furnished it with copper pots and linens, things Marie now had at her disposal? He even ordered shoes for Marguerite through the Company's stores.

If he hadn't let her change the subject, they'd have argued. He didn't want his limited time with her embittered by their differences. He knew what she was doing, how she'd ask to hear of the doings of that chief factor, McLoughlin, the big man with flowing white hair; and the rest of them. She'd even asked his opinion of how the Company's pension worked. She didn't seem to understand that everything affected everything else in the Company, even how happy the chief factor's *métis* wife might be in the dwelling house.

Jean would tell her how he served as interpreter for some of those Eastern men who visited. Those men wanted to mix with the natives but were worried by the closeness of men they thought less civilized than themselves. Jean enjoyed taking such plant and birdmen or artists out at the Company's direction. It kept him from having to do the strenuous work that required two strong arms. Building the new fort and then transporting even the cannons to it in the cedar canoes had taken weeks of effort. Jean much preferred the company of gentlemen making notes about grasses and geese. All in all, he enjoyed the work he did and could imagine doing it until he was old and sent back to Montreal to retire. Sometimes he even said such thoughts out loud.

"You let yourself be assigned to things you don't want to do," Marie said. Jean ate a slice of cold ham placed between two halves of corn biscuit. François rode in a sack on his mother's back while Marguerite, now nearly six, wove mats of dark grasses, kneeling in that way all native women did on their furs, her little fingers stuffing the grass strands through.

"It's what to do in the Company, Marie," he told her.

"If they told you to shoot someone who did not deserve it, you would do this?"

Where does she come up with this? "I'm not part of the jail detail," he told her.

"But they could assign you there."

He nodded. "If they did, then I could be here at Walla Walla all the time. Would you approve of that?" He risked the next. "Maybe you prefer your time away from me." Silence. "Maybe it isn't your snarl with the Company that keeps you from coming with me. Maybe you trick me into thinking that. You're a resourceful woman, Marie. Maybe to stay here without a husband around to make his ways known to you, maybe this is what you prefer, eh? This is what a marriage is to you, two people who go their own ways. Separation. Maybe safety lies in distance." Silence.

Marie picked up the sewing kit. *Did her hands shake? Did he speak unwanted truth?*

His wife squinted as she pushed the steel needle through the leather, one bead at a time. Did he see sweat on her upper lip? Maybe he'd gone too far.

"The new chief factor is a better man than George Simpson, his boss," he continued. "When Simpson places his napkin at his chin, his eyes count even the peas that each man gets served. To make sure no one receives more than his share, you ask me. He announced that we spend too much of the Company's money in the Columbia region. Tom McKay tried to explain how things work here, differently from back at York or Fort Williams where supplies arrive easily from England. But he listens only to himself, that Simpson."

François started to cry, and Marie laid her beadwork down and took him from the sack. She sat him down among the pups who nuzzled him, and the boy laughed. She said then, "Or perhaps because McKay, as the son of a Scot and mixed-blood woman, holds little weight with that Company man. See it for what it is, Jean Toupin, and what you are within it. A Company man pays a price a free man wouldn't."

"You, too, woman," Jean said. "The Company meets your needs too, *non?* Keeps me separate and away."

Marie remembered the first time she saw the great governor of all the Hudson's Bay. His name was George Simpson, a cylinder of a man as narrow as dentalium and just as pale. He carried a cane. Jean told Marie that Simpson required the *engagés* and *voyageurs* to beach their craft miles before they would arrive at a fort. "So they dress themselves in their best, but it's to allow him time to don a high beaver hat, vest coat, and smooth leather shoes." Then he'd order them full speed into the forts, sometimes after sixteen hours on the river, while Simpson arrived looking refreshed from his catnaps.

Marie could tell much about a man by the way he walked among people who served him or the distance he put between himself and Cayuse children and their dogs as he paraded between them to the dwelling house. For Marie, the native families and their painted leather lodges brought color to this place of dust as more and more brigades brought people to tramp the grasses. George Simpson treated the landscape and children equally, as though they were there to get out of his way.

The trip he made in 1825 would be remembered.

"You have to help serve," Sally told her. "He's accustomed to English ways, and we have just our little doings here." She was dabbing at her wrists with a perfumed handkerchief, a habit she'd formed of late. "It will reflect on my husband," she said. "How we do this."

"I'll help. But I'll work in the summer kitchen," Marie told her. "Have Jean Toupin serve. He knows how to do this and can understand what might be asked."

"You could too. And it would please him knowing a person of high honor waits on him."

"High honor?"

"People talk about you, Marie. They know what you did to save your sons. They know how it was across the trail with Hunt. The men use your name…well, not your name but that you were the wife of Pierre Dorion and the mother of his sons and you did remarkable things."

"I'm best in the kitchen. That's where I'll help."

Sally had relented, sighing. "At least you'll be there to assist with the cooking of that soup. The grouse, the pork, the venison and elk and salmon will be enough to keep a dozen capable cooks busy, and we've but two. And the first course," she waved her handkerchief before her face. "He insists on the French dish, egg soup *à la Paysanne*. He's even brought his own red wine to add at the table, but Mr. Ross says the heat must be perfect or the eggs will curdle and so will his chances."

"Mr. Simpson is inspecting the cooking too?" Marie said.

Sally wiped her nose, dabbed at tears. "He's already been at a big council of Spokane and Flathead and even Kootenai who came down all the way from the north. But this is the truly fine fort, Mister Ross says, and we need to show it so."

The events consumed even the native families encamped around the fort. They were urged to bring the freshest game, tidy up as Ross ordered—now that he was back and in charge once again.

The time of feasting arrived, and after the meal was served, the men rose to retire to a room in the dwelling house where they chewed on tobacco and ideas. As expected, Mr. Simpson brought out cigars for some of the men that he handed out while they milled their way from the shiny dining table to a parlor with cloth carpet covering the rough wood floors. Marie carried a platter of glazed pecan-stuffed dates. Jean passed her as Ross waved him to join the men. Marie backed out, over-hearing Jean introduced as an "interpreter" and a man who was "willing to do whatever was asked."

"Including serving dignitaries, it appears. Didn't you tend us at the table this evening?" Marie heard Simpson say as the door closed behind them.

Marie and several other women and girls cleared the white china from the long table. They'd have to finish this work before sitting for their own meal, much less splendid than the men's. The plates and plat-ters and tiny cups were white with pink flowers surrounding the dips in the edges. Sally called them Spode china and told her they were light as eggshells but much more expensive.

Marie and the other women sat down to eat nearly two hours after the men had finished their meal. The eggs had indeed curdled, and the garlic and vinegar that brought such a spice to her tongue when she tasted it hot before serving the men now made Marie's stomach roll. She wrinkled her nose, and Sally laughed.

Marie felt more than heard the presence of someone. She looked up.

In the doorway stood two young Indian boys, no more than ten or eleven summers old. They wore English style clothes, vests, and leather shoes that one boy now wiped on the back of his other pant leg. Each had his hair pulled back into a queue, but Marie could see by the swing of the tallest when he took a step closer that his hair had probably never been cut. He could easily sit down on it. The shorter of the two moved to stand next to the other now, his large hands still at his side, his shoes, shined. They didn't appear menacing, but their silent arrival surprised.

"May I help you?" Sally said, turning when she saw Marie's upraised eyebrows. The taller of the two put his little finger at his waist as though slicing his body in two. "Ah," Sally said. "You're hungry. You're dressed to eat with the men but…?" Sally left the thought as a question, but neither boy acted as though they understood. Now the younger repeated the sign for hungry.

Marie didn't remember seeing any boys included at the men's table. But they weren't from here, not from any tribe she recognized. By their dress, they must be part of the governor's entourage.

Marie rose, motioned to them to sit, and went to the food store to bring out the remainder of the whole hog that had been roasted on a spit and some of the greens from the kitchen garden, as well as the apple ambrosia that had brought an "I say!" to the mouth of Simpson.

"Do you think we should let them have that?" Sally said. "Those apples were brought from the East."

"It will spoil soon in this heat," Marie said. "That's what I'll say if I'm asked."

"You won't be," Sally said. "I will." With her finger, Sally tapped her lower lip, then said, "Go ahead then. The men have their cigars. And if it spoils, the pigs won't eat the marshmallow anyway. It would be a shame to waste it."

Marie waited until the boys sat down, impressed that they looked about for a napkin, which Marguerite handed them, her little hands having brought François for his dinner as well. And then both boys did an amazing thing. They bowed their heads and began singing one of Sarah Shonowane's Christian songs of grace.

It was as though her friend Sarah stood in the room with them.

Marie asked them when they finished, using sign, "Question, your name?" and the boys answered with Indian names Marie was trying to decipher when Alexander Ross and George Simpson shadowed in the doorway of the kitchen.

"That one is Spokane Garry," Ross said. Simpson pointed his cane to the tallest. "And this," Simpson tapped the shoulder of the second young man gently with his cane, "is Kootenai Pelly. Their fathers are chiefs. The Company appreciates your tending to their bellies."

Sally blushed, curtsied. Marie stared. She'd never seen Mister Ross near the kitchen.

Simpson raised a brow over blue eyes as intense as a preying eagle's, stared at the whipped ambrosia sitting in the center of the table. "In a most accommodating way."

"They sing," Marie said, violating everything she'd learned about an Indian woman's manners in the presence of her betters.

Simpson stiffened, frowned. He turned to Ross, who cleared his throat, spoke quickly.

"For their supper, no doubt," Ross said. "'Tis part of what will get them East, to the Red River Settlement south of Winnipeg. These boys have asked for Christian education, Mrs. Ross. Their request, mind you. Quite impressive for someone perhaps only eleven years old."

"The songs—" Marie began.

Simpson glared at Marie; Ross answered, "Madame Dorion was with Mackenzie." He rubbed his hands together. "They learned their lessons through some Iroquois teachers up there among the Flathead. Taught them all about the Christian faith, so that they've asked to go back and discover for themselves how to read the Scriptures. Shonowane. Ignace, I believe he said his name was."

"And his wife, Sarah," Marie breathed to herself. *She who listens to her inner voice.*

"Come along, boys. You've had enough excitement for one day," Ross said.

"As have we all, apparently," Simpson said, turning his back on the women.

"What's wrong?" Sally said when the men left.

"I cry a thankful song," Marie said, her fingers wiping at her cheekbones. "It's what we Ioway do when we learn of the safekeeping of a friend."

❖

"You've done well," the commander told Baptiste. "For a half-breed. We'll sign the treaty, and your own people'll be proud they surrendered with the Tetons. You'll sign here, at the end, after the listings of the officers."

For a half-breed. He would always be less than enough, even here among his mother's clan and his father's people.

The commander moved on then, his sword swinging at his side against the blue wool uniform. A warm June wind off the Dakota hills brushed his face, snapped at the tent awning over the table where the treaty would capture the signatures of military and braves. Baptiste blinked, expecting to see hair over his eyes, but he could see clearly. He still missed his long hair, but the military required a dress code along with codes for everything else.

He'd arrived well after the fighting. He was sorry for that. But the months of arranging the details of the signing, the terms of surrender, had all demanded the efforts of someone who spoke English and Sioux and Ioway and Chippewa. French, too. He could maneuver through those languages, and he had no history here, or so the military thought, so he was neutral. He was someone who could be trusted to convey both military and Indian meanings without interjecting his own.

His Dorion name had helped him back here too. So many of his grandfather's brothers, his uncles' sons, made their way here as interpreters. Even the famous William Clark had reason to request the help of a Dorion. His own father had been an early part of that historic journey, in fact, something Baptiste had never known. His name opened doors here, not as in the Columbia country where it was associated either with a massacre or the endurance of a mother.

He hadn't found Paul, though. He'd looked, the search taking the edge from his anger over time, unfolding pleasant surprises instead. Being a part of the treaty signing was one. Meeting his grandmother, Holy Rainbow, was the other.

Holy Rainbow was as he'd remembered her, though he'd been barely four when he'd seen her last, not long before they left with Hunt. She was shorter, a little wider than he'd thought she'd be. But she pulled him into herself, pressing his face against the elk's teeth decorating her skin dress.

"My beloved," she called him when he told her his name. She had poor eyesight, but she told him, "I would have known you anywhere, son of my son. Tell me of your mother. Your brothers and sisters. I know how your father died. The story told over campfires. That and how you lived in the mountains for months."

He'd told her he looked for Paul, that he had a little brother and a small girl-child sister in the Columbia country, that his mother had remarried, twice.

"No other brothers?"

Baptiste frowned. "No," he said. Then: "I have this dream, grandmother. A looping dream, over and over with a boy, older. In my father's house. Does this have meaning?"

"We sometimes remember what we once knew, inside dreams," she said. "If it's full of meaning and not just the weaving of longings, it will reveal itself soon enough."

Her eyebrows furrowed, then formed a question she didn't speak. After a pause she said, "You have a wife?"

"No wife. A daughter."

"There was a wife once, then," she said and smiled. "There will be another." He shrugged his shoulders. "When the wound is healed enough. It is our way," she said. "To grieve long and hard, but then to let our souls fill up. We are a family known to keep company with love."

16

Métier

Marie held a new infant at her breast. She called her daughter Marianne while waiting for Jean to return and discover that his family had grown. "I paint the year 1826 with a baby," she told him. "An honoring thing."

"At least you listen to some things I say," he said. "Marianne. A good mothering name," Jean told her.

"The Company takes the cows north," Marie said. They watched as *engagés* drove the four calves arriving from Fort Vancouver, as they called the main fort now, into the corrals at Walla Walla. The animals didn't look as small and neat as Marie had imagined. When she said as much, Jean told her there'd been a few imports brought from the Sandwich Islands that were spotted with red and were leggier than those cows the color of sand that had been brought out of the Northern California province of Mexico.

"Going all the way to Fort Colville, not far from the Okanogan country. Maybe you should ride with us, see old country you once knew," Jean said.

"I don't see why the factor doesn't allow us to have cows at this fort," Marie complained.

"We're horse country," Jean told her. "That McLoughlin knows exactly what he wants, where. They say he even wishes to control the shipping from here, put the captains under his thumb instead of them taking orders from back East. So all we can do is watch these calves move through to Colville country now."

John Work had already ordered Jean and several others to help drive horses north since the Walla Walla herd grew large with the Nez Perce and Cayuse help. Jean knew the route, so he was asked to ride herd with the calves, pushing them along the dust of the horses to keep them protected from raiders.

"The factor would allow you along," Jean continued. "You know the country. Maybe you could ask after Paul?"

The baby fussed. François pulled at her skirts. "Up," he said. "Up."

"Sister will be tall like you, Mama," Marguerite told her, lifting François. "And see her long toes?" Marguerite tugged at Marianne's feet.

Marianne's dark hair grew thick as spring grass around her head in swirls of ringlet curls. She had tiny ears, a mouth with a perfect upraised lift to her upper lip and one dimple in her right cheek that grew deeper as she fattened on her mother's milk. She'd been both wanted and expected, and Jean was at the fort to hold his daughter in his arms a few days after she arrived.

"She reminds you of the one you lost, eh?" Jean asked. He looked at his wife.

Marie nodded. Jean seemed to know her thoughts without her speaking them, at least at times. Had she looked sad? She hoped not. Marguerite had afforded relief she could birth a healthy child; François a gift to give his father; Marianne added comfort.

Still, she suspected Jean spoke of her missing Vivacité, but her thoughts wrapped Paul's absence into the loss too. And now Baptiste's, though he at least had told them he was leaving, heading back East.

She should be enjoying this new child, be excited by seeing cattle again. How quickly her thoughts could turn to sadness, worry, regret. Why did joyous times always ride on the back of sad ones?

Marie rarely spoke of Paul with Jean. She watched Jean make a final brush of his beard to his daughter, brush his son's thick head of hair with his hand. He saluted Marguerite, who held François on her hip. He so loved his daughter and his son. What could she say to this giving man? How could she explain what she didn't understand about what had happened with Paul, that no mother or father could predict the choice of their own? There was no explanation for why a mother failed her son in such a way that he chose to leave and never turn back to her nor let her know if he still lived.

It had been five years now since Paul's leaving. Six years since she'd wrapped red strips of gurrah cloth around his wrists, his ritual he'd made up; and six years since she'd found the sign of her husband in the tangle of a beaver's lodge.

She wished again, as she had so many times before, that she could have talked with Sarah about this all. Perhaps Sarah had a song for Marie that would soothe her when the thoughts of Paul came to her in the early morning stillness, when his years of silence spoke as loudly as thunder, as burning as lightning.

Could it be worse to not know what happened to a child than to learn that the child was dead? Did she grieve Vivacité more than Paul? Or did hope stay living as long as there was silence?

Sarah had said Marie had a friend she could always speak to, but how could she tell her darkest secrets to someone who didn't know her name? How could a woman speak into the night sky the unspeakable things of her unworthy heart? There were things even Sarah didn't know about her, things Marie didn't even want to tell herself.

"Marie?" Jean said. She blinked, came back from her thinking. "We'd be back before the month is out," he told her. François held a small bow up to his father. "Yes," Jean said. "We'll go hunting soon." Jean had dark circles under his eyes. Perhaps he got less sleep than he needed, what with the sounds of babies filling the night. "I know you worry when a husband leaves," he told her. "You should think of coming along, eh? Kilakotah goes with her LaBonte, her children go too."

"François needs you now," she said, shooing him out. "You come back quick."

He walked stoop-shouldered, this young husband of hers. Maybe she didn't have the right to deprive a father of time with his son.

❖

Marie cried her Ioway departing song for Sally. She and Ross, Jemima and James and a new baby were headed east. "We'll see each other again," Sally told her. "Don't you know that? Marguerite will come back to school. Maybe François and Marianne. I'll see what happened to

Sarah's singing boys, to Garry and Pelly. I'll write and maybe you'll yet learn to—"

"Here," Marie said. She handed Sally a present. She'd worked late into the night to finish a flat bag for her friend, woven with grasses laced with a purplish tint.

"What's in here?" Sally said, slipping her hand in.

Marie dropped her eyes, wishing she'd remembered to put something inside, the way European women might. "It's the container that's the treasure," she said. "I hoped it would be enough."

"Oh, it is, it is! I just didn't think before I spoke. Forgive me, please?"

Marie smiled. One accepted a friend with the wrapping they came in.

Then Sally handed her a small canvas bag. "Here," she said, pushing it toward Marie. "This one isn't the container but what's in it that matters. Take it." Marie hesitated, then opened the drawstring. "Seeds," Sally said. "Grain. Wheat. So you can make bread and so someday you'll have grain to feed those calves of yours you plan for."

Marie cried again, then watched as her friend and her children stepped into the canoe to head north, then across New Caledonia east to the Red River Settlement. Mister Ross had not set her off; he was taking Sally with him.

"You'll ask after Paul?" Marie whispered as she said her last good-byes.

Sally nodded. "And Baptiste, too. We might see him."

"Tell them they are missed at home," Marie told her, patting her own heart. "And that home for me is when we are at the fire circle, all together."

❖

Kilakotah didn't go north with the calves. Instead, she stayed behind and made a board for Marianne, decorated it with beads and willow grasses woven into a little bridge out and over where the baby's head would lie so she would be shaded from the hot summer sun.

"You did not flatten your baby's head," Kilakotah said as François waddled by, stumbled over a mat, lifted himself up and tried again. He never stopped moving; he reminded Marie of Donald Mackenzie in that. Kilakotah's youngest lay sleeping and François came closer, peered at the child, moved on.

"No," Marie told her. "It's not our way."

Kilakotah ran her hand over her own child's forehead as he napped, pulled François onto her lap. He squirmed, got down. "I did not do it either," she said. "My mother says I try to be white and that people will think my children are slaves. But she didn't press my head very much. And she didn't flatten my daughter's head either."

Marie remained silent. She hadn't known of Kilakotah's daughter, wondered if the infant had died. Kilakotah seemed too young to have had a child before Louis LaBonte II.

"Your mother planned for your future," Marie said.

"My husband wouldn't let her. My first husband. He was a clerk. An Astorian," Kilakotah told her. Then so quietly Marie could barely hear her, she added, "He set me off, William Matthews did."

"I'm sorry this happened." Marie reached to touch Kilakotah's hand, patted it gently.

"And then another took me, James McMillan. He was a clerk like William Matthews. But he rises to a high post. He set us off while my daughter was not yet born."

"You've had three husbands, like me," Marie said. "Two of them clerks."

Kilakotah raised her eyebrows, then looked away. "I'm selfish. I didn't want Louis Two in the board so much because then I couldn't feel his skin on mine or hold him close."

"I don't think you're selfish," Marie said. "I know mothers who do selfish things, and that isn't one of them."

Kilakotah sat with her hands folded in her lap. "My mother raises my daughter, Victoria. She is Marguerite's size. Someday Mr. LaBonte takes his children back with him, to Montreal, even if he doesn't take me. They will be…welcomed there if their heads are round, like yours."

"He'll take you," Marie said, though she wondered. Who could be sure of such a thing in a place where the Company ruled? It might be best to remain strong alone so what the Company did couldn't hurt.

"I go with LaBonte everywhere so he won't forget we are here. And I leave my daughter somewhere else to be raised so he's not reminded. You see how I put myself before my children? No mother should do such a thing as that."

Marie came close to telling Kilakotah what selfish was; she kept her silence.

When Jean returned, she asked if he'd heard any of the tribes he'd seen singing Sarah's songs.

"'Une Jeune Pucelle,'" Jean said. "They sang 'Let Christian Hearts Rejoice.' There is a verse in it I had not heard," he said. Marie adjusted Marianne at her breast. "About 'three chiefs together made a pact' and how Jesus is the Chief they welcomed at Bethlehem. The Iroquois teach it to them."

"You saw Sarah, then?" She felt an ache of disappointment that he'd seen her and Marie hadn't. In the songs, Sarah's work of waiting, of witnessing through her life, had acted as a riverbed for God's spirit to flow through.

"No. Just evidence of her *métier*," Jean said.

Her friend had found work that blessed. Marie suspected Sarah wouldn't call her effort work, just the privilege of giving. It would be good to visit with a friend again. The baby's small hand shifted on Marie's breast. She looked down into the child's round face. "You are my calling," she said. "I will teach you to sing welcoming songs." And maybe Sarah's songs, Marie thought, though she didn't know all the words, just the melodies. "Your grandmother would have liked that," she told Marianne, her third daughter, second one to live. "And your mother Sarah would be honored too."

❖

Baptiste heard about it first from Tom McKay one day while he hoed the kitchen garden at Fort Vancouver. He'd come back, but here at Fort Vancouver he didn't have to watch his daughter grow, didn't have to be reminded of her mother's death. He felt like a rat for not being there to tend his mother-in-law's needs. But Narcisse was there. Josette was a capable girl who might be like a mother to Little Marie, able to fend for herself and her children.

Still, Older Sister had no brothers to help her family. He'd been the responsible man in her household. And he had married her when she was young, too young. His stomach knotted. Her family didn't have any other daughters of marrying age. Little Josette couldn't be more than ten years old. Baptiste's mother-in-law couldn't expect any time soon new sons to bring in game or pay a bride's price.

He didn't like to think about it.

At his request, he'd signed on with the Company and asked to be posted somewhere other than at Walla Walla. He'd sent word to his mother that he'd joined Hudson's Bay, but he let her believe that the Company had just sent him away, that it was another example of the "powers that run our lives," as his mother put it, having their way with them.

He hadn't found the Company to be anything but fair to him. He wasn't sure why his mother held such aggravation toward it. The Company was just made up of men, that's all it was. And for most, it was directing, protecting, advising, and even providing a place to eat and sleep. Family, that's what the Company was. His mother just couldn't see that.

He wouldn't ever tell her that he'd raced enough horses, drunk enough whiskey, lied to enough women that even Older Sister's uncle, Narcisse, had suggested he make a change.

"I'll miss the horse racing, though," Narcisse told Baptiste. "You always won, and I got my payoff in handsome ways."

"Even against Tom's ponies," Baptiste said.

"Even Tom's. But you'll be dead before long you keep this up. You've met your duty as a son of my sister. When you witnessed the treaty, you signed your change, too. The army wouldn't contract with a drunken interpreter. You did well. You can be clear-headed when men are warring. You go now. Make a different way here."

"My mother—"

"A fatherless son straddles a difficult stream. He has to make his way through lots of eddies and backwater that can hold him without moving and then spit him out before he's ready. And when you have two streams of blood rushing through you, the way can be even murkier." He'd clapped Baptiste's shoulder, then pulled Baptiste to him in a bear hug. Baptiste bit back tears from this loving grasp. He'd left the following day.

Baptiste figured it would be construction that would consume him at the Fort. He'd been assigned instead to the Vancouver farm.

He could see the Columbia River from where he hoed. A green carpet spilled down to the water dotted with canoes and larger supply ships arriving downriver from Fort George. To the east and west, horse-drawn plows continued to break more soil for fields in which they'd plant barley, oats, wheat, and peas. They'd already planted over three hundred acres, and the potato and bean harvest promised to be "bountiful" as the chief factor said when he surveyed the fields. A peach orchard grew off to the west, and a vineyard of table grapes kept the children busy chasing at birds who might get the crop before anyone else did.

Activity swarmed around the fort. Visitors came upriver from aboard big oceangoing ships. It was rumored that McLoughlin hoped to someday dock them right there in front of the fort. The river was deep enough and wide enough, and some Boston ships with masts had already come up, or so the stories of it were told. But the tidewaters pushed the mud flats around, and it could be a dangerous trip certain times of the year. Still, it promised a future here, with things happening all around. And no day was the same. When he lay down in the bunkhouse at night with dozens of other *voyageurs* and *engagés* and trappers and hunters, Baptiste was almost too tired to hear the stories.

The hard work had been good. The rationing of whiskey had been better. He found that if he drank none at night, his days went smoother. The Company took good care of them.

A shout from the docks drew his attention to the men loading kegs of tallow. Potatoes recently dug were loaded also. He'd heard the wind and sun had wiped out much of the crop at Fort Walla Walla. This shipment was headed for that fort, though they provided stores for almost all the forts inland. Still, it pleased Baptiste to think that he'd had a part in sending foodstuffs that would reach his family there. It was his way of still being responsible even though he'd deserted them.

"Got yourself some girl's work, I see."

Baptiste turned, his hoe raised like a weapon ready to swing before he realized who it was.

Tom McKay leaned against the split-rail fence, favoring that bad leg of his. He grinned, and Baptiste shook his head. He could see why the ladies chased after the man with his wide smile flashed now and then, just enough to warrant interest. Word of his prosperity preceded him too.

"Girls get first pickings," Baptiste told him. "Except for your Billy. With his curls, he could pass for a girl, though."

"You insulting my kin?" Tom asked, but he didn't sound upset. He looked around. "Where is Billy? Hey, Billy!" Tom shouted.

Tom's first son had been born at Fort George two years previous. His wife had already delivered a second, and rumor was, she was waiting on a third.

"Billy slipped into the melon patch and picked himself one so big he couldn't lift it. I watched him rolling it around the sleeping house," Baptiste said. "Took him most of the morning, and I hate to tell him, it isn't even ripe."

"He'll adjust. Get his grandma to give him some maple sweets instead," Tom said.

Tom scanned the landscape, and Baptiste let his eyes follow toward a meadow where horses grazed among blue flowers and grass so tall and lush it looked like a painted picture. A plant man had been staying at the fort ever since Baptiste had arrived. He was out there now in that field, making sketches. There were always guests: painters, scientists, curious Americans, he figured, who were cruising the competition.

"I always thought this place would make a good horse farm," Tom said. "Told my old man and behold, it's the Company's now." He had an edge to his words. "Not that anyone can own the land outright. Joint occupancy." He said the last with a kind of sneer, his demeanor already shifted as quick as the river's winds.

"It's lots easier with the fur factory closer to the water," Baptiste said.

"Don't kid yourself about the motives of those in charge, my friend.

Ledger books decide what matters for the Company. They don't make changes for your benefit. You're the only one who can do that."

❖

"More and more Americans push into our rivers. They ignore the boundaries," Jean had told Marie. "So we're being sent to new places, to counter them."

It would mean a long separation, and he'd once again urged Marie to join him.

"No," she said. "I stay behind with Kilakotah and Ogden's wife."

"It will be long months this time, maybe years." He'd miss his children, and he'd miss Marie, too. Why couldn't he convince her to come with him? Didn't she love him enough? That was what he feared, what he couldn't bring himself to say.

"You went with Pierre when he was sent out," Jean said. "You didn't want to be apart from him."

"See what it got me? The name of widow."

"And a new husband, because you came west with him. Me."

"Pierre needed help," she said.

"You only follow weakness?"

"I was weak then," she said.

"Maybe you're afraid to find out you aren't so strong. Maybe you fear discovery of something hidden." He was a fool to say such things. It would only force her into silence.

It did now.

He was right, but the argument hung between them, even as he saddled up and rode away with the wild man Peter Skene Ogden.

❖

She should have followed him, at least let him know she held no hard feelings. The children were better here, where there was routine. She could help look after Little Marie. That child needed her too. Who knew what trouble Ogden would put them in if she'd gone along? Even

Ogden's own wife hadn't gone. Didn't that say something to Jean? But she could have let him go with a lighter heart.

Marie ripped at the willow strands, tearing them into long fibers she'd use for matting. The effort felt good, her whole body pressed into the work. Why did this happen whenever he prepared to leave? Always the same argument. He could either find work as a free man and stay at home or he could accept things as they were and let the Company determine his comings and goings. Why couldn't he see that?

Why couldn't she? That was a question too.

Sarah would say, "Why do you expect wheat to be other than wheat or weeds to be other than weeds? It's what they are. You be wheat," she'd say. "You do what you were made to do and trust God for the rest."

Sarah had words for everything. *Do what I am made to do.* What was that? Marianne squealed her high-pitched call that meant a mother must come running. Words didn't matter here. Choices did. She knelt over Marianne's board and smiled at the child. She looked so much like her father.

Marie unwrapped the laces on the board, cooing and singing as she did. She'd set herself to making Jean's time when he returned strong times, without arguments or expectations. She wouldn't let him bait her with his talk of how she'd gone with Pierre those years before. She wouldn't say, "Yes and see what it got me? The name of widow." She'd say, "This is what I am now. What you chose."

She'd chosen too.

❖

Jean had heard that Peter Skene Ogden was a wild man, both in his thinking and appearance, but he had a reputation as someone who'd risen up in the Company too, so he was a man to be reckoned with. Wild men often are. Now, Jean'd been sent out with him as part of the Snake River brigades, and the beauty of the aspen and cottonwood leaves turning gold wasn't enough to make him ignore his uneasiness with Ogden's wild ways.

Jean and Ogden's groups followed a river four days south from the

Columbia. They left the river at the falls. This river rushed wild, eventually plunging between high rocky ridges almost as formidable as that Mad River they'd been on those years before.

Now, in the September heat, they also trapped. The pelts were coming into prime. Ogden hoped to trap early, make trades with pockets of Indians along this river and the others of this region, urging the Indians to trap for the Company's camp before the American's offered more money for their pelts. The Americans encroached on the Hudson's Bay Territory and even in this section, jointly held, they often acted as though it belonged only to them.

Ogden led the brigade of fifteen men, five wives of trappers and their children, and forty horses down a treeless ridge, with Captain Hood's mountain white and steep on their right. They'd split the group earlier in the month with Tom McKay taking the other half and moving farther south.

Soon, the mountain was out of sight and they switched back down rugged canyons with coils of rocks that stood on end and soared into blue-beaded skies. A four-day march from the long falls on the Columbia where the Celilo and Wish-ram people fished brought them to a place in the river where other Indians dipped spears or nets dyed to match the river's muddy color. Now the stream they'd followed swirled around black rocks and appeared turquoise in places with white froth streaking through it. *Rivière des Chutes,* Ogden called it because it emptied into the Columbia near the falls.

It was a good adventure so far. No bad encounters. Ogden behaved, even keeping nightly records with his writing pen. Jean would have good news to report to Marie of Ogden's actions this trip.

But at a falls where the whole river poured between a narrow ledge of high rocks, Jean remembered Michel LaFramboise's saying, "Very smart stands next to very *stupide.*" He couldn't be sure which one was what Ogden demanded.

"Looks like the Lord's given us a natural bridge," Ogden said, pointing to two logs lying like sticks across the river that was perhaps fifty feet wide. Below them, the water swirled turbulent and deep. On one side, the trees' rootballs reached up like fingers, and on the other side, the logs, wet from the spray of water, narrowed out to the rock ledge. The strength and breadth of the entire river rumbled beneath the logs like black thunder. Jean lay awake that night, wondering what it was this man would ask of them in the morning.

At dawn, Jean had stared at what Ogden called a "crossing." An Indian family of twenty or so camped near the water, a canoe tied to a boulder nearby. Jean was asked to talk with them. They were Sahaptin-speakers, possibly Wasco or Yakima or Warm Springs Indians. They fished for the big salmon that pushed up to the falls. Those standing on the wooden platforms that jutted out over the water wore ropes around their waists as they lowered their nets. As Jean understood what they were telling him, the ropes wouldn't keep them from dying if they slipped and fell, but would help their families pull their bodies to the surface.

"He says the currents beneath here are treacherous," Jean told Ogden.

Ogden said, "Ask them if they use the bridge."

Jean slipped into using Chinook jargon, which he understood better than Sahaptin, and some signs, and one of the men shook his head and pointed to the canoe. "Maybe ten or twelve miles upriver there's a ford. They cross on canoes. Farther up, above these falls. They could help us swim the horses across. He shakes his head at us. He says it isn't a bridge at all here. Just where two trees fell together."

"They're just wanting us to pay them for transport help," Ogden said. "Those trees've been dragged here from some beaver stream. There aren't any that large just growing here; the rocks prevent it, gentlemen. They want to take us upriver and make us pay. Probably been paid off by some Americans already in these parts. To stall us."

Jean shook his head. It didn't seem that way to him. He suspected their judgment of the crossing came from experience Ogden didn't have.

Ogden ordered the men to slope up an entrance onto the timbers with dirt. It had taken them the day. Then they'd chopped trees from a west-feeding creek, removing branches so they could be laid like a flat ladder across. The next morning, they'd been given orders.

"Come along, ladies. No time to play coy for your dance cards. You've got a dancing partner waiting," Ogden said.

The horses stomped and turned and raised their heads up and down, clanking bits and rein rings, kicked up dust beneath the blue sky. When no one moved, Ogden finally said he'd go first, and he pushed his horse to the edge of the root ball. His horse whinnied and neighed, pulled back. Ogden dismounted, yanked on the rein, pulled to lead him. Finally, with careful steps and coaxing, the two moved out onto the bridge, the horse frothing with sweat. They made it successfully across.

Ogden's boldness strengthened the next man, who led his horse forward saying, "May as well get it over with." Before he even got onto the flatter planks that crossed the twin logs, the animal reared, yanked back, shoving its leg into one of the holes that marked the bridge like netting. Jean heard the horse's leg splinter, followed by a scream of quivering pain.

"Shoot him," Ogden ordered from the other side.

The shot rang out against the canyon walls.

"Maybe we could just return as we came," Jean shouted. He turned toward the west side trail. "Cross back at the mouth. Or travel farther west."

"What? No. Here we cross. All of us," Ogden shouted across the chasm, the rocks creating an echo barely heard above the water's roar. Ogden tied his horse to a boulder and nimble-footed his way back, not once looking down. "Unsaddle your mounts and get the dead one out of the way. Don't want to lose tack in case one falls into the river. I'll lead one or two to assure you ladies it can be done since, even seeing with your own eyes, you doubt."

Two more horses were lost, legs broken or twisted, as men tried to lead them, did lead them, onto the logs.

The Indians murmured with each step. Jean didn't think they looked like wealthy people, and the loss of the horses must have seemed extravagant. It did to Jean.

One of the younger men of the family group approached Jean. He spoke and signed in such a way that Jean was sure he was telling them they'd show them a better way, take them upriver, "No trade," he kept saying. "No trade."

"There's another way," Jean shouted to Ogden, knowing he pushed beyond his role but he couldn't imagine the women and children being able to cross safely here.

"Order's been given," Ogden shouted. "Take the horses across."

Another three men and animals made it. Then, a fourth horse that Ogden led himself slipped at the far side. The bridge was slickened from the spray of water reaching up from the gorge.

Jean knew he'd never forget the cry the animal made or the wildness of its eyes as it plunged into the turbulent river below.

One woman lifted her chin, stepped out and, with a child clinging to her back, led her horse across never looking down.

Another horse was led to the edge. It bolted and pulled itself over backward and plunged into the water. Five animals gone. What a waste.

And then it was his turn, his horse Jean would lead—if he chose to go this way. What choice did he have? The order had been given. He worked for the Company. Was he prepared to be insubordinate? They'd need every mount with five already gone. Some men would be walking as it was to get back safely. Jean wondered at the wisdom of this man who ordered this senseless challenge. He'd vowed those years ago under Hunt that he wouldn't do what a leader said unless he really believed it was the best thing to do.

But what was best? More mounts had made it across than not. Some of the women had succeeded, and several of the children, too. Maybe he was making the ones who held back more worried than need be. He guessed the vote to cross would win if a vote were taken. The acts of the others were their votes.

"You coming, Toupin? It's time."

Jean was grateful for the years he'd had with the horse, to know it as he would a friend, its ways and quirks. He'd given it a long French name but shortened it, the way the Americans always did. He called him Lumière, meaning light. A guiding light was what he needed, all right.

It was a hot September day. Eagles drifted above him, and he felt a kind of stillness in his soul as he stood, rubbing the velvet of Lumière's nose. "You think we can do this, eh?" Jean said. "These Indians think we're crazy."

He wondered what Michel would tell him to do if he were here; where did smart stand? Where was *stupide*?

And then he pictured Marie's face and wondered what good sense might she give? He ached for her presence, for her quiet wisdom. How he wished that she'd come with him, never more than now.

"Toupin!" Ogden shouted. "You're holding us up."

He was a Company man. He'd cross. And if he made it, he would tell Marie it was his last brigade without her and his children. What good did it do to be a responsible family man out for adventure if he only longed for the former and the latter brought about nothing but a good story of his death for men like Ogden to share?

He took a deep breath, led the horse to the edge.

17

Little Letters

Marie only knew that her husband didn't return with Ogden's men. Her Little Letters, as she thought of the children, had come bustling ahead with news of Ogden's return, and she'd handed out slivers of maple cone and sent the children off. She hurried Marguerite, urging her daughter to scurry about, putting things into their places. Jean was a tidy man and always liked his lodge "scrubbed," he said.

She'd rinsed her hair with herbs, run an ivory comb Jean had brought her through the lengths of hair that touched the floor when she bent over, pulling the strands like soft rain out over her face. It was almost cool inside the hut, though the October sun burned the day hot outside. She stood, twisted her hair back at her neck, and held it in place with twists of cloth and round, beaded hair picks. She'd created them after looking inside one of Sally's books she said were drawings of "Orientals." The women in the pictures resembled Marie in some ways and wore their hair as she did too, held in place with large needles sticking out of the black knots of hair at the sides and backs of their heads. Marie wished she knew what the words beneath the pictures said.

Beading the sticks had taken some time, covering them around wood, but she'd done it. And today she would wear them for Jean Toupin, to welcome him home.

François grabbed for the dog's skinny tail, and the animal snapped at him, though Marie had never known First Lick to hurt the boy. The dog used its growl to set limits, and François could use that. He was more like his half-brother in that way, always trying things he couldn't quite accomplish.

"Your papa comes soon," she said. "Leave First Lick. You don't want to be crying with a wound when he arrives, *n'est-ce pas?* Come tell your mama how she looks." She smiled at him.

He gazed up at her and grinned. He had few words yet. Marguerite at that age had chattered Marie to shushing. More like Paul, he was. Marie sighed.

But he had her upturned nose and his father's high forehead and eyes the color of acorns, similar to the rock Jean had given her after they had said their marriage vows. This child had been their first melding together, and she could see the two of them reflected in his face.

"François is a handsome boy," she said and leaned to kiss him. He pressed his lips together and blew the way Baptiste blew on his jaw harp.

A mingling of remembering one son while enjoying another filled her. Her sons. For a moment she allowed herself the joy of anticipation, the bubbling up of contentment that arrived with a loved one's return to the fire of his family.

She felt herself bustling about, giving directions to Marguerite, telling her things to which Marguerite said, "I already know this, Mama!" Marianne pulled on the dog's tail. The animal turned and snapped, causing Marie's youngest to go from whimper to wail.

"Oh, shhh," Marie said, swatting at the dog who scooted out the door. Marie lifted Marianne, who pulled on her beaded hair sticks. "No, no," Marie said. She took a deep breath. "Your father comes soon, very soon. Be good now, *oui?*"

Butterflies filled her stomach, and she no longer cared about the hide she'd been scraping earlier, hoping to get it finished before the evening meal. It lay where she left it when the children brought word of the brigade snaking their way beside the Columbia, riding and walking high above on the treeless bluffs when the sharp rocks kept them from the shoreline.

She nursed Marianne, then, rocking the board on her knees when the child finished, singing an Ioway sleeping song.

Marie waited.

The children had long since curled their fingers around the maple candy and scampered off toward the fort to tell Julia Ogden, the factor's wife, and any of the other women of the brigade's soon arrival.

Marie waited.

The sun set over the distant ridge, and she heard shouts and even a fiddle playing. She wondered why Jean didn't ride in on Lumière. He always made his way to their tent within minutes after checking in at the fort. Had the Company required some new task of its men before they could rejoin their wives? She would wager Julia Ogden wasn't wondering where her husband was.

And then the night had come. Marie wrapped Marianne in her board, sang an Ioway song to her that put François to sleep too. Marguerite's eyes stayed open. Next to her sat Little Marie, who had come to spend the night.

"Will you tell us a story, Mama?"

Marie sat beside her elder daughter, ran her fingers through her mop of curls. Louis's curls they were, with just a hint of red in them as she grew older. They were the color of cattails. "I tell story," Little Marie said.

"No story tonight," Marie told them.

"Are you tired? Can I get you something, Mother?" Marguerite offered.

Marie said. "I'm to take care of you, Marguerite. You're my little girl."

"I help too."

"Yes, you do." She brushed the curls from Marguerite's cheeks. "You're both good girls."

"Your hands are cold," Little Marie said. Little Marie's palm felt warm to the touch.

"White like shells," Marguerite added.

"Are they?" Marie turned her palms over to look at her fingertips. They were icy white. "I'll go outside where it's still warm," Marie said. "You two rest now. Tell each other stories."

"You tell," Marguerite begged.

"I'll tell you two tomorrow," Marie said.

"And one will be where Papa is?"

"We can hope," she said, pleased that the child saw this man as one she could claim as her father. She'd tell Jean that when he returned. It would please him.

If he returned.

He'd be dismissed, he was almost sure of that. Well, Jean had dismissed himself by his choices. He could count himself lucky to be let go and not be flogged or fined for his insubordination, which was what it was, of course.

But he could not bring himself to risk Lumière at that crossing. It might be called cowardice, but he didn't see it that way. It was questioning the wisdom of the order and, of course, that alone would make him forever suspect in the Company, at least where Ogden was concerned.

He'd had his hopes. He'd shouted across that he would take care of the horsemeat first and then follow as ordered.

"Just bring the animal and join us, you Canadian coward," Ogden had screamed at him. "Forget the meat."

Jean had acted as though he couldn't hear him above the roar of the ropy waterfall that pushed beneath the fallen trees. "We can always use it," he shouted. "I'll bring it along and catch up with you."

If nothing else, it would show the natives watching that these Hudson's Bay men weren't all so crazy as to let good meat rot in the sun or risk another good animal at an ill-conceived crossing.

Ogden had shouted a few more choice words. Jean had kept a smile on his face, pretending confusion, holding his ears as though to hear better, then lifting his shoulders in an exaggerated shrug. Then he'd knelt down, took his knife from his sheath and began slicing the hide off the animal's carcass, enlisting help from the Indians by using motions and a few Chinookan words. His heart pounded as though he'd just run a race, waiting to see how long Ogden might harangue him.

Finally, Ogden had given the order to mount up and had led the brigade up the east side of the river. Jean cast a look that way but kept himself busy with the meat.

Jean's plan was to cut up the horses that had been shot after they'd broken legs on the bridge, then use the meat to trade for a ferrying across the river. If these Indians wouldn't trade for the meat, he'd load Lumière with as much as he could hold and walk the animal upriver until he found a suitable place to swim across.

It had taken him the better part of the day to cut up the horses and lay the strips out on rocks to dry. A couple of the Indian women brought what looked like drying racks that still held bits of fish on them. They motioned for him to use them. Jean hesitated, then decided it would speed the process even if it did give the horseflesh a little river flavor.

His eyes had adjusted to the growing dark, and he finished with the moon not yet up. The Indians had shared dried fish with him and some roots, and then he'd laid his head on the saddle and rolled into his sleeping blanket as he listened to the soft chatter of voices carried over to him in the sporadic bursts of wind.

He thought of his Marie then. He hoped he could catch up with Ogden before they reached the fort. Ogden would trap as they went, and that might give Jean the time he needed. Having fewer horses would slow the brigade. At least he assumed Ogden wouldn't attempt to push so hard. More women and children would be walking, and there'd be even fewer mounts to haul the pelts. Maybe the added time would allow Ogden to reconsider his outrage toward Jean. Maybe the time would increase his disgust with Jean.

But Jean's real worry as he lay there beneath a night sky as black as good molasses was what Marie would say when he told her what had happened and what he'd done. He hadn't outright disobeyed...well, yes he had. No sense making it into something it wasn't. He'd disobeyed an order. He'd not be trusted again, at least by that man. He wondered if Marie would be pleased with his choice or pained by it. It bothered him that he didn't know her well enough to predict.

For four days he waited for the meat to dry, then loaded what he could of the meat onto his horse. He motioned to the native people starting to rise from their own mats that he was leaving some of the meat for them. They said something to him, but he didn't understand it. He wasn't even a worthy interpreter, Jean decided.

Then one of the men used an English word Jean knew. "Follow," he said, and Jean did. The big-chested man led Jean upriver where a crude raft awaited, lashed by ropes to a rock. Another rope stretched across the river at this spot as though strong arms could pull themselves and the raft to the far side and then pull the raft back.

And that was what the Indian had done for him, pulling and poling the craft across the river while Jean held a rope as his horse swam a length behind the raft.

Lumière resisted the raft, its pitching and yawing into the fast-flowing stream. Jean hadn't enjoyed the ride either all that much, but it had worked, and the horse was strong and the two arrived safe on the other side. They could have kept all of Ogden's horses alive if that leader hadn't been so stubborn.

The native shook his head, no, when Jean tried to give him something for his effort.

Walking the rest of the way back to the Columbia, then east, Jean kept hoping each day he'd encounter the brigade, but he hadn't. He was alone on this journey but for the thoughts of his wife and his vow that he'd not leave on another expedition without her. If the Company would still have him, which he doubted.

By the time he arrived at Fort Walla Walla, he'd consumed a fair amount of the dried horsemeat he'd carried on Lumière. All he had to show for his effort was his own well-fed body and a horse that whinnied recognition of Janey as they approached the compound outside the palisades.

He usually returned in daylight, and he wondered if as before, Marie would somehow have known, be smelling sweet and waiting for him.

He loosened the reins, slipped his leg over the side and dismounted, both feet landing at the same time beside his horse. Janey nickered to him and he walked over, leading Lumière, to rub Janey's nose as she hung her head over the driftwood corral. *"Oui,"* he said. "We're home for you, eh?"

"All your girls wait," Marie said.

She walked up behind him, put her arms around his waist. He could smell smoke in her hair from a cooking fire but that lavender smell too, though not as strong as sometimes. He turned and she put her cheek next to his. She had something new in her hair. Round, beaded sticks he felt when he put his hand at the back of her neck and pulled her to him to kiss her.

"You missed me," he said.

"So did Ogden, I hear."

"What's the story? From your end?"

"That my husband made a poor choice. His hearing was so bad he couldn't know to follow orders to cross where everyone else crossed. He has poor eyes, too. He couldn't see what they'd done either."

"That's the way it's told?" He had his warm hands at her waist now, firm and welcomed.

"The Company won't want a man who can't hear well and whose eyes fail him. They weren't sure you still lived. Ogden worries about what those Indians might do to you, alone on that side of the river. This is what Julia Ogden says."

Jean snorted. He pulled himself away from Marie, untied the leather strap that latched the entry to the corral, and lifted the gate. Marie took the reins, held them while Jean removed the saddle and set it, cantle down, on the ground. He stroked the gelding's back for a time with the brush Marie handed him. She lit the lantern hanging near the gatepost and held it above him.

As Lumière cooled down, Jean removed the bridle and patted the animal's rump, pushing it into the corral. The horse bolted away into the darkness.

"The Indians were nothing but helpful," Jean said. They walked toward the wood house. "And Ogden didn't seem too worried about my fate. He just rode off." Jean had his arm around Marie's waist and pulled her toward his side. They walked in step. The moon cast a feathered light brushed by billowy clouds.

"Bad ears and eyes, eh?" he said then. Crickets chirped as he held her hand in his. Her fingers felt cold. They always felt so cold.

"The Company undervalues what a man has most to give," she said.

"Good eyes and ears?"

"Your kindness, washed with wisdom," she said.

He was glad it was dark so she couldn't see how his face turned hot with her words. She wasn't upset, at least she didn't seem so. If anything, tonight, she was a stake beside him, one set to stabilize a wind-whipped tree.

"Not sure what we'll do now," he said. "Company's the only sure wage in these parts. Not even the Americans pay out without pelts."

"I have a plan," she said. "You have suffered enough."

He was silent for a time, then said, "The Greeks say wisdom's born of suffering."

"Then together, we give birth."

❖

Little Marie waved, her small hand smudged with tear-stained dirt. Beside her stood Josette, her arm around the child. Marie and Jean's wood structure where Josette and her mother and brothers and sisters would live shadowed their faces, so Marie couldn't see the ache in their eyes. It was just as well. Marie hurt enough already.

She'd given a spinning top to her granddaughter, showed her how it worked, just once, and Little Marie could repeat it. She was quick, that one. Marie wouldn't be around now to watch her learn new things.

First Lick barked, yap-yapping at the commotion of horses and long poles loaded with *shaptakai* and baskets dragging behind. Little Marie grabbed at the dog and knelt down, her arms wrapped around his neck. At least the dog would be there to comfort the girl. And she had Josette. Marie had to remember her granddaughter had Josette.

❖

Baptiste said some man named Pambrun helped plant it, the first apple seeds placed in Fort Vancouver ground. It was the first in all the Northwest, the gardener said.

The head gardener, Bruce, sent Baptiste to bring the boxes which he filled with dirt. The gardener had the privilege of holding them while a Mr. Parker, and an English sea captain, and Mr. Pambrun pressed the tiny apple seeds into the soil.

McLoughlin looked on, his white hair lifted by the breezes.

"Mark the year, gentlemen," McLoughlin said. "Eighteen and twenty-seven. Give it three, four years, and we'll have an apple or two to bite into. They'll squeeze the juices out. From then on, we'll be shipping apples inland and all the way to Russia."

Baptiste kept glass over the boxes after that. He checked the sprouts often. Such a precious thing, apples. With ripe ones would come cider and ways to fight the bone diseases, and, of course, feed them with the fine taste of pies.

For Baptiste, the apple seeds in the boxes marked his own time of maturing, of growing in new ways. He found he had a knack for growing things, and even the factor's wife sometimes brought him sickly plants to nurse back to health. He liked the challenge of taking something weak-stalked and leafless and finding what it lacked so he could make it strong.

He'd picked up other skills, too, at this Vancouver place. He apprenticed in the blacksmith shop, rebuilt boats, even ran errands for the factor's wife. There was always someone to assist.

He understood quite a bit of the Chinook jargon too, and could distinguish the sounds of Warm Springs from Wasco and Clatsop. He could separate the clicks of the Wish-ram tongue from the Tillamook. He had even learned a few Sandwich Island sounds while those round-faced men helped work the ever-growing cattle herd.

His father might have been proud of his ear for languages. Four generations of men who could interpret the words of others. His mother, too, might have noticed.

He'd heard she'd left the Walla Walla area. Maybe returned to the Okanogan country, for all he knew, probably still looking for Paul. Paul had always been first in her heart, that much he knew. His brother hadn't been the easiest seed to bring up to fruit, but she still took more time with him than Baptiste ever received.

He felt a rush of anger rise up, not sure if it came with the thought of Paul or his mother. His mother always said a man's action spoke louder than words. What had his brother been trying to say by his simply disappearing? What had his mother meant to say by sending him away when his wife was about to give birth? Now she'd gone, hadn't even attempted to send a message to him about when she might be back. Maybe adults didn't convey those things to their grown-up children, but they should. A son still wondered about his mother.

Some languages weren't ever learned, he guessed, especially not those spoken inside of a family. Yet within kin, the most important messages were passed, parent to child and back. He was an apprentice interpreter in that area; of that he was sure.

❖

They took the children with them.

They left Fort Walla Walla, Nez Perce country, in the time of yellowing leaves and followed the river to the Clearwater. Marie hoped to find her friend Sarah there.

She hadn't. Jean's use of words helped them learn that Sarah and Ignace and their sons had returned to the East. A rock of disappointment settled in Marie's stomach. Somehow believing Sarah was close made it possible for Marie to not miss her so much, to know that if she did want to hold her friend for a time, she could do that without wide travel. Now that choice was gone.

Marie noticed that many of the Flathead people bowed their heads before eating and didn't eat pork on a day Jean said was the Sabbath. They wore crosses around their necks, not unlike the one Sarah had given Marie. When she pointed to them and her own, they smiled. But they didn't seem to have that look of peace that Sarah's eyes always held. Instead, these eyes had a seeking look. She recognized it from the reflection of her own when she scrubbed her face in waters of a quiet pool.

"I wonder if Sarah's calling is complete, then," Marie asked Jean as she handed out tufts of cheek bread baked over an open fire. She heard disappointment in her own voice and wasn't sure if it was because she missed seeing Sarah or because she was troubled by the idea of her friend leaving behind unfinished work.

"A *métier* is seldom complete," Jean said. "Your *métier*, as a mother, you think this ends, eh? No. It changes only."

They continued east into mountainous country where streams ran swift. The first season they set steel traps, stripped the hides, salted and baled the pelts with good success, taking them to the rendezvous point north of a great salt lake that was said to look like the ocean in white desert sand.

Marie met a number of women at the rendezvous point. Wives of trappers, "mountain men," they called themselves, who chose independence rather than being moved here and there at the whim of some Company.

Marie looked for Sarah, to see if she might have traveled this way. Her eyes always scanned for Paul, too. Yet she never saw either.

The work was hard, harder than she remembered. The horses carried the fur bales and the younger children. Marie and Jean carried nearly as much on their backs. Horses pulled travois behind them. The packs had to be loaded and unloaded daily, ties tightened, animals soothed when they skittered. And still they followed the trap lines, seeking streams that would give up their furs.

Setting traps in the icy water, pulling the drowned beaver to the surface, Marie's hands were always cold, her fingers white as bone even when she buried them inside fur-lined mittens she sewed herself. Yet one couldn't wear mittens pulling beaver from icy streams.

It was work she knew, work she'd done in her previous life with Pierre. She knew how Louis's hands had split from the cold; recalled her sewing the cracks closed. Now she had no time in the lean-tos set beside fast-rushing streams to do beadwork or make baskets. Her eyes were constantly watching for her children's safety and her hands put to use making meals and keeping the hides from spoiling and rubbing grease onto her husband's chapped hands and her own. Their wealth was salted with those hides.

Her plan, their plan, was to cache as much as they could so they could someday, sometime, store up seeds and plant and have a farm with a cow or two in a place the Company could not touch. Maybe south of the Columbia River. Maybe in the rich bottomland beside the Willamette.

They'd chosen hard work, but it would pay off, Marie was sure of this. She would make it successful, her husband's decision to make his way separate from the Company. That was her *métier*, to make him successful.

✦

In their second year out, away from the Walla Walla River, they made their way to the rendezvous at the south end of a place called Bear Lake, where they crossed a mountain range, tramping through snow even while she could see flowers pushing up as though ready for spring. The country reminded Marie of the land where Hunt had led them astray not far from the Snake River.

But Jean had a good sense of direction and used a needle-piece that gave him confidence in their path. In places of towering timber where Marie couldn't see the sunrise nor take her measure from the dusk, Jean's compass, as he called it, gave guidance.

He worked as a free trapper, which was what he claimed himself to be even though he hadn't "gone back" to sign off at Montreal. Still, he didn't want an argument if they encountered Ogden's men or Work's. So they'd trapped mostly east and south, in the American sector trading with American traders.

"I come from the American section," Marie told him. "If anyone questions. Say I lived in St. Louis and on the Des Moines."

Patchy snow still settled on the north side of the ridges. But in the bowl where tents were pitched for the 1828 rendezvous, the meadow ruffled green and the horses hurried toward the lush grasses despite the loads they carried. Marie could already hear music, flutes and jaw harp twangs, and fiddles, too. She anticipated seeing the women she'd met the previous year, catching up on news of those present and those whose stories the others carried with them.

When they rounded the last ridge, the valley opened, and Marie gasped at the sight of thousands of horses grazing, hundreds of skin tents pitched, and children and dogs racing about as though set free from a wintry den.

Marie looked for women she knew, wives of free trappers who would bring their pelts so the mountain men could barter for needed ammunition, better traps, flour, and whatever other supplies they'd seek for the winter.

But even more, Marie hoped she and Jean had enough pelts in the finest shape that they could get three or four large steel traps, perhaps trade for an additional horse, fill all their basic needs and still have some remaining to make a special request of the supplier. They were beginning their third year as free trappers, and next year Marie hoped would be their last. Next year, she wanted the supplier to bring them seeds.

She touched the faces of some of the women she recognized from the previous year, marveled at the growth of their children. They nodded and smiled their broken-teeth smiles at Marie's brood. Whenever she stopped to consider this family of five, she always felt something was missing: then she realized it was always Little Marie.

"There are more languages spoken this year," she mentioned to Jean after she'd made the rounds at the traders' blankets where they'd laid out their wares. "It took some time before I found English and French speakers."

It was where she'd learned of LaBonte and Kilakotah.

She heard the story as she stirred fresh elk meat in her old copper pot. She could use a new pot. Maybe there'd be enough for an additional kitchen purchase this year.

"LaBonte asked the Columbia chief factor, that McLoughlin, for permission to settle on the Willamette. He wanted a few seeds and a plow. The rest he'd manage himself," related one of the men. "But the white-headed eagle refuses. He tells the French-Canadian he has to go back home, back to Montreal if he wants to start farming. As though his home wasn't the Columbia country he'd lived in for twenty years. Says it's Company policy." Others murmured, nodding their heads.

"McLoughlin doesn't want settlers in that Willamette country. Worried more will come and then it'll go with the Americans 'stead of the Brits. That's the way I hear it." This new speaker had a Boston accent; at least it was how Marie distinguished it from the mountain man's words.

"So LaBonte goes," said the latter. He leaves his wife and his son and heads for Montreal. Eight thousand miles, if he comes back."

"No man'll do that," said the Boston. "Not for a woman already had two husbands in tow."

"Brits would let them settle on the north side, in that Cowlitz country," the mountain man said.

"Can't grow nothing there," said another. "No, LaBonte's found a good place."

"By the time he gets back to Montreal, he'll be glad he returned," Boston said. "Quite lovely country, Montreal, and the women more splendid than the wide one he left behind."

Marie ached for Kilakotah, wondered where she was now, if she was waiting for her Louis or if she had found herself as Marie once had, alone, making her way in the Company's world.

Jean walked up, holding a copper pot. "You traded?" she asked.

"Lead at a dollar a pound. Flannel, a dollar-fifty a yard. Buttons, five dollars a gross. Vermilion and thread, all three dollars a pound. A copper pot, too."

Marie looked at her husband. "These are the prices? And a copper pot the same as vermilion?" She rubbed her sleeve on the pot. "It has smudges on it. Yet they give us only three dollars for a made beaver?"

"It's the going rate, Marie," Jean told her. "Some are getting only two dollars for their pelts. Ours are in good condition. We can be grateful—"

"But he must get five dollars each back in St. Louis," she said. "And we need more traps. He wants nine dollars for one? This is too much."

Jean shrugged his shoulders. "He has his expenses in bringing supplies here. He lost men to warring tribes, and it's a journey of hundreds of—"

"I don't want to hear his sad tales," Marie snapped. "We work hard. We deserve fair treatment. First the Company and now the Americans, too, find their way to take advantage."

"Fair gives everyone what they deserve," Jean said. "He treats us all the same." He picked up the copper pot, rubbed a dark spot with his handkerchief.

"You gave one dollar and a half for a handkerchief, and you use it to clean an unworthy copper pot," she said, taking the cloth from his hands and spitting on it, then rubbing the smudge as though it were responsible for ruining her day.

Jean put his hands over hers and stopped her efforts. "Little lies untarnished, wife," Jean told her. "It's not anyone's fault. It's just what is."

❖

Tom McKay filled Baptiste in on the goings on here and there whenever he visited Vancouver. Tom's stepfather had him leading brigades and making a name for himself. *It would be nice to have someone in a position of power making a way for me,* Baptiste thought, though he appreciated that Tom didn't flaunt his influence the way some did.

"You remember Lucier?" Tom asked Baptiste. The two men rode among a herd of horses that grazed at the edge of a fir forest. Tom had an eye for a good horse.

Baptiste vaguely remembered Lucier, the Canadian who'd been with them when they traveled with Hunt. He'd been a *voyageur* with a deep booming voice.

"My old man refused his request for seeds and tools to settle on the Willamette but paid his passage for him and his kin to return to Canada. They started out but came back. He's pushing again to be allowed to stay without returning to his point of enrollment." There was something different in Tom's tone this time. Baptiste couldn't place it.

"I've been that way, along the Willamette," Baptiste said. "We planted a little garden somewhere there. My father'd been hurt. Me and my brother and mother hadn't been with him. I don't know why. Maybe she didn't want to go. Then we did go. I saw her take a deer for us, in the Wallomat place, she called it. Didn't want to be in debt to the Astorians, so she did it all on her own. Trapped there, too. Made me work, watching Paul."

"Good pasture land for horses. Not so full of trees and hills as this country," Tom said. "Less rain, too. Fever hits in the late summer there. Not so good then."

"She made a dogwood bark tea. I remember. Kept the fever down. The factor doesn't want people going there, does he?"

Tom took out a twist of tobacco and bit it off. "Time I was doing things on my own," he said. His mouth twitched in that way he had sometimes when he was thinking.

"Will he send you back to Montreal too, to part ways with Hudson's Bay?"

Tom laughed. "I was eleven when my father set my mother off and we came out here. Wasn't employed by the Company then, no sir. So I think the old man will have a hard time trying to send me back. Besides, my children's wails would reach their grandmother's ears. And they may be just loud enough he won't object to their voices rising up from the Willamette country."

Tom moved the chew from the side of his mouth, pulled a stray flake from his tongue with his fingers. "He sent Louis LaBonte. Remember him?" Baptiste nodded. "Had a son he left behind."

"My mother spent time with his woman."

"She says he's coming back," Tom said. "But he's been gone a year already. She's staying with her sister, who's married to Joseph Gervais. Remember him? Suppose he'll get sent back too, another French-Canadian."

Tom chewed on the side of his cheek. He stared out, talked now as though Baptiste might not even be present. "My own sons, half Chinook, me half Ojibway, they've got a harder trail to ride. A man without a family to worry over might be better off than some."

The scent of ripe blackberries heated by the afternoon sun came to Baptiste, and he dismounted, reached into the tangle of vines. He pulled the plump berries and tossed them up to Tom.

"You ought to come, too," Tom said as he grabbed at another fruit lobbed his way.

Baptiste let the soft ridge of berry skin roll to the back of his tongue. Warm and soft and sweet. "We could get ourselves quite a horse ranch going. There are good streams there, for a gristmill. Much better country than north, across the Columbia, for growing things. You're good with plants. Just go there and turn the soil."

"Just up and leave?" Baptiste licked the palm of his hand of the berry juice.

"You entered into service here. You wouldn't have to travel back to any place except Fort Walla Walla. You got any stake money? For supplies and whatnot?"

Baptiste shook his head. "I spend as much as I make. A Company benefit, I guess. Always have a roof over my head, food to eat, and any time now, even an apple to crunch into."

"Think about it," Tom told him. "There's a price to pay for contentment, especially if it's dependent on someone else's."

❖

The rendezvous was at Popo Agie, east of a gentle pass. Marie said if they'd known of it, perhaps her daughter Vivacité might have survived Hunt's winter crossing.

Once there, Marie traded her round beaded hair sticks for a knife with a blade of smooth black stone the woman who had it called "obsidian." The edge was sharper than anything Marie had ever felt. She hadn't had a good knife since the one Sacagawea gave her years before. It was the first trade she made, and she hoped it was a sign of a good rendezvous this year. She'd had no time to paint on her hide calendar, but if she had, this year of 1830 would have been marked by a beaver hide. A good year or poor, their lives were driven by the furry pelts.

Prices were even higher than the two years prior. So, together, wrapped inside their robes, she and Jean came to a new conclusion: there was no way to make this trapping world work. Too much had changed. Too much depended on others, how the companies and traders and land set the prices.

There was no way to live unaffected by the Company.

"When you worked for Hudson's Bay, we paid off debts," she said. "And had enough to set aside. Maybe it's time to do this again. Maybe we must put up with the Company for a time in order to make another way."

Jean dropped his jaw. "I never expected to hear you say these words."

"I can change," she said. She tugged at a loose tooth of Marguerite's. The girl stomped her feet up and down and begged her to wait, wait.

"It will be better, faster, daughter," Marie said. "One yank—"

"No, no, no."

Marie sighed, paused. "I'm sorry the dog ran into you, but the tooth is loose and will only turn black. It must come out."

"If they'll take me back," Jean said. "Ogden knows me as a 'trouble-maker.' That's what I hear."

"Maybe you can convince him you can make things besides trouble," she said. Then she yanked once more at her daughter's tooth.

Marguerite cried, held her finger to her top lip. "Who will want me now?" she said. "All ugly with a tooth missing? Who will want me now?"

"My thoughts exactly," Jean said. "Not about you, daughter, but of your Papa."

Marie lay quiet beneath a summer sky. She could hear Marguerite jabbering to seven-year-old François, telling him to be still, to stop teasing First Lick. She said the dog's name strangely now, without a front tooth.

Marguerite could already salt the hides nearly as well as Marie. She was tall for a child with twelve summers, and Marie noticed a few whiskered men eyeing her at the fire, glances Marie met with glares. Her daughter was too young to make a match. Her daughter would make her own choice when that time came.

The dog still growled and tore at sticks as though he were a pup, and François encouraged it, even while they were asleep. Marianne's soft snores already filled the tent behind them. Closer to the river, a har-monica and a fiddle livened up the night. Marie knew there'd be headaches in the morning.

Jean held Marie in the crook of his arm, her hand resting gently on his chest. He stroked the side of her face while they talked, a gesture as soothing as silk. Jean was a steady, patient man who put each foot before the other in predictable fashion, rarely out of step with what she'd hoped for in a husband. As long as his family was near, he was content. That he'd earned a reputation as a 'troublemaker' seemed the greatest injustice.

Once, she'd used it to advantage and he'd become a free man. But he'd only done a righteous thing. He deserved better than to be discred-ited on account of it.

And yet they had no future that she could see except to go back to the very place, the very people, who had named him so.

"If we go back to Walla Walla and the Company takes you on, you'll become part of a brigade," she said. "Do what they tell you."

"You'll go with me, eh? The work will be much the same as what we do here. But there'll be many more of us. And the food will not be ours alone to give our children. But we could put some aside as before."

She was thoughtful for a long time.

"Or we could secure a loan. From the factor perhaps."

"Go into debt?"

"Your debt brought you to me," he teased.

"No," she said.

Jean's breathing slowed, and she thought he might sleep. But he said, "Did you see that? The star that falls. Another, there." He pointed, his voice excited. "Beautiful, eh?"

"Oui."

He sighed. "It doesn't matter where we go, Marie. We are guided by a good God. He writes our *métier* across the sky. Even these past years, hard as they have been, we have been well kept."

Marie couldn't help but think of the separation that existed between her and her sons. The deaths they'd endured. Her loss of two husbands. These parts of her life had not been well kept. But Jean was right: His children were safe. They'd had enough to eat. What more did they need?

"You think it is God's *métier*," she said, "to keep us?"

"Wherever we are," Jean said. "He knows the name of each star, my Marie. And our names too." He squeezed her shoulder. "God's *métier*," he said. "This is a good thought, eh? And that he helps us find ours, too. Marguerite's and François's and Marianne's."

"And my sons?"

"We are not alone in this, eh? *Métier*." Jean said, "It is an unattested word. Did you know this?" She shook her head, no. "In a language," he told her, "as in Chinook or Sahaptin or English, *unattested* means there is no direct evidence for the meaning of the word, but it is known and believed just the same. Everyone accepts it in all languages, just as it is. Unattested."

She'd forgotten how much words and their meanings, translating, interpreting, fed him. Maybe he could do that again instead of this hard work of setting traps. And maybe if she traveled with him she could find new places where word of Paul might be found.

"A calling that is suited best, this is unattested?"

"*Oui*. The work for some is in finding what that is," Jean said. "And accepting it as so. We trust in One who takes time to name each star and see where he leads us."

"Even back to the Company?"

"Even there."

18

Riverbed of the Spirit

It felt like home, a welcoming of rounded hills, towers of rock watching over them as they approached, the shimmer of warmth off the river. Walla Walla, again. Much had happened here; many joys and wounds had found their carving at this site. Perhaps that was all life was, pleasures chiseled out of disappointments with the hope that the strength of the former outweighed the latter.

It was a mature landscape, Marie thought, as her eyes settled on the distant hills. One with many rounded edges, not jagged spires and peaks of mountains or the cuts of waterfalls and ripples that marked the Snake River or the Shining Mountains. Age weathered, the wind and rain took soil down to foundation. Perhaps that was what was happening to her. She was finding her foundation.

Marie craned her neck as she rode to see if she might recognize Little Marie, Josette. She spied their old house with a garden green beside it.

"We check in first, at the fur house," Jean said.

They met the new factor, Pierre Pambrun, in charge of sending out brigades under the leadership of John Work. Ogden had been promoted to factor at another post.

Pambrun's Indian wife, Catherine, looked barely older than Baptiste, Marie realized when she saw the young plump woman beside her husband. Marie wasn't all that good at judging age, but Catherine's fingers on her clay pipe were unlined and smooth as dough, so she couldn't be much beyond twenty-five summers.

Catherine treated Marie as though she were a long lost friend when she arrived, and said she knew her son Baptiste, had met him at Fort Vancouver and watched him tend the orchards there. She said he was known for his gift with plants.

Marie warmed with the praise of a son. "He works there?"

"Here, too," Catherine told her.

"Where?" Could she really have such a pleasure as seeing both her granddaughter and her son? To have everyone together? Almost everyone.

"Somewhere, there," Catherine said, waving her hand toward the palisades. The young woman wasn't interested in talking more of Baptiste. Instead, she inhaled her clay pipe and told Marie she'd refused to give it up even when her husband had offered her a pair of diamond earrings if she would. "He has his books to read, dozens of them," Catherine said. "I gave up my blanket in order to wear the cape he says is more becoming of my station. But I refuse to give up my pipe."

Tom McKay brought news of Kilakotah. "So you've returned, and LaBonte has too," Tom said. "He traveled eight thousand miles and surprised the old man by showing up eighteen months after he was sent packing back to Montreal. Probably surprised his wife as well."

Marie shook her head. "Kilakotah believed in him, that he'd come back for his son if not for her."

"Well, now he's back, and he again asked my father for some seeds and tools. The old man agreed this time. Probably humbled by LaBonte's devotion to his kin. They're settling in the southern section, on the Willamette River. Lucier is already there, farming. Lucier finally worked the old man down to an offer of assistance too.

"I've broken ground there myself," Tom continued, his long dark mustache bouncing as he spoke. "Get a little more time there now, and I've received permission to step aside from the Company."

"You've found another way?" Jean asked.

"Free trap some. Hit the rendezvous, but mostly trade in horseflesh. I still do well at racing. And I guide some of the botanists and artists and such heading this way. My father says he read an article from a Boston paper about colonizing the Willamette, so I expect there'll be even more of such folks before long. Spies, even, from America."

"Kilakotah is on the Willamette," Marie breathed again.

"With her daughter and son. And her sister, Yaimust is there too, with her husband. My own place at *Cantonment du Sable* is just above the falls. Regular little village forming up."

"That's where we were, where Wallace built the fur house," Marie said. She could hear the excitement in her own voice. "Kilakotah will walk where I walked!"

Her friend had not been set off, she'd had a long, no doubt grueling, wait with no word sent, no letters—at least none Kilakotah could read—telling her of her husband's intentions. She simply had to trust that he'd return. And he had! And as her reward, she was now at a place separate from the Company, the very place where Marie had once wintered, dug the soil, and planted seeds.

"We can go there, maybe," she said, tugging on Jean's sleeve after Tom left.

"Sometime," Jean said. "We could ask the factor for seeds. They did. He gave some to them."

"It would be a loan," Marie said. Then, backing off: "With your record, they wouldn't even make the loan."

"They'd insist I return to Montreal, eh? Would you wait so long for me?"

"I'd go with you. All of us would. But not to come back to a debt."

Jean smiled at her. "No, let's do what we planned now. See if Pambrun will have me back. Save what we can, and in a few years or so—"

"She has her sister there, too," Marie said, the ache of having a full family around her tugging at her heart. "Her family present in one place."

"And you've got yours here."

Marie turned to the voice she knew.

❖

Baptiste had only intended to see his daughter from a distance. It had been seven years, by his calculations, since he'd ridden away from Fort Walla Walla. His daughter wouldn't remember him, and maybe that would be all right. He hoped she didn't look too much like her mother; that was what he really hoped. He wasn't sure if he could face a child with Older Sister's dimples or her skin, the color of sand.

It had been bad enough to be left without a father when he was young, a loss followed by his wife's death. Baptiste had a fleeting memory of his mother kneeling in the snow when his father'd been killed. They shared a grieving, and he'd just now understood it.

He shared it with his daughter, too. She'd lost her mother, and he'd drifted away from her.

He wished he'd found a way to avoid this place of bad memories. But he'd made the journey from Fort Vancouver as part of an assignment for McLoughlin, bringing with him starts of grapes and peaches and one small apple tree that had delivered up a perfect green apple after barely two years. He hadn't gotten to taste that apple, but the factor had sliced many thin pieces he shared with his family and visiting guests. Soon, they'd have more than enough so all could have a bite or two. Baptiste took it as an indication of trust that the factor sent him and none other with the starts.

Several canoes carried supplies east, but Baptiste, not wanting to put the plants in the hands of those who wouldn't share his concern for them, had ridden his own good horse and packed two of the Company's animals. Tom McKay rode with him, heading for a rendezvous. The canoe handlers and he and Tom McKay camped together at night, but during the day, the horse riders would often be well away from the canoes, crossing overland, high above the river where they could see snow-capped mountains and the Columbia, twisting calm as a fat snake.

They didn't worry about assault or attack. The presence of people moving up and down the river had become routine over the past few years. A far cry from the danger experienced by the first expedition of Lewis and Clark. Twenty-seven years had passed since they'd made their way along this river; twenty since Baptiste had passed by here as a boy. East and West were meeting faster and faster. Pretty soon his having been part of the Hunt overland expedition wouldn't even mean anything, there'd be so many people who'd come across the mountains with their own stories to tell.

Baptiste had heard that a new group of Nez Perce, sons of people he might know from his time at the fort, had headed back East. A young man named Richard was one of them. Baptiste remembered he rode with the reins in his right hand. He was unusual that way. They were said to be looking for the "Book of Heaven," they called it.

"Inspired by the lowly Spokane going back East first with Simpson, you ask my opinion," Tom said when Baptiste asked if he'd heard of this eastward trek. "The Spokane boy Pelly died, they say, but not before he wrote a letter, using English. Simpson delivered it to his parents last time he was out. In twenty-eight. Garry's still back there at the Red River Settlement. A 'highly educated Spokane' is what they call him. And the Nez Perce, they want some of that influence, too, I suspect. That's why they're heading back."

"You don't think they're really looking for what's inside the book?" Baptiste asked. "My grandmother always said the book was real, that its words helped a man know his way around the world."

"Help him know who he is if he studied it, I'd guess," Tom said. "My own mother says as much. Raised Catholic, she was. Yours?"

Baptiste said he wasn't sure about his mother's training. Or his grandmother's, except that Holy Rainbow did indeed speak of baptism and such, urging him to trust in something larger than himself.

What good was a God who left a child without a mother?

Baptiste had fidgeted in the saddle, remembering Holy Rainbow's words of wisdom and his own wide berth around them.

"Don't know that I'd be willing to ride across the continent to find out more about that Holy Book," Baptiste said. He knew he sounded bitter. "God's revealed himself well enough right here."

Tom shrugged. "Something made them do it. Fame maybe. They'll be noticed if they make it, just because they had the interest and it took them over the mountains."

"Where're they heading then? Red River, where Spokane Garry is, or—"

"St. Louis. Said they'd find Captain Clark, and he'd direct their way from there. Twenty-some years, and they still think of Clark as a king. They're asking for him to send long robes or black robes or preachers and such. Maybe priests will get schools out here. Simpson promised those three years ago, but it never happened." Tom was quiet as they rode. "My own sons and daughters need schooling," he said.

"Maybe they'll do all right without it," Baptiste said. "Look at me. Who would have imagined that a half French-Canadian and half Indian would be tending treaties one year and planting seeds from London's soils the next?"

Tom said, "Without European blood or military backgrounds, our children don't have much chance out here. Not without schooling. It's a different place than the one you were brought to. Or me either. We've got to do something to help. It's a father's responsibility, that's sure."

Tom had given Baptiste all those things to think about on his trek upriver.

He'd known he needed to see her, Little Marie, to see what she might need from him.

When he arrived at Walla Walla, Narcisse told him that Older Sister's family had moved into his mother's wooden house that looked no more prosperous than when he'd left. Yet Narcisse had kept them as comfortable as he could, Baptiste decided. He dismounted, his eyes scanning until he saw her. His heart pounded. *Strange.* She had long, graceful arms. *Like her mother.* He inhaled deeply, for the first time wondering how his daughter would receive him.

She beat on a blanket draped over a rope, dust causing her to cough. Marguerite—his half-sister—beat beside her, and the two girls laughed through their chokes. That little peak of hair that dipped into her forehead named her. She'd been born with it, all tiny and dark. Now, nearly ten years old, she wore her hair like her grandmother's, knotted at the back of her neck. A young woman.

He watched for a time, hands crossed over the pommel of the saddle. Marguerite turned to see whom Little Marie stared at.

"Baptiste!" his sister squealed. "You're back. It's your papa, Marie, your papa's come home."

She ran to him, his sister, and he pulled her up onto the horse behind him.

"As beautiful a woman as I've seen in some years," he told Marguerite.

"Days, I'd say," she said. "When did you get here? Where have you been? How long can you stay?" She squeezed her arms around his middle.

"Oh, shhh," he said, peeling her hands free.

"You sound like Mother," she said. "Come here, Little Marie. It's your papa. He won't bite you."

Careful as a doe, she walked toward him. When she looked him full in the face, he saw her mother's eyes, her chin, her nose. His heart ached. He swallowed. He didn't want her to see his pain, so he quickly converted it to the pleasure of her presence.

But it was too late. Tears pooled in her eyes, and she ducked her head and ran inside, braids flying out behind her.

That was when he'd ridden away and come upon his mother.

❖

"The rumor is, you went back, you met your grandmother," Marie said. She'd turned to the sound of her son's voice, her arms at her side, held back from reaching out. She wanted to reach out.

Baptiste dismounted, the reins in his hands. She walked over to him, close enough that he could smell the lavender in her hair. If he were a hugging man, he would have done that now. But he didn't. He noticed that Jean and Tom moved away from them, took sudden interest in the hoof of a horse, in running their hands over the rump of the animal, their backs to him and his mother.

"Is she well, Holy Rainbow?"

Baptiste nodded. "We had much to talk about. She knows about treaty signings and Dorions. My father's grandfather was an interpreter too. And his. I didn't know this."

"I didn't keep you from it," she said. "Some things I did not know."

"A boy needs to hear good things about his father and those before him," Baptiste said.

He held his elbows out, hands at his hips, as he had when he was young. He made himself drop them to his side. He looked more confident when he held his arms loose. Older Sister had taught him that.

"Did you see…others?" his mother asked.

"Say it," he said. "Did I see Paul? No. I didn't see your son. Not then, not on the way, not coming back. Not in all the years since I've seen you. Did you come looking for me, Mother? Did you send someone to find me?"

"I knew where you were."

"No one has seen Paul, Mother. If he lives, he chooses to make us wonder. If he's dead, then we are blessed."

She slapped him then, the flat of her hand to his face.

He saw Jean and Tom turn at the sound, watched his mother put her fingers to her mouth, her eyes water. *"Pardon, pardon,"* she whispered, turned, and ran away.

❖

"I helped Work move equipment and supplies from Fort George to *Belle Vue,"* Jean said. "He remembered me."

"So he'll hire you back?" Marie asked. She'd been looking at Little Marie drawing in the sand. She looked up, smiling.

Jean nodded. "It surprised him that I'd had a bad report, he said. Then noted it was from Ogden and while he didn't grin, it looked as though he wanted to. He asked what would be different with this brigade, and I told him I had a wiser leader, I thought; that I was older and smarter, too; and that this time, my wife and family would come with me."

"He agreed?"

"I know you must want this very much, to wish me in the Company's employ and to agree to go with me. You will come along, *oui?"*

"We'll have time here, to visit with my son's daughter first?"

"Work returns to Vancouver within the week to supply the brigade. Then we head out, from here, south."

Jean continued, "You could stay and enjoy your family, I guess, join us when we come back through."

Marie heard longing in his offer. "A mother should stay with her children. Baptiste is here. I must…"

"You're not leaving are you, grandmother?" said Little Marie.

Jean tried not to let his disappointment show. He'd hoped she'd travel back with him, show Work that his words carried weight even before the brigade set out. He didn't think time with Baptiste now would resolve a conflict that seemed to get worse with time instead of better.

"I thought we'd crossed that river already," Jean said. He lifted the end of Little Marie's braid, ran the smooth strands between his fingers. To the child he added, "Your grandmother is a good traveler. I need her to see things I'd miss."

"She squeezes her eyes to see my drawing," Little Marie told him. "She sees better when she's with you?"

Marie nodded. "Seeing me reminds Baptiste of things he wants to forget. And I become someone I don't want to be. Little Marie is well-raised by Josette. I think your family goes with you now," Marie said.

Jean reached to pull her up to him, his face bathed in gratitude and grin.

"Baptiste will forgive you in time," he said. "First you must forgive yourself."

✛

She was slender as a cattail and just as a brown. All the rest were out berry picking, Baptiste supposed. Only a dog with pups at her side lay in the shade of the hides. He'd spoken little to his mother, his eyes cast down. He didn't know why he couldn't reach out to her, let himself be held. He could feel her wanting that from him.

And then he spoiled it, said things with a spite he hadn't intended. And she'd struck him.

He deserved it. Just as he'd deserved it from his father, or Paul had deserved it from him. It kept being handed down, this dishonoring. If only he had honored her by stepping away. If only he hadn't jabbed at her about Paul. What kind of son was he?

What kind of father?

He'd done almost nothing for the girl. His mother would know that, probably judged him as a poor father in addition to being an ungrateful son. He'd mounted up and ridden away, leaving them both licking wounds he'd given.

Then just beyond the lodge, he saw her. She looked up at him, this Cayuse girl, no, woman. He felt as though he'd had another looping dream, as though he saw someone he'd known before. It wasn't Little Marie, the one he'd come to see, hoped to see even through the pain.

This one wore a question on her face, slender brows raised up, her mouth slightly open. She called him by name.

"Do I know you?" he said, pulling up on the reins. As he got closer, his heart seemed to stop then begin again, pounding loudly in his ears.

She nodded. She had brown eyes like sable he could sink into. She looked so much like Older Sister he'd thought at first she was.

Her hand shaded her face from the sun. He moved to cast a shadow so she could drop her fingers that now held the ends of her long braids. "Who are you?"

"Your wife's sister," she said. "You used to call me Josette."

She'd been so very young when he left, her bare feet muddied by the pies she played in. No, she hadn't played much at all, as he recalled. After Older Sister died, Josette had taken on the tasks of tending younger brothers and sisters, of putting soft cloths to the forehead of her weakened mother. He'd not looked at her much at all, and when he did, he looked away, guilty for how his choices had touched hers.

But now, he held her gaze. Here was the one who most resembled the woman he'd loved and lost. And yet she looked different, had a welcoming smile, more than a sister to a brother. And she had a name of her own.

❖

Marie sat with the children while they ate, while the fires drifted from cooking into soft light that filled the growing dark. Marie discovered interests of this child who called her Kasa, grandmother. The tender tie they had for each other, from the year she lived with Marie, stayed strong, even through the distance since. Maybe she should stay here for a time, to be with this child. Maybe through this child she could reach her son, ask his forgiveness for her temper, for who she was.

But it couldn't be, not with her younger son's and daughters' arms looped around her neck yet, growing, needing her. And this child belonged with her father, if Little Marie took on any new ties at all.

"What's this?" Little Marie asked. She pointed to a scar Marie had on her hand, one received when she'd cut herself years past while helping her own mother strip a hide from a buffalo. Marie told her. "And this?" She pointed to the cross Marie wore at her neck.

"A gift from a friend," Marie said. "Whenever I see it, I think of her."

"What makes you think of me?"

"Ah, well, whenever the sun comes up, I think of you. I see the round, warm ball and know it warms you and lights your way so you will not stumble or fall. Whenever you see it, you think of me, too, *oui?* Then we know we are thinking of each other."

"What about nighttime?" Little Marie asked. "Should I think of the moon and you?"

"Yes. That would be good. The moon watches over you while you grow during the night."

"Sometimes I get asked to dance at night when the fiddler plays."

"I suspect you do." Marie touched her forehead with the respect due such an act of intimacy before seeking permission.

"But I fall over my feet. And the trappers' feet, too."

Marie looked into this child's face, could see her own mother's nose, a glimpse of her eyes. "Nighttime especially I think of you," she said. "Whenever the stars come out."

Something her mother once told her came to her, about each star having its own name, given by God. Marie wasn't sure how that was possible, that each tiny speck of light could be so precious as to bear a unique and individual name. "When you look up at night and you see each star, know that I see them too, wherever I am. And that they are over you just as they are over me, signs of great, glowing, singular love."

"And if I fall down in the dark?" Little Marie asked, teasing. "You'd catch me if I fell down?"

"Always know when you fall, even in the dark, that someone who loves you will be there to pick you up. Let the stars remind you."

❖

They left soon after, in the Company's employ under the guidance of John Work. A fever raged at Fort Vancouver when they arrived, so they stayed but one night, sleeping far from the other tents. Jean had told

Marie that she couldn't even look at the cattle barns. "Too dangerous."
First Lick had to be called back more than once as he sniffed farther
away to the new smells of outlying places.

They headed south in the morning, just Jean, Marie, and their children. Near the falls they located the place Tom McKay spoke of, the
beginning of that little village.

Marie remembered Etienne Lucier, the man who owned the homestead they encountered first. In the field she could see him, still a tall,
strong *voyageur*. He'd been polite to her on the overland journey. He even
seemed to notice her children and speak kindly to them. He hadn't been
near when Pierre had lost control, her husband's wisdom beaten by the
whiskey. But she had believed of Lucier that he would have intervened if
he had known how Pierre had hurt her. Some Astorians had known and
done nothing. Jean Toupin, young as he had been, had tried to help.

Lucier walked toward them from his small field of wheat. He'd
roughed out a story-and-a-half house, a smokehouse, even a pen with
one hog. A few chickens scratched near a lean-to meant to protect them
from the coyotes and raccoons.

"Madame Dorion," Lucier said, his voice booming out. "Such a
surprise. And who are these then, these little cherubs?"

"My children," she said. "And my husband."

Lucier cocked his head.

"You remember one of Hunt's camp boys?" Jean said.

The taller man pushed his sleeves up as though a habit and shook
his head. "*Oui,* I remember. The horseman. And you took a liking to
Mackenzie's dogs. And the Dorion boys, too. Do I remember well?"

"You do," Jean said, and he reached to shake the man's hand. Wheat
headed-out, the stalks heavy with rope grain, in the little field they stood
beside. It was clear Lucier intended to begin his harvest, a task they'd
interrupted.

"Come inside," Lucier said. "My wife will serve you well. She's of
the Nouete tribe. You've heard of them?" Marie shook her head, no.

"No matter. We'll eat and talk. Your dog won't run off?"

Marie looked around, not wanting to be impolite, but it was
Kilakotah she wanted most to see.

Jean said, "LaBonte lives close by?"

Lucier started to speak but was interrupted then by Louis Two. The boy huffed and puffed from around the corner. He was taller and certainly leaner than when she'd seen him last.

"Ah, my Little Letter," Marie cooed and stood. The boy's face turned to rose. Then he stepped aside, and Marie walked into the arms of her friend.

❖

"I've always been old," Kilakotah told Marie as they sat on a stump near the log house. Marie threw a stick for First Lick to retrieve. The dog moved more slowly, as did she. Even Its-owl-eigh had slowed down so much they'd left the dog with Little Marie rather than strain his efforts on this journey.

The children chased butterflies near the field. Her friend touched Marie's cheeks. "Smooth. Waiting made my face rain wrinkles."

"But you knew he'd return, that LaBonte would come back to you. The worry choked you?"

"I heard a man at the fort say my husband received money to take me on after McMillan set me off. A third hand. Someone had to pay him to take me." She lifted her chin. "I thought maybe he used up all the money going to Montreal and couldn't come back. There are younger, stronger women he could have found. I'm so old. I've always been old. I even remember seeing the woman who came with Lewis and Clark, what was her name?"

"Sacagawea," Marie said. "You saw her?"

"I was little. My father's a Clatsop chief, and my sister and I were allowed to stand beside him when he spoke with those men and that woman with her child. She carried a knife and had a pretty beaded belt the color of the sky."

Marie felt tears form at her eyes. "She told me of the belt. She gave it away so that Lewis could have a sea otter cape. And I once had that knife as mine."

"You will stay the winter," Kilakotah said then. "My sister has room for some of you. We have room for the rest."

The log cabin was small, the invitation generous. "When Jean goes back, I go with him," Marie said. "I go everywhere with him now."

"Ah," Kilakotah leaned into her as they sat in front of the hut LaBonte had built. "You grow wiser with age."

LaBonte worked a plow behind a horse, the black earth turning over like a twist of tobacco. Jean walked beside him, bent to lift some of the loam.

"It's good land," Kilakotah said. "We raise enough to feed ourselves. All our family," she said. "Victoria joins us, too, my daughter. And we have some left over."

"Your daughter comes too, after all this time." Marie knew she sounded wistful, and a face came to her, distant as a dream. She couldn't bring it to the surface. "Are you well?" Kilakotah asked, touching her hand.

Marie looked at her. *"Oui."* She touched her temples with her fingers. "Is it warm?"

"I'll get you water," Kilakotah said. "The water here is very good."

Marie drank, then asked, "Will the Company buy what you raise?"

"My husband says the time will come when this will be a busy place. More French-Canadians will come back here, even if the Company allows them only a few seeds to get them started. See how far Lucier has come with his seeds. And this place will be called French Prairie, for so many Frenchmen breaking the soil. And we will sell to each other and trade for what we need."

"There has to be a way to live here and prosper," Marie said.

"Bear fruit, that's all a tree is meant to do. My husband says we are all trees in this place." She pressed her hands against her thighs to stand. "I take cold tea to my husband. It keeps him from the fever and ague," she said. "Will your husband want some?"

Marie nodded, stood to follow Kilakotah. "There has to be a way," Marie said, fingering the cross at her neck.

❖

They spent the winter at French Prairie, the chief factor willing to have men in the outlying areas rather than consuming resources at the fort. Marie walked the lands where she and Pierre had once set their sights. Jean trapped some, but for Marie, she spent her days sharing the work of tending children, mending clothes, preparing hides for storage. They did what they could to help Kilakotah and her husband become farmers.

They talked about the land, the resources. Kilakotah had been promised one of Lucier's hogs. LaBonte hoped to purchase some chickens at the fort. No one knew how any could get a neat milk cow, though, in time, they could purchase oxen to lessen the workload.

The weather, though rainy and cold enough to make Marie's fingers ache, still permitted work. They felled trees for building corrals and outbuildings, the crack of a falling fir muted by the damp earth that lawned the forests.

The natural prairie opened into tillable land. François and Jean helped clear brush and burn it, the smoke a help against the bugs. And when a pale, hazy sun shown through the firs and the ground was not too spongy to walk on, they broke more soil, preparing it for seed.

Marie thought of her older sons often while she watched her second family. She remembered where Paul had slipped into the stream, and she found the place where Baptiste had encountered crayfish. She even thought she'd located where they'd had their lodge and nursed Pierre back to health. Where were her sons now? Had they found peace despite the intrusions of their mother?

They met some Kalapuya people, and Jean's ability with words helped them learn of leaves to supplement the cornmeal and dried fish that were the staples of their days. And when spring came, and Tom McKay rode in, they learned that the rendezvous Tom had been headed for the year before had not been held. No eastern supplies arrived with Ashley that year.

"We did well to leave the trapping when we did," Jean told Marie when Tom left. "We had someone looking out for us."

"Did we?" she asked. Was there pattern in her life, some mapping done by an all-seeing hand? She looked at the painted hide marking the important events of her days. Was there another artist's hand in the overall design?

They helped LaBonte plant spring fields, brought in meat to share, and rode their horses out across the meadows at fast paces. Even Kilakotah rode a horse, though she claimed that Marie's speed and skill on one of Janey's colts left her so far behind as to be out riding by herself.

"This is a good place, husband," Marie told Jean as they watched the sun set behind the oaks and cottonwoods that lined the Willamette. "We prosper here."

"With the gifts of our neighbors," he said. "But to make it on our own…" He shrugged his shoulders.

They left their winter of the Willamette and returned to Fort Vancouver. With the brigade, they reached Fort Walla Walla in early September. Jean wrote the month and day on a pad while Marie watched Little Marie and Marianne play together.

"Are you back to stay, Grandmother?" Little Marie asked. Marie shook her head no. "More to see with Jean?" she said, and Marie nodded in agreement.

Little Marie called Josette "Mother," showing her bugs kept alive in the small of her dark hand, and allowed Marianne to elbow her way in to look as well.

"I remember the stars, Kasa," she told Marie. "It's our secret," she whispered then, her finger over her mouth to indicate silence.

"Me too, Mama?" Marianne asked. "I want a secret."

"It's nothing we can't share," she told the girls. "There are enough stars to go around to remind each of you of how special you are."

Little Marie frowned and crossed her arms over her chest.

"There's enough of me to go around too," Marie told her, opening wide her arms. The girl hesitated, then flung herself at her grandmother's lap. Marianne pushed in behind her, and Marie held them both tight to her.

Marguerite came around the house with a basket of roots, and the girls deserted Marie for her. "Good root-diggers make good mamas," Marguerite told them as they spread the white tubers out onto a mat for drying.

How Marie wished she could leave these children something more than the thought of the stars watching over them, as comforting as that image was. She tried to remember her own mother's teachings. How had it begun, a mother's building up of confidence, of a child's trusting that she was precious, valued as a treasure's worth? Her mother had given her this. Yet something had washed it away.

Once she'd believed she could do anything, pushed her way to places where men did not expect to see a woman's shadow reflected in their light. Once she'd stood firm, lived with the choices she made without the constant fear of choking if she found a moment filled with joy. She could push unbidden thoughts of danger away. She loved without hurting others.

Somehow, she'd been given strands of ancestral stories—their strengths, attachments, and uniqueness. She had drawn on those. Even when she'd wondered if she'd be enough, in her times of greatest trials, she had discovered an untapped pool beneath the surface.

Something had changed along the way. The deaths. The losses. Her loss of control with Paul and Baptiste. They'd dried her up.

Her mother had been a riverbed of spirit, someone who let God's strength flow through her to reach her daughters. Sarah had been this kind of mother too. But Marie had built a dam and only let a spillway open when the waters pushed hard against her life. In the calmer days, her riverbed ran dry. She had nothing to give to sustain those she loved. She just could not discover why.

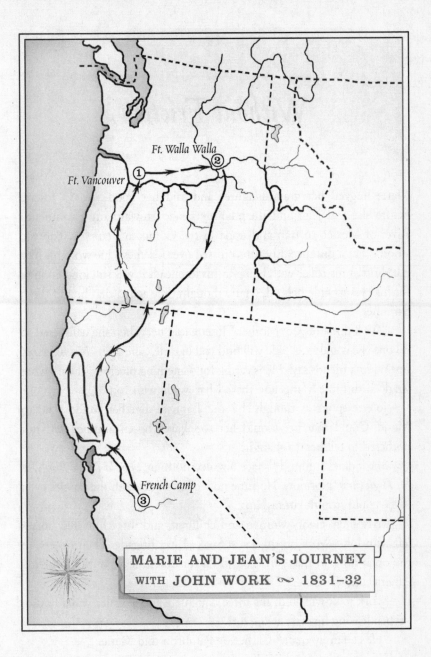

Ft. Walla Walla

Ft. Vancouver ①

②

French Camp ③

MARIE AND JEAN'S JOURNEY
WITH JOHN WORK ∽ 1831–32

19

Without Friction

Marie hugged her granddaughter and said her good-byes to Josette before she and Jean and their family headed toward the Sacramento River of Mexico to trap and trade in the Company's employ. Baptiste stood off at a distance, his arms crossed over his chest. He wore his hair cut short at his collar with bangs at his forehead. It was still long enough for his eyes to hide behind, Marie thought. She ached that he hid them from her.

"We'll think of you, Mother," Josette told her. Then she whispered so no one else could hear. "He will find you in time," she said. "*Naknuwisha,* my Yakima friends say. 'He is caring for something precious.' That's what we do with Little Marie, and that's what we do with you."

Josette spoke as though she and Baptiste together would tend to Marie. Could that be? Could her son have chosen another and not bothered to tell her, to share it?

She looked at him. His face revealed nothing. *Should I go to him, ask his forgiveness?* Not now. No time now to work through the tangles even if she could stop the unraveling.

Sixty men, eighty women and children, and three hundred horses left with John Work on this latest Snake River brigade. Their orders, in the open now, to make the country a fur desert, leave nothing for the Americans.

Work took with him his three daughters and a Walla Walla house-keeper, leaving his wife at the fort.

"He's a family man," Catherine Pambrun told Marie.

"He doesn't bring his wife with him."

Catherine took a draw on her pipe. "Only the wives of laborers go," she said. "I mean no offense."

Marie remembered that Ross had left Sally behind, too. It was a salute, not a slap, but Sally hadn't seen it that way.

Marie assumed duties of tending her own children as well as helping with Work's girls. The housekeeper seemed at a loss with no house to tend, though she claimed to always be warm at night.

They'd be out for two years at least, wintering at a place on the San Joaquin River, even farther into Mexico. "There are good meadows there," Jean told her. "Michel, our friend, has already wintered there, Work says. They call the place by us French Camp." He seemed proud of that fact. "And our hands will not get so chapped in that warm climate. It's not so wet as your Willamette nor as snowy as Fort Walla Walla. Maybe we'll stay there."

If all went well, in two years, they would have what they needed to secure what Marie believed was her *métier*. A farm. If all went well.

The journey took strength and patience. Illnesses struck the children. There were surprise attacks by tribes fiercer than those along the Columbia. Some days the men returned with nothing in their traps because they'd already been checked, the treasure taken by others, Americans already in the area or local tribes planning to sell to the highest bidder.

Horses were picked off as though they were tree plums.

Even Marie could see why local people challenged their efforts. Three hundred horses tramped the land, broke through vines, and consumed grass that deer or elk would need, that the tribes' own horses would need for winter survival.

Hunters spent long days circling farther and farther out to feed the nearly 150 people daily, further depleting the local food supply. The men especially needed extra fuel for the hours spent in the streams setting traps and recovering their kills. They took all the pelts they could, not leaving any for seed for the next year. The Company didn't care about the next year, so sure were they that the Americans would be the ones cursing the losses. And they overfished…the horses and people fouled the streams, and what they didn't catch to smoke and eat left little for those who'd lived beside the rivers for as long as anyone could remember. No wonder the Indians hurried the brigade along with thefts and frights.

Closer to the Sacramento River, one of Jean's colts was stolen along with six others. Work noticed, said he wrote it down in his book and would replace the value of the horses when they returned. "We need closer guards," Jean told Marie, "not just notes about replacements. We tempt them."

"What could be worse than to tempt someone in need?" she agreed.

The winter at French Camp near the Sacramento River proved pleasant enough with the addition of nearly one hundred more men, women, and children brought in by Jean's old friend, Michel LaFramboise. As always, the stocky French-Canadian charmed them all with his stories of men he'd met along the way.

"Once I was separated from my horse," Michel said as they sat around the evening fire. "Around San Jose, they say. I wander for days with a very bad head. I see long-horned bulls and fat cows that I think are bad dreams. These is not good, I tell myself, but I have no way to make my way back. *Mon Dieu,* I pray. Help me. Then these man finds me and takes me to a room with no window and a bed and a candle and I say, '*Mon Dieu,* I am in jail! I pray for help and you bring me a jail!'"

"That's when I met Michel," John Work said. "I was asked to come interpret for him. By the priest who rescued him."

"*Oui!* My prayers were answered, and I did not know it." Michel laughed at his own mistake. "I prayed to God, and he gives me a priest not a jail cell. I did not recognize the gift!"

Marie could see why Jean enjoyed the Canadian's company. Everyone was his friend, and he never made a joke at another's expense, only his own.

Still, the presence of so many people told Marie why extra guards began being posted nightly by both Michel and Work. The Columbia River horses were desired here while they camped at the confluence of the Sacramento and Feather Rivers.

In the spring, the brigades remained together but a short time, camping on buttes above the rivers, posting extra guards before separating. By July, Work had moved his brigade into the thickness of the tules and the brambles of the coast. He hoped for improved trapping and to avoid tempting the Indians with his horses, which appeared to be slipping away in the night despite the extra guards.

"The men go out and come back with fewer pelts," Marie commented to Jean one evening in mid-July. She whispered because they made their camp not far from Work's. Sarah, Jane, and Letitia, the three Work girls, had curled up with Marguerite and Marianne. Marie could hear them swatting at mosquitoes even while they gave the breathing rhythm of deep sleep. The insects had thickened of late, and only heavy smoke from the cooking fires seemed to discourage them at all. Marie's throat burned from inhaling the smoke as she worked. She worried about the children's throats. Even now, the smolder of leaves and green sticks didn't discourage the buzzing at her ears.

"I miss your earrings more today," she told Jean as she poked at the fire.

"This I know," Jean said, distracted. "The people here want us gone."

"It's as though a cougar watches us, and yet when I look, I can see nothing."

"*Oui*. And Work brings out his Wilson pistol and keeps it loaded. Be wary, Marie," he said. "I will watch too."

The next morning, as the men were dispatched to the streams, Marie held Jean back. "Something's wrong," she said. Jean looked around.

"I see nothing," she said. "But I feel something—"

"If I sound an alarm and there's no danger…" Jean said. He patted her hand. "You worry over much, maybe. Because you have Work's girls underfoot. Send them to the housekeeper today."

"She's of little use without a house," Marie said.

He smiled as he mounted up, then leaned down to stroke his finger across her cheek. For a moment, it reminded her of Louis's leaving and that he had never returned.

On the morning of July 12, 1832, Marie lifted her eyes from a vine where she'd plucked a ripe berry and saw the men of the brigade ride hard into camp.

"What is it?" Work asked, his over-and-under Wilson drawn as he stumbled from his hut. "Why are you back?"

"Trouble," one said. "We were told our families were in danger. Toupin told us that he'd seen Indians."

"Do you see any trouble here? No. Where's Toupin now?" Work asked.

Jean cast his eyes down. He'd ridden in last and made his way toward the front where Work stood, the sun beating on his bald head and the breeze lifting sprigs of hair like crumpled mistletoe at his ears. "I must have mistaken the women and children picking berries for men creeping up on the horses," Jean said. "My mistake, Monsieur Work. *Pardon.*"

"Ach," Work said. He stabbed the air with his pistol. "This will cost you, Toupin. Ach. You're all back now. May as well stay put and tend to tack. Go out early tomorrow. Wasted day," he said. "Because of you, Toupin. You're dismissed. Take your horses and your worrisome ways and your children and, at first light, you go."

"He would send us out, alone?" Marie asked. "Did you really see something?"

"It could have been intruders," Jean said. He smiled at her, that half-smile that drooped on the same side as his shoulder.

"Thank you," she told him.

"For what? Getting us dismissed? Putting us at risk?"

"For trusting my worry, even though it meant nothing. We'll find a way without the Company. They're as predictable as skunks and not nearly as welcome."

❖

Josette's uncle, Narcisse Raymond, had not aged a day it seemed to Baptiste. He laughed a big belly laugh when Baptiste approached him. It was probably not the right sequence, but talking with Narcisse would give him practice.

"I don't see you for six years, and then you come to claim another of my nieces." He looked grim, but Baptiste could see he kept the corner of his mouth from rising to a grin. "You'll stay here. Take care of her. And your Little Marie."

Baptiste nodded. "We'll share in the keeping of her family."

"I can use some help," Narcisse said. "She only has sixteen summers. You know this." Baptiste nodded. "And the bride's price, you can pay it? If she'll have you."

"That's what I've come to discover," Baptiste said. "I'm not a rich man. I've worked for the Company for—"

Narcisse held his hand as though to silence him. "We'll have no arguments over this bride price." He rubbed his chin. "We'll have a horse race," he said. "If you win, you take the wagers and hand them to me. And if you lose, you hand over the horse. You don't need it if you stay here tending those weeds you bring us from the west."

"Agreed," Baptiste said. "Now all I need is to see if the bride will have the groom."

He'd yet to have a satisfactory meeting with Little Marie. She usually sat sullen if she remained near him at all. It had been Josette's persistent reassurance that he give her time that had him coming back at all.

That and the smile on Josette's face whenever he stopped by.

"Do you see me as a brother-in-law, then?" he'd asked one day as they rode horses up the Walla Walla River. "Or as a suitor?" He supposed he was too blunt for a young girl, but it was his way. She'd have to take it or leave it.

"What about as a protector? A provider? I could give you many names," she said.

Baptiste grunted. "Which of those, then?"

"With what eyes do you see me?"

He'd pulled up on the horse, adjusted his hat to see her better. Her dress had slid up along her thighs, revealing nut-brown calves without leggings. "With loving eyes," he said. "Of one who is not a brother, though I would protect you as a brother would. And eyes not of an uncle, though I would watch out for you as Narcisse does. But with eyes that seek to sink into yours, every day of my being."

She dropped her eyes, played with the ends of her long braids.

"I'm not my sister," she said.

"You don't need to be. I have let her go."

"You still hold anger toward your mother," she said. "How will I know that if I do something that upsets you that you won't hold yourself away from me?"

"For someone with few years you ask old people questions," he said. "And your answers?"

"I have no answers. Only that with you to guide me, I will make wiser choices all the days of my life, even when I'm old."

❖

Gunshots from the sentry alerted the camp as it burst into a swirl of disarray and panic. Marie grabbed for the children, shoved them under the lean-to of branches, looked for a weapon while Jean crept with his rifle toward the cluster of men finding targets in the rushes. John Work stood, shouting orders as horses whinnied and yanked at their tethers. Children cried, and mothers grabbed them and placed hands over their mouths. Marie clutched an axe, crouched low, the eyes of her children like frightened birds hovering beneath their mother's wings. Marie put her finger to her lips, a sign of quiet. Marguerite held Marianne, her hand lightly over her sister's mouth.

Marguerite's eyes grew larger, and she raised a shaky finger to point. Marie turned her head slowly.

In front of the lean-to, standing between them and Work's camp, stood a face-painted Indian. Beyond, Marie could see Work himself gesturing with his Wilson, suspenders like lost thoughts clinging to his waistband. His bare back stood exposed as he'd flown from his tent at the dawn attack. He yelled, pointing while Marie watched the Indian crouch to lift his bow and arrow. The Indian took aim. Work would be dead in seconds.

Marie stood up. She screamed, then struck the stranger with the axe.

❖

Baptiste had never been called in for a private meeting with Factor Pambrun before. He tried to think of what he might have done, what unwritten rule he might have broken. He stayed to himself, he and his wife and daughter. He socialized with Narcisse and Josette's brothers and sisters only. No horse racing. He hadn't touched whiskey for years now, and only rarely sat for games of cards at the men's quarters. What could he have done?

"Take them Bostons just between here and Fort Vancouver," Pambrun told him. "Or south if they request it. These are Americans, but we've been told to dissuade them from competition in whatever gentle way we can. I suggest you tell them the worst about your overland journey with Hunt."

"I was pretty young, sir."

"Well, make sure they know about the flash flooding, the hostilities of natives. Exaggerate a little. You can do that, yes?"

"Who are they? Exact."

"One's name is John Kirk Townsend. He's an ornithologist. Birds. He paints birds. Another is a businessman, Nathaniel Wyeth, who swears he has no intention of fur trading or trapping. It seems he knows a Boston in the business of making ice, and he intends to dry salmon, ship it back, and make his fortune selling it hither and yon. Obviously not something the Company is interested in. The ice shipping part. But we need to make sure he's not infiltrating under the guise of salmon. He was here before, two years ago. Whatever he had planned then didn't work out."

"The ice does sound a little suspect," Baptiste told him.

"See what you can find out as you talk with them. Take them wherever they want to go, but encourage them to stay on the south side of the river. Especially if they start to talk 'settlements.' We don't want Bostons considering land north."

"There's good land south. Do we want to give that up so easily to the Americans?"

"We'll have all the streams and land above the Columbia. That's what we're counting on. And Work and Ogden are out there doing what they can to clean the country of furs in the south so we won't be leaving them much. Drat this tooth," he said. He held his hand over the side of his cheek, which Baptiste realized now was swollen.

"There are Methodist missionaries by the name of Lee. Jason Lee, too. He even drove two milk cows with him all the way from Independence on the Missouri. Got them here over the Rockies, through

Blackfoot and cougar country. He'll need extra protection, or at least his cows will. Not sure what he intends to do with them."

"Trade for supplies."

"Are you willing to guide them, then? We'll provide a Company barge and some individual canoes, but they'll need someone to help them through at the portage of the falls."

"Methodist," Baptiste said.

"Seems those Nez Perce and Salish boys that headed back to meet Clark succeeded. And someone wrote about their quest in a missionary journal, and now there's growing interest in bringing teachers and preachers out. Lee's coming to see what might work. I already told him he should go to Fort Vancouver first, but he seems to want to follow up on the Salish request and go on up the Clearwater where those Iroquois did their missionarying."

"To the natives."

"There aren't enough Protestants among the Company to warrant him being here. Company men have been seeking priests. Guess I'll ask him to speak at our Sunday services just the same. Of course the Holy See might be a bit busy, what with the Mexican government taking over all the Catholic missions in the south. Well, are you interested in leading them or not?"

"My wife expects a baby," Baptiste told him. *Can this be happening again?*

"She'll foal whether you're here or not, I suspect," Pambrun told him. "If you want to stay here tending the garden, I can find someone else." He raised a bushy eyebrow.

"Why me, sir? If you don't mind my asking."

"They asked for you. Wyeth remembers hearing your name, from when he was here before. Knew of your mother. And Lee heard there was a son or grandson of Pierre Dorion who started out with Lewis and Clark. Thought he'd heard somewhere you and your mother and brother were still out here. Told him you were. Didn't know where your brother was nor your mother at the moment, for that matter."

"I'll go," Baptiste said then.

"And there's a botanist. I nearly forgot. He remembers you, too, he said. He started out with Hunt but turned back. You remember him? Thomas Nuttall, he said his name was."

Baptiste smiled. "We called him *Le Fou*. He collected plants and medicines from the Omaha and Osage. He can probably help your toothache, sir, if you ask him."

❖

Marguerite watched the brave come at John Work, watched her mother raise a hatchet to his head. He was all painted colors of a slippery snake. She held her ears; the sounds hurt. Horses snorted. Her papa Jean shouted, loud, so loud. Her mother screamed.

John Work swung his pistol. His suspenders bounced up and down. The housekeeper never came out, but Work spun around, saw what her mother had done to save him. He saluted her, then leaned over to see if the man lived.

"Mamama," Marianne wailed.

"Shush, now," Marguerite said, but her mother, breathing hard, put her arms around them.

"Still," she whispered. "Pretend to be rabbits. Burrow deep under the leaves and grass."

Marianne closed her eyes. Marguerite thought, "Maybe they can't see us if we close our eyes." Marianne squeezed Marguerite's leg; the Work girls leaned into her farther. François grabbed a knife left on the ground and crawled out.

❖

Baptiste was sure Josette would understand. Their separation wouldn't be for long. And if he did well, he might be invited to take on more such expeditions. He could move up in the Company, the way Tom McKay had, even without the influence of a powerful stepfather. Maybe the influence of a grandfather still carried some weight. Or his father, God rest his soul.

He finished checking his horse's hooves, used a tool to remove packed mud. His mount was sound. He'd ride beside the canoes or let another ride his animal when he wanted to point something out to the "guests," as Pambrun said he should call them. "Guests" who contributed more to the conversation when they were absent than when they were present. Pambrun had said little after Baptiste had been introduced, and the Bostons spoke mostly to each other on the journey.

He'd have to ask Tom about such things. Tom understood the Company ways and these other ways, of those who walked with one foot in two different worlds. It was no wonder the man limped.

The Company had sent Tom on a dangerous task to build a post along the Boise. They must have thought him up to it. He'd make his name there just as perhaps Baptiste could make his name, guiding a naturalist, a botanist, a rich man, and a missionary.

Tom's kids were even going to a school at Fort Vancouver. Maybe Baptiste could get that for his children if he performed this mission well. That was what he'd tell Josette.

She might not be impressed. She didn't want him going anywhere that she couldn't go with him. Her mother lay ailing again, and there were all those younger sisters.

"It's a position of authority," he practiced telling her. He wished his father could have been here to see him asked to do it. Baptiste would make him proud. And make his own child proud too.

He just had to tell Josette and not look too closely at the eyes of Little Marie when he told her that her papa was once again leaving.

❖

Is he dead? Is he dead? The question repeated itself in Marie's mind.

Work turned, bent to the man, placed his fingers at the Indian's neck. "He still lives," Work told her, "but not for long." With the man apparently incapacitated, Work continued giving orders, setting men to protect horses and supplies. He even sent his little housekeeper to Marie's lean-to, saying, "Hold the children until this is over."

Instead, the woman rocked with her arms around herself, no others. Marie shook as she held Marianne, François, and Marguerite. The

Work girls sat as close to her as they could get, huddled back inside the lean-to. Poor little Jane pounded her ears with her fists, the action making Marie realize she was crying, her wails probably scaring the child, and she stopped. Soon Jane did, too.

"It's all right," Marie said. "It's over now. We're safe." She said it to herself as much to them, the smell of wounds and fear mere smoke hovering over them. These were words she'd said before to her sons. Baptiste had heard them and come through that violent storm; the other's life had continued like a whirlwind and, for all Marie knew, Paul was still being tossed to the winds of his memories, unable to move to the moment.

She thought she should go to the fallen Indian, see if she could bind his wounds. How strange, she thought. To want to mend what she had torn.

And then while she rocked the girls, her own children, too, safe in the shadows, the man lying in front of them groaned. She felt the girls stiffen, and just as quickly, two braves with painted faces slipped in, quiet as a clear conscience. They knelt to their comrade and, looking around, lifted him. They raised his arms around their shoulders. One scanned the leaves and grasses and noticed her there, a mother hen with her chicks. He looked into her eyes.

Marie saw understanding there. No condemnation. No judgment over what she'd done. Perhaps they hadn't seen that it was Marie's axe that felled their friend. But even if they had, they hadn't chosen retaliation. Sorrow filled his eyes and Marie knew then she wanted no more of this brigade, no more invading what did not belong to them, no more asking landscapes to give themselves up to those who'd strip them clean. She was glad Jean had been dismissed.

She'd defended, yes. But why were they here, needing such defense? She wanted to go home, wherever that might be.

The warriors made no move toward them, just looked away, then carried the wounded man off.

When the skirmish was over, Work ordered the injured to be tended and posted extra guards for the horses.

"You're hired back," John Work told Jean. "I was…too hasty, it seems. Maybe your false alarm allowed our rifles to be ready, our ammunition where it could be reached. And the men rested for the test."

"I suspect your saving his life is the real reason," Jean told Marie.

"I may have killed that man," Marie said.

"You did what you had to, to protect the children, to protect Work. That's all that matters."

She wasn't sure anymore that it was.

Marie never expected to harm another, to kill a man. Jean's words held truth she let herself receive. Yes, she did what had to be done in the moment's calling, to keep her children safe, to save another's life. She accepted her action as part of the unexpected color unfolded from that day's fabric. Many weeks later, Marie remembered this feeling of acceptance as she watched stars spill across the night sky and streak to the ground like handfuls of sparks. A meteor shower, Jean called it, something one sees once in a lifetime. She never expected to see such beauty, but there it was.

❖

"She's going to operate the dairy," Baptiste said. He kept his words even, flat, without emotion, but he answered Jean's question. Jean and Marie met him at Vancouver.

Beyond them stood the chief factor with white hair flying. He bent slightly toward a woman who wore a hat and pointed this way and that. The hat wasn't to keep the summer sun from her freckled face but to make her appear taller. At least that was what Baptiste supposed the flowers and straw was meant to accomplish. Mrs. Capendal was squat as a mushroom and just as pale. Her husband was lean as a bacon strip. He stood beside her, wordless.

"She's not too happy with the accommodations, it appears," Jean said. Baptiste stood with his stepfather, leaning at the corrals. He swatted at the mosquitoes that plagued the late summer heat.

Baptiste hardly recognized his younger half brothers and sisters, they'd grown so tall. Marguerite stood pitchfork straight, even when she ran, which she did now, chasing after the younger ones in play. He hadn't expected to see them at Fort Vancouver. He hadn't planned on seeing his mother.

"Josette has a baby soon," he'd told Jean, just in passing when they'd met. "She's my wife now." He'd thought a grandmother would want to know. Jean could tell Baptiste's mother, or she could eavesdrop. Women did that well.

"And you're here," Marie said. *Accusing him.*

"I was asked to lead some Americans." He said it louder than intended. He supposed that was why she winced, nearly stepped back at his words.

"She'll be happy to have you back. Will the baby come before you return?"

"Not this time," he said. "She's strong." *Did she think he'd marry a weak woman?*

"You guided Americans," his mother said then. *She always wanted to know things, always probed and picked.*

"*Le Fou* asks for me. He says he remembers you. And a preacher. He goes to where we stayed one winter, where Tom's place is on the Willamette. He brings two cows and says he'll start a stock company. With two cows." Baptiste laughed. "The preacher, too, starts a mission there. For all the Catholics. The chief factor sends for priests from the Red River."

"This is good," Jean said. "When this happens, we'll have a proper marriage with baptisms for the children. Your children, too, Baptiste."

Baptiste glanced at his mother. Her face showed no emotion. Baptiste fidgeted. He changed the subject. "None of the buildings are finished. Even the factor lives without paper on his walls. His wife doesn't complain. A good wife doesn't."

"Maybe you could put in a word for your mother to tend the cows," Jean said. "She'd be happy to stay here and encourage the dairy. She wasn't happy that Work took back his dismissal of me."

Baptiste glanced again at his mother, grunted. "I've no influence."

"They asked you to come here," Jean said.

"It's a long story," Baptiste said.

"She'd do it for pay in butter, I'd wager."

Marie stood a respectable distance from the factor and the Capendals, even though Baptiste suspected she could hear every word that Mrs. Capendal said. Even he could hear the dairywoman's complaints, and he stood several yards away.

"The house is less than promised," Mrs. Capendal said. She straightened her hat. "The animals are…fractious. No wonder. The birthing paddock is disgraceful." Baptiste had never seen the factor so silent. "What kind of man are you to allow calving in such wet and muck?"

"Calm yourself," Mr. Capendal told his wife. "It's likely the rains here that—"

"Calm? Calm? When a maternity pen is filthy? Who can be calm? How a firm treats the mother cows says much of what kind of company it is."

Baptiste listened, thinking about his trip with the Americans. He'd delivered the men, learned a thing or two about ice-making and birds. *Le Fou,* Nuttall, had reminded him of long forgotten events, perhaps things he'd never really known about, things his mother had kept hidden from her sons. It had been an interesting journey, and then he'd readied himself to return, hopeful for more such assignments.

Instead he'd been relegated to fieldwork. Even telling the factor that his wife waited and she expected an infant had failed to influence his assignment. He wouldn't tell his mother that.

A father should be there for the arrival of a child. Hadn't he been taught that lesson well?

He knew this even though he didn't remember much about his own father being where a boy would expect him to be.

Nuttall's story of Baptiste's father's beating of his mother, where all could see it happen, bothered him now while he watched Mrs. Capendal and the factor. That woman didn't have any trouble stating what she wanted. But according to Nuttall, when Baptiste's mother stood for herself, his father had struck her. Not just once, but many times. Nuttall himself seemed embarrassed a bit by the telling, but he had told anyway, finishing with statements of admiration for his mother. "But she proved herself worthy on that crossing. Something changed between them. Your father changed. Yes, she's an Indian to be reckoned with," he'd said. "A woman to be honored."

As a young boy, had Baptiste seen these sides of her, of his father? Had he pushed it aside? Could a person push such pains aside? Nuttall had spoken with such regard for his mother, as though she'd done something almost saintly in how she'd handled herself with "a most difficult man," as Nuttall said. He seemed to think the fact that they all arrived, alive, at Astoria was some grand feat. Nuttall said he'd turned back after he realized that the expedition leader had some judgment difficulties that might "render the party incapacitated."

His mother and father had continued on. Faithful, maybe. They were in service to the Pacific Fur Company. He wasn't sure how he and his brother and mother ended up in Okanogan, only that when they did, they were no longer connected to a company and his father was no longer connected to them.

Baptiste watched her now, this tall woman with children not much older than his own Little Marie hanging at her side. Marguerite brought Marianne to her, and his mother settled some dispute between her and François.

Had the journey across been that bad? Maybe that was why she pushed him so to read and write, so he could make choices instead of having to follow the directions of those who could, like the expedition leader that Nuttall had questioned.

Maybe she wanted more than just an ordinary life for him. But an ordinary life was no sin, was it?

Maybe he should talk to his mother about all that, about what it had been like for her to make the trip, to keep them safe. For the first time, he wished he could have asked Paul and not had to admit to his mother that there were things he wanted to know, without the risk of finding out more than he wanted.

"My mother would do nothing to make the Company rich," Baptiste said to Jean. "Not even milk their cows. I'm surprised she lets you work for Hudson's Bay, and that she goes with you these past years."

Jean straightened the cross strap that held his powder horn, nodded his head. "You don't know your mother, then," Jean said. "She's like a good saw. When she must, when she sees a thing that has to fit, she can change direction quickly without causing a lot of friction."

Part 3

20

Settlement

1836

Marie sat astride her gelding, her eyes scanning the Walla Walla hills. She could remember the first time she'd seen them, when she'd been rescued by these good people who now called themselves Nez Perce. Names changed. The fort they lived near had once had a different name. Certainly she'd had her share of names through the years. But the hills had remained the same, a safe refuge, for more than twenty years.

Pambrun said they'd nearly seen the last of 1836. And Marie had long since stopped painting events onto her calendar. There were too many events to remember.

She heard hoofbeats behind her, and she kicked her horse forward. He leaped with the startle and then galloped out. The wind blew the knot in her hair loose, but she didn't care. She never felt freer than when she rode a fast horse, astride; to be accompanied by her daughter was a cool breeze on her hot back.

Marie laughed as she dismounted, sliding off the back of the horse, her calf-length skirt billowing out over the horse's rump. "I win!" she shouted, patting the horse's wet neck. The dropped reins told the horse to stand, which he did, the wind splaying its mane. She missed riding Janey, but the old mare needed her rest time and Marie gave it, saving her for short rides to visit her grandchildren, who clustered at Josette's knees.

A stiff wind spanked the Walla Walla River and sent sprays their way. Across the rolling ridges, wind swirled dirt. Marie turned her back to it just as she heard her daughter's shout, a plea for dignity wrapped into the words. "Mother, please." Marguerite rode up beside her. "You'll hurt yourself, or worse."

"What worse do you worry over?" Marie said. "Losing a race?" She looked up at her elder daughter, motioned for her to dismount to avoid the wind-whipped dust.

Marguerite was already seventeen years old and as fine a daughter as any mother could want. She reminded her of Sally sometimes, blunt and opinionated, but she also heated stones for her mother's feet at night and reminded her to rest during the day. Marie chose compassionate friends who weren't afraid to speak their minds, now that she thought of it. Sarah had been much like that too.

Marie had never known her own mother when she was Marguerite's age, so she had no map to guide her as to how to be with a daughter. Perhaps it was just as well. She'd treated her as a child with a name of her own, not just daughter, and as a result, they threw banter and badinage about as old friends.

Marie scanned the horizon. The other children were well occupied. François, her youngest son, hoed near the fort's garden; her youngest, Marianne, looked after free-trappers' children tossing stones near the Walla Walla River's edge.

"Mr. Townsend writes down what he sees of us, our places of belonging," Marguerite said, catching her breath.

Marie lifted her hand as though brushing at dirt. "Jean says he writes about birds and plants. 'Naturalists,' they call themselves. Such men don't worry over women," she said. "Especially not women like us."

"Papa Jean says he writes about how we dress and what we eat. Alexander Ross wrote such things down too, Mother," she said. "I remember Jemima Ross telling me that. Men do this, write what they see. Then they judge us. So you should watch how you dismount your horse." Marguerite pointed with her strong chin. "They'll wonder about us, the way we are. Catherine says we must use decorum."

Marie grunted. "Catherine hangs on to her pipe," Marie said.

Her daughter scowled.

"What is this decorum?" Marie asked.

"Manners, Mother."

"*Pardon.* I have manners. Romping with a friend on a windy day and winning a race with dignity. This is manners."

Marguerite smiled.

After she and Jean returned from the Snake River brigades, Marie had made it a point to spend more time with her children and her children's children. One didn't become friends just because blood was shared.

While some would say she'd danced with death more than once in her life, it had been the almost taking of another's life that had set her feet on a new trail. She would do what had to be done for her family; but she would not assume that few choices or hard choices were the same as no choices at all. There had to be a way to live with your neighbor without taking away their way of living each day.

Marie and Jean believed they'd found it.

"No more trapping," Marie had told Jean when they arrived back at the fort. "No more stripping the lands south of the river. We'll grow things and sell it as sharecroppers, the way Etienne Lucier did on the Willamette."

"He didn't do so well, from what I hear," Jean said.

"He's still there. And he doesn't trap. He doesn't take away from land."

"I can go back to interpreting," Jean had said. "Maybe with more Americans coming, that'll be a needed service. Baptiste was enlisted for it. Maybe I could take visitors to places, show them the lands south of the river."

"Baptiste does well?"

"Words don't disappear," Jean said. "They can be used to make poor neighbors, but they can also make new ones."

"This is a good plan, husband. Words don't get used up."

❖

"Who do you think it is, Mother?" Marguerite asked, bringing her back to the present.

Marie hadn't noticed the entourage arriving at the fort. She did now, the dust rising behind a group of riders. She squinted, in her forty-sixth year, maybe more, she found she had to concentrate to see in the distance. She put her hand at her forehead to shade her eyes.

Three days previous, the fort received word from Tom McKay, who was returning from the rendezvous, that a "singular" party followed them. "Missionaries, including two women. And they aren't Catholic," Tom said. "The old man will have trouble shipping these out."

Marie had heard about one of the Willamette missionaries that her son had guided to the river. Jason Lee. He'd brought cattle with him, and Kilakotah said he'd built a mission house in the bottoms maybe a half-day's ride from her place. He apparently intended to stay. He'd already been "winning souls," Kilakotah said. And he'd opened a school that Tom McKay had enrolled his sons in. "Many orphans go there too," Kilakotah had told her. "So many orphans. The fever and ague has devastated so many families."

Everyone talked of the fever and ague as though it were one word. Sometimes Marie wondered if men like Lee might have brought it, those who came from other places. Maybe it was passed through a family's line and some would get it and die while others would be passed by.

But it appeared in Fort Vancouver and even when they'd been in the French Camp of California. It was almost as though it followed the trappers' parties.

Now more missionaries arrived while Marie and Marguerite watched. Marguerite pulled long hair from her eyes, the breeze so blustery. Neither of the Company men had stayed for the arrival of these missionary men and their women. Instead, Tom had limped aboard a *bateau* to Fort Vancouver, no doubt to tell the chief factor that the first overland "immigrants" approached, as though the Astorians' coming those years before didn't count as overland arrivals.

Or maybe it was the presence of "women" they wanted to announce. "One with wheat-colored hair and a voice like a morning bird, soothing and sweet." Pambrun had teased Tom about his description of the women. But women arriving overland was nothing new either. Hadn't Sacagawea come that way? Hadn't Sarah? Hadn't Marie?

But those had not been white women. That was what Tom announced without ever using the word. They weren't white anyway, these people. Not white as shells, not white as dentalium. They were the color of ham.

But the presence of them, these *white* women, was what mattered.

Marguerite looked at where Marie pointed with her chin. "Who's that?" Marie thought she recognized a Nez Perce youth as the dust settled near the fort's gate. This man rode with his right hand holding the reins. And his left shoulder sloped lower.

"Is that Richard?"

Did her daughter look even more excited by Richard's presence? He'd left some years back, heading to St. Louis, seeking priests who would bring "the Book of Heaven" back to them. Yet she was sure that was him, even if he had aged. Maybe Marguerite expected him.

Richard was the same age as her son Paul. Twenty-seven. She wondered how Paul would look now. Might she someday pass right by him, not recognize him? Could a mother forget her son? She stopped herself from remembering.

"It is Richard," Marie said.

"The woman with him rides her horse wrong," Marguerite said.

"Just because someone does it differently does not make it wrong," Marie chided. "We survive in this place when we do not judge harshly what we don't understand, Daughter."

"She'll fall off, Mother," the girl said. "I'm just stating what is."

The woman did look unbalanced, perched like a bobcat hunched at the lip of a ledge. Her leg was draped up over the top of the saddle, and both slippered ankles hung on the same side of the horse. The woman wore a long dress, a bonnet on her head, and she carried a shredded cloth on a stick that she held above her. "A parasol," Marie said out loud. "I haven't seen one in a long time. Small-waisted women ride that way. Or did when I was younger, back in St. Louis."

"Ah, your St. Louis," her daughter said. "If it's Richard, then where are the priests?"

"Jean said they looked for priests, but others said they went seeking the Book of Heaven. The Bible, your mother Sarah calls it. Spokane Garry learned to read it and they wanted to read it too."

"It should have been priests who came," Marguerite said. "The missionaries must have changed his thinking that priests were needed, that only holy men would do."

How had she raised such a child of judgment? "Change is salt in everyday stew," Marie said. "Sarah says the Book is the same no matter whose hands hold it."

Marguerite opened her mouth, but François rode up, interrupting, "Mrs. Pambrun says come. She can use help."

"Did you get the woman's name?" Marguerite asked her brother. "The one with the parasol?"

"The what?"

Marie made a gesture to demonstrate the umbrella. "Oh. Whitman," François told her. "Her name is Narcissa Whitman. Pretty, *n'est-ce pas?* And her husband is a doctor. They say another woman follows. They didn't wait for her. Richard's taking them to the Clearwater."

"She'll finish Sarah's work there," Marie said.

"See what they bring with them, Mother?" He pointed.

In the distance, then, Marie didn't just see a woman on horseback nor young Richard returning. What she saw was the future, her future, if she could bring it about. Tears came to her eyes as through the clearing dust she watched a small herd of dairy cows shake their heads of the flies and the heat.

❖

"Women arrived and they have cows. They even left some at McKay's Fort Boise in exchange for stock they'll get at Vancouver. The Company will be unable to stop the Americans from coming, and they'll bring with them all they need." Jean heard the excitement in his wife's voice. They lay in the feather comforter, the September evening cooler than usual. Jean had built a log house for his family, not far from the fort. Even Baptiste had come around some to help with the chinking. Over the past two years since the birth first of Denise and two years later of Pierre V, Baptiste had mellowed toward his mother, at least a little. Jean didn't think there had ever been words spoken to break down the wall that had been built between them, but at least Baptiste could be in the same area with his mother without quickly walking away.

"Missionaries," Jean said. "They're different. They come because those Spokane and Nez Perce invited them. Few others will have the same grit to pull across the mountains."

"The woman, Mrs. Whitman, doesn't appear gritty. She lounges in the chair and eats her fresh salmon, potatoes, bread, and butter as though she has always been served. If one who uses a parasol to ward off the sun can come with her knees on both sides of a horse, then anyone can come. And will."

"The other one is sickly," Jean said.

"It's a shame. I like Mrs. Spalding. She listens with her whole being," Marie said. "And is less interested in her mirror reflection than Mrs. Whitman."

Jean grunted.

"They bring cows, husband. Cows. This is what matters." Marie was up on one elbow now, her hair in a long braid falling over her bare shoulders. "These Americans will make their own way, and the Company will not be able to stop them."

"Baptiste tells me that the goal of six hundred head of cattle in the Columbia country has been met now. So the Company will begin slaughtering cows. People will have beef to eat and tallow candles that burn well, and we'll have hides without having to ship them in. The Company will continue to do right by us, Marie. Americans will not be able to compete with that."

"No, husband," she said. "You're wrong." She lay back down, arms crossed across her breasts, the comforter pulled up and held tight at her neck. "What we have been putting aside so we will be able to go to French Prairie country in a year—without a debt—I have a new place for it."

"Marie…" Jean cautioned.

"It will all change now. You men fail to see it, but when a woman comes to a place, it means change. We alter things. We don't wait for it to sneak up on us like a snake and then wonder why we didn't see it before we stepped. And it's not just because we have Indian blood or white. It's not about our blood at all."

He wanted to ask what her plan was, but he was patient. He'd learned through the years that she talked only when she was ready. He had no complaints at all about his wife except her silences. He supposed he should be pleased that she wasn't a woman to prattle. Instead, she'd talk of what the children did or the condition of the horses, their herd having increased each year, first by one foal, now two. But the silences still surprised him. He never knew what new thought would break them.

"I hear the French-Canadians at the prairie build a church there," he said, cautious. "There's a gristmill." Jean stroked the side of her face. Perhaps he could risk a subject more intense. "They'll finish the church and then ask again for a priest. When one comes, we will have the children baptized, *n'est-ce pas?* And be married by a priest."

She lay quiet. He wondered if an ember burned that would soon ignite.

❖

The Whitmans began building at a soft, green place that grew lush roots and grass on the north side of the Walla Walla. It was a hard half-day's ride, east from the fort. Marie learned that Mrs. Whitman was not there yet. She remained at Fort Vancouver until her "home" was ready.

"They build at Waiilatpu," Josette told Marie. "Place of the rye grass. And the doctor, Mr. Whitman, he acts as though it is his land. My uncle, Narcisse, grazes two or three cows there, ones they took in trade from the doctor, but they did not intend to give them the land. They only use it in exchange for beef and food as needed. My uncle's cows make milk but also get ready to give calves. The doctor acts like they're still his cows."

Marie wove the tule through the matting, listening. "They cut trees and build," Josette said. "And the men argue, the Whitman with that Spalding. He wants to go and begin his house on the Clearwater where the Nez Perce invite them. No one invites them to stay at Waiilaptu. This is what Baptiste tells me."

"Baptiste helps them there?" Marie rarely got information directly from her son, always a reflection of someone else's awareness of him.

"He was sent by Pambrun to help," Josette said.

"It's only the beginning," Marie said. She watched Little Marie pound the dried berries into salmon pemmican and form the cakes with her hands. "It's how my mother would have done it, but she used buffalo meat," Marie commented. Her granddaughter asked her what a buffalo looked like, and Marie blinked. How to describe an animal as grand as that? "I'll paint one for you," she said, but she felt a catch beneath her heart. It had been a long time since she'd seen one. Perhaps her grandchild would have only a painting as a way to know what once was.

Josette nursed a newborn baby and another slept in her board. The baby was fat and crabby and insistent, tugging at his mother's breast and then pushing her away. *A Dorion child,* Marie thought. *One who knows his own mind.*

"I tell Jean it is only the beginning," Marie said. "We must act before much more time passes."

"To do what?" Josette asked. The dimples in her cheeks made her look as though she were always happy.

"To make our own way," Marie said.

❖

"She teaches us to read and write English," Catherine Pambrun said. "The girls learn. You could too. Mrs. Whitman is a fine addition to the Fort. She should stay as long as she wishes."

Marie shook her head. "Marguerite and Marianne, yes. But I'm too old. The words swim," Marie said. And she didn't share the same confidence in this woman's teaching. Marie couldn't name it, but Mrs. Whitman saw all of them as one, not as individuals. She began her words with "You people" or "The Indians" and never seemed to recognize Marie as someone she'd met before.

Eliza Spalding went with the men, listening to the Cayuse helpers, asking questions of Jean and even Baptiste, Marie noticed. She drew pictures with dark pencils, and like Marie, smiled at pretty flowers and gasped, pointing to the reds and oranges of a deepening sunset.

That woman carried Sarah's *métier* upon her shoulders.

❖

"Richard urges the Spaldings to go to the Clearwater," Marguerite told her mother. "It didn't matter to him whether priests came or these missionaries. He just wanted those who could read the words."

"You talk often together," Marie said.

Marguerite's face blotched red. "He…is interested in horses. And catching up on old news." She looked away.

Marie hung linens on a line stretched from the side of their log house to a tree. She earned trade money by washing the fort's linens. Napkins, tablecloths, even white aprons had to be boiled and lifted, steaming, with a stick. She stopped now, listening to her daughter's words. They said Richard held more meaning to her daughter than someone sharing traveling stories.

"The words matter to Richard, not who reads them."

"Your papa says the priests are the ones who will lead us," Marie said.

"The priests are who Richard went back for."

"Maybe in time you'll find out why he left to ride with the missionaries."

Marguerite blew her nose. Her eyes were red, and she took short breaths. *My daughter cries?* "He leaves as soon as the Spaldings listen to him. The Nez Perce at the Clearwater wait for them. When the priests come there, it will be too late." Marguerite cried openly now.

Marie let the washing stick sink into the iron pot. She wiped her hands on her dress to dry them, then pulled her daughter to her. *What can I say?* To Little Marie she sometimes said reassuring things her mother-in-law once told her, even though she wasn't sure she believed the words herself. But Marguerite was older. And this wasn't just about words.

"Wait to see what happens. Where there is great love, things happen, surprising us." Were the priests so important to her? Had Jean influenced Marguerite so that she feared to love a man who followed a missionary instead of a priest? "We wait to see what Richard finds when he brings the Spaldings. Maybe we even follow sometime, to see if the words touch the same no matter who brings them."

❖

Marie and little Marie sometimes made the long ride to where the men worked so the child could see her father and Marie could visit with the Spalding woman better. There had been no white women in Marie's life, no women of that other world whom she could claim as "friend," yet this Mrs. Spalding came beside her with a hopeful step.

Mrs. Spalding spoke with gentle words, and Marie noticed she looked at the person speaking, always seeking more from their face than just their words.

Even Jean told her that Spalding's wife had asked him for a way to learn the Cayuse language. He'd told her of the sounds and such that had helped him understand, and she'd made scratchings on paper.

"She has an ear for sounds," Jean said. "She asked how to say the Cayuse word for the place where Whitman is building. I told her if it were in English she'd say, Why-e-la-poo. She laughed, but she says it well, now. She thought they would all remain together where the Nez Perce wanted them, on the Clearwater.… The Nez Perce ask for them. Richard asks for them. But these Whitman people want to be closer to the fort, I think. And he's the doctor. And Mrs. Spalding… needs one."

"I like her mouth," Marie said. "She waits until another's mouth stops before she starts her own."

The two women walked the rye grass, Marie showing her plants and Mrs. Spalding sharing sewing needles and patches.

Then before Marie was ready to let Mrs. Spalding leave, 125 Nez Perce men arrived on horseback, summoned by Richard. They came to take the Spaldings to the Clearwater River, to "Lap Way," as Mrs. Spalding spoke the Nez Perce word, *Lapwai*. "What does it mean?" she asked Jean.

"The place of butterflies," Jean told her.

It was 120 miles away. Mrs. Spalding was leaving, just as Sarah had.

❖

"We can't put in as much as some," Jean said.

Michel LaFramboise nodded. Jean had made the journey from Walla Walla to French Prairie with all the cash they could spare and the hopes of his family. At the head of the table sat William Slacum. Rumor had it he was an American spy sent by none other than Andrew Jackson, the American President, to see how things looked in the West.

Ewing Young tapped a metal pen on the table. "Jason Lee puts up four hundred dollars. For the Willamette Mission," Slacum noted. "And, gentlemen, here's the surprise. Chief Factor McLoughlin puts up seven hundred dollars of his own money. Up to eight hundred dollars, if need be."

This last would surprise Marie, Jean was certain of that. If the Company man was joining the stock company of the Americans, he was obviously covering both sides of the river, not unlike him and Marie, still working for the Company while taking a chance on this new venture.

"The factor probably wants to run cows on Sauvie's Island," someone said. "Wyeth's deserted salmon drying operation did little good there but construct buildings."

"Got Young a copper pot for his distillery," the owner of the gristmill said.

"The illness took Wyeth back East, but I believe he's a man who'll be back," Young said.

"None of us has done good here, just being a sharecropper for the Company." A former teacher turned farmer reached for the pen. Ball, his name was, and he started coughing, so George Gay grabbed the pen to sign. This whole venture felt less risky with his old friend George Gay involved. Jean had given his money to George so no one from the Company need ever know of his and Marie's involvement.

"Each needs to sign this Willamette Cattle Company agreement, that we all concur. We're doing this not only to make our own livelihood here in this settlement, but because we can't purchase cattle from Hudson's Bay. This is our only choice. We do this for the benefit of the entire settlement, not just for ourselves. Agreed? Good."

"We expect to pay three dollars per head," he continued. "From the Mexican government. It's a good time, gentlemen. They're slaughtering thousands to meet the hide market and turn their Mission cattle into cash. We pay a tad more than they'll get for a hide and get a cow on the hoof. All we have to do is drive them north. Ewing will head the party, if that's agreeable."

Slacum looked around the room to the nods of heads. The gristmill owner cast his eyes down. "Will he give up his distillery? The Temperance Society would feel better about his leading if—"

"Ewing's been blacklisted by McLoughlin," another man defended. "For no good reason. He didn't steal no horses from Mexico. He was driving his own north when those renegades pulled in with him. What was he supposed to do? He just wants to be independent. You've been converted, Webley, so you don't approve of liquor any more. But that don't mean the rest of us have been touched by Rev. Lee or that it's the only way to see a thing."

"Fact is, I'll be happy to give the distillery up," Young said. "If I can make money with cattle, I'd prefer it. Keeps me from relying on the Company. You want me to direct this operation? Glad to. I've been to Northern California State. I'm putting my faith in the cattle business." He reached for the agreement and signed.

"We board the *Loriot* in January," Slacum said. "Until then, I suggest we keep our own counsel. No need for word to get out prematurely and tip the Company's hand. Eleven Americans and three Indians will go. Your boy Baptiste counts as an Indian, right?" Slacum looked at Jean, who nodded. If only Jean could convince Baptiste that he should go.

❖

"Why me?" Baptiste told Jean.

"Your mother…we thought it a chance for you to…support your family. Get out from under the Company. That's why we're in."

"Josette won't approve."

"Your mother's going to speak with her."

It was a risk, and Baptiste knew it. He'd felt badgered into it, his mother haunting around the wood home he'd built for Josette, talking in the sideways habit she had about "cattle this" and "cattle that." She never came right out and asked him to go, but she kept saying they'd need good people to take the ship south and then herd the cattle back. Now she'd sent her husband.

"Any who participate will be able to buy the cattle," Jean said. "It's a way for any man interested to get a step ahead for his family."

What was wrong with the step his family was on anyway? What he did was never good enough for her, Baptiste thought.

Before deciding, he wanted to talk with someone outside his family. He'd heard that Tom had gone in on the deal and that even the chief factor had put money into it. In a way, the factor's choice seemed disloyal to the Company, the way Baptiste saw it.

But Jean pushed that as one more reason why Baptiste should arrange to go with the cattle company, help them out, help the family out, and bring new distinction to his own. What could they do to him? Even the factor had invested.

"I'll decide after I talk with the factor," Baptiste said.

✦

"I guessed it'd be all right with you, sir," Baptiste told McLoughlin, his hat in his hand after he'd finally gotten his courage up to seek the meeting. The factor had eyes like an eagle's that pierced into a man's soul. His face looked frozen as he stood beside the polished table in his office.

"Why ever would you believe that?" the factor asked.

"You putting your own money into the cattle venture and all," Baptiste told him.

The factor's face flushed red.

"I invest on behalf of the Company," McLoughlin said.

"But isn't it a policy that no individual can own cattle here? Just lease."

"Sometimes we do things that may not seem rational to everyone," McLoughlin said. His eyes glared into Baptiste's. "I keep the names of French-Canadians on the books, make loans to them, and report that they are still employed when they're not, just so they don't have to go back to their point of enrollment. I do this for the benefit of us all."

"But isn't it…dishonest?"

Now McLoughlin's nostrils moved in and out, and his fingers gripped around the cane.

"You are free to name it anything you wish," he fumed. "But it should pose no problem for you as you are no longer in the employ of the Company!"

"I work here. I haven't quit."

"You're discharged," the factor shouted.

"I'm discharged?"

Baptiste couldn't believe it! After all these years, after all his time tending vines and apprenticing in the blacksmith shop and coopering and herding and doing whatever was asked of him, after all that, because he asked a question, he got discharged!

He stomped out of the factor's office, brushing past men and animal alike, stepped up onto his horse and rode hard away from Fort Vancouver. Cows mooed in the distance, and he took it as another insult.

He rode back to Fort Walla Walla and told Josette what had happened.

He didn't even bother to tell his mother. Let her wonder why he hung around and didn't have work to be doing. His wife had another baby coming; Denise was ill and hacking, and even Little Marie looked so—he couldn't describe it—but he never would find a husband for her. She was already fifteen and ought to be spoken for by now, but she was too outspoken. She argued with Pambrun over how the garden produce was distributed and how long Waiilatpu should be used by the Whitmans.

He grunted. Poor child. She'd gotten his challenging blood too, it seemed, asking questions that got a man fired.

No, she spent too much time with his mother, that was what it was. The girl set men off, acted as though she didn't need them around, that she had another trail to take. If they wanted to be on a trail with her, well fine, but otherwise, she wasn't interested in their wants. Yes, even his elder daughter acted disloyal.

For the first time in years, the whiskey he'd given up and nearly forgotten was calling his name. All because he'd let his mother push him and his into places he knew no one should go.

❖

Ewing Young's party had been scheduled to leave in January of 1837. But an accident on the Columbia held the ship back. The new departure time—Jean told him—would be spring. By then, Baptiste had drifted into an ale fog.

"You have scowled long enough," Josette told him.

"What?" Baptiste said, surprised. Usually his wife hurried the children out when she wished to speak with him of things that mattered. But something had sneaked in and straightened up her back. She held their youngest to her chest.

"Your mother says we do not need to put up with such from you," Josette told him. "You find somewhere else to waste away. Not where my sons and daughters can watch it happen. I won't help you destroy who you are. I won't watch it happen."

His mother, again.

"I'm not welcome in my own house?"

"Always. When it is you here and not a whiskey-driven man. You have a place here, the man I chose. That man does what he must for his children." She patted the baby's back as she paced. "That man keeps his word. That man doesn't place blame at the feet of any, except for himself. The man welcome here starts new. His feet aren't hobbled. He can move anywhere he wishes because his mind isn't fogged by whiskey. That man is welcome in my bed."

Baptiste blinked through the fog at her. "You think I choose these things that happen to me? A mother who sends me away? A father dead? A wife stolen from me? A job lost for no reason?" He made fists of his hands, sent his rage to keep them at his sides.

"You did not choose those wounds," Josette said, her voice low yet firm. "But how you heal them, that you choose. Whiskey heals nothing. Disappearing covers no pain for long. It is time your heart directs your feet. I married a loving man. If his feet serve his family, they can walk this man to me. If they serve whiskey, they should take him out of here. Now you choose."

❖

Ewings Young took Baptiste on. "If you're sober, son," he told Baptiste when he reached him at Fort Vancouver. Baptiste had thought they'd never set sail. Then when they did, he worried they'd never reach California.

Baptiste's stomach ached constantly, and whatever he ate soon quickly made its way back up and over the side of the ship. At Monterey Bay, Ewing Young made the final arrangements, purchasing not only cattle but also horses for the herders. The animals, yellow and beige and spattered with spots of reds and whites, all sported long horns that demanded respect.

Baptiste remembered his mother years before trying to rope a wild Spanish cow, and now he marveled at her courage if not her wisdom in taking such a foe. The woman had wanted a cow for as long as he could remember. She was persistent, someone who set her sights and then didn't let herself get swayed away no matter what rivers had to be crossed. Stubborn was what she was.

The cattle drive started out well enough, but the San Joaquin River in mid-May ran swift and swollen from the winter rains. Those animals they managed to get into the river panicked and bolted. They tore at each other, attacked the men on horses, and allowed themselves to be frantically dragged downstream.

That evening Ewing requested a meeting of all parties. "Ideas, gentlemen? We've got to get these cows across the river."

Suggestions ranged from waiting until the river was less swollen to sending parties ahead to secure more funds to try to contract for a ship to bring them to the Columbia and just drive them south from there.

"We could build rafts," Baptiste said.

Young looked at him. "You crazy, son?"

"There's plenty of timber. We know how to do it. We could ferry them across."

Which was what the Willamette Cattle Company did, one cow at a time.

At night, Baptiste longed for a bed warmed by his wife. His mother was the one who should have gone on this drive. She was the one whose eyes sparkled with the talk of cattle and living on their own. It was her wish, not his, and her pushing that had ended him up here, beaten and tired as a used-up ox.

He was dismissed from the Company, had distressed his wife, was distanced from his kin, and suffered from the flooded landscape and the poor, pitiful state of his own soul. It had to be someone's fault. It surely couldn't have been his.

He heard the bellow of cows. He stood up. The night sky was clear with stars so close together they looked like dribbles of milk. He'd helped move over seven hundred head of cows on rafts. Perseverance. He'd shown that. And he'd thought up a new solution and then followed through on hard choices. At least tonight he could sleep with a clear conscience. He'd been steadfast. That ran in Dorion blood, too, he guessed. Steadfast was the other side of stubborn.

21

A Reflected Name

"Let me help you with that, Madame Dorion," Jason Lee said. "Surely you don't plan to lift such a heavy—"

Marie shook her head at the missionary. She and Maria Pambrun and Marguerite stood together in the pouring March rain, blankets over their heads as they helped Rev. Lee toward his appointment with the Whitmans. He'd spend a night at the fort first, then travel on to their site.

"Here, my writing desk weighs less… Well, I'll just carry myself and hope I don't fall in," he said.

The late afternoon sky was as gray as a duck's bottom. Water poured off Lee's beaver hat, too. They were crossing a small stream that separated them from the fort, stepping on rocks and branches that bent with their weight.

"Truly. Madame Dorion, I—"

But she'd already lifted the heavy saddle-pack onto her shoulder and steadied it with one hand. With the other, she grabbed the writing desk, tucking it up under her blanket, then stepped her way across the stream already swollen from the rains. "Follow," she told him, wondering how he knew her that he called her by that name.

Madame Dorion. Marguerite had asked her once why people still called her that name. She'd always told her daughter that people from another time used it, those who knew her when she came across with Hunt, but this missionary Lee hadn't known her then. He'd obviously gotten the name from someone else.

Yet no one would take the time to describe an Indian woman to an American. She laughed at herself. What would they say? "She has dark hair and dark eyes." What would be distinctive about that?

Perhaps she'd been described to him by Jean, who'd known her longer than anyone here in the Columbia country, knew her from then and from now, the name a way of granting her respect with those Jean guided. The Dorion woman as she was known. Perhaps a way of raising his own esteem.

She hadn't ever considered that before, that her experiences might reflect well on Jean. It was good they reflected well on someone. She was certain Baptiste didn't see it that way.

Marie placed her feet carefully and hoped in the gray downpour that Lee could see the edges of rocks and would step solid so he wouldn't slip or fall. These missionaries could be fragile, easily taken by the challenges of this country, at least that was how she saw the Whitmans' efforts this past year. They'd done little to "win souls" the way she knew Sarah meant it those years before. If anything, they were plowing sprouts under rather than planting new seeds.

Little Marie had gone to Waiilatpu curious with eyes wide as a child's in wonder at the pretty lady's musical voice. Little Marie had even helped Mrs. Whitman with the laundry sticks, since Mrs. Whitman's work was restricted as she awaited the birth of a child. Later, Little Marie had cared for the little girl, but not to Mrs. Whitman's satisfaction. A Sandwich Island couple had arrived to serve the missionary's wife.

The girl often visited Older Sister's burial place, placed strips of cloth and beads on the branches near her grave. She was a respectful child, but she returned from those visits with complaining words about the Whitmans' tilling more soil at the rye grass place, news she brought back and told the Cayuse elders.

"Mrs. Whitman treats me as though I'm not there, Kasa," Little Marie had told Marie once. "Like I'm one of the dogs she chases away from her chickens."

"She's new. She doesn't know our ways yet."

"They're the strangers. They should make the changes."

"Shoulds are heavy *shaptakai* to carry," Marie told her. "Give the newcomers time." Marie tried to be reassuring, though she agreed with the child. Her own time with the Whitmans carried prickles on her arms like the air that carried lightning storms. She wasn't sure how this

Mr. Lee behaved among the Kalapuya people at French Prairie. He'd had "converts," Jean told her, people who came to believe in new ways because of words he said. And he'd started an orphanage for the many children whose parents had died of the fall fever and ague, so he must have been a good man.

The Whitmans had started nothing but buildings and plantings and disagreements.

The rain chilled her; the drenched blanket smelled wet. Marie coughed.

"Are you all right, Mother?" Marguerite asked. Marie nodded her assurance.

Fortunately, this March month wasn't the season for the fever and ague. That usually happened in the late summer and ended with the first freeze. Even Michel's little *Lapine* had succumbed at Fort Vancouver last year, and she'd never been anywhere these missionaries had been. The child had been buried at Vancouver. Jean had attended and told Marie that the new reverend and his wife had suggested that these bad things were happening because of the people's living in *sin,* a word the missionaries used often.

Marie didn't remember Sarah talking much of the dark places in people's hearts. Sarah spoke not of a father who punished those he loved for doing wrong, but of one who loved regardless of how that child behaved, and how once his child sang a welcoming song and asked to be lifted, so all men could be held in the palm of his hand. "God thinks of you," Sarah had once told her. "If he should count the thoughts of each one of us, they'd number more than each grain of sand."

This can't be, either, Marie decided. *God must lie somewhere between Sarah's sand and that reverend's message of judging words.*

Mr. Lee headed overland again, to spend a night at the Whitmans. Marie had heard that a ship had come, bringing ten more men or so and a wife for Mr. Lee. Perhaps he needed more help for the growing fields of melons and corn and potatoes he tilled. Maybe the Whitmans had decided to team up with the Methodists, to support Lee's efforts of bringing more Americans because the Cayuse workers weren't working hard enough for them.

The Whitmans' cattle herd grew. But he hadn't butchered a one yet according to Little Marie. The Indian workers there and the Whitmans all still ate game or horse meat that he bartered from the Cayuse.

Even the arrival of little Temi, as the Cayuse called the baby, Alice Whitman, was not enough to warm up the frigid relationship between the Whitmans and their neighbors.

Lee would pick up horses from here, the best the Company had to offer for his return trip East. Walla Walla was known for its fine horses. Marie might ask him to look for Paul. If she described Paul to him, maybe he could look out for an Ioway-Sioux-French-Canadian boy on his ride east. But what would she have him say? No, better not to stir up ashes already long cooled.

Marguerite followed behind her mother. She carried equally heavy items, a saddle and valise. Marguerite was a strong girl. Louis would have been proud. The Pambrun girl brought up the rear with Lee, who turned to help her with her step. He was a gentleman, that was sure. Full of manners, as Marguerite no doubt noted.

Marie set her load down, adjusted her blanket around her shoulders, and watched the others as they wove their way across the stream.

Marie heard the Pambrun girl laugh. She was slender; Marguerite an oak next to that one's sapling shape. Her daughter would need a strong man to share her life, a fir tree tall and towering and comfortable with his own height, not worrisome over the shadow his wife might cast his way.

Marie had such a fir tree of a man. She'd had three, once Pierre had changed his ways.

Richard might be such a man for Marguerite, but when he hadn't brought priests back, Marguerite's interest in him seemed to falter. Jean's passion for the ways of priests had rubbed onto his stepdaughter.

Josette had a good man too. The cattle drive had proven successful for Baptiste. Josette said when it was time, she would join him south of where Kilakotah and LaBonte stayed, the latter now watching Tom McKay's horse farm in a place called Scappoose. South of the Columbia. Everyone Marie knew chose land south, in the American sector.

It was woodier and a little more rolling, good cover for cattle with enough open meadows for grazing. Baptiste kept in touch with Tom, and that was good. She just wished her son had time for her.

The rain-drenched party arrived at the fort, and Marie walked around to the back where, once she dried off, she would help Catherine Pambrun serve any guests stopping at the fort that evening. Little Marie, already sixteen, spent the night with Marie and Jean's youngest this night.

"I'm to meet Tom McKay farther north," she heard Lee tell Pierre Pambrun and the men settling into the parlor. "Taking his sons with me to an American school. He wants the best for his children. He knows it won't happen without a good education. Not for mixed-blood children…well, it's just better that all children have proper schooling."

"Perhaps we should send our girls back," Pierre Pambrun said. He motioned to Marie, as she brought a tray with cocoa, to open a window and let in the rain-freshened air.

"Boys more easily learn the alphabet," Lee said. "Even Spokane Garry reads now. I hear he works well with the new missionaries up that way. More settlers will follow. And we'll have proper families living all over this northwest country then."

"Got proper families," Pambrun said. "Mine. Whitmans. Even the Maki, arriving from the Sandwich Islands, are as good a workers for Mrs. Whitman as I've ever seen, helping her with that new baby. What's not proper about my family?" His voice turned sharp.

"Nothing, I assure you," Lee said. "Thank you." He nodded to Marie as she served him the hot cocoa Catherine had ordered prepared in the kitchen. "It's just that communities, well, they…stabilize with…weddings and baptisms and churches and schools. That's what a settlement is."

"We've held church services here since '28," Pambrun said. "And it's commerce, that's what makes a community. Look about you. People making money make a place. You think this fort isn't a settlement? Nearly eight hundred people live at Vancouver. Almost as many here."

Lee nodded. Marie cleared the dishes from the room. Catherine remained behind, she and her girls, each stitching while they listened, Catherine's pipe set aside.

"The chief factor apparently lost his temper with the Church of England's representative," Lee told them. "This after he'd had a civil ceremony performed between him and his wife of many years, just to placate the man. The reverend was quite concerned that so many at the fort are French-Canadian and therefore Catholic, though that's the field for harvest as we Methodists see it. He calls them 'papists.' McLoughlin takes offense at how he insults the officers and their wives."

Marie had heard that word *papist* used before, back in St. Louis, and it had not been said with respect. Some words stayed in a memory, even now, nearly thirty years since she'd first heard it.

Lee sipped his cocoa. Put the Spode china cup down. "Not something to be feared, the presence of Catholics, but favored, for the opportunities among all God-fearing people."

"So you head back to bring new Methodists?"

Lee nodded. "And supplies, on board ship. We won't return overland. Let the Presbyterians and Congregationalists do that, as I see they've done in numbers."

"And the Catholics. They'll follow," Pambrun said. He smiled. A clock ticked. Then he added, "If you're returning by ship, you'd have room for books?" Lee hesitated, then nodded agreement. "I'll advance you a hundred dollars to have you purchase a few for me. Pack them in tin and send them out."

"That could be arranged," Lee said. He turned, then spoke directly to Marie. "Speaking of books," he said. "Madame Dorion, are you aware that you're in one? Published two years past. My new bride brought it with her. It's a title called *Astoria* by a quite notable author, Washington Irving. He says kind things of you and what you did to keep your family alive. And even Hunt's men."

"She's in a book?" Catherine said, settling her needlework on her lap. Was that a different level of interest Catherine's eyes now showed? "How distinctive," Catherine said. "But now surely you've got to let Mrs. Whitman teach you to read, Marie. If only to see your name."

❖

Jean didn't think he'd ever understand her, his wife. All this pushing to get cattle had just added more pressure to their future rather than less.

He agreed, they had gotten into the cattle at the right time. The price had risen to over sixty dollars a head now, while the 603 Spanish cows that survived the trip north had been distributed at $7.67 per cow. Even the chief factor had proved a kindly soul in this matter. He'd replaced several of the wild Spanish cattle for some of the tame ones held at the Fort. The women at French Prairie could milk the tame ones.

He and Marie had received ten heifers, three of them tame, needing milking. They'd spent all the cash they had for those. Jason Lee had nearly eighty head for his investment. The mission apparently gained money in addition to new converts.

Baptiste's efforts added another five cows to the Toupin-Dorion herd. Jean had arranged all that, Baptiste not wanting to talk business with "a woman," even if she was his mother. Especially his mother, Jean imagined.

Jean had suggested they combine their cows with Lees and Youngs or others of the Willamette Cattle Company, each put in money for a wage of some herders. That, too, had been arranged. Baptiste earned a little income from the labor and received his board along with the other men who seemed to accept the company of cattle as well as people. And so Jean and Marie's efforts helped sustain Baptiste's family back at Fort Walla Walla.

They were all separated, Baptiste from his own; Jean from his when he moved back and forth; Marie from Baptiste. But the separations had been chosen, which meant they could be changed.

Fifteen head, hard earned. They had no money to fence them, and few did anyway. But it meant taking them to meadows, bringing them back for twice-daily milking, and otherwise riding through bramble and brush, keeping them grazing, getting them familiar with "their home." Baptiste couldn't herd the wild ones alone, keep coyotes and wolves away and milk them, so he'd sent word to Jean to have his half-brother François "join him in the brambles."

"No," Marie had said. "I've given up all my sons. I'm not giving up François." She kneaded bread dough, the scent of yeast and dark grain filling their small cabin.

"You asked Baptiste to herd the cattle," Jean told her.

"Yes. But he doesn't need François's help."

"It's a tough job, Marie. He's without his family. He's living in a lean-to, and the rainy season will make that even more miserable. The weather's different there—"

"He's young. He's strong."

"He's not made of iron." She'd continued to press her knuckles into the dough, sprinkle more flour beneath it as she rolled the edges up. "Maybe we could assist with Josette joining him there, eh? I believe she'd like this. I know he would."

"Little Marie won't want to go."

"You don't know that. Maybe we should all go, now. Not wait. That would solve all the problems. I could sleep in a warm bed with my wife each night and Baptiste would have his—"

"If we could do this, we would. You talk nonsense, dreaming nonsense."

"There's a way," Jean told her. He cleared his throat. "We could take a loan."

She turned to him. "Go into debt? *Non.*"

"But this is what you long for, to live in that French Prairie country, to be with your family all together, to have your precious cows to milk. Yet you resist this, you put it off so that you owe no one. This makes no sense to me. What if something happens to me, to you, and we never see this dream come true because we waited and waited for the perfect time. Going into debt is an act of love when it serves others. Don't you see this?"

She kneaded the dough. She knuckled it so hard the table she stood at rocked against the log wall. She greased the iron bread pan, split the ball in half, dropped each into the two-sided cheek bread pan. She patted them both so hard that he wondered if his aging teeth would be able to chew it once it baked.

"Non," she said spanking the bread. "François stays here."

❖

The four rode horse together, Marguerite's mother on a mount more green broke than her own, twelve-year-old Marianne, the youngest, riding the oldest horse, plodding Janey, Little Marie on a fine white Cayuse mount.

Marguerite appreciated watching her mother work a young horse. The way she positioned herself on its back, the softness of her words, even the degree of tension she placed on reins spoke to the horse of disciplined love.

That was her mother, all right. Disciplined love. A broken or trained horse was asked to surrender, to give up a bit of its will. The animal learned to trust that the rider wanted only the best for it and, once learned, they'd share times together without the worry of wondering what either might do next. Her mother trained with tenderness, not the way some of the men worked the horses. Even some of the Cayuse men were rougher than Marguerite thought needed. The horses wanted a relationship with their riders. There was no need to overpower the way some did.

They rode down into a dimple of land, a place her mother found to take young mounts. It formed a natural corral, and she often let them graze on long ropes, a reward for a trouble-free ride. Marguerite had packed food, and she unloaded it from the *shaptakai*. Marianne rubbed at her backside. Little Marie gathered up water in jugs.

"You need more riding time," her mother said to Marianne. "So your bottom isn't so surprised on a horse."

"She'd rather sit in the shade and draw pictures," Marguerite said.

Marianne stuck her tongue out at her sister, but she smiled, then lifted her pack of brown paper and chalk. She found a spot beneath a willow and sketched.

Marguerite laid out the cloth, set food down, and called for the others to eat. Marguerite made the sign of the cross as her father always had. But this time she also spoke words of blessing.

"Where'd you hear that?" Marianne asked.

"Mrs. Whitman says a blessing," Marguerite said. "Little Marie taught it to us."

"It's a nice thing to do before a meal, to pause. Isn't it mother?" Little Marie asked.

Marie nodded, took a drink of water.

"There's a priest north of the Columbia now," Marguerite told her mother. "Isn't that grand?"

"I hadn't heard that. A priest?" Marie said.

"And Papa Jean says the factor thinks if he gets enough people out here, they'll need even more priests. He hopes the Columbia country people monopolize the markets with the Russians so the Americans will only be able to sell their milk and grain to each other, or to him. He's hoping any new arrivals will stay loyal to the Company. They'll share-crop there at a place called Puget Sound. They're recruiting from the Red River area where Spokane Garry went to school. The Company'll lease them a thousand acres for half the production," Little Marie said.

"Will they bring cattle?" her mother asked.

Little Marie shook her head. She took a drink of water from the jug, the twine around it wet against her fingers. "No cows, and they can't own the land. They can lease the stock, but the increase always goes back to Hudson's Bay."

"As it was in France," Marianne said. "Papa said it was a bad thing in France. People made huge payments every year, regardless of the yield, with lords and such collecting rent and only the king allowed to hunt the fields."

"The only real hope is doing things on your own," her mother said. "See how that story shows that?"

"Papa says to serve the people. Our people," Marianne said.

"Indians, too," Marguerite corrected.

Butterflies settled on the rye grass surrounding them. Horses nicked at each other. "Papa says we can be baptized," Marianne said, soft, her eyes lowered. "I want to be baptized." She moved her drawing aside, reached for the jam she spread on the bread. "Don't you, Marguerite?" Marguerite nodded. "Papa says the ceremony brings tears to his eyes."

"Your father is soft-hearted," her mother said.

"Me and Marguerite and François and even you, Mama. Baptiste, too, and Little Marie. We can all be baptized together. Or was Baptiste already baptized?"

Marguerite wasn't always sure her mother heard things. She stayed silent. "Was he?" she asked.

"Your brother? No. He wasn't."

"Weren't there priests where he was born?" Marianne asked.

"There were."

"And you weren't baptized either, Mother?"

"I wasn't," her mother said. "It's time we finished up here."

❖

They were round men, Marie thought to herself. Both of them. Or perhaps it was the size of their flowing cloaks that made them appear that way. The one looked as though he wrinkled his nose up at something foul, but the expression didn't change even when he smiled, which he did now as he stepped out of a Company boat. Several others stepped out now too, a woman with eyes red as though she'd been weeping, a small child, a few other men and women. They looked…troubled, eyes darting here and there, as if seeking something.

A storm the night before left a clear October sky soaring over them, the air as fragrant as a lily, dust settled by the rain.

The taller of the black-robed men turned back to the other. Marie could see his round belly as the wind whipped his cloak tight against him. But he laughed as he got his land legs back. Both men stood, inhaled the air, and placed their hands on the long crosses and string of beads at their necks. They gazed around, then turned to assist a woman who leaned heavily upon a child. The party moved toward the fort's gate.

Black robes, that was what they were. Priests, along with some French-Canadians and their native wives, returning, coming back. It had been—Marie counted—twenty-six years since she'd seen a priest and that one had been walking the streets of St. Louis. Her last encounter with one close up was in the fog-days after her sister and mother died. The priest had arrived too late to save them.

They were too late, too, these priests. The Spaldings and Whitmans and even Lee and those he recruited by ship were already ahead of them, making changes.

The taller of the two, Father Blanchet, spoke in French-accented English. Pambrun, who had been summoned at their arrival, spoke back in French with a hearty welcome. "Father Demers," the first priest said, turning to introduce the shorter priest.

It was all very cordial and quick, then Father Blanchet said, "There was a tragedy upriver. Drownings. Americans and the native woman, there." He motioned toward the woman Father Demers helped. "She lost a child."

Even with priests present, death had slipped in and taken a child away.

The party spent only the night before heading downriver.

❖

"They're going to Cowlitz," Jean corrected Marie when she told him she'd seen priests on their way to Vancouver a few weeks before. Her husband had arrived back from Fort Vancouver, and it was good to have him home. "They'll establish a mission there. One has already arrived. There'll be masses held."

"Did you see him?" Marie asked.

"The priests? No, I must have—"

"Baptiste. Have you seen how he's doing?"

Jean nodded. *"Oui."* He finished eating roasted salmon, liking the way it flaked pink as a dog's tongue. She served him a slice of fresh melon.

"Like me, he is tired of the separations. Marie—"

"Do these new people come as missionaries? They'll have competition now, the missionaries."

"I know this," Jean said. He bit his words off as though they were tough. "At Vancouver, they served mass in the schoolhouse. McLoughlin is on furlough, and Douglas, the acting factor, gives them permission. I know all this already." He took another bite of his salmon. "I attend the mass, Marie."

"Did you?"

"Oui."

"What happens at the mass?" Marianne asked.

"Will you have more melon, husband?"

"I had forgotten how it feels to receive the wafer, to remember what

I first knew and trusted." His eyes said that his thoughts went far away. "There is more, my Marie," Jean said. "Two weeks later, when I returned from Fort Langley, I learned the priests had gone south to French Prairie. The log church our people built there, they hold a service. Kilakotah and LaBonte and our friends there, they all attend. We should go there, Marie. It would mean change, but we would live with less certainty. We would live together."

"The new missionaries bring twelve cows," Little Marie told Jean. "And two are fresh."

Marie's mouth watered with the thought of fresh milk sliding down her throat. It had been so long since she'd tasted it. Why did she deprive herself of this?

They could have milk daily at French Prairie.

"We could tend the tame cows," Jean said. "Baptiste and François could ride herd. They are deprived of more than fresh milk."

Jean spoke in a stern tone Marie rarely heard from him. And he had stopped eating. He was pacing now, wiping his hands on the leather leggings all the horse and cattlemen wore when they had to be in heavy brush. "When a child of mine, almost ready to marry, asks 'What is a mass?' then I know they are deprived of more important things than milk. We will go, all of us, for a mass."

She opened her mouth to disagree, but he put his hand up. "The children will be baptized. We will marry. It is time a man decides such things."

❖

Jean and Marie argued through a fall and winter of strain. Small things took on more meaning. They disagreed about whether the down should be replaced in the comforter or whether Jean's old horse, Lumière, should be put down or allowed to limp from his aging. She gave the children directions; then Jean redirected them toward some other task. Marie knew the tension arranged itself on the sharp edge of her decision to be baptized, for them to go into debt, to do what Jean wanted even though it wasn't what she thought best.

When Jean left on a task for Pambrun, Marie felt relief more than grief.

Sometimes, when she told the truth to herself, it wasn't the debt that concerned her. It was all of them being together, it was depending on Jean. It was his wish to bring the priests back into her life.

"We will all go, all of us," Jean said one summer morning after he'd returned from Vancouver yet again. "It is decided. There will be a large mass on September 24. As many who wish will be baptized. And vows repeated. It will be at Vancouver, and we can stay for a time and visit your friends. Maybe see Kilakotah, eh?"

"I do not trade baptism for a visit with a friend," she said.

"You believe you have nothing to confess?" Jean said. "We all have things to confess. It is a sign of being human, *n'est-ce pas?*"

"Why should I tell anyone of what I do wrong? I make my own trouble. I cause my own feet to stumble. Telling someone else does nothing."

"It lets another help hold us up, my Marie," Jean said. "God wants us to hold each other up. We pay attention to our bodies for years. Now is the time to feed our souls. We do that in the presence of a priest, yes, but in the presence of each other, too. I only want to lift you, my Marie."

"And I am too big for you to do this alone."

He wasn't sure if she teased him. It would be her habit to do that, to throw him off the path like a dog distracted.

Marie knelt and pulled weeds in the rows she'd planted that spring. She did her best to ignore him.

"Think of it as talking only," he said.

"Fruit will not come to plants tended by angry hands," she said. "Go away now. My fingers get angry with this talk."

"I confess." Jean said. "I tell the priests my sins. It's painless." She looked at him. "Well, a little pain is good. To remember all the things I wish I had not done, the words spoken in anger, the—"

"There are too many for me to remember," Marie said. "It would slow the day, and everyone would leave, waiting for my long list."

"You don't need to say each one, Marie. He knows already."

"You've told this priest of me?"

"No, no, my Marie." Jean was being kind, his voice soft as a lamb's ear.

"Then why must I—"

"It is a gift," he said. "The baptism is simply a sign that you accept it. You never want gifts, and yet this one..."

She shook her head. How could she tell him that it wasn't the saying so of her errors that concerned her or the saying so of her strong and sometimes angry feelings she didn't want to confess? It was knowing that what she had to say could not remove the stain of what she'd done long years ago, and since. It was those choices that would keep her separated forever. She wasn't worthy of this gift he wanted for her soul.

Hadn't her one son abandoned her as payment for the way she raised him? Wasn't another son as distant as a ship's bell heard through the fog but never seen? What hope was there that she could ever earn the quietness of spirit Jean said the baptism could grant her—if she let it?

"No. I'll not go," she said.

"They are my children, too," Jean said. He straightened to his full height. He lifted her arms. "For your children's sake... Do not deprive them of this."

He was right. She had no right to make up their minds for them.

"If they decide, then yes," she said. "But I will keep the name my mother-in-law once gave me. Her to Be Baptized."

❖

The entourage that made its way up the Columbia River could be heard long before its members arrived. The creak of wood, the awkward gait of the horse, and the rattle of the unusual cargo formed a natural melody in Marie's ears. In a canoe, moving at a slower pace, was a woman with a parasol held over her face. A white woman, coming upriver. They must have come west by ship.

Marie set her water bucket down. It was so very hot this summer day, and her sprouts withered quickly if she didn't bring water to the little troughs she'd dug between the rows. She wiped her eyes of the sweat.

They carried the woman in on a stretcher of sorts. Four men. One of the riders, dressed in a dark suit, dismounted. He hovered near the woman, walking beside her while she was lifted gingerly up the bank, then moved into the fort. Before long, Marianne came running from the courtyard where she'd been collecting eggs with a Pambrun girl. "They want you to come, Mother," she said. "The lady is ill."

Her name was Sarah Hall. She and her husband, Edwin Oscar Hall, had arrived from the Sandwich Islands. They brought a "printing press," they called it, an item sent by the "Christians of the Sandwich Islands" to the Spaldings at Lapwai.

"She's expecting a child," Catherine Pambrun told Marie in the kitchen area. "And she has a weakened back. She can't walk on her own. She's been teaching English classes at the mission while lying down. Imagine that?"

"Her husband—"

"He's a printer, and they're taking the press to make books, Marie. Mrs. Spalding apparently wants them, the Nez Perce, to read the Bible like Spokane Garry does, but not in English, in their own words. So it will mean more to them."

Marie looked out at the canvas-covered chunk of wood. It appeared square with strange rolling tubes in various places. "The Nez Perce language is in there?" Marie said.

Mr. Hall heard the question and answered it, saying yes, it was in the right hands. "Every language is there if we know how to put the letters together," he said. "The signs some people make to talk with, do you know those?" He was a young man, not much older than Baptiste, Marie thought. Dressed in an English suit and wearing a stiff collar similar to the one Mr. Pambrun wore. He stood firm as a fir tree, but his eyes were kind. "Like signs, or designs on native tents I've seen, drawings are put onto a little block of wood, and we put ink on the wood, then press it onto paper. Together, they tell a story."

"They've even brought paper," Catherine said. "All the way from the Islands."

Marie still tried to grasp how it worked.

"Perhaps if we have time later I could show you a piece of type," he said. "We'll be awhile setting it up once we reach Lapwai. That's how you say it, yes, 'Lap way?'"

Sarah Hall had her own intrigue. She was tiny, not much bigger than Marianne in fact, and pale as sun-bleached parchment. If she was expecting a child, there was no evidence of it yet.

"Do you have something that might strengthen her legs?" Catherine asked Marie.

Marie nodded and began making a mixture of sage and rosemary, lavender and thyme, chamomile flowers and melilot from the kitchen garden. Marie showed her what she'd mixed. "Sweet clover," Mrs. Hall said. "I had no idea." Marie stewed it all in some red wine Mr. Pambrun approved of for the purpose.

"Place it in cloth," Marie told Catherine. "We'll put it on her back and legs."

She did seem to improve through the night and in the morning. Mrs. Hall commented that she wouldn't have such ingredients to take with her. "Lye, oak leaves, vinegar, and salt will help, too," Marie said.

"What a gift you have, making healing things up from whatever God provides," Mrs. Hall said.

"She's quite good. A long time ago, she helped a woman who could hardly walk and who had lost all her hair," Catherine said. "The woman put her feet inside slaughtered—"

"It was a long time ago," Marie said. She wondered how Catherine had even heard of it.

"We need to be going," Mr. Hall said. Another printer named Rogers would ride with them, and four Indians would row the canoes.

"Maybe the milk they have at Lapwai will help your bones," Marie said.

"They have milk cows there?" Mr. Hall said.

"Would you consider coming with us, Mrs...."

"Toupin," Marie said. "I'm Mrs. Toupin."

"French," Mr. Hall said.

"I could use your help," Mrs. Hall said, her eyes pleading. "It would be good to have a woman in the canoe."

"And I could show you how the press works. You could see your name in type," Mr. Hall said.

✦

"If you don't go for the baptism, then I won't go either," Little Marie said. "I'll go along with you to Lapwai."

Marie shook her head. "You do what your mother wants you to do," she said. "I help this woman a little, and then I'll come back. I may not be here in time for you to go if your parents choose that for you."

"I have seventeen summers. I don't need for them to decide. I could already be married if my uncle or my father approved."

"So you found someone at the root feast and you wait for your uncle to decide this for you?" Marie smiled, wiped a smudge of dirt from the girl's cheek. Marie wondered if her granddaughter knew how much she was loved, this firstborn child of her son.

"No. I have no one. But if I did—"

"If you did, your father and uncle and grandfather Jean and your mother and me would all come up with what was needed for you to have a good life."

"I know this," she said. She dropped her eyes and rubbed her elbow with her opposite hand, hung on to herself that way Baptiste did when he was younger. "But I want you to go along for the baptism. I don't want to go alone."

"There's nothing to fear," Marie said, her words a warning in her own ears. She felt a tightness in her stomach, talking of soul things. She didn't want to mislead Little Marie into a certainty Marie didn't know for herself. "You say words the priest asks you to say, you listen to hear if your soul fills up in new ways, and then they sprinkle water on you."

"And you know you're loved that way?"

"You should know you are loved even before that," Marie told her. "You know this, don't you? That you are as precious as every star in the sky?"

Little Marie nodded. How she ached for this child of her flesh, for all she wanted for her to have, to be. Marie hoped her own reluctance didn't stand in Little Marie's way.

"The Halls carry something called 'type,'" the child said then.

"Strange words."

"Would they make my name in the type?" Little Marie asked.

Marie smiled. "If they make mine, then yes. We have the same name. The time will come when you will have another name, if you wish it. For now, I'll bring back the piece of paper with your name on it. And when you get back from the baptism, you will have it as another worthy gift."

❖

It was late September. Jean thought his heart would break when he gathered up his brood and Marie was not among them. This had been his fear all along. That once he stood firm she wouldn't bend, and that what they'd had for years would break. Marguerite had remained behind at the last minute too. She said she hoped she could go with her mother to Lapwai.

"But you'll miss being—"

"I want my mother there," Marguerite told Marianne. "You'll at least have your father and brother with you."

So only he and François and Marianne had headed west to Vancouver for the baptism.

And then, only his daughter had come forth to accept the baptismal water.

A French-Canadian boat maker, stationed at Fort Vancouver, acted as her godfather, promising to keep to her religious instruction as best he could, long distance, and knowing she would soon be of marriageable age and chances were, soon enough, her husband would be helping with her catechism. If Jean found the right husband for her.

Jean had to concentrate on the fact that his baby had maintained an interest in the faith, asked the questions, made him rethink all the things he'd once known by heart and hadn't said for years. The special prayers. The reasons why he lit a candle in memory of someone lost or loved.

Even the chanting words of the priests came back to fill him up, make him feel that he was where he was supposed to be, inside that log structure serving as a church at Fort Vancouver.

François had hesitated, then decided not to go at the last minute. Maybe that was as it should be. A man should make such a choice only when he was sure. At least the boy had come with them, been there for Marianne's great day. Jean's own wife had chosen not to join them. She was with that printer at Lapwai and the Spaldings. Doing what? He didn't know.

She'd done it on purpose, leaving when she did so she didn't have to face the choice to be baptized or not. And so the marriage banns would not be read either. She needed to be baptized, accept the gift, for herself alone, not just for the marriage.

At least Baptiste had surprised him, showing up at Vancouver for the September service. Several hundred were there, residents of the forts, some coming south from Fort Langley, others north from French Prairie. Baptiste's presence had pleased Jean, more than he realized. "Your daughter didn't want to come," Jean said.

"She stays to help her mother."

"*Oui*," Jean said. "This is probably the reason why. She is being helpful and waiting until you come home. Help her decide things then, you and your wife."

"I've decided to bring them here," Baptiste said. "I may not be able to be a cattleman. But Tom McKay has work he needs done. I could do that and have Josette here too. I've been without them long enough."

Jean coughed, felt a pounding in his head. It was the beginning of the fever and ague season. He'd be glad to leave Vancouver where it seemed all who had it converged each fall. McLoughlin usually had some potions that helped ease it, but it was worse in this region than closer to Walla Walla.

"We may have to find other help for the cattle," Baptiste said.

Jean nodded. "Today I tell myself the truth. This being here and there has gone on long enough. I take us into debt and bring my family here. I'll tend the cows. Your mother must decide then, if she belongs with us or not."

22

Reunion

Baptiste came straight from Marianne's baptism.

"The Whitmans let us have butter and cheese," Little Marie told her father. He sat in the wood house that had once been his mother's, surrounded by his daughters, Little Marie and Denise, and his son named for his father. Josette kept a constant smile on her face. A load had been lifted when he'd told Jean of his choice. He knew he would feel even lighter once he faced his mother and told her of his intentions.

That could wait. His mother wasn't even here.

He thought of François's decision to wait to be baptized, to turn back at the last moment. The boy hadn't seemed troubled by his choice, just wanting to be sure, he'd said, "before committing my soul. Leastways, I was there for Marianne."

Baptiste envied that kind of confidence. When Baptiste had been fifteen, he'd been troubled by the birth of a baby sister and his own part in the departure of his brother. He'd wooed and won a wife and then lost her.

He'd failed his own family, he supposed, by not offering them the rituals and routines that helped a child make choices about their spirit life, about knowing that part of himself that was not just eating and sleeping but dreaming and finding what a man or a woman was best suited to in life. He hadn't had that himself. A flash of resentment heated his face red. He could lay much of the blame for his life at the feet of his mother.

"But no milk," Marguerite continued where her niece left off. "The Whitmans won't let us have milk."

Marguerite entertained the baby and tickled Denise's fat belly. Marguerite was good with children. Baptiste wondered why she hadn't found a husband yet, started a family of her own. Here was another he didn't know well, a sister. He'd neglected much. But he could change that and he would.

Little Marie prepared a flat cake she dropped into heated oil. Baptiste watched it bubble to the surface, turn into a snowdrift of dough. "And the one missionary, Mr. Smith, he says no giving cows to the Cayuse or other Indians, either, the way the Spaldings do."

"Where do you hear this?" Josette asked.

Little Marie shrugged her shoulders. "I listened when I looked after the child at Waiilatpu," she said. "They pay in cows at Lapwai. To workers there. Old trappers who find their way. Those who tend the fields. Mr. Beers, the blacksmith at the Whitmans', he tells me these things."

"Maybe not all stories told are true," Josette said.

"He has the writing desk of Rev. Lee," Little Marie insisted. "He can write things down, so his stories are true."

"Written words don't make it true. It's what words mean," Baptiste told her.

"Maybe even those who paddle canoes for ill women, as Kasa does, will get a cow from the Spaldings. Even Indians get cows at Lapwai."

After all Baptiste's hard work of riding herd on Spanish cows, these missionaries were just giving cows away? Baptiste couldn't imagine that. They were too precious, those animals. No one would give away something of that kind of value.

"The Spaldings give the cows to workers," Josette said. "You're certain of this?"

Little Marie lifted the dough, crisp now and folded in onto itself, out of the hot pan. "Let it cool," she told her father. "Then put this jam on it. It's good. I made it myself. Kasa showed me."

"They give cows away," Baptiste repeated. "How can they do this?" He wondered what his mother would have to say about this when she returned. He might have to ask her why she thought these missionaries would do such things. It might be an easier conversation to have with her than talking about…what separated them.

◈

"Does that feel better?" Marie asked. She placed poultices on Sarah Hall's limbs each morning so the woman wore them while the canoe was rowed upriver. Marie was careful to lift the skirts so that little of her legs showed, in case either of the Cayuse paddlers might see. Sarah's limbs felt limp as wet grass, pale as shell.

Sarah nodded. "The heat helps. And whatever you're putting in the cloth. I might try standing on my legs. Perhaps at the fire tonight, when Edwin meets up with us."

"A little soon," Marie told her, shaking her head, no.

"Do you think so?"

She sounded so disappointed that Marie smiled. "Tomorrow. Gives us one more day for the medicine to work. We'll try it tomorrow."

The lines that formed pain on her face smoothed out as she lay back onto the heavy buffalo robes forming her bed in the canoe. A feather-filled comforter acted as a pillow around her shoulders. Marie rolled a cloth casing stuffed with the same goose down beneath her knees. Sarah's white-and-pink calico skirt billowed out in a bell and covered the pillow Marie had laid there.

"Your hands are so small," Sarah said. She reached as though she wanted to take Marie's hand but she hesitated. Marie took it as a sign of respect that she waited, didn't assume Marie wanted to be touched.

"My feet are large," Marie said, and Sarah laughed.

"The fingertips are white as snow. Are you cold?"

Marie nodded. "My hands know cold best," she said.

Tiny tucks of cloth from the shoulder of her dress converged at Sarah Hall's slender waist, which was circled with a leather belt. She wore long sleeves but no gloves, and her hands were brown as nuts. Her bonnet shielded her face, keeping it pale.

Marie wore a calico dress too, though without an underskirt. She still wore leggings, but they were of cloth, not leather. More practical if she wasn't riding a horse and easier to keep clean. She saved the buckskins now for dancing and special occasions. Jean always liked her in them best, he said. The smoke-tanned leather smelled better than the Company's cloth. Marie hadn't worn them now for a while.

"You are comfortable?" Marie asked, and when Sarah nodded, Marie signaled the Cayuse paddlers who pushed the boat out into the river.

The journey proved peaceful. The men on horseback rode away from the water at times, dipping into valleys and ridges. The women could see them occasionally, tiny figures high above the river. "It's nice knowing they're there, even when we can't see them," Sarah said. She used her straw-formed hat to wave away bugs from her face.

"Do they know they're held in the mind of another?" Marie asked.

"What a lovely way to word it," Sarah said. "Could there be a more precious gift than that, to know one holds another in her mind? I must tell Edwin that tonight. May I repeat your words?"

Marie shrugged. Such an emphasis on words felt strange, at least that someone considered her choice of words worthy of remembering felt strange.

Deer sometimes lifted their heads at the water's edge, not startling, just watching as the craft moved past. The heavy scent of mud and earth and overripe berries wafted in to them from the shoreline.

"Have you met Eliza Spalding?" Sarah asked.

Marie nodded. She moved her paddle from side to side, helping as she could. But mostly she knelt where she could adjust Sarah's comfort. "We had time together while they built at Waiilatpu."

"It will be nice for you to see old friends, then."

Marie nodded. She'd see her friend Mrs. Spalding and walk where Sarah Shonowane might have walked. And she'd get to see the mission's cows. That she was doing something helpful, too, for this woman along the way pushed aside the words that Jean had spoken before she left, asking that she go with him to Vancouver to meet the priests instead.

She didn't want to think about it.

At the evening fires, Marie watched as they unloaded the bulky cargo carried on the horses—a printing press, fifty "reams of paper" and "fonts of Pica and Long Primer"—all things that Marie marveled at. She had no idea what some of the words the men used meant, but Mr. Hall had promised to explain when they arrived. The items filled the side packs of three horses.

During the day, Sarah Hall let her hand drop over the side of the canoe and into the cool water. "The paddlers make a good speed," she told Marie. "To bring the water up over my wrist this far."

They spoke of landscapes. And they talked of women within these hills and of women far from home.

"My daughter is a good woman," Marie told her.

"I hope mine will be," Sarah said. "Or if I have a son, that he'll be so. You have only the one daughter?"

Marie shook her head. "Three daughters. The youngest goes with her father, to be baptized. One is buried in the mountains. Marguerite is the first to live." She pointed southeast.

"I'm sorry," Sarah said. "I met your…Marguerite. That's her name, right?"

Marie nodded. "It was kind of her to stay to help your son's wife. I hope she feels better soon."

"The fevers come this time of year. Usually it is worse for the very young or very old. Josette is sturdy. Marguerite serves her well."

"Service," Sarah said. Her hands languished in the water. "We came by ship from Boston to be of service to the Father." She said the word so it sounded like a place of distance, somewhere "farther." Marie squinted. "We married and took our honeymoon to join the Christians at Honolulu."

"Honeymoon?"

"It's a time of special loving, after marriage vows are spoken. To get to know someone, apart from family or familiar. To make new memories that belong to each other now, and not those who went before."

"You stayed on the Sandwich Islands?"

"Yes. When the believers there wanted to do something for people in Lapwai, the printing press was the perfect solution." She spoke differently than Mrs. Whitman, the sounds of her words telling Marie that she'd come from far away even if Mrs. Hall hadn't told her.

"And have you always lived here?" Mrs. Hall asked.

Marie shook her head, no. She rested the oar across her upper thigh as she knelt, allowed the other three paddlers to continue the push upstream. "In a place back that way," she pointed east. "On the Des Moines River, then to the Mississippi at St. Louis, and then to Fort George."

"You came by ship too?"

"Overland. We lived for a time at the ocean place. It was called Astoria then."

"Oh, that's right. My husband says there's a book about Astoria. I hear that your story is in it. And does it tell why you came?"

"It was not a honeymoon," Marie said.

Sarah laughed. "I gathered that from what Mr. Hall said about Mr. Irving's book."

The canoe hit a snag, thumped from under the water. Sarah Hall gasped, a flash of pain severe enough to make her cry out, something she rarely did.

"Did you have this pain on the big ship that took you to the Islands?" Marie asked.

"It came after," Sarah Hall said. She panted a little. "I handled it…all right in the Islands…for a time…but then had to lie down…all day long. We hoped…I might get better with a change of climate. I do think it is better," she panted, straightened herself on the comforter. "With your ministrations and the dryness here, I think I'm better." Her eyes cast toward the already yellowing grasses that flowed like ocean waves away from the riverbanks. "It doesn't rain much though, does it?"

"Snow in the winter. And more in the mountains where you'll be."

"Are you a missionary to the Indian people too?" Sarah Hall asked then. "Is that why you came all this way? Or should I just read the book?"

Marie shook her head. She did wonder what had been said of why she came, what words with her story on them now appeared on a piece of paper written by someone whom she'd never met, never knew. Hunt wrote in his journals. Sacagawea said Clark and Lewis wrote often of their journey. It was an important part of the expedition, she'd learned.

Even Rev. Lee took a writing desk with him, at least as far as the Whitman mission.

Words appeared to be the reasons the Nez Perce and Spokane had wanted to learn to read, because they'd seen men coming from the east who did, and they were men who brought change.

Had Hunt mentioned her in his expedition journal? All the Company factors made notes. That was how Jean's name had become wrapped up with "troublesome" when Ogden wrote up his report.

Jean could write words down about her if he chose that. She wondered if he had.

Maybe her husband wrote about his disappointment in her, that she had refused to go with him for the baptism and their own marriage blessing. She swallowed. Another emptying of the basket of her soul at a time when she should have nursed it, could have helped fill Jean's basket up.

She didn't know how to make him understand that she wasn't worthy of the gift, could never be.

"No," Marie said. "I came for other reasons. My friend and her husband, they came for your reason, to this place, even before Eliza Spalding came with her husband."

"I just thought, with your necklace," Sarah Hall pointed, and Marie fingered the cross at her neck.

"It was a gift from her," Marie said. "To remind me that I was loved."

"A lovely way to put it," Sarah Hall said. "Gifts do that for us. Is she still there? Will I meet your friend?"

"Maybe her work was finished. She has your same name," Marie told her.

"Sarah? It's an old name, written in the Bible. You've seen it?" Marie shook her head. "No? Well, it is. Sarah was a woman who laughed at a promise. Her husband told her that God had promised them a child under very unusual circumstances. She was a very old woman. And she laughed when her husband told her. She couldn't speak for the whole time of her pregnancy. She'd been quite a chatty woman, so to not talk was quite an undertaking."

"God caused this suffering?"

Sarah Hall was thoughtful. A family of mergansers moved away from the shoreline, causing a silent V in the water that spread across toward them. Sarah pointed, and Marie told her the names. She seemed familiar with the word. "We have them where I come from too," she said. Then dropping her hand over the side again she said, "I suppose God did allow Sarah's problem, her suffering as you say, but it was not to punish her. It gave her time to think, time to reflect on his wonderful promise and on the gift God was about to give. To her," she clarified when Marie furrowed her brow. "And I think it's a story to remind us that we don't always know the good things that await us. We must simply trust. If we do that, we can submit as a good horse does to a tender master, knowing it won't be led into troubling places. And that he can get us through anything, even if we don't understand why we're there at the time. Sometimes misery, despair, and pain ride in the same canoe as faith, hope, love. They're passengers together."

"As we are," Marie said.

"One of us isn't pain or the other hope," Sarah Hall told her. She smiled. "I don't want to suggest that. All the choices are given us, as gifts. Your kindness to me, your healing hands, those are reflections of him that I see in you. And I hope you can see something of him in me, not just my complaints."

"I see he must be someone wonderful that you would come so far, endure so much to tell others of him. If that was your choice, why you came."

"Oh yes. It's a privilege to be here. Why, I wouldn't have met Mr. Hall if I hadn't followed my heart. We wouldn't have brought his words to the people of the Islands. The Maki family, who look after the Whitmans, they discovered him through me and my husband, and they came to help the Whitmans because of him. You see how it all works? People are touched by him even when they don't believe in him. And with the printed words, we hope the Nez Perce people will discover more of him too. To hear God's words in your own tongue brings him closer. Words bridge the separations." Sarah removed her hat, waved it gently so Marie would have a breeze. "We go where we are called. We never know what our lives will reflect or how they'll touch others."

"You found your *métier*," Marie said.

"I'm not sure I know that word," Sarah Hall said. "It sounds French. Lovely."

"My husband can tell its meaning better than me, but I think it means finding work for which one is especially suited."

"Is that why you came here, then?"

"I came to do what was best for my family," she said.

"Isn't that what we women all want, deep down?" Sarah said.

"And to not forget our own names on that journey of giving."

❖

"She just started shaking," Josette said. "It happened so quickly."

"Burning up," Baptiste said. He pressed his hand to the forehead of his Denise, his and Josette's firstborn. Denise's fever-moist eyes looked through him.

"Papa?" she said. Her teeth chattered.

"How long?" he asked.

Josette paced with the baby on her hip. "Two, three days ago. People came from the fort, traveling through. It's the season for it. Others have it too, but young ones…"

"She's not that young."

"She was at the dock where they unloaded. She and Little Marie. There might have been some sickness there. She complained of a terrible pain behind her eyes and in her back. Her arms burn. And now the fever."

Baptiste didn't remind his wife that she'd been fevered lately too. "You're still weak yourself, Josette," Marguerite said. "Maybe I should take Denise with me to Mother and Jean's. Give you a chance to recover your strength."

"Jean was ill with a cough and fevered, too," Baptiste said. "He could have brought it?"

Josette shook her head. "I don't know where it comes from. And the doctor doesn't know." Josette was crying now. "I gave it to her, my own daughter."

"I can take care of her, Mama," Little Marie told her. She patted Josette's arm, then knelt to replace the cool cloth on Denise's head.

"I should have taken the cowpox awl pricks for her," Josette said. The factor said we should all have the awl pressed into our arms. Two years ago. When you were chasing cows," she told Baptiste. "I had to decide on my own. I said no. Where were you when I had to decide such things?"

She was sobbing now. He reached for her, but she brushed his arm away.

"Maybe we take her to the sweat lodge, break the chills that way," he said.

"I don't know. I don't know." She shook her head.

Marguerite said, "Mother would give dogwood bark. But not to sweat and not to go into the cold water after. Too many die that way."

Baptiste nodded. He had to agree with his mother about that. Denise shivered her blankets off. How could she be so hot and yet chatter, even with the robe pressed around her?

He wished his mother were here and, at the same time, was glad she wasn't. He didn't have time for her long looks, didn't have time to wonder if she would think he was doing the right thing for his child or not.

Maybe the steam from the hot rocks of a sweat lodge would help Denise. But no, at Fort Vancouver a few years back, when the apple trees were still young sprouts, many had treated themselves that way for the fever and ague and they'd died. Whole families had died within days of each other. So many canoes with bodies in them had been hung in trees for burial that the forest had looked as though the crafts grew there as dead and silent poisons, waiting to be plucked off all eerie and silent. Even the birds had quieted.

Factor McLoughlin had used something called quinine. Baptiste would go to the doctor here and see if they had this medicine.

"Marguerite, you take Josette. See if the factor has quinine. You take

it, Josette. Marguerite will bring some back here. I'll stay with Denise."
It was all he could do for his daughter or his wife. All he could do.

❖

They reached Lapwai while the leaves were in full gold and red. Before
them stood a gristmill, a blacksmith shop, a church-school building
marked by a cross on top, and several houses. One of the crude buildings
had been bare when they arrived, and now the paper and printing press
filled it. Henry Spalding referred to it as "the print shop." Within days of
their arrival, families from near Spokane, the Walkers and Grays, had
come down for the occasion of the annual gathering of the missionaries
in Columbia country. The Halls and their press were an added pleasure.
Children raced about, mixing with the several hundred Nez Perce who
came for the Sunday service. Singing and drumming and preaching, with
Eliza and Henry Spalding translating the English into the native language took most of the morning. Marie heard them sing the "Three
Chiefs" song, as she thought of it, "Let Christian Hearts Rejoice."

"Isn't that a lovely version?" Sarah Hall said while Eliza nodded
agreement.

Eliza beamed when she handed Marie her child following the service. "Little Eliza, we call her."

"This Lapwai, this Butterfly Place, is good to you," Marie said.

"It has been," Eliza said. "Such provision. See our cows, Marie.
They grow healthy and strong. And our work here, too. We have bap-
tized two Nez Perce, Joseph and Timothy. Our first Nez Perce converts.
Joseph is a chief who carries his New Testament with him everywhere.
And now this," she nodded toward the printing press. "Now we'll be
able to give them God's Word in the Nez Perce language."

Eliza spoke with many of the native women, using their own words.
The women laughed and smiled as though they were friends. Eliza told
the Halls that they'd already taught the people the alphabet, and soon,
with the printing press, they'd each have their own book to read.

"They have their own sounds," Henry continued after Marie handed
Eliza's baby back to her.

"All babies do," she said.

"No. The letters of the alphabet. Here." He wrote on a piece of paper. "This is an em. Em-m-m," he said, "is the *M* sound. For Mmm-Marie." He exaggerated the first sound of her name. "Then comes 'ah' for this letter." With each sound he pointed to scratchings on the paper. They all blurred together, sands at the shore. She kept her face free of expression, not wanting him to see her disappointment at not knowing what he meant.

"Come outside." Edwin Hall said then. He squatted at the hard dirt beside the print shop. He scratched an area free of dried grasses so only loose dirt remained. "See here," he said. "May I?" He reached for Marie's hand, and with his over the top of hers, he used her finger to trace the letter *M* in the sand. Then *A.* Then *R,* repeating each sound as he did. He made it big so she could see. "Can you feel it? It's your name being spelled out. Everything we can say can be spelled in this way. It doesn't have to be on paper at all."

With her fingertips, Marie could "feel" the sound. She had never experienced this before, this knowing of her name through the feel of it.

"Yes, I think you're getting it," Hall said. "And if we know the letters and sounds, we can know the words, and then our minds can imagine all kinds of things. We can know places we've never been to just by the words that someone else writes about them. We can remember something just by seeing the word about it."

"Heart knowing," Marie said.

"What's that?"

She signed the word for *memory* as *heart knowing.* "It means to remember something."

"That's the beauty of language," he said. "Words bring us the knowing of our hearts. Yes. And truly this is so when the words are Scripture. In the beginning was The Word," he said. His eyes were shining.

❖

"Here, Papa," Little Marie said. "Put this on her forehead."

Baptiste had taken the cloth from his daughter, placed on another.

Denise lay quiet as snow, but she opened her eyes when he touched her.

"Good now," he said. "You get well. I'll get you your own horse to ride when you're better."

Denise smiled. "Little Marie, too?" she asked.

A generous child. "Yes," he said. "For your sister, too. Go ask Marguerite if she got the quinine," he told Little Marie without looking at her, still stroking Denise's hair.

"All right," Little Marie said.

Her voice was so breathy that he lifted his head to look at her. "Little—"

"Papa…" He caught Little Marie as she sank to the floor.

He hoped Marguerite would come. He hoped Jean would return. He wished his mother were there. But none were, just him, just helpless him, not able to stop a fever, not able to fix what was wrong.

He felt tears, jabbed at his eyes. He couldn't, not now. He held his eldest daughter, lifted her to a mat. Little Marie struggled for breath. Her skin felt hot as a poker left in a fire. Should he lay her beside Denise? Would that spread this disease? Was Denise past the worst of it? What should he do? What could he do? Maybe it was good he hadn't been there when this child's mother died, maybe he'd have felt as helpless as a motherless fawn, exposed by his labor, so lacking.

"Papa?"

"Not now, Marie. Get strong, now." *Don't die, please don't die. No child should die.* And yet they were each someone's child, no matter how old they might get.

❖

In the days following the service, the missionary women sewed and chatted while the men gathered to do the Society's work of setting up the press and having their annual business meeting to discuss mission efforts. The Whitmans had not joined them. Eliza told her all the others from the region were present. "Mrs. Whitman has a little one now, so it's harder for them to travel," Eliza said.

"Sarah Hall came a long way," Marie said.

"Yes, she did. And we are grateful."

Sarah Hall's panting in pain became more frequent. She could stand for a few minutes at a time, but as Marie prepared to return home with the Cayuse paddlers, the mission women said they thought Sarah should return with her.

"You came all this way for nothing?" Marie said to her.

"Not for nothing," Sarah told her. "I'll stay at the Whitmans' where the doctor will be close at hand for the delivery of my baby."

"Wouldn't the doctor come here if summoned?" Marie asked.

"He…doesn't, always," Eliza said. "He's supposed to provide our medical needs, but they're so busy there. Narcissa has her little Alice now too. So many more people come by there than here… It would be better."

"Can't I stay so Edwin can set up the press?" Sarah asked.

"Oh, he can still do that," Henry Spalding said. "The woman can take you back and send word when…your husband will be summoned."

And so Sarah prepared to go back with Marie and the Indian paddlers. But not before they saw the stack of four hundred copies of an eight-page book come off the press—the primer that Eliza Spalding would use to teach the Nez Perce people to read.

"We already made a few dozen handwritten books they took home," Eliza said. "They're so quick, these people. They learn so quickly."

"And someday soon," Edwin Hall said, "We'll print the Bible's words. That will truly be the accomplishment of a printer's call."

Marie looked at the stack of papers. So many words, and all the same words in each book.

"Here," Edwin Hall said to Marie. He handed her five little blocks of wood, each barely larger than a tear. "Type," he said. "Feel the face of each block."

"Face?" she said. She touched her cheeks.

"Interesting word, isn't it? Outward features of a thing, something prominent, that stands out. Can you feel it? Think of the surface of a rock, the landscape of it. In Hebrew, *face* means 'presence.'"

"I didn't know that," Eliza said.

"As in, God makes his face to shine upon you, that he's present with you. I find the meanings of words so fascinating, don't you? The word for *comfort,* for instance, in Greek, means 'to come along beside.' Isn't that interesting? And—"

"Edwin," his wife cautioned.

"Oh. Yes." He turned back to Marie and the objects she held in her hand. "Just feel the little edges, that's the face of the type."

Marie could feel the ridges with her fingertips.

"There is one for each sound in your name, Marie. We could do more and say Madame Dorion, as I hear you're known as. M-A-R-I-E. Your name," Edwin Hall said.

Marie felt the landscape of her name on the page.

"Yours is a mother name," Edwin Hall told her. "It comes from the word Mary, the mother of our Lord. There were many women named Mary in the Bible," he said. "Did you know that?"

"And named Marie?"

"None translated as such. But Marie is a reflected name, from Mary just the same. The way these letters reflect the word. See here now."

He placed the little blocks from her hand into a tray beside several other rows of type. Then he rolled a long tube across them that left the type wet and glistening, and then he put paper on top of that. He and Spalding lowered a heavy block of wood over it and turned a knob at the top. They counted several seconds, then unturned the knob, lifted the square, and Edwin gingerly pulled up on the paper. Rows of dark scratchings broke the white of the paper. Tiny little letters. Marie squinted, the distinctions blurring.

"It's your name in printed form," he said. "Right there." He ran his finger beneath the first word. "Marie."

"What does it say behind it?"

"The whole thing reads thusly: 'Marie. "He telleth the number of the stars; he calleth them all by their names." Psalm 147:4.' It means that to God, you are as precious as every fixed star in the sky. He calls you by name, Marie."

"Can you make the name 'Little Marie,' too? For my granddaughter," Marie said.

"Certainly," Edwin said. "He calls her name, too."

❖

The canoe moved swiftly downriver. Marie rode high in the bow, so filled with a presence. She had a piece of paper tucked into her treasure pouch that Sarah Hall reminded her was not "who you are" but just the face of who she was. "It's that each of us is loved just for ourselves," Sarah Hall told her. "To name something is to love it. And that is enough."

"We are enough just by being created as a reflection of him," Marie said, awed by the thought. "All goes well then."

Sarah Hall laughed. "Look at my body," she said. "No. Not all goes well on the outside, but it means all is well on the inside, that we are never separated from love no matter what we do, how many mistakes we make. We are never separated from him, and so we can do things we are called to do, things we otherwise could not imagine doing." She removed her hat and fanned her face that was the shape of a serving platter and just as pale. "I couldn't spend months on my back being carried here and there all by myself. It's only because I believe I am where I'm supposed to be. I have help, not perfection. No. Don't hope for that."

Marie felt for her pouch. Something had been freed within her with the words of Scripture that Edwin Hall had added to the paper, about each star being named. That was written down too! She'd said something similar to Little Marie once long ago. She was named and called. She didn't know to what yet, but she believed it was so. She had a *métier*, a way of reflecting. She would tell Jean as soon as she returned.

Her husband's look stopped her joy. Her eyes searched for François and Marianne. She could see Marguerite in the distance, her tall slender body leaning in the fields. Baptiste. She couldn't see Baptiste.

"It happened quickly," Jean said. "The fever and ague. One day she was tending Denise and the next day, she was fevered and gone. Our Little Marie. Gone."

"Our Marie?"

He nodded. "Everyone did what they could."

"Our Marie?" she said, the name catching in her throat. "I should have let her come with me."

"No," Jean said. "It is not what this is about. You did what you did. You do not get to wallow like a buffalo in regrets. It's a robe you've worn too long, eh?" He took her shoulders in his hands. "Marie." She nodded. "I know this robe, too," he said. "And I take it off." He took a deep breath. "We will go to French Prairie, Marie. We will all be in one place. It will strain us, but no more than these years have strained. I decide this. I want you to come, but I will take the children whether you come or not. Baptiste had already decided this for his family."

"How is Josette? The other children?"

"As expected," Jean said.

"And Baptiste?"

Jean shrugged his shoulders. "She was his firstborn daughter. You know of this kind of loss. Maybe you go to him, see for yourself."

"I don't think he wants me around him," she said.

"A father's loss changes everything, my Marie. Go. See."

And so she'd gone to find her son. She rode up into the hills, taking the trail along the red rock towers that drew Mackenzie to this place those years before, marking it as the fort where he would build, take on the landscape and its people in so bold a fashion. Here was where they'd come when they survived the winter in the Blues. It was a place of new beginnings, always new beginnings.

Where the valley opened up, thousands of Nez Perce horses grazed, neck over neck, legs bent in rest for some; young colts chasing the wind and each other.

She rode old Lumière, Jean's horse, steady along the trail. No dogs chased after them.

When Lumière nickered a familiar call, Marie squinted. Yes, there he was, her son, set on his horse, his hands folded over the pommel. He turned at the sound of Lumière. He must have recognized her, though he didn't ride off.

"It's a good herd," she said as she approached. Baptiste nodded. He wore a felt hat. His dark eyes sank beneath a high forehead, a nose that looked larger in his now gaunt face. He looked at her, then turned away.

She plummeted like a falling star.

The pain in his eyes burned through to her core. It was one thing to experience her own regrets, her own sting of loss and death, but for a parent to see their child's agony and not be able to quell it, this was the ultimate grief.

She ached for Little Marie, for the things she hadn't done for her, for being too late to comfort her when she was ill. Too late for so many things.

This last was the only loss she might do something about, but only if she said the right words. Always words. *Give me healing words*, she prayed, *words to come beside him.*

"Sometimes cougars prowl these hills," she said. Her eyes scanned the treeless ridges formed of grasses and waterfalls, of pebbles that started high and dribbled to the valley floor. Where springs flowed, green squeezed out of crevices, and shrubs poked up hopefully through an otherwise dry land. "Have you ever seen one in all your years riding herd?"

He shook his head that he had. "First one I saw was at Okanogan."

"I remember. You and Paul and me, out gathering berries, wasn't it? I can't remember now."

"Sarah came upriver that day."

"Yes. That's right. She wanted us to go with her to Lapwai. Did you know that?" He shook his head, no. "I wasn't sure what to do. All alone with two sons. I wasn't always making the best choices then."

Was she talking about herself too much? Were these the words he needed to hear?

"I wished we could have stayed to bury him, your father. I wished lots of things."

"Maybe if we'd gone back, Paul would still be with us," Baptiste said.

No regrets, Jean had said. No regrets. "This could be. Maybe Louis would still be alive. Maybe I would never have met him. He was good to you, wasn't he? Louis?"

Had she comforted him enough when Louis died, when his father died? When his first wife died? She had done the best she could for him, each time. She'd taken care of business, getting her sons away from the danger. She had even been right about Older Sister being so young, but being right did not bring her joy nor comfort to her son. Perhaps she had lacked the words to lift him then. She mustn't let healing words be taken now by the wind.

"Louis was a good man," Baptiste said. "Little Marie was a good child." His voice broke, and he thumbed his eyes now, cleared his throat. He removed his hat and swatted at flies hovering over his horse's ears, replaced the hat on his head.

And then she moved old Lumière closer to her son's horse and tied the reins around her saddle. She reached over to her son, this grown man of hers, and she pulled him to her and he let her. She wrapped her arms around him and he wept, the deep, hacking sobs of a father grieving for his daughter but so much more. Grieving all the losses, all the separations of times past.

"You did the best you could for her," she whispered. "I am so sorry, Baptiste, that it was not enough to keep her living on this earth, only in our hearts." He nodded and seemed to burrow deeper into her as his shoulders shook. She didn't flood the space with words of wishing she'd been there, wishing she'd done something different, wishing she could fix it when she couldn't. She simply let him be, warmed by the feel of her son back in her arms.

His muscled shoulders were familiar even after all these years, the ridge of his spine as easily read as Edwin Hall's type. She could read what he needed, and at that moment, she reflected the love she'd been given. It was the reunion long hoped for. A gift she accepted.

23

Every Fixed Star

More missionaries arrived at the Willamette Mission, men with wives and children too. The printing press returned downriver, ending up for a day or two at the bottom of a deep ravine where the horse carrying it went over the side. All survived.

Mr. Hall and a man named Rogers easily repaired it and printed more books, including the book of Matthew, just as Sarah Hall said someday they would.

Little Alice Whitman drowned near Waiilatpu.

Sarah Hall gave birth to a healthy baby boy. The Halls stayed in one of the many small cabins Dr. Whitman had built for visiting guests. Barns housed more cattle and Cayuse horses.

"It's been such a tragic time," Sarah told Marie, who brought her melons that Marguerite had nurtured in the garden. "And yet so wonderful, too. I'm walking now," she spun around as though she were a young child, her skirts flowing full. Marie held her baby.

"You'll go back soon," Marie said.

"You're moving too," Sarah noted and Marie nodded.

In the spring of 1840, the Halls returned with their new baby to Honolulu, but it was nearly June of 1840 before the Toupin family set their sights on a tract of land not far from the Methodist mission at the base of French Prairie. They'd chosen a portion east, where little streams broke up gentle rolls of hills covered with vines and oak that had been burned out more than once, as was the practice of the Kalapuya.

McLoughlin assured them, along with the other French-Canadians settling there, that if the boundary put them in British hands, their land claims would still be honored as owned, not leased. And he said he suspected the Americans would see it that way as well.

"There is some risk," Jean said. "Either way. So we must just choose the spot and hope for a miracle when the boundaries are finally decided."

These Methodists would be their neighbors, of sorts, closer to them than where Kilakotah and LaBonte had made their place.

Family would be their real neighbors. Josette and Baptiste and their children. Josette announced shyly that their next child would be born in this valley.

Yes, there were deaths in a family, accidents unexpected, disappointments and draining away. But there were also joys and new life to celebrate, which they were doing in this French Prairie place.

Marguerite became engaged to a French-Canadian named John Baptiste Gobin. A farmer. "He'd been waiting for me all this time, Mother," Marguerite beamed. "I just had to leave Walla Walla." The women sewed together in the lean-to they lived in while Jean and Baptiste and the other French-Canadians helped fell logs for the expanded Gobin house.

"You stepped out onto a cloud of faith believing you wouldn't fall through," Marie told her.

Marguerite smiled. "He's Catholic, too. So Papa Jean approves."

The marriage banns announcing the couple's intentions would be spoken the next year after Marguerite was baptized.

"Perhaps we all get married on the same day," Marguerite said. "John and me, Baptiste and Josette, and you and Papa Jean."

"We'll see," Marie said. "A marriage should be a special day that you don't have to share with another."

"But it would please me to share the day with my family," she said.

"We'll see."

But the greatest gift for Marie had been the ease with which she'd accepted Jean's decision that they would all come here, even though it meant a debt. Once Jean said it would be this way, that he believed this was what his *métier* was after all, and he was willing to go into debt to be there, all of them, in that place together, she'd felt a great weight lifted from her.

It was a horse trusting its master, submitting to the gift of another watching over her. She didn't have to take the trail alone. Why had she resisted it so long?

Her heart had been lifted by wings of trust. She'd never been carried that way before.

At French Prairie, Jean and Baptiste worked the land together, François too, bringing a scythe across the tall grass so they'd have feed for the cattle in winter. When they needed more tools, more supplies, he could earn extra money at Fort Vancouver working on the wood detail. They always needed choppers for the hungry little steamship that had joined the wooden crafts and was not dependent on the wind but on the backs of those who piled the wooden fuel.

Jean's shoulder didn't work as well as it once had, but he could still chop a stump up, still provide for his family.

On the Willamette River, a log house marked the halfway place between the Willamette Mission and McKay's old beaching place. A halfway place. It was where she felt she was in her life, halfway between young and old. A good place to begin anew. Marie was certain that someday, that log house would grow into a fine little town.

For now, she watched her grandchildren grow and gather at her knees. It was her calling after all.

The settlement, their neighbors, had reasons to gather, for celebrations, for exchanging news, for keeping track of commerce. They met to discuss new settlers coming from the Red River country and how it might affect selling their grain and butter to the fort. They talked of how to tend the orphans whose parents died of fever and ague. They made plans and carried them out together.

"There are some good men here," Jean told her when he returned. "Josiah Parrish is a blacksmith and a preacher, but he speaks good sense. And Ewing Young is a good man. He quotes poetry words from two big books he always has in his saddle packs. Shakespeare, he says. People listen to him more since he removed the distillery. There's talk of forming a government, maybe. To do things together as we did to get the cattle north. There's to be a meeting. Even Father Blanchet says we can go."

"Which government will it be? Under the Company or the Americans or who?"

"Maybe just our own," Jean said. He shrugged his shoulders. "Who knows what lies ahead? We meet again next month. I'll know more then."

But before they could discuss things further, Ewing Young died, leaving wealth no one knew how to distribute.

"My people would give it all away," Marie said. "It would find its way back in time."

"Not how they do it, these Americans," Jean said.

"There are more French here than Americans, *n'est-ce pas?* You can decide what will happen."

Jean shook his head. "Men plan things, but I believe more and more, it is God who decides, eh?"

❖

Marie found more time to spend with Denise. To comfort when someone had lost an older sister, this Marie knew something about. Little Marie had been Denise's older sister, in spirit as well as sharing half her blood.

"I loved her so much, Kasa," she told Marie as her grandmother bent beneath the cow for the twice daily milking. No need to say her name. The people here rarely said the names of one who died, for at least a year, though they spoke them in their hearts. But Marie knew whom Denise spoke of.

"We all miss her," Marie said.

"How will I know what to do, who to follow? I watched her to know what to do."

"So think of what you remember. She can still bring you nurture as you remember her, what she believed in, even if she's gone away."

"She didn't spend time with boys. She was too busy, she said."

"Her time was coming."

Denise pulled at a sticker hung up in the cow's tail. The cow swatted its tail from her hand. "Mama said she caused trouble," Denise said.

"For things that mattered."

The sound of the milk hitting the side of the wooden bucket filled the silence.

"She laughed with me and held me when I cried. I'll remember that." She paused. "What did you put in the treasure basket at her grave, Kasa?"

"Words," she said. "Just words."

"Do you remember them?"

"Yes. She wanted her name written down. And there are other thoughts there too. I gave what was written to her."

"I can write. Maybe when you tell me stories, I'll write them down. So I can remember them when you go away."

Marie set the bucket down. She moved to the wooden stall where Etoile, the tamest cow stood waiting, flicking her tail at flies. Marie bent to milk the animal.

"Would you write things down for me, Kasa? When I die, will you write for me?"

"We should make a snow mountain," Marie said. "As soon as we finish this milking."

"Before we churn the butter?"

"Before we churn the butter. We'll whip the cream into a mountain with a wooden spoon and sweeten it with maple."

"Your arms will dance," Denise said. She laughed.

Marie placed Denise's hand on the skin that hung beneath Marie's upper arm. "It's hanging on to my muscles," she said. "I'll need those to whip that cream."

"When it's huckleberry time, Mama says we'll make sweet cream for François's baptism. But we don't have to wait for sweet things? We could eat it right now? Not just for a special time, Kasa?"

"We could. Right now. We may not have sweet cream when François is baptized. Your mama might burn her cake. Etoile may decide no, she won't give us milk. What then?"

"We deserve it now. Right now." Denise stomped her foot in the dirt, laughing.

"Your older sister used to do that," Marie said.

Marie felt tears press against her nose. She sniffed. "Here's another gift let's give ourselves. Who cares if we look foolish?"

Marie stood up, stepped over the milk bucket she set well away from the cow. She bent over, put her head and hands to the ground and pushed herself over. She rolled and rolled, her skirts flying and her hair picking up new grass and yellow flowers with the red bugs that lived on them.

"What are you doing, Kasa?"

"Making *sombresault*," she said, puffing. "Right now. "Come on. It's a good day for it."

"Somersaults," Marguerite called them. Denise's sister and Marie's sons called it that too. The words, English or French or Sahaptin or Cayuse, whatever language she chose didn't matter. The words all meant the same.

❖

In 1841, Father Blanchet came south to the Mission of St. Paul on the Willamette, using the little log church to hold mass, baptisms, weddings and funerals. Baptiste was not interested in such activities, he told his mother.

In July of that year, François said he wanted to be baptized. He met for instruction with the priest. His mother sat in with him, asking questions, nodding to the answers.

"With your mother, eh?" Jean said. "You'll be baptized with your mother. And we'll say our marriage vows that day, too. What do you say, Marie?"

"It should be a special time for François," Marie said. "Let it be his day. We will take another."

"This is true? You do not tease your husband of these many years by putting it off still another year?"

"It's true," she said. "I give you my word."

"What makes you do this now?" Jean said, those acorn eyes cautious but sparkling as well.

"I have asked all the questions for now and the priest has answered. He and my Sarahs say similar things. Their crosses mean the same." Jean nodded. "And something more. Your granddaughter Denise said words to me about not having to wait. A seven-year-old with such wisdom should be honored. And so we set our date. July. The huckleberries should be ripe for a feast."

On July 25, François came forward to be baptized. And after some discussion with his mother, Baptiste brought his eldest son, Pierre, age five, to do the same. Godfathers and godmothers were announced and the service completed. On that same day, Jean Toupin served as a witness to the marriage of a friend's daughter and the legitimizing of their one-year-old son. They rejoiced in the gathering.

Marie celebrated with them. She had known what to expect. Because the week before, on July 19, 1841, Marie l'Ayvoise, wife of Pierre Dorion, Louis Joseph Venier, and Jean "John" Toupin, knelt before Father Blanchet at the log church at the Mission of St. Paul on the Willamette. Water from the wooden font was placed on her forehead, and the priest spoke words in a language she didn't understand. But somehow it did not matter if she understood him exactly. She understood the meaning of the words and what she brought to them. That was what mattered.

Jean helped her to stand, and he kissed her on both cheeks, his own face wet with tears.

"Can we have the vows said, then?" Jean asked. And when those were completed, Marie's small hands in Jean's, his fingers moving gently across her fingers, "Can we legitimize the children?"

"Oui," Father Blanchet said. "Their names?"

Jean gave out Marianne and François. And from Marie's other marriages, he named Baptiste and Marguerite.

"Marguerite will be baptized next month, when she marries Monsieur Gobin," Marie told Jean.

"Oui," Jean said, corrected, "but she can still be legitimized. Baptiste, too. Maybe it will inspire him to come forward for the water and marriage."

And then Marie reached up to touch her husband's arm, to remind him of her other children. Jean raised his eyebrow, waited for her to speak, but she didn't.

Those others belonged to the winds of this world. She had done the best she could for them.

Marie knew that Holy Rainbow had kept Paul in her prayers, though his own mother had failed him in this. But she'd begun to forgive herself for even that, if what the Sarahs said was true. Accepting forgiveness was the most difficult gift of all.

Children were given as gifts for however long a parent was allowed their presence. Parents helped create them, name them, hold them in their hearts. But parents were not responsible for everything that happened after that. It was a weaving of many strands: parent with God, parent with child, child with God as well. The rock Jean had given her long years before with the red layer holding them together could have stood for a parent and a child.

She looked across the room at Baptiste, Josette, her family gathered around her. Why had she resisted this ritual for so long? What had she feared in it? There was nothing but promise in the words the priest spoke over her, in the smell of incense and good tallow candles, music sung by Sandwich Islanders and natives, the presence of family and friends with good wishes.

Kilakotah caught her eye as she held her youngest, Julienne, already three. Her other daughters were with her too, now, and Louis, already a young man, stood taller than his father. Kilakotah began a chanting song. Soon other native women's voices blended in with words Marie didn't understand. A Frenchmen broke into a voyaging song then, the men's and women's voices moving back and forth across the room like coyotes calling across rivers. Two worlds, blended into one.

"We will complete the nuptial benediction, now," Father Blanchet said. "The banns have been read these past days, and with no objection, we will continue." And so they did.

"Who can sign?" the priest asked when he'd finished. The witnesses came forward.

"Here," Jean said when the service was complete. He pulled from his pocket a slender box, the size of a flint kit. He handed it to Marie. She should have known he would give her a gift! And she hadn't thought of doing the same.

"I didn't—" She tried to push it back to him.

"I know," he said. "Here. I open it for you."

Even then she wasn't sure of what it was until he unfolded the thin wire and the glass as clear as tears. "Spectacles," he said.

He helped her put the wire loop over each ear. Only clerks wore such things. She'd seen no pictures of spectacles perched on a woman's nose.

"They will make the words larger, maybe make them distinctive so you can see your name. Here, on this priest's certificate, eh?"

"Can she write her name?" the priest asked. Jean shook his head, no. "Then have her make her mark here." He pointed to a place and Marie marked an *X* there. But she could see her fingers holding the lead, the wrinkles at her knuckles, the scar in her hand.

She made each line of the mark precise. Someday, maybe, she would even write her name. She handed the lead back to Jean. His eyes were even darker than she'd realized, and bigger through the spectacles. He had lines flowing out from his eyes she'd never noticed before, and little nicks on his face, dark little circles. This was what living looked like, then, these nicks and scars and his enormous grin, his warm and inviting smile.

"You are a married woman, now," Jean told her. "Wife. *L'épouse.*"

She hadn't been set off. She wasn't just "I follow after him," but "married," a name with a choice wrapped into it. Once she said the words that mattered, told of her wish to diminish the division of her heart, then the face on which he wrote her name wore new etchings, freed of the sharp edges that kept her separate and apart.

The baptism meant she was loved and that she chose to love back. Despite her mistakes and poor choices, she was still worthy of love.

Author's Notes

In Every Fixed Star, I've woven the life of Marie Dorion through the development and settlement of a landscape veined with rivers as roads, scarred by the choices of commerce, and wounded by family separations and losses. I've tried to stay true to "shared knowing," beliefs about the historical record, what is known about fort life and native women's roles and the ways that people made their living, traveled, or thought about the world around them and how they intervened or changed the landscape. Where facts were missing or were in dispute, I speculated in ways I believe are consistent with the remarkable woman of Marie.

Details of Marie's life after her arrival in the northwest and her survival, in what became known as the Blue Mountains of Eastern Oregon in 1814, are formed from fragments. The name of her daughter Marguerite Okanogan suggests the girl was born in the Okanogan country of what is now Washington State. Little can be found about Marguerite's father, Louis Joseph Venier. Even his name is spelled in various ways (Vernier, Wagnier for example) and the lore is that he worked for the Hudson's Bay Company and was later killed by Indians. No evidence for his employment with the Company and none about his death have been found to date, so who he was and how he died are speculation. Descendants of Marguerite have origins dating to the Okanogan/Colville, Washington, area. They remain in Oregon today.

The date of Marguerite's birth is listed in two different years by two valued sources; but the date of her baptism and marriage are recorded by the priests and, as translated by Harriet Munnick, they offer the best authority to use for dates, and thus I used 1819 as Marguerite's beginning.

Information about Marie's third husband and the two children from that marriage are documented by Munnick, as are their baptisms. The *Journal of John Work* provided additional documentation that Jean Toupin was believed to have been a part of Hunt's party, though others contend he did not come to the Columbia country until 1835. The

Hudson's Bay Company records state 1821 to 1827 "in the Columbia country" and that he had "12 years experience" by that time, making it possible that he was connected as early as 1809. He would have joined Hunt's journey in 1810.

That the Company had a policy of making the land south of the Columbia a "fur desert" is fact. That Ogden crossed the *Rivière des Chutes* (known today as Sherar's Falls on the Deschutes River in Central Oregon) in 1827 and lost five horses in the crossing is based on fact, though it's not known if Jean Toupin was with him. Jean and Marie's stay in the Walla Walla area seemed plausible given the Hudson's Bay employment reports. Jean's dismissal in 1833 is fact; his rehiring is as well, though the causes are not known. That Marie and Jean were part of John Work's party into California is based on John Work's journal entries. An Indian woman did save the life of John Work (who did bring his three daughters and his Walla Walla housekeeper with him), but the name of the woman saving his life is not given. Marie was present. The keeper of the records rarely included the names of women, especially Indian women, even if they saved a man's life.

Cattle and the lack of them, the Company's control of them and the settler's desires to have them, and the anthrax outbreak "back East" are all based on fact. Four cows did arrive at Fort George (Astoria) in 1814, and none were slaughtered until six hundred head were counted. The first cattle drive from California north occurred in 1837 as a result of the Willamette Cattle Company, and John McLoughlin contributed a significant share. Whether Marie and Jean did is not known; but they did come to the French Prairie not long after the arrival of the cows, and it seemed within the realm of feasibility. Whether Baptiste participated in the cattle drive isn't known, but he was discharged from Fort Vancouver that year and returned to service in 1840 back at Walla Walla, so he went somewhere. It may have been helping bring cows across the San Joaquin, one at a time.

Thomas McKay did develop a limp as a result of a mysterious accident. Alexander Ross and McKay were part of the trip to negotiate for horses with the Yakima people where a "chief's knife" did save their lives.

Louis LaBonte and his wife Kilakotah and their son Louis LaBonte II were in the places where Marie was likely to be, including their time at Walla Walla and later at French Prairie, and they did manage the horse farm of Tom McKay at Scappoose, Oregon. That Marie and Kilakotah might have been friends is highly plausible given their backgrounds and the documentation of their travels. Michel LaFramboise was a dynamic French-Canadian well-remembered. And Sally and Ross Cox did leave the Okanogan to help build the fort built by Mackenzie. They may well have helped draw Marie to that more southern fort as well. The need for horses and the transporting of them north and west out of Fort Walla Walla is based on fact, as is the Nez Perce skill in horse breeding.

Baptiste's time at Vancouver and Walla Walla and later as a signer of the Teton/Ioway treaty in 1825 is factual, as is his presence at French Prairie. His first wife, Older Sister, was given that name by me; but there is evidence Narcisse Raymond was the uncle of the first two wives of Baptiste, his first wife being unnamed; his second wife known as Josette or Josephette or Josephine Cayuse. That there was another child, unnamed in the record, is noted by the Raymond family line. I gave that child the name of Little Marie.

That there was a separation between Paul and his mother has basis in fact. She did not name him at the time of the blessing of her other children, just as she did not name her first daughter who died. Unlike some who have speculated that she "hadn't seen him for so long that she'd forgotten about him," a more plausible explanation is that she thought he was dead. Whether he was or not is a part of the rest of the story.

The interest of native people in the gospel, in the "Book of Heaven," and in the Christian story has many rocks of foundation. Early trappers did record hearing Christian songs sung among the Flathead people in 1818. "Pious Iroquois" were said to be evangelizing among western tribes. George Simpson did take two young men back for religious instruction, and Spokane Garry returned to read the Bible to his people after being taught in the Red River school. Four youths did attempt to find the "Book of Heaven" and met with William Clark back in St.

Louis seeking instruction. The Nez Perce sent Richard (and others) to ride back and bring the Whitmans and Spaldings to the Columbia country. The Whitmans chose instead to go to Waiilatpu on the Cayuse land. What happened there is a part of the continuing story of relationships and loss.

The plea of the French-Canadians and Chief Factor John McLoughlin to send priests to the Columbia country was answered in late 1838 with the arrival of Fathers Blanchet and Demers. The first mass was celebrated as noted in this story, and the deep faith of the people and their hunger for spiritual connection after a long separation is both documented and understandable.

That Marie was known to the Whitmans is documented by Jason Lee, one of the Methodist missionaries who wrote in his 1838 journal on his way to the Whitmans, "...overtook a...woman who crossed the mountains with Mr. Hunt, and a grown daughter...to my astonishment, I was followed by the females with larger loads than I should probably have ventured with, consisting of children, saddles, bridles, blankets, saddle bags, dogs etc. and all came over safely." He also noted the presence of the Pambrun girls. His traveling desk is today at the Mission Mill Museum in Salem, Oregon.

The Sandwich Island (Hawaii) mission did send the Maki family to assist the Whitmans as part of their missionary support to the tribes in the Northwest. And Sarah and Edwin Hall did indeed bring the first printing press from Honolulu in 1839 to what is today Lapwai, Idaho. Whether Marie was present to assist Sarah Hall is speculation on my part, but Sarah Hall was taken in a canoe by "four Indians" while her husband rode with the printing press on horseback. It seems feasible that Marie, as a strong woman, may well have been one of those Indians sent to assist a pregnant white woman unable to walk.

That printing press is now housed in the Oregon History Center in Portland, Oregon. It survived the fall down the ravine and is noted for printing the first books west of the Rocky Mountains, including the book of Matthew in the Nez Perce language.

As the story notes, Marie was baptized on July 19, 1841, a year after her daughter Marianne and a week before her son François. Baptiste was not baptized nor his marriage blessed until years later and yet his son was baptized the same day as François. It is speculation—since Marie left no written record—that Marie's greatest sense of worth came when she chose to accept the gift of baptism and understood the true meaning of a debt paid.

It was shortly after this date that Oregon land records indicate that Jean Toupin and his family began farming on French Prairie. The nearest settlement would become known as St. Louis, and within a very few years, a log church would be constructed by the residents.

The second book in a three-book series is always a challenge: how much to repeat of book one and how much to leave unfinished for the third novel while still allowing satisfaction for any reader who may only dip into book two. It's my hope that I have met this challenge and that readers will continue to seek themselves inside these stories and be intrigued by this journey of a native woman, a wife, a mother. Marie.

Thank you for reading *Every Fixed Star*.

Questions for Reflection and Discussion

1. *Every Fixed Star* is in part a story about a strong woman in the wilderness places of landscape, relationship, and spirit. What are some of the specific wilderness experiences confronting Marie? What strengths help her persevere? Are you aware of times in your own life when you triumphed in a wilderness place? What enabled you to succeed or what got in your way?

2. What might have been different if Marie and her sons had gone with Sarah instead of remaining on the Okanogan? Is her insistence to be free of the Company a sign of her independence or is she being stubborn? How can we tell the difference?

3. The word family comes from a Latin word *famalus,* meaning "servant." What choices does Marie make to serve her family? How do her choices reflect her commitment to do the best she can for her family without losing herself in the process? Are families today defined by their service to each other? What separates a family servant from a slave?

4. Strong evidence supports that Marie was both a compassionate and intelligent woman. However, she demonstrates what some might call "blind spots" when it comes to her family. What contributes to her poor vision with regard to Paul and Baptiste? What keeps her from moving to the Willamette Mission with Jean earlier in their marriage? Do we all have blind spots related to those we love? If so, what strategies have you used that allow you to see more clearly?

5. Based on historical evidence, the trappers or Company men who kept the records seldom recorded native women's experiences. Absence of their mention is conspicuous considering women were essential for the survival of their husbands on the trapping expeditions and significantly contributed to their

family's wealth. Sadly, their efforts were rarely acknowledged, likely causing many women to feel inferior to men, even value less. Does Marie eventually define herself as worthy? In what ways? How does her awareness of worth change her behavior? How do women today struggle with feelings of worth? What factors influence their feelings?

6. Our shared experiences of landscapes, both geographical and spiritual—our upbringing, our memories, our faith, our work, even the losses we may have lived through together and the family celebration stories we tell and retell—these all unite family and friends even as they can often separate us. What shared elements separate the characters in this story? How does Marie overcome the separations and bring about reunion?

7. The concept of *métier* suggests that we are all given a passion in life, a purpose that may require some risk, going out beyond our safety and comfort. What is Marie's passion in life? How does she honor it? Is what drives Marie the same as Sarah's *métier*, "finding work to which one is best suited"? What happens in our own lives when we seek the "limits of our longing"?

8. What kinds of gifts did Marie eventually accept on her life journey? Who opens the doors for her? What does she have to do to receive them? What role does her faith play in her acceptance? How has God gifted you on your life's journey?

9. The author believes we can all choose to be clear about what matters in our lives and to have the courage to act on what we believe. What evidence supports that Marie was both clear and courageous in her life? How clear and courageous do you consider yourself about what matters most to you? If someone were "reading" your life, what evidence supports your own clear purpose and courageous actions?

Thank you for participating in the telling of this story through your reflection and discussion.

Acknowledgments

...alued people contributed to this work. A list of historians and ...works accompanied *A Name of Her Own,* and it has grown for this ...ook as well. Please see the "Suggested Additional Reading" pages for this updated list. Many more could be added who gave texture and authenticity to this work. A few people must be given special recognition.

Brenda and Roger Howard of French Prairie, friends and keepers of the story; Marianne Long and Victor Robidoux, historians of the Iowa Nation; Leonard Dorion, keeper of the Canadian Dorion story; Patricia Smith, Dorion family historian extraordinaire; Bob and Nancy Noble, Oregon historians and lovers of story; Madeleine Ladd for her language gifts; Kit and Naomi Hall for attending a wedding and telling me they had the Hall diary of the printing press's journey north and sharing it so easily; a special thanks to George Thomas Brown for his kind letter and conversations about early French Prairie life and for his book; Laurie Carlson for her *Sidesaddles to Heaven,* her fine work about the missionaries, and *Cattle: A Social History;* friends Annabelle Prantl and Erhard Gross for speculating with me; Susan Holton, publicist, for making it look easy; Eileen and Bob Berger, for locating a probable early hymn from the Algonquin peoples; Joyce Hart, agent, for a belief that never faltered; Carol Tedder for love and prayers; Blair Fredstrom, Sandy Maynard, and Kay Krall for unending encouragement; nieces Michelle Hurtley and Arlene Hurtley for computer skills and good humor and faith; Barb and Craig Rutschow, sister-in-law and brother, for being there; and Jerry, for being my rock.

The cocreators at Random House and WaterBrook Press are too many to mention. But editors Dudley Delffs, Erin Healy, and Traci DePree and Publisher Don Pape have put new meaning into the words *publisher support.* I'm grateful.

For whatever in this story rings true and touches a life, I share credit with these fine people. All errors I claim as my own.

Finally, to you the readers who found a place in your hear
Marie: I thank you for giving us the means to provide her with a na
of her own.

Respectfully,
Jane Kirkpatrick
www.jkbooks.com

gested Additional Reading

. B. *Early Catholic Missions in Oregon.* Seattle: Lowman and
anford, 1832.

croft, Hubert Howard. *Bancroft's Works,* vol. XXVII, *History of
Northwest Coast, 1800–1871.* San Francisco: A. L. Bancroft and
Co., 1884.

Barry, Neilson. "Madame Dorion of the Astorians." *Oregon Historical
Quarterly.* Portland: Oregon Historical Society, September 1929.
Numerous additional articles from the *Oregon Historical Quarterly.*

Betts, Robert B. *In Search of York: The Slave Who Went to the Pacific with
Lewis and Clark.* Boulder: University Press of Colorado and the
Lewis and Clark Trail Heritage Foundation, 2000.

Blaine, Martha Royce. *The Ioway Indians.* Norman: University of Oklahoma Press, 1995.

Boyd, Robert, ed. *Indians, Fire and the Land in the Pacific Northwest.*
Corvallis, Oreg.: Oregon State University, 1999.

Brown, George Thomas. *The Hand of Catherine.* Fairfield, Wash.: Ye
Galleon Press, 1998.

Carlson, Laurie Winn. *Cattle: An Informal Social History.* Chicago: Ivan
R. Dee, 2001.

———. *Sidesaddles to Heaven.* Caldwell, Idaho: Caxton Press, 1998.

Dee, Henry Drumond. Introduction to *Journal of John Work,* January to
October, 1835. Victoria B.C.: Charles F. Banfield, 1945.

Dobbs, Caroline C. *Men of Champoeg.* Portland, Oreg.: Metropolitan
Press, 1993.

Hafen, LeRoy R. *Mountain Men and the Fur Trade of the Far West.* vols.
I, II, VI, VII, VIII, and IX. Glendale, Calif.: Arthur H. Clark, 1971.

Haines, Francis. *The Nez Perces, Tribesmen of the Columbia Plateau.* Norman, Okla.: University of Oklahoma Press, 1955.

Haines Jr., Francis D. "The Snake Country Expedition of 1830–1831,"
John Work's Field Journal, vol. 59, *The American Exploration and
Travel Series.* Norman, Okla.: University of Oklahoma Press, 1971.